D0543361

BRUNT BOGGART
A Tapestry of Tales

David Greygoose

Brunt Boggart

Text copyright©2015 David Greygoose
Cover design©2015 Daniel Allan
Original artwork©2015 Cate Simmons

ISBN 978-1-908577-44-3

The Author has asserted his rights under the Copyright,
Designs and Patents Act 1988 to be identified as the author
of this work.

British Library Cataloguing in Publication Data.
A catalogue record for this book is available from the
British Library.

1 3 5 4 2

First Published in Great Britain
Hawkwood Books 2015

Printed and bound in Great Britain by CPI Group (UK) Ltd.
Croydon CR0 4YY

"These are utterly wonderful new-old tales. In his bones, David Greygoose understands the rhythms of great storytelling, with its incantations, repetitions, knowing asides and snappy dialogue, and he has a frankly marvellous ear for the music of language. This tapestry is inventive and witty, dramatic and moving, and deeply earthed in the superstitions and folk beliefs of old England. Now that I've stepped into Brunt Boggart, I know that part of me will never leave it."
KEVIN CROSSLEY-HOLLAND

"David Greygoose is a master-storyteller, creating the visceral netherworld that is Brunt Boggart. Greygoose draws deeply on the riches of Britain's folklore to conjure up dark and whimsical tales of an imagined village. I found myself lost in the wildflower meadows, mossy hollows and wolf pits of Brunt Boggart."
EMILY PORTMAN

"Brunt Boggart is a skilfully crafted collection of timeless tales which connects the reader on a visceral level. Each is as true a tale as ever was told. Just as a great sculptor sees the divine form within the slab of granite, Greygoose has stripped away all that is extraneous exposing the primal folk-tales which lay buried within us all."
JOHN REPPION

"It tastes fabulously medieval, it smells uncanny, it looks like the roots of half-forgotten herbs, and it sounds like verbs of thunder and earth."
JAY GRIFFITHS

For

K.F.W.

ACKNOWLEDGEMENTS

Thanks to Eleanor Rees for editorial advice,
encouragement and support and to Freda Davis:
The Original Blue Ball Press Moon Calendar
for information on the naming of the moons; to Cate
Simmons for original artwork; Daniel Allan for cover
design; Mandy Vere and all at *News From Nowhere*
bookshop, Liverpool; Ellis Delmonte at Hawkwood
Books for his insight, enthusiasm and dedication.

Let me tell you... I lived in this place before you were born - when it was just a tiny village on the banks of the river, where I used to fish. The river flowed down to the city beside the great blue - and yes it was truly blue - ocean. I still live here now. And I am still fishing. I fish for dreams. I am the dream-fisher. I catch the dreams of the sleeping-wakers, of the waking-sleepers. And what do I do with these dreams? Why, I hang them up in bottles. I tie them onto leaves. I leave them under flowers. I freeze them in a snowflake. I let them rest, and sing, and listen - and then, when they are ready, I turn them into stories.

Let me tell you... I can see it all. Remember, I can see you now.

I know what you are doing. You are part of someone's dream - not mine, not your own. Maybe someone you do not know, someone you only saw once, one day in the street. You may not have noticed them, but they saw you, and they remembered - and now you are in their dream...

The Tapestry...

BRUNT BOGGART

THE PEDLAR MAN'S TRACK

ARLECCRA

BRUNT BOGGART

CROSSDOGS AND THE WOLF PIT

Let me tell you. Let me tell you... once there was a village - not a big village, not a small village, just a middling village, much like this place used to be. And what was the name of that village? - I know what you're asking. Why, that village was known as Brunt Boggart. And who was it who lived there? Let me tell you. I can see that you're curious. I knew that you'd want to know. If I didn't tell you, you'd make up your own stories.

And that's just what the boys did who lived there: Hamsparrow and Bullbreath, Larkspittle and Longskull, Shadowit, Scarum, Scatterlegs and Crossdogs - they all made up stories. Every night when the old'uns were busy, weaving and sewing and sleeping off their supper, all the boys who thought they were men and all the men who wished they were still boys, they'd all come and gather in the mossy hollow that lay in the middle of the Green that was in the middle of Brunt Boggart. A middling village, just like I told you. Much like this place used to be.

What stories did they tell? I knew that you'd ask me. Every tale is worth telling, even if it's half-forgotten. And for every tale there is to tell, there must be someone to listen. So - are you listening? Good. Let me tell you...

The boys would sit around in the mossy hollow and tell each other stories of the wolf who lived in the woods: how big he was, how strong. How sharp his teeth, how long his claws. In each boy's tale the Wolf grew more terrible. They said he did dreadful things. They told how he came to the village each night and gobbled up all the food. He broke down the fences and tore leaves from the trees and smashed the window of Old Mother Tidgewallop's cottage. He drank the water in the well. He stole the wine from Snuffwidget's cellar.

"That's nothing," said Longskull, the next boy in the circle. "I know the Wolf steals more than food and wine. I think he tries to steal our sisters. Why, where are they now while we're all sat here? They're not indoors neither, safe and sound. They've sneaked out same as we did while the old'uns are creeping and slopping and sleeping. Listen - you can hear them laughing, hear them tittering, hear them shrieking - over there by the woods. That's when the Wolf comes to take them."

Bullbreath and Scarum looked over and nodded. They could hear the wind howl through the tall whining trees. They could hear the snapping of branches. They could smell hot smoke like wolf's breath in the breeze.

Then Larkspittle spoke. His voice was so quiet it was almost a whisper. All the other boys gathered round, crowded in close, so that they could hear.

"I think my sister's new baby must have come from

the Wolf."

The boys were aghast. They were shocked and surprised. But then they realised - yes, it could be true.

"Her baby does not look like us. It is hairy and howls every night at the moon."

"It is not one of us. It does not have our ways. It has a long chin, long ears and a long pointy nose. Larkspittle is right. His sister has been taken by the Wolf!"

Across the way and over they could hear their sisters laughing. They could hear their sisters skittering, screaming and shrieking.

Crossdogs sprang up.

"We must drive the Wolf away!"

Hamsparrow nodded. "Better to catch him. Catch him and kill him."

"How shall we do it?" Larkspittle asked them.

"With a net!" bellowed Bullbreath.

"Dig a pit!" clamoured Scarum.

"Hit him and hit him..." Scatterlegs gibbered.

"... with sticks," muttered Longskull.

"... with staves," echoed Shadowit.

"... with stones!" they all cried.

The boys danced in a circle, in the middle of the Green. They were maddened. They were angry. They fixed their gaze on each other's eyes.

"Listen!" hissed Longskull.

They stopped their cavorting.

"I can hear nothing," Scatterlegs wheezed.

"Nothing is not what we heard before," Longskull retorted. "We heard our sisters laughing and shrieking. Now it is silent."

"Where have they gone?"

"The Wolf's come and taken them!"

"Let's go and find him and bring our sisters home."

The boys stood quite still and watched each other, waiting to see who would move, who would lead them, who would be the first to tread the path to the edge of the wood. Out of the darkness they heard an owl's mournful wail, the whisper of the wind. The crack of a branch. And then silence. Nothing more. Nothing more. None of them moved.

Where were their sisters? I know what you're asking. Why - they'd crept up behind the boys on their way back home. Ravenhair and Silverwing, Moonpetal and Dawnflower, Duskeye, Scallowflax, Dewdream and Riversong: they rushed out of the darkness, chasing their brothers all the way to the cottages where the old'uns were waiting beside warm glowing fires.

Who would be Wolf Slayer? All the next day, all through the village, the boys watched each other with wary eyes - circling and staring, growling and crouching, like wolves themselves. Then as late day turned to evening, turned to dusk, turned to night, by the light of flickering torch flames they sat in a circle, squatted in the hollow in the middle of the Green. And they raised the torches high as they began to dance, whirling sticks, clashing staves, dashing stones.

"Wolf Slayer."

"Wolf Slayer!"

They shouted and taunted, each of them trying to hit harder, throw farther, leap higher than the rest. A glint in the eye. A flashing of teeth. Arms grabbing arms to wrestle, to grip. Tippling and rolling across the hard ground, punching and clawing, pulling each other down. Muscle and sinew, spittle and blood - they struggled and grunted and threatened and stood. Until Crossdogs, the tallest of them all, howled "Stop!" And they stopped. And they listened. And from the woods they heard a wailing.

Could be owl, could be wind. Could be Wolf.

And then a snapping-off of twigs and a clatter through the branches.

"Wolf is come!" they cried, "Wolf is come!" snatching up sticks and staves and stones.

But it was only the girls running home before Silverwing's mother came out to fetch her daughter and drag all of the rest of them away from the woods.

Night after day after night the boys would meet and fight. Fight each other for the right to be "Wolf Slayer". But none of them deserved it, for they would only fight with each other in the middle of the hollow at the middle of the village green. None of them would go into the woods. No-one would go alone. And the girls would watch them and jeer them and taunt them, crying, "Who is Wolf Slayer now?" And the boys would grow maddened and chase them away but then rush after to save them.

"From what are you saving us?" Ravenhair asked them.

"From the dark."

"From the night."

"From the Wolf."

Then Silverwing laughed and Dawnflower giggled and Scallowflax tittered behind her fingers.

"We're more afraid of *you*," cried Duskeye and Dewdream, while Riversong and Moonpetal said nothing at all as they linked arms and walked away.

Day after night after day, the old'uns would wake and find fences broken and food had been stolen and daughters had been dragged to the dark wood and back. But no-one ever saw who had done it.

"Wolf," they muttered.

"Wolf," they cried.

"Wolf!" they howled.

"Wolf has been and gone again and no-one saw him come. But Wolf has been here, we know."

"We will find it," cried the boys, brandishing their sticks and staves. "We will slay the Wolf." And they marched up and down the village streets, smashing fences as they went, grabbing food to give them strength and chasing after the girls.

"Look at them," Old Mother Tidgewallop exclaimed. "There is no Wolf at all. Only the boys. Not fit to grow into men. Why, my son Larkum is worth ten of them."

The girls got to hear her and the gossip spread in whispers and the whispers spread in catcalls, leering and jeering.

"There is no Wolf," taunted Ravenhair. "You only say there is so that you can march around the village with your sticks and your stones and your staves. As for trying to save us, you're as useless as a cuckoo. We'd be safer with a wolf than any one of *you!*"

Crossdogs gathered all the boys together, the boys who thought they were men and the men who still wished they were boys.

"Listen to what the old'uns are saying. Listen to what our sisters are whispering. We've spent too long watching and waiting - it's time to go to the wood!"

Suddenly silent, the boys picked up their sticks and

reached for their stones and their staves. Then they shuffled single file towards the shadows of the wood. They trudged between the tall dark trees, dragging their feet through crisp fallen leaves.

"Perhaps there is no Wolf," whispered Shadowit. "Perhaps we imagined it all."

"Shsh..." cautioned Hamsparrow. "The Wolf will hear you. And there must be Wolf. Remember Larkspittle's sister's baby. Remember its nose and its long pointed ears."

"Look!" cried Scatterlegs.

He pointed to the trunk of a tall gnarled tree. Its bark was scratched. The twigs on its lowest branches were broken and snapped.

"Wolf has been here," Scatterlegs said.

The others nodded.

"Look! Look at this."

Strands of grey fur clung to the thorns of a bramble bush.

"Wolf been here. Wolf been close."

Scarum shook his head.

"Could be anything, that," he said. "Could be tomcat, or badger or an old mangy fox."

"Could be, true," Shadowit replied. "But tomcats don't break fences, badgers don't steal our food and foxes don't take our sisters."

Longskull shook his stave with his strong hairy arm. His long chin quivered, his long nose twitched and his pointed ears flushed with anger.

"No-one must touch our sisters. Anyone who does must be punished. That's why we come here. Come to find Wolf."

"Find Wolf!"

"Find Wolf!" they chorused, rattling staves and banging sticks and flinging loose stones into the bushes.

"Look there! Look there!" Hamsparrow shrieked.

What did he see? A shadow running. So quick that before the others could look where he was pointing, it was gone. Just a darkness of quivering leaves and snapping of twigs. And way in the distance a lost howling sound.

"It was here. Was Wolf. I saw him. I'm sure!"

The boys stood rooted as the trees around them.

"Wolf!" howled Crossdogs.

"We found him," Hamsparrow gloated.

"Let's chase him."

"And catch him."

"And stone him."

"And kill him."

But none of them moved.

Crossdogs stood and looked at them.

"We'll never find him now. He knows this wood much better than us. Let's go back to Brunt Boggart and plan what we should do."

"Yes!" cried Hamsparrow. "Let's go back. Let's tell old'uns and sisteren what we seen. They got to believe us now."

Next day the boys gathered again. Gathered up all the things they needed to go and hunt Wolf. Nets to drag the undergrowth. Axes to hack a way through the woods. Horns to blow to make a hubbub - to drive Wolf into their trap.

"There they go!" laughed Moonpetal and Riversong as they waved them on their way. "There they go with their sticks and stones and those daft silly horns that will let Wolf know a mile off that they're coming!"

"Tain't to frighten the Wolf, my dears," Old Mother Tidgewallop nodded. "Tis to scare their own fears away."

But the boys set off all the same, clamouring and chanting and blowing on their horns and rattling their staves in the air. Into the woods they came stamping and hacking and thrashing through the brambles.

"This is where he was. This is where we saw him!" shouted little Larkspittle.

They looked for the shadow. They tried to find the signs. They even stopped blowing on their horns to listen, to catch the echo of a distant howling. But there was nothing. Only the scuttle of a startled rabbit, a hare clattering out to the open fields, the dirt from a newly-dug badger's burrow. The flash of a red fox's brush.

"Wolf ain't going to come," Hamsparrow muttered. "The girlen were right. We make too much noise. Wolf can hear us, see us coming. Best we go back, come again another day."

The next day the boys all waited till dusk. They left those great horns behind and they set out stealthily, just as the moon rose, wearing dark colours so Wolf wouldn't see them - moving like shadows from ditch to hillock to tree. Instead of the horns they carried shovels and torches, and in the centre of the wood they started to dig. Shallow at first, then deeper and deeper, throwing up the dark earth to make a great pit. Down at the bottom they spread out a net then covered it over with branches and twigs. On top of it all they placed leaves and dry grass till under the stars no-one could tell that the trap had been set.

The trap had been set, but would the Wolf come?

They watched and they waited, shivering and coughing behind the dark crouching bushes.

"Tain't coming," mumbled Hamsparrow.

Larkspittle chided him. "He won't come at all if he hears you chittering."

"Shshsh, stop your racket," Crossdogs commanded.

They kept quiet. They waited. They waited and listened, but there wasn't a sound.

"Maybe there ain't no Wolf after all," Larkspittle stuttered. "Maybe Old Mother Tidgewallop is right."

"Then who is it steals all the food from the larders and drinks all the wine from Snuffwidget's cellar? Who is it breaks the fences down?" Hamsparrow reminded him. "Tain't none of us."

"And none of us steals away sisteren, neither. Specially not yours," Longskull said quickly.

"Stop your chattering," Crossdogs cut in. "Something is coming."

A snap of a twig.

A light padding footstep.

A smell on the breeze.

"Wolf!"

"Wolf!"

"Wolf!" they all whispered, gripping their sticks and flourishing staves.

"Down, stay down," Crossdogs snapped tersely. "He won't come by the trap if he hears all your noise."

They watched and they waited but no Wolf could they hear.

"He's gone."

"Let's go after him. Let's chase him back here to the trap."

They moved through the wood, smelling out Wolf.

Padding and pausing, loping and stalling. Listening to the wind. Then they saw the shadow again, just the way they did before - running and skittering in between the trees. The rustle of leaves, the cracking twigs. The howl.

Then a shadow running through the shadows, a figure hunched and hurrying. This time they gave chase - beating sticks, swinging axes that glinted silver in the moonlight. Their own jaws set and snarling, teeth bared, dribbling spittle. Baying and howling they ran through the wood, chasing the shadow, chasing the Wolf, back and forth through the brambles and nettles, back and forth, back and forth till they came to the clearing where they had laid the trap.

The Wolf-shadow broke out into the moonlight, heading straight for the branches with the grass strewn on top which hid the pit beneath. With a snap the trap gave way and the darkness swallowed him up. Crossdogs stopped and waved the others back. They all stood still and silent, ranged around the edge of the clearing. Then slowly they advanced towards the pit, holding up torches to see what they would see.

Larkspittle ran forward.

"Wolf! Wolf!" he spat.

But Crossdogs grabbed him quickly.

"Stand away. Keep back. If Wolf is cornered he'll be twice as dangerous."

They waited. Watched in the shadows, in the torches' flickering flames. But Wolf made no move. Wolf made no sound. So then they stepped forward, staves at the ready, to peer down into the bowels of the pit to see the Wolf creature thrashing round at the bottom. Thrashing then whimpering. Whimpering then howling.

"Wolf!"

"Wolf."

"We have him now."

Crossdogs stepped right up to the mouth of the pit. He raised his hand and paused.

Hamsparrow leaned forward.

"Tain't no Wolf," he exclaimed. "Tis a Boy!"

"Tis a Boy..."

"Tis a Boy....."

The others whispered in puzzlement.

"What is a boy doing in the Wolf Pit?"

"How did he get there?"

"Twas Wolf we chased through the woods."

"Sure enough - I saw him."

"I saw him too."

"Maybe he's a shape-changer, like the old'uns told us."

Crossdogs shook his head.

"No - maybe just boy. Just boy like me and all the rest of you."

Crossdogs dropped into the pit and held out his hand to the skinny bundle of bone and rags that was cowering there, wide-eyed and shivering. Crossdogs tried to grab him but the Boy just flinched away.

Crossdogs spread his hands and whispered gently.

"Come on. Come on. We ain't going to hurt you."

He waved to his companions.

"Put down your sticks and staves."

One by one the boys dropped their weapons.

"Put out your torches."

The clearing was plunged into a sudden eerie darkness. The Boy darted past Crossdogs as if he might run. Scrabbled at the sides of the slippery pit, but then slithered back down. His shoulders shook with sobbing. This time he did not resist when Crossdogs took his arm and pulled him to his feet. Hamsparrow and Bullbreath leaned down and slowly they raised him out of the pit. He stood there looking at them, blinking in the moonlight. His breath was quick and even from the chase. The boys all gaped at him. He was boy, right enough. Same age as them. Dressed in a strange mess of rags and pelts and bits of dried leaves. His face was grimy, just like them, and strands of whisker were beginning to appear, except that maybe his had grown longer, more straggly.

Longskull strode forward. "What's your name?" he demanded. "What are you doing, hiding out here? Are you the one? Are you the one who steals food, steals wine and breaks all the fences? Are you the one who took Larkspittle's sister? I know you must be. You may not be Wolf but you look like Wolf. If look like Wolf then act like Wolf."

Longskull swung round, addressing his companions.

"And if act like Wolf then *is* Wolf, true enough. And if Wolf, then I say killum. We come here to kill Wolf, and this be Wolf now!"

He grabbed up his stave, but Crossdogs and Hamsparrow held him back.

"Tain't no Wolf, Longskull. Tis boy. You can't be killing one of our own."

Larkspittle and Scatterlegs threw their arms round the Boy. His eyes were wide, bewildered, as he knelt at the edge of the pit they had dug - one moment minded to dart away, the next too scared to move. And as he shivered in the moonlight, he looked at them and they just looked at him.

"Who are you?" Crossdogs asked.

WolfBoy's eyes were wide and soft. He opened his mouth. No sound came out. He pointed at the woods, at the darkness. At the trees. He pointed at the wind, and then at himself.

Crossdogs shook his head.

"I am Crossdogs," he said. "Who are you?"

The Boy shook his head, just as Crossdogs had done.

"I am Crossdogs. This is Hamsparrow, this is Bullbreath. This is Larkspittle, Longskull, Shadowit and Scarum. And this is Scatterlegs over here."

The Boy listened, shuffling, his eyes darting from one to another, his lips reading Crossdogs' words, shaping the names. Then he smiled. Slowly he started to make a sound. It was not a howling. It was not a wailing. It was a soft voice, gentle and high. It did not seem to be his own. It was a lost voice he remembered as his eyes roamed up to the stars:

"Coddle me, coddle me,
My darling son.
I'm leaving you here
Till the crying is done.

Back in the village
They'll look at you strange,
But here in the forest
You're safe from their gaze.

Coddle me, coddle me,
My darling son.
I'm leaving you here
Till the crying is done.

I'll bring you sweet milk
And I'll fetch you fresh bread.
The trees are your chamber,
Green moss is your bed.

Coddle me, coddle me,
My darling son.
I'm leaving you here
Till the crying is done."

And then he sat down. Sat down on the ground and wrapped his arms around his head and curled like a baby sobbing. His body shook, but he did not cry.

"Tell us more," demanded Bullbreath.

"Who are you?" quizzed Shadowit.

"Where did you come from?" Larkspittle asked him.

"Why are you here?" Hamsparrow prodded.

"Is it you who steals food from the village?" Longskull snarled darkly. "Is it you drags sisteren into the wood?"

But the Boy just covered his ears to the gibbering.

"Stop, stop. He's confused. One at a time," Crossdogs commanded. Then he turned to the Boy and started again, speaking very soft, very slow.

"I'm Crossdogs," he gestured. "Who are you?"

He paused while the Boy sat up. He had stopped shaking now and opened his mouth, moving his lips. He was trying to make words. They all craned forward silently, waiting to hear what he would say. And what did he say? I'll tell you. He sang the song again. But slower, lower, more in his own voice. More like the voices of the boys. They waited till he'd finished and then stepped away, confused.

"It's a trick," hissed Longskull. "How do we know he's not dangerous? We set a trap for him. How do we know he's not trapping *us*? I say we kill him still. Still while the moon is high."

"No, no," Crossdogs insisted. "He's no Wolf at all. He's Boy - you can see that. He's Boy, same as us. Take him back with us. The old'uns will know. They'll know what to do. Take him back to the village."

So they took the Boy, who was Wolf, who was Boy, all the way down the long path home. And on the way they tried again to tell him their names, and the Boy tried again to say them, but all that would come from his trembling mouth was the song that he'd learnt so long ago. And by the time they got back to their homes round the hollow in the middle of the Green, the boys knew every word.

And the Boy who was Wolf who was Boy, where did he stay in the village? I knew that you'd ask me, and I'll tell you. He stayed with Old Granny Willowmist, whose house had been empty for many a year. He stayed there and she loved him like a son, and all of the old'uns loved him too. And all the girlen as well. Straight away next day they crowded round to see him, this BoyWolf the boys had brought home.

"Isn't he pretty?" Moonpetal crooned.

"What shall we call him?" Scallowflax mused.

"Call him Greychild," Old Willowmist had suggested. And from that moment on, Greychild was his name. And all the girlen wanted to touch him and stroke him and run their strong fingers through his long matted hair.

But Greychild was scared. His dark eyes were

staring. Where was he gazing? Back to the forest, back to the sky. Back to the trees and the fields. He skittered and scatted this way and that, running round the village while the girlen chased after him, trying to tug at his raggedy clothes.

"Look at him go," muttered Longskull. "He knows his way around. He's been here before, let me tell you. Tis him that drank the wine from Snuffwidget's cellar and knocked all the fences down."

"Maybe so, maybe so," said Crossdogs. "Course he's been here. He had to get food. But don't mean he's Wolf. Only boy, same as us. Same as us he came from here. Someone took him out to the woods. Someone left him there. Someone used to take him food. *I'll bring you sweet milk and I'll fetch you fresh bread'* - just like it says in the song. That's why he sings it - it's all that he knows."

Way over on the village green they heard laughing and singing. The girlen had caught Greychild and sat him in the middle of the mossy hollow and they'd twined his hair with flowers and covered his cheeks with kisses and now they were trying to mend his clothes and wrap a long shawl around him. And Greychild had stopped running. He seemed to be pleased, he was smiling. And he was teaching the girlen the song, till they were all singing it too.

"Tain't natural," muttered Longskull. "He shouldn't be here."

And some of the old'uns agreed.

"Tain't natural," they said. "He'll just bring bad luck. Look at him there with the girlen, hugging and kissing with eyes like the moon. Tain't natural at all."

"Where did he come from?"

"He came from the wood."

"How did he get there?"

"Nobody knows."

"Let's take him back," said the men. And the men were bigger than the boys. They drove the girlen away, screaming and shrieking back to their houses. And then they turned to the Boy who was Wolf who was Boy, who was Greychild. The crows in Black Meadow scattered and cawed, flapping their wings in the darkening sky. Then the men took up cudgels and stood round the Boy with fists huge as stones and dull loathing in their eyes.

"Stop!"

Who was that? Quick as fox, Crossdogs leapt between the men and the Boy, between the Boy and the men.

"Stop!"

"Out of our way," snarled Oakum Marlroot, who stood head and shoulders above the rest of them. "Who are you to be meddling? You're a spit of a boycub, you ain't one of us."

Crossdogs stood up straight and proud, as tall as any of them.

"You know who I am. I'm Crossdogs. I am son of Redgut, Slipadder's son. This is *our* Boy. We brought him here: Hamsparrow and Bullbreath, Larkspittle and Longskull, Shadowit, Scarum and Scatterlegs. Tain't none of your business. When we thought there was Wolf - old'uns, young'uns, girlen - who was it went to go get him? Was it any of you? No, it was us boys. You were too busy in the taverns and the fields. You were stinklazy, gutted up by the fire. This is our Boy. This is Greychild. We brought him here. He's one of us now.

Old Granny Willowmist has taken him in. Put down your cudgels. Leave him alone."

Even the yard-dogs were silent. The leak of the water-butt stopped dripping. The rooster in the scrat-pen ceased crowing. A cloud crept in front of the sun. But as it stole on, the light tumbled down on the buttercups twined in Greychild's hair and one by one the men dropped their staves and trudged off sullenly while the old grannies stood and watched as they leant on the steps in front of their houses.

Old Nanny Nettleye folded her arms.

"Look at him - look," she said. "Shouldn't be here. Shouldn't be there." She nodded her head towards the wood and spat. "Shouldn't rightly be anywhere."

"But he's here now. Now he's here," Willowmist insisted.

"Sure he's here. You've took him in. You always were too soft. He don't belong here. Don't belong nowhere. I says send him back."

"Can't send him back if he don't belong nowhere. Where's your sense, you great lumpen? He came from here, as much as you or me. Look at him now, running with the girlen, wrestling with the boys. He's one of us, sure enough."

"Then what was he doing in the woods?" Old Nanny Nettleye quizzled. "All by himself - all of this time? How did he get there?"

"How did he get there?" Willowmist reasoned. "How do you think? Nobody lives there. And he ain't no acorn, no child of the trees. Somebody left him there."

Silverwing's mother came sidling over.

"My sister had a baby. None of you knew. None of us said. Nobody knew whose baby it was. She never said any one man. She just waited round the woods at night when that feeling came on her, just like the girlen do now, and all the boys would go there. Nothing seems to change. Then she grew bigger and bigger, and then the baby came. No-one would come to help her, we were all too ashamed. One day my sister went out to the woods and then the baby was gone. We never saw it again."

"Coddle me, Coddle me, my darling son..."

They heard the girlen singing, sitting in a circle holding up their hands, clapping and slapping along with the song, while Larkspittle's sister held her baby and looked on. Greychild was rolling and tumbling in the dust, spitting and gnawing, laughing and falling as he wrestled with the boys.

"We would watch our sister every night, stealing off to the woods again. At first we thought she was back to her old ways, waiting to meet the boys, the boys who would be men. But no - she did not run with them. Every night she took a basket, covered with a soft linen cloth. And sometimes we noticed that milk was missing from the top of the pantry shelf. And sometimes bread and later tatties and sometimes turnips and apples too. But no-one said anything. Baby boy was gone and she was gone too, some while after. Died of the shivering fever."

The old'uns nodded, listening, thinking. Figuring it all through. Greychild was playing chase with the boys, fleetfoot down the alleyways in between the houses.

Old Nanny Nettleye pointed.

"In and out and up and down. He seems to know his way around. And twelve moons back the first food went missing and then Snuffwidget's wine. And then all the fences got broken down."

"And then boys said there was Wolf."

"There was Wolf, there was Wolf," muttered Longskull, as his long chin quivered, his long nose twitched and his pointed ears flushed with anger. "This ain't no Wolf. This just boy. I could snap his neck with a twitch of my thumb. But must be Wolf in that wood. I could feel it. I could smell. Could sniff it in the wind. Crossdogs ain't no wolfslayer. Look at him now. First time he takes us there and finds this boy he kids us it's Wolf. But not Wolf. Won't killen. Says his work's done. Tain't done at all. Must be Wolf, Larkspittle. Who else took your sister into the woods? Who else give her that child?"

Longskull was talking to Larkspittle. Longskull was twisting Larkspittle's arm high up his back. Longskull was shoving his fist in Larkspittle's face.

"All your fault. It's all your fault. Want to take better care of your sister. Shouldn't let her roam off into the woods. Anything could happen when there's Wolf about."

Larkspittle whimpered, a muted smothered moan. Then a shadow came.

"Let him go."

Longskull looked up. Crossdogs stood over them as they wrestled on the ground. Far off in the houses they heard a baby cry.

"You be so sure there be Wolf," Crossdogs declared, "then you go there and finden."

Longskull stood up.

"Wolf - there was Wolf," he snarled. "Come Hamsparrow, come Bullbreath. Come all you boys. Don't need Crossdogs no more. He can't find no Wolf.

Can only find Boy. Come all of you. Come with me. Blow horn. Gather staves, sticks and stones. Come with me. There was Wolf. Wolf is there. Wolf is there."

And the boys all came. Came as he called. And what did Greychild do? It wasn't him they were looking for now. He watched as the boys all rattled their sticks and waved their long staves and blew on the horn, and uttered a cry:

"Wolf must die. Wolf must die!"

Greychild clutched at Crossdogs' arm.

"Hush," whispered Crossdogs. "They mean you no harm."

And Greychild stood and watched as the boys ran and ran, ran with their sticks and their staves and their stones. Ran and ran with their loud hunting horn. And they ran and they ran, beating their way, lighting torches, swinging axes - their jaws set and snarling, teeth bared, dribbling spittle. Ran and ran after Longskull, all the way to the edge of the wood.

"Wolf must die! Wolf must die!" Longskull cried.

"Wolf must die!" the boys replied, as they raised their weapons high to the sky.

"Into the wood!" Longskull commanded.

"Into the wood, into the wood," chorused Hamsparrow, Bullbreath, Larkspittle and Scarum.

"Into the wood," echoed Scatterlegs.

Deep in the wood was a rattle of crow wings. Deep in the wood a fox's voice wailed. Deep in the wood the dark shadows beckoned.

"Into the wood," croaked Longskull again and turned to look at the boys. The boys who stood behind him, brandishing stones and sticks and staves. He looked into their moon-struck eyes.

"Into the wood, Longskull," Larkspittle told him.

And Longskull ran. Ran and ran into the darkness of crackling branches. But the boys turned around and marched back, back to Brunt Boggart. Not a big village, not a small village. Just a middling village, much like this place used to be.

SNUFFWIDGET AND THE CROWDANCERS

Let me tell you... Let me tell you... as Snuffwidget woke in his cottage he could taste a taste dark as thunder deep at the back of his throat, sharp as ginger, sickly as cinnamon. He stumbled across the cluttered room and stood in the doorway, shivering. In the street outside, dull puddles squinted between the ruts, but the rain had gone and the dust was slaked. Snuffwidget stretched and turned to look round his room. It was full with barrels of wines and potions brimming with goodness. Goodness of bluebells and tatties and clover. Goodness of honey and heather and dew.

Snuffwidget had been brewing potions and wines for all the folk in Brunt Boggart for as long as he could remember. He used to help his Grandmother, old Corbin Night-thorn, used to help her gather the goodness, used to help her stir the brew, used to help her fill the barrels, then tap out the ferment into old stone bottles - and then sit on the doorstep and sell'em.

Oh yes, Snuffwidget knew everything that old Corbin Night-thorn knew. Or almost everything. All except one thing. Old Nanny Corbin had one special brew, they called it Night-thorn's Morning Sunrise. People would queue round the houses to buy it when word went out that she'd brewed a new brew. It was a special recipe all of her own, though some say she got it from *her* grandmother - and *she* got it from her grandmother before her.

She would pick forest berries, just before daybreak and mix them with elderflower, nutmeg and basil and simmer them with sugar in a big mixing vat. And when it was ready and when it was bottled, mothers would use it as a healing potion, fathers drank it to bring back their strength, while children would clamour at the doorway for Snuffwidget to sell them a glass for a penny, mixed with fresh water from Old Mother Tidgewallop's well. Back in Nana Night-thorn's day they would line up down the street to taste her new brew, but now bottles of Morning Sunrise sat covered in cobwebs on Snuffwidget's shelves. He tried his best to make it just the way that his grandmother had, just the way that she'd whispered it to him as she lay on her dying bed - but it never came out the same.

Mothers complained that as a cure it was no use at all. They used to take a spoonful for dropsy and coughs but now they said they might just as well drink water from the muddy ditch out by Oakum Marlroot's fields. Fathers said it took more strength to open the bottle than ever the brew gave them back. And little'uns would rather play hopscotch in the dust than line up for a glass.

Snuffwidget didn't know what to do. The other potions and wines all sold well enough, but anyone could make them. Corbin Night-thorn's Morning Sunrise had been his pride and joy. He had waited all his years to be the one who brewed it, but now it just came out wrong. He was sure there must be something Nanny Corbin had not told him. She must have forgotten one last ingredient - but it was too late for her to tell him now.

Snuffwidget looked at the barrels and sighed and went back to stand in the doorway again. The street was silent, no-one had woken - then out of the alleys which leaked between the shadows, the dancers tumbled one by one by two by two - dressed in tatters, dressed in rags, their masks askew and dreaming still. They danced in silence, their heavy limbs dragging to the beat of the drum which sounded out from the distant field: footstamp and handclap, twisted wrist and backsnap. Snuffwidget looked on, his fingers twitching. Snuffwidget stood in the doorway and listened, his spindle limbs thrilling to the echoing rhythm, watching as the dance moved on, waking the morning between the squat houses, crawling away down Brunt Boggart's narrow streets and out to the waiting fields.

Snuffwidget watched the procession move off - Hamsparrow, Ravenhair, Scatterlegs and Silverwing, Scarum and Moonpetal, Shadowit and Dewdream. He remembered seeing them grow, all of them little'uns, younger than him. Remembered them struggling and fighting and running, roaming the backstreets and tossing up pennies as they chased the sun; the days sharing sweets under the shadows of the chimneys, the nights stealing secrets when the starlight had gone. Now every morning Snuffwidget watched them leaving, out to the field by the Fever Tree. They left every morning and trailed back in the evening, just as the sullen sun was sinking. They trailed back decked in night-dark feathers, flowers dangling from their brightly-patched tunics, streaked with daubs of tawny clay. They came back laughing, weary from dancing, spinning words in broken whispers which Snuffwidget could never understand.

He turned around and started to count the bottles, just as he did every morning. Then he sluiced his face with a shudder of water scooped from the bucket in the corner. He paced up and down the dusty room and began to sieve the sediment of fruit which had mulched overnight, and then poured the clear liquid again and again. But his hands were trembling and he set the jug down. He could still hear the rhythm of the distant drum, beating from the Echo Field. Snuffwidget's limbs were shuddering and shaking. The sunlight was calling from the open door.

He hauled on a shirt and paused to snatch a scrag of mottled feathers and twist it through his hair. And then he ran. He raced, gawkish and squinny-limbed, away from the house where Nanny Night-thorn had lived. He raced down the clumsy-footed street, following the trail of the morning dancers, following the beat of the drum as he stumbled between dull-eyed houses. Dogs appeared at bleary windows, clawing the shredded curtains, singing in twisted shriveled voices. Snuffwidget ran, skittering between the crawling puddles, glints of thunder still reflected in their sheen. Snuffwidget ran, away from the suffocating stench of the village, out to the mud-slicked lanes.

He could hear the beat of the drum, pounding from the Echo Field. He could hear the trudge of the morning dancers slipping between the cross-tracked ruts. He pounded on, his legs mud-splattered, till round the next bend he spied them, stumping sullenly between silent hedges, stumbling through slurry and overgrown ditches.

Snuffwidget called out - but they did not hear him. They just gazed ahead, their eyes glazed with hunger, clutching gouts of silent thunder, lured by the rhythm of the beckoning drum. He tagged on at the back of the procession, prancing and pirouetting, spinning round and round. But the others still did not notice him as they trudged on, mulligrubbing and muttering till they came to the gate of the field. The field was filled with a fever of poppies, red as boar's blood, swaying and beckoning. In the corner beside a stricken tree crouched the figure of the hooded drummer, his long hands moving in a blur of shadows, beating out the pulsing rhythm under the blackened branches.

Snuffwidget watched as the dancers moved around the field, plucking the heads from the wafting poppies, smearing the petals across their faces, across their arms and over their bodies, stuffing the redness into their mouths, choking on the heady nectar, until the petals dribbled out again, through their nostrils, through their ears. Red tears trickled from swollen eyes.

Snuffwidget watched. He saw how the dancers gorged on the poppies. Saw how Ravenhair tossed her tresses and how Hamsparrow pursued her. Saw how Ravenhair seemed to encourage him, even though Snuffwidget knew what everyone knew, that Ravenhair yearned after Crossdogs. Snuffwidget watched Silverwing flutter her eyes at Scatterlegs while Moonpetal danced a slow dance, winding herself around Scarum, wrapping him in ribbons. And Shadowit and Dewdream, they just lay there in the ditch and giggled as they covered each other all over in a bed of petals, warm and red.

Snuffwidget watched, then joined the dancers, joined their swirling dervish dance, a frenzy trance, driven by the rhythm of the crouching drummer in the corner of the Echo Field. Then one by one the dancers stumbled, tumbled into the arms of the waiting ditch. The drumbeat slowed. Slowed to walking, slowed to heartbeat. Dark crows flapped across the field, shadows black against the scarlet poppies. They sat in lines along the fences, perched on thorn bushes, massed on hedge tops, ranged along the branches of the Fever Tree. Their heads nodded in time to the rhythm of the drummer as his hands beat slower, slower than breathing, slower than dreaming. Then the drumbeat stopped and the dark crows rose, spiralling high above the poppies then swirling downwards, lower and lower till they plunged to the ditch where the dancers lay.

Snuffwidget screamed. He felt his body rack and shake. He screamed out names he could not remember. He clenched his fists and arched his neck. One huge crow straddled over his face, drawing sharp claws across his flesh. Snuffwidget screamed, but no sound came. No sound left his muted lips as the crow flapped and strutted, clattering its jet-black wings. Snuffwidget screamed, but no sound came as the crow lurched down with baleful beak and plucked away his eyes.

Snuffwidget writhed and shuddered, then in the ditch he slept. Slept in blinded, wild-eyed sleep, slumped against the other dancers - propped up next to Hamsparrow and Scatterlegs, lolling into Silverwing, toppling into Moonpetal's lap. Snuffwidget slept, lost in the depths of the ditch at the end of the Echo Field, the heads of the poppies drooling their redness, while the drummer played on and on.

Snuffwidget dreamt dreams he had never dreamt before. Dreamt he was flying, dreamt he was spinning high above treetops, plunging down to skim just above the reach of the hedgerows, swooping over the rough stone walls. He could see. Could see the scrawny-tailed cats who glowered at him from the dank shadows of backyards. He could feel the breath of the ravaging dogs who snarled at his tail feathers as he twisted away. He could smell the dew of the morning's awakening turning sour as it seeped into moss-festered walls.

In a clearing in a forest, he saw a house crouching, walls of grey silence spun with silver webs. The door opened slowly and out stepped a woman, taller than her shadow, her hands reaching up for the sun. Her hair was long and black, spilling across her shoulders, cascading in rivulets down towards her waist. She wore a gown of darkness, darker than the night, darker than the darkness sealed in a cellar for an age of sleepless years. Her house was surrounded by a ring of moon-white stones and as she walked around them she reached inside her dress and placed a bright red seed on the top of every one.

Snuffwidget gazed at the woman. He knew that she was beautiful. He knew he wanted to embrace her and kiss her full on the lips, but as he hurried forward he heard his dark wings clattering and saw her face turn from the hack of his bone-sharp beak. Snuffwidget flapped away and perched on the branch of a nearby tree. He tried to call out to her, but he knew she could not hear him. Only the broken darkness of his rough and rusty "caw". Instead he sat and watched her, his head on one side. He could see that she was singing but he could not catch the words.

He sat with his head cocked, watching as she continued, placing a bright red seed on top of every milk-white stone. Then when she had completed the circle of her house she went back inside and closed the door. Snuffwidget hopped down from the tree and strutted round the clearing. Then he flew up onto the window-sill and peered in through the glass.

She was combing her hair in front of the mirror and as he watched the movement of her long pale hands he was struck by something familiar about the way she was standing, the rhythm of her arm, the way she tilted her head. For a moment he blinked and imagined her hair not black but silver - and knew that this could be none other than his own grandmother, Corbin Night-thorn. Except that he knew this could not be, for old Nana Corbin was long since dead. But this was her, and she was alive. And she was not old, she was here and young.

He could see her eyes smiling at him, just the way his grandmother had, and he could see that she was singing, but he could not hear her song. He felt his head spinning and he hopped down from the window. He hopped out to the circle of milk-white stones and pecked at one of the bright red seeds that Corbin Night-thorn had placed there. The seed was sweet - sweeter than honey, sweeter than dew, sweeter than the rainbows that float in the river and run to the ocean when the moon is still new.

Snuffwidget rose with the seed in his beak and felt himself flying away from the clearing, high over the forest, away from the house, away from Corbin Night-thorn and her ring of milk-white stones. He soared and he soared till the sun scorched his feathers and then he dropped down towards the Echo Field once more, where the drummer still beat out his rhythm in the corner, hunched in the shadow beneath the Fever Tree. And the poppies still nodded, their heads torn and ragged, their petals strewn across the dancers who lay sleeping in the ditch.

Snuffwidget woke. Felt the weight of the crow who perched on his face. Felt the clutch of the claws which clung to his neck. Felt the pulse of his eyes as they opened soft and gentle as the crow pulled back its beak then slowly flapped away.

Snuffwidget could see. See daylight and field. See drummer and poppies. See the lengthening shadow of the Fever Tree. Could see Hamsparrow and Ravenhair, Scatterlegs and Silverwing. Could see Scarum and Moonpetal, Shadowit and Dewdream. Then the drumbeat stopped. Darkness was crawling. All around the field, sleepers rose from the ditch, reaching out to pluck fresh fistfuls of poppies, frail petals spilling from their mouths to the ground.

Bedraggled down the rutted lane, the procession struggled home, decked in crow-black feathers, their masks askew, flowers dangling from their tunics, streaked with daubs of tawny clay. Back to Brunt Boggart, back to the alleys, back to the warmth of their homes.

Snuffwidget stumbled in through his door, sleepy and tired from the long dreaming day. His head was spinning, his pockets still stuffed with fading poppies. He slept long and dark. He dreamt of his dreams.

Dreamt of the crow and Corbin Night-thorn's cottage. Dreamt of the poppies and the straggle of dancers. Dreamt of the drummer out under the tree.

Snuffwidget woke early next morning. The sun shone brightly in through the window and his head felt as clear as a fast flowing stream. He sprang out of bed and opened the door to let in the light and the blackbird's clamouring song.

The Crowdancers were leaving already. One by one, by two by two, silent as shadows as they wandered off along the lane in their ragged tunics still smirched with clay and feathers. Snuffwidget sat on the step and watched them disappearing, out beyond the edge of the houses. He could feel the drum-beat throbbing as if it was inside his head. His fingers twitched restlessly and his toe tapped out of time. But he didn't want to dance. The sleep was stealing into his head and he could taste dark thunder at the back of his throat, just as he had the day before. He could see the dreams in front of him, more real than the dusty room. Could see the crows come pecking, could feel the tug in his arms, as if they were wings. Could see the cottage in the woods and Corbin Night-thorn come to the door. Could see her face smiling, could feel her eyes turn on him. Could read her lips as she spoke.

"Where is the seed?" she seemed to be saying. "Where is the seed that I put on the stone? Was it you who took it, Snuffwidget Night-thorn?"

Snuffwidget stood up. His hands were shaking.

"Oh, Nana Night-thorn, I didn't mean to. I'll find it in my pocket, you know that I will. I'll find the seed in my pocket and then I'll bring it back."

Snuffwidget thrust his hand in his pocket to find a

pebble, a string, a rusty old key. A dead moth, a penny, a dry shrivelled leaf. But the seed wasn't there. Then he put his hand in the other pocket, thrust deep and groped along the lining. There in the shadow of the shadows, there was the bright red seed that had lain on the stone in the woods outside Corbin Night-thorn's cottage. But how could he take it back to her? He would have to go with the dancers. He would have to go to the Echo Field and dance around the Fever Tree. He would have to lie in the dreck of the ditch and wait for the crows to come. He would have to give them his eyes again and see what he would see.

Snuffwidget rushed around the room, grabbing up his coat and pulling on his boots.

"But what if the crows don't come?" he asked himself as he tied his laces tight. "Or what if they do and they take me somewhere else? What if I never see Nana Night-thorn again?"

"Stop!" Her voice came again.

"Snuffwidget, there's no need to bring the seed to me. The seed is for you. Take care of it. Plant it in your garden. Tend it and water it well and see what will grow."

Snuffwidget looked around. He could hear Corbin Night-thorn's voice though no-one was there. But he did what she said. He took the tiny seed out into his garden, the little plot of dark black earth out at the back of his cottage, where he reared his spinach, his turnips and his tatties, where he tended his long white parsnips and his sweet green beans.

Snuffwidget scooped out a hole in the moist rich soil and dropped in the bright red seed as the morning sun rose high in the sky and peered down over his shoulder.

He scattered warm earth on top of the seed and patted it flat with the palm of his hand. Then he fetched a can and watered it and trod the soft mulch down. And the warm wind blew and the sweet rain fell and the sun gazed down every day as Snuffwidget tended his seed, every moment he could spare away from the bottles and the barrels and the brewing.

Still they would come, the mothers and the little'uns for a pennyworth of gobstopper and a taste of lemonade. And the Crowdancers would stop by too on their way to the Echo Field. He was always pleased to see them but he wished that they would leave so that he could go out into his garden and see if the seed had started to grow. Finally they drifted off to the beat of the distant drum.

Moonpetal waited behind.

"Why don't you come with us, Snuffwidget? Come back to the Fever Tree. You've only tasted the poppies once. Come and dance and lay down with us."

She smoothed her skirt and fluttered her eyes, but Snuffwidget looked away.

"Not today, Moonpetal," he said.

Moonpetal sighed and planted a playful kiss on Snuffwidget's cheek, then hurried away to catch up with Scarum and all the other dancers. Snuffwidget closed the door and sat in the shadows of his room, counting up the gleaming bottles which were glinting in the gloom. He put on his coat and went outside and then his tired eyes opened wide.

The seed had sprouted! One tender green shoot had sprung up from the ground. Snuffwidget seized his can and watered it again. And day after day he did the same, until the shoot was a stem, was a bush, was a shrub, was grown almost to a tree. And blossom flowered and faded and fell and then there were berries which bore the branches down. And the berries were green, then red, then golden brown.

Snuffwidget took a basket from the cellar. He wiped it around to take the dust away and inside it was stained the colour of the berries and then he knew this basket must have been old Nana Night-thorn's own, that she used for gathering-in the berries. So he went out into the garden and he picked and he picked just as quickly as he could till the basket was brim full and all glistening with dew.

That day when he brewed Night-thorn's Morning Sunrise, the elderflower, nutmeg and basil, simmered in sugar - he mixed in the berries too. Then he sat and he waited and watched the street go by, the mothers and the babies who came knocking for their sweets, the men on their way to the fields who needed a jar of lemonade to help them on their way. And the draggle of dancers still tottering on to the beat of the distant drum out under the Fever Tree.

One day passed, and two, and three. Snuffwidget's fingers were trembling as he unscrewed the lid on top of the brew. He drew in a breath and his cheeks became flushed as his nostrils twitched and his lips felt as though they'd been kissed, though no-one was there at all. Snuffwidget raised the jar. He took a sip. His tongue was dancing. He took another, then more, then more. He felt a warmth inside him and as the sun streamed in through the window, he thought he could hear Corbin Night-thorn laughing happily and feel her arms embracing him as she swirled him round the room.

There was a knocking at the door. Snuffwidget flung

it open wide. Ravenhair and the dancers were standing right outside.

"Snuffwidget, why are you smiling so much?" Moonpetal cried.

"Step up, step up." Snuffwidget beckoned them in as he held out a glass of Night-thorn's Morning Sunrise.

"Not this again," sighed Scatterlegs.

"It's only old rot-gut," Hamsparrow complained.

"We've all tried it before," said Scarum, shaking his head.

"We've got better things to do," Ravenhair declared. "Can't you hear the drummer's started, out under the Fever Tree?"

And they shuffled all away, leaving only Moonpetal sitting on the step.

"Here," she said. "Let me try."

She took a sip from the glass. The Sunrise was sweet. Sweeter than honey, sweeter than dew. Sweeter than the rainbows that float in the river and run to the ocean when the moon is still new. Moonpetal smiled and stretched her arms wide as she arched her back.

"Should I come with you, out to the field?" Snuffwidget asked.

Moonpetal shook her head.

"It's too late," she said. "The dancers have gone."

As Snuffwidget gazed into her eyes which shone as bright as berries, twas as if Corbin Night-thorn sat right there beside him.

"I think I'll stay here instead," she said, as she shook the dead red petals out of her hair.

They climbed the step together and as they closed the door, the street outside filled slowly with a dark cluster of crows.

RAVENHAIR AND THE PEDLAR MAN

Let me tell you... Let me tell you ... around Old Granny Willowmist's cottage the cats would slink scowling by day and prowling by night, all marl eyed and belly crawling, crook backed and yowling. Once Greychild heard them he could never get to sleep - and sleep came hard enough for him, here between the four walls of Granny Willowmist's cottage, for he was a child of the woods, remember? He had grown up under the trees, with the moon in his eye and the wind in his hair. He sang his own songs, he played his own games. He could not settle in the village. On hot summer nights like this, those old cats would watch him steal out of Granny Willowmist's house and pad down the silent streets, while everyone was sleeping.

Greychild would make his way to the woods again, the woods that he knew, the woods where he grew. He would run through the trees, tearing loose his shirt and he would howl a sweet release. Not the howl of the

Wolf the village boys took him for, but a howl of his own tongue. Howl of wind, of sinew, of bark rough against skin, of brambles gnawing at his legs, of the sweet kiss of dew at the waking of dawn.

And he would howl for mother, though mother had not come here these long moons gone. But he howled for her still and he felt an emptiness aching inside him bigger than the hunger he first knew when she stopped coming, stopped bringing him food. And he would sing again, the song she sang for him: "*Coddle me, coddle me, my darling son...*"

But the wood was empty now and he howled one last time to the moon which hung between the trees. She was not here - and she was not in the village, he knew that. But he set off back, grateful again that at least he had his long narrow bed in Granny Willowmist's cottage, where the cats sat and waited, watching for his return.

Greychild was tired now, loping sleepily across dull colourless fields. As he reached Brunt Boggart's twisted streets, the first squat cottages lurking in the dark, he heard a sound. Sound like banshees, wailing, howling, clattering and beating. Greychild stopped. He remembered the boys had told him how they thought he was Wolf. Told him they all felt safe now, now they knew he was Boy. But maybe, true, there was Wolf, and this Wolf was coming now. Coming down the narrow streets. Coming down the rattle of cobbles. Beating against locked windows. Greychild shivered. Wolf was here. Wolf was before him as he hid in a doorway, shivering and shaking as Oakum Marlroot and his men rounded the corner. Not Wolf, but wolf in them. Their eyes were wild, their fists were hanging - beating and brawling, singing and wailing. Filled with the best and worst of Snuffwidget's ale which he stored at the back of his cellar. They had been there and drunk it all.

Oakum Marlroot stood big in the moonlight. He could see Greychild cowering in the door.

"WolfBoy!" he spat. "You know what you are. You know that we know. What you been doing out now on your own? This been night. All good people sleeping. What you doing out here under the moon?"

Greychild's jaw fell slack. A stream of words which could not find their shape slithered from his mouth and turned to a wail, to a cry, to a howl. Oakum Marlroot seized him triumphantly.

"See!" He turned to his companions. "See - when he's out at night, alone at night, alone like Wolf - then *is* Wolf. Can't talk at all. Only howl."

The men around him bayed in agreement.

"What shall we do with him?"

Oakum Marlroot pinned Greychild against the door. Greychild felt the hard wood press into his back. Felt Oakum Marlroot's breath hot on his face, stenching like a rancid dog. Greychild cast his eyes to the moon. At last he found one word.

"Mother!"

"Mother..." echoed around the empty streets where all seemed asleep, in spite of all this racket. Not a curtain twitched. Not one door opened. Except this one. The door behind him. Greychild fell into the darkness inside and the door closed quickly again, leaving Oakum Marlroot and his men pounding their fists against the heavy wood. Greychild looked around. He wondered where he was, whose house this might be.

But then he heard a voice, a voice firm and sure.

"Greychild! Are you hurt?"

Greychild shook his head, confused. It was Crossdogs. He had fallen in through Crossdogs' door. The boy stood above him and offered his hand. Greychild sprang up, pressed his ear to the door. It shook with one kick from Oakum Marlroot's boot. Shook but did not budge - and the hinges held firm. Greychild listened. He could hear the men cursing, then muttering, then hear them shuffling away. He looked at Crossdogs. There was silence. Then a crash as one hurled bottle shattered against the door. They waited, but no sound came anymore.

"Greychild - what are you doing?" Crossdogs chided. "You shouldn't be out at night. Should be sleeping in Granny Willowmist's cottage. Does she know where you are?"

Greychild shook his head.

"Not sure if I know where I am. Anywhere I go don't seem right somehow. Have to keep running. Have to keep looking."

"What are you looking for?" Crossdogs asked.

"Looking for home."

"Granny Willowmist give you a home."

"Granny Willowmist is kind. But her house is her house, not mine. My home isn't here. Not in the village. Not in the woods. Home is where my mother is."

"Your mother's..." Crossdogs began.

"... not here," Greychild concluded. "I know, I know. Not here, not there. Not anywhere. But somewhere after all. I have to find her."

Crossdogs shook his head as he filled the kettle and placed it on the hob. The two boys sat in the kitchen while his family were upstairs sleeping. He made a brew of fennel tea. Greychild sipped it slowly as the light from the moon outside glinted on the plates and the cutlery stacked along the dresser.

"Where else is there?" he asked.

"Let me tell you..." said Crossdogs, as Greychild sat and listened. "Let me tell you - there is a place. They call it Arleccra."

"Where is it? Where is Arleccra?" Greychild leaned forward eagerly.

"It is far away from here. A day's walk and a day's walk and many days' walk from there. No-one from Brunt Boggart has been there. Nobody has seen it."

"Then how do you know of it?" Greychild enquired.

"We know enough and we know too much and we know nothing at all. The Pedlar Man who comes here tells us all he knows and more."

"Who is the Pedlar Man?" Greychild looked puzzled.

"He's come this way every month for many a year. Since as long as I can remember and a while before that, I reckon. Don't bring nothing useful, only bracelets and rings and shiny things, and bright ribbons to tie up the girlen's hair. But he brings stories too and tells tales of Arleccra."

"What does he say?" Greychild's eyes were shining.

"Says it's filled with markets that sell treasures you've never dreamt of - brought by ships that sail in from the ends of the world. And taverns and food and wine that tastes sweeter than any potion that Snuffwidget has ever brewed. And there's dancing and music and everyone's happy and laughing all day and singing the long night through."

"I'd like to go there," Greychild mused.

Crossdogs shook his head.

"Wouldn't we all? But the way is long and weary. Some set out, but they always return. They always come back to Brunt Boggart."

Greychild was sitting on the edge of his chair. In the far distance, in the shadow of the night, he could hear Oakum Marlroot's men banging at their own front doors as they stumbled back to their houses. Then there was silence. An owl called, way off in the wood.

"I'd like to meet the Pedlar Man. I'd like to hear for myself everything he can tell me."

Crossdogs smiled.

"You have to be quick to catch him. I only ever see him once in a while. Truth is, mainly it's the girlen and the mothers and the old'uns who bother with him. All he's got is bracelets and trinkets. That's no good for the likes of me."

Crossdogs paused and poured out another round of tea.

"But let me tell you... let me tell you about Ravenhair. You must know Ravenhair, everybody does."

Greychild nodded. "She tried to knot my hair with ribbons."

"Hope it wasn't her own ribbon," Crossdogs replied. "Ravenhair had a ribbon that was darker than night so you couldn't see it when she had it tied in her pitch black hair. It was the only one she ever wore - it was the one that her Grandmother Ghostmantle gave her. And then one day she lost it. Couldn't find it anywhere. At first she never minded. She told me it held her hair too tight and now she could shake her tresses long and free and feel the wind as she ran barefoot through the dew-drenched fields all the way to the wood.

"But then her hair flew into her eyes and she couldn't see where she was going and her foot slid on a slippery stone and she tumbled down to the ground. As she lay there, her head all spinning, staring up to the sun, she knew that this was no good. She had to have the ribbon, the ribbon her grandmother gave her, the black ribbon she'd always worn. So she limped back to the village and she asked the girlen one by one. You know them all - you know who I mean - Silverwing and Moonpetal, Dawnflower and Duskeye, Scallowflax, Dewdream and Riversong.

"She even checked through Silverwing's hair, picking through all the many-coloured ribbons that were tied and knotted there. She tugged at Moonpetal's one gleaming thong. Dawnflower's hair was trussed up with daisies, she had no ribbon at all. Duskeye fixed her with a smouldering glare as she raked her fingers through her hair, but all she could find was a comb of white bone. Scallowflax's tresses were scrabbled and lax, the ribbons hung loosely, while Dewdream and Riversong were braided up tight - but her Grandmother Ghostmantle's night-black ribbon was nowhere to be seen. None of them had it at all.

"Ravenhair stamped her foot and then regretted it, for her ankle was still sore from her trip on the slipperty stone.

"'Someone must have seen it,' she winced. 'Don't all just stand there, looking so innocent.' Dawnflower and Moonpetal pretended they hadn't heard her while Silverwing and Duskeye looked the other way. Dewdream and Riversong shrugged.

"'Ribbons come and ribbons go. It's nothing to fuss

about,' they said. 'If you can't find this one, you can soon get another one, next time the Pedlar Man comes.'

"Ravenhair folded her arms. 'The Pedlar Man won't be here till after new moon. But I don't want a new ribbon - I'm not like you. I don't keep on changing and trying out new colours. I've only had one ribbon since I was a little one - the ribbon my Grandmother Ghostmantle gave me, the ribbon dark as night.'

"The girlen ran into the darkness and Ravenhair was left standing, her long tresses hanging loose around her shoulders. She was sure that one of them must have taken her ribbon, but unless they were brazen enough to start wearing it in front of her, she had no way of knowing who that might be.

"Ravenhair wandered away sadly. Perhaps she was judging too harshly. Perhaps none of them had taken the ribbon. Perhaps it had just come loose and blown away in the wind. She peered down the alleyways and rooted round the pigmires. She squinnied the roof-tops and rattled at the leaves of low-hanging trees with a length of willow-stick. But the ribbon dark as night that her Grandmother had given her was nowhere to be seen. How could she go home? How could she tell her mother that she'd lost the only ribbon that she'd worn all her life?

"Then she saw it. A dark ribbon, a long ribbon, draped over the top bar of the gate to Oakum Marlroot's fields. She grabbed it up quickly and swung it in the air, flinging it over her head to tie up her flowing black hair. But then she stopped. The ribbon felt different, not so smooth somehow - it was coarser and rougher. She let her hair fall loose again and ran the ribbon through her fingers. It was dark, sure enough - but not as deep as night. She held it out in front of her. Not as dark and not as long. And at each end was a thread of silver, woven into the black.

"'This is not my ribbon at all!' Ravenhair exclaimed. 'It must belong to Moonpetal - she's always copying me. It's fine enough in its own way, but she must have bought it from the Pedlar Man. Maybe I should wait till after new moon and go and see him myself.'"

Greychild leaned forward in his chair, drinking in Crossdogs' words.

"What did she do? Did she keep Moonpetal's ribbon to tie up her hair so her mother wouldn't notice?"

"I knew that you'd ask me," Crossdogs said slowly. "What do you think?"

Greychild rubbed his chin.

"I think she might try it. Them girlen sure like their ribbons. Always trying new ones. Long'uns, short'uns, pretty ones, tatty ones - just to see how they feel. They always done that with me. A-tying up my hair and stroking of my face. And kissing me all that way and this."

Crossdogs shook his head. "But Ravenhair, she's different - not like the other girlen. She'd never wear Moonpetal's ribbon - she had to find her own. So she searched day after day. Searched in the alleyways, searched every street, searched in the gutters up under the houses. But it was nowhere to be seen, so she wandered off out into the fields, thinking maybe the wind had taken it.

"She searched and she searched till at last the new moon rose, a thin sliver of silver, high up in the sky. And then she watched, and then she waited, till just as the other girlen had told her - next night as she sat out by the track, she heard a song in the gloaming and she heard tired boots a-trudging, and then round the corner came the Pedlar Man, with a sack tied on his back. His face was worn with the weather and his beard was long and grey. His eyes had seen the rising suns and his lips were cracked with the stories that he bore from town to town.

"'Oh Pedlar Man, you're here at last,' Ravenhair cried. 'Where have you come from and where are you going and what do you carry in that patched old sack that hangs from your shoulders so heavy and full?'

"The Pedlar stopped and looked at the girl and lowered the sack slowly down to the ground.

"'Why, I come from Arleccra and I'm going as far as my feet will take me, then all the way back again.'

"Ravenhair shifted from foot to foot and tossed her long flowing tresses.

"'Pedlar Man, Pedlar Man, let me ask you again. What's in your sack so heavy and full?'

"The Pedlar Man unknotted the string that bound the top of the sack.

"'I've got bracelets and rings and glittering things. I've even got a ribbon for you to tie back your flowing black hair. Your tumbling tresses are handsome but your face is prettier still. I'm sure you don't want to hide it away, or how will the boys ever kiss you?'

"Ravenhair danced round and round. Now she had decided. Much as she was saddened to have lost her grandmother's ribbon, she had to have something to tie up her hair. The Pedlar Man pulled open the top of his sack and let her peek inside. There was a glitter of trinkets and bracelets and beneath them she glimpsed the ribbons, the sheen and the lustre of silk brocade.

"Ravenhair was so excited, the words came tumbling out.

"'Oh tell me, please, just how much these ribbons cost?'

"The Pedlar Man scratched his head. 'Each one is a shining penny.'

"Ravenhair pulled out her pockets. 'I'm sorry, I don't have any.'

"She scuffed her toe in a circle in the dust as one teardrop fell to the ground.

"'I set out this morning, as I have every morning, to look for my ribbon, my Grandmother's ribbon, that was stolen away by the wind.'

"'Don't look so sad,' the Pedlar Man said. 'I'll tell you what I'll do. I'll give you a ribbon, especially for you, if you'll just sing me a song.'

"Ravenhair felt so grateful she almost flung her arms around the old man's neck and kissed his leathery face. Instead she sat on the grass by the roadside. What could she sing, she wondered."

"I know what I'd sing," said Greychild.

"I know what you'd sing as well," Crossdogs replied. "You only know one song - *Coddle Me, Coddle Me* - the song your mother taught you. Well Ravenhair had a special song too. It was a song her Grandmother passed on to her, the one who gave her the ribbon. I know it because, some nights when we'd sit out together, under the stars, she'd sing the same song just for me:

> 'Tie me a ribbon,
> I'll wear it so well;
> It will whisper me secrets
> That I'll never tell.

It will whisper of rivers
That shine in the sun,
Carrying tears to the ocean
When the long day is done.

It will whisper of mountains
That rise to the clouds
And gather the silence
While the wind blows so loud.

It will whisper my true love
Who I've never met,
But he'll bring me sweet happiness
I'll never forget.

Tie me a ribbon,
I'll wear it so well;
It will whisper me secrets
That I'll never tell.'"

Greychild rubbed his eyes. Crossdogs' voice was hushed to a whisper.

"When Ravenhair had finished her song, all the birds fell silent. There was no breeze in the trees. The Pedlar Man wrenched open his sack and let the ribbons spill onto the grass. There were yellow ribbons, red ribbons, purple and green. Long ones, short ones, wide and thin. There were ribbons striped and mottled and ribbons plain and trim. But none as dark as Grandmother Ghostmantle's ribbon that Ravenhair had worn all her life. But now she didn't care anymore. She flung up her hands in delight.

"'I want this one - no this one!' Each one was so beautiful she just couldn't chose. 'I want them all!' she cried.

"'Each one's a shiny penny,' the Pedlar Man reminded her.

"'And my Grandmother's song is worth all that and more,' Ravenhair replied.

"And so she sang the song again and again, while the Pedlar Man sat raptured, there by the roadside. And each time she sang he twined another ribbon around her wrist, until in the end there were no ribbons in his sack - Ravenhair had them all. The sun was nearly setting down. Ravenhair had been singing her Grandmother's song all the long hours long. She eyed the bracelets and trinkets and rings, but the Pedlar Man shook his head.

"'Save your breath,' he said, as he tied up his sack. 'Leave me something for the other girlen. I can't sell it all for a song.'

"He tipped his hat back on his head and set off down the dusty track that would lead him straight to Brunt Boggart. Ravenhair watched him go, then she seized up her precious ribbons and ran off into the woods. She picked her way between the tall dark trees until she came to a pool. There she knelt by the edge of the water and tied the first ribbon into her hair. And then another and then another until her long black tresses were festooned with colours as she stared at her reflection.

"'Now my hair's just as fine as any of the girlen - and the boys can see my face again and they'll all come flocking to kiss me!'

"And she picked up her skirts and she ran and she ran, skipping quickly over knotted roots, twisting and turning between bushes sharp with thorns. But then in the creeping dullness of dusk, her foot slipped under a fallen branch and she tripped to the ground. She lay in a bed of fallen leaves, staring up to the stars. Then she turned and she peered into a brackish puddle and she saw her hair, a tangle of raggedy ribbons - but none of them suited her like the ribbon dark as night, the ribbon her Grandmother Ghostmantle gave her. And how had she come by these ribbons? She had sung her Grandmother's song, the song she never sang to anyone."

"I thought you told me she had sung it to you?" Greychild interrupted.

"That's what makes it so special," Crossdogs explained. "I'm the only other person who's ever heard it."

"'Now I've given my song to the Pedlar Man,' Ravenhair wailed, 'And he'll be singing it to everyone, not just in Brunt Boggart, but in every town and village along the road.'

"She tore the ribbons from her hair before she reached the lights of the houses. In the mossy hollow that lay in the middle of the Green, all the girlen were sitting.

"'Ravenhair, Ravenhair - see what we've got. You missed the Pedlar Man again.'

"'Look,' cried Silverwing, 'I have a comb as white as ivory.'

"Moonpetal showed her a glittering ring with a stone that glowed a shimmering green. Dawnflower laughed as she twisted a necklace between her long pale fingers. Duskeye smiled and clutched a box, but wouldn't show what was in it. A gaudy bracelet dangled from Scallowflax's wrist, while Dewdream gazed into a looking glass and Riversong threaded a needle of silver. But Ravenhair stood and stared at them all. Somehow she sensed that they didn't seem truly happy with their trinkets.

"'What's the matter?' she asked.

"'The Pedlar Man came, just the way he does after every new moon. You know how much we all look forward to seeing him again. These gimcracks are fine, but you know what we long for most of all?'

"Ravenhair shrugged and raised her eyes to the sky. 'No - I don't know. Please tell me.'

"'Oh Ravenhair - of course you do. We buy new ribbons every month, but this time the Pedlar Man didn't have any. He told us he had sold them already, and he always has so many.'

"Ravenhair smiled at her friends' frowning faces. The trinkets that they had bought looked dull and tawdry now.

"'Don't be sad!' Ravenhair exclaimed. 'I have ribbons enough for everyone.' And she pulled them out from under her coat and threw them amongst the circle of girls.

"Then Ravenhair ran to her mother's house and found her sitting by the window with a far-away look in her eyes.

"'Ravenhair, Ravenhair, where have you been? I've been worried about you, child.'

"'Mother, oh Mother - I've lost my ribbon, the ribbon I've worn all my life, the ribbon your mother gave me. All the while I've been without it and had to tie my hair in a scarf when I came home so that you would not see. I've looked for it everywhere, the ribbon dark as night. I've asked Silverwing and Scallowflax and all of the others. None of them have got it, none of them have seen it. I've searched through the streets and the alleyways and rooted through the pigmires. I've squinnied the roofs and the gutters and rattled the leaves on the low-hanging trees with a length of willow-stick. But I cannot find the ribbon that Grandmother Ghostmantle gave me.'

"Ravenhair's mother put a hand on her daughter's shoulder. She spoke to her softly, in the way only a mother can.

"'Last new moon when you were sleeping, I wanted to visit the Pedlar Man. I wanted to buy a necklace to make me look young and pretty again. Now that your father has gone, I hoped I might find a new man to keep me company and to be a father for you.'

"'I don't want another father,' Ravenhair replied. 'Foxbriar is all the father I ever had and all the father I ever knew. I can keep his memory. I don't want someone new.'

"'Forgive me child, if I was wrong. But I wanted to look my best for the Pedlar Man - and so I took your ribbon, the ribbon my mother gave you. I took it while you were sleeping and tied up my own tawny hair. Then I went out to the track by the woods and waited until he came.

"'He told me I looked so fine, with my nut-brown hair all tied up with a ribbon dark as night. I begged him to open his sack and I pawed through the jewels and the trinkets until I found a necklace which sparkled like ice against the bronze of my skin. I implored him to let me buy it, but he would not let me have it, not for all the gold I could give him, which I have to confess was not very much. But then he told me he'd give me the necklace if only I'd take off the ribbon and let down my hair for him.

"'And I did, my child, I did. I wanted that necklace so much that I parted with your precious ribbon, the ribbon my own mother gave you. And though I knew it was wrong, I loved the way he looked at me with my hair so loose and long. But all this time, though I've worn the necklace and smiled at every man I've met, not one of them smiled back at me the same way as the Pedlar Man.

"'And so last night I set out early to catch him before he even reached here with his sack. I told him I still had the necklace, but that none of the men had looked at me, and I knew that you'd been missing the ribbon, even though you hadn't told me - so I asked if he still had it, anywhere in his sack.

"'He rummaged through all the ribbons and in the end he found it. We exchanged the necklace and the ribbon again, the necklace which sparkled like ice and the ribbon as dark as night, there beside the rutted track.'

"'But Mother, Mother,' Ravenhair cried, 'I went to the Pedlar Man myself today. Now I know why he did not have any ribbon black, but others of every hue and colour. I sang him Grandmother Ghostmantle's song, again and again and again until he'd given me them all.'

"Ravenhair's mother clapped her hands. 'Let me see! Let me see!'

"Ravenhair shook her head. 'Mother, you know that the ribbon dark as night - the ribbon your own mother gave me - is the only ribbon for me. The other ribbons were gaudy and brash and I gave them all away to the girlen who sit by the mossy hollow that lies in the middle of the Green.'

"Ravenhair's mother took her daughter's face and held it between her long dusky hands. 'My child,' she said slowly, 'Now that you've met the Pedlar Man, alone along the rutted track, you can tie up your hair on top of your head, the way that the women wear it, not loose down your back like the girls.' And while she spoke, she took out the ribbon, the ribbon dark as night, the ribbon that Grandmother Ghostmantle had worn, and her grandmother before her. And she combed her long fingers through her daughter's hair and braided the ribbon around it. Ravenhair didn't know what to say. She felt as tall as a woman and as small as a child.

"'I'm worried about my Grandmother's song,' she said as she smiled and looked away. 'Now that the Pedlar Man has heard it, I'm afraid he will sing it on street corners for pennies and everyone will know Ghostmantle's secret song, and I will feel ashamed.'

"Ravenhair's mother placed a finger on her lips. 'What the Pedlar Man remembers and what the Pedlar Man forgets is a mystery to us all. I know he did not sing the song here in the village tonight. If he had, why then Silverwing and all the other girls would have been the first to sing it to you. But leave it to your mother. Necklace or no, ribbon or no, I will go after the Pedlar Man and meet him under the stars. Just one taste of your mother's sweet kiss will make him forget every song he's ever heard!'"

Greychild tilted his empty cup and Crossdogs rattled the earthenware pot, but they'd drained it of fennel tea. Through the window dawn was creeping and the first birds of the morning broke into song. Greychild leaned back in his chair and stretched. In the room upstairs they could hear Crossdogs' father stirring in his bed. Greychild stood up.

"I knew there must be worlds beyond Brunt Boggart," he said. "I'm going to find the Pedlar Man's Track to see where it will lead me."

Crossdogs shook his head. "First journey you must make is back to Granny Willowmist's house before anyone sees you. Oakum Marlroot and his men will all be snoring now. There'll be some fat heads among them today. They won't be out in the fields till near noon, that's for sure."

Greychild opened the door. He could hear the cats squawling round Granny Willowmist's cottage. He smelt the morning air, the scent of dew wet flowers, the dull waft of dung from the pigmires and the dust on the path that wound away from Brunt Boggart. Now he knew where it led, out towards the Pedlar Man's Track and a day's walk and a day's walk and many days' walk from there, all the way to the city of Arleccra.

RIVERSONG, LARKSPITTLE AND THE MOON OF BLOOD

Let me tell you. Let me tell you... cold was on the world, gripped in a fist of frost. In Brunt Boggart, all around the Green, fires flickered in the crofts and the cottages, but still it was cold. Cold was in the sky as the stars glistened clear, searing through the emptiness of cloudless night. And early the next morning, rooks pecked at the thin ice down by Pottam's Mill, while ducks upended, searching for grubs in the muddied water. Cold was on Larkspittle's hands as he blew on his fingers in the pigmires, in the slurry yards, as he slopped out the troughs. Cold was in his back, in his belly, in his bones.

But his eyes shone brightly with a warmth he'd never known, when he looked up and saw, just for an instant, Riversong standing next to the old barn door. It was like as if he'd never seen her before, but he knew that wasn't true. Larkspittle had known Riversong ever since he could remember, ever since they'd been babes together, ever since they was little'uns running and laughing, tumbling and singing ring songs down by the meadow, beside the eddying stream. They grew up calling and shouting, climbing trees and falling, getting wet-footed in the spring-time puddles, gathering berries from branches and bushes, then lying in the shadows turning green with belly-ache.

Now here she was standing, watching him - and he was watching her in that moment so short it went on forever - before she smiled and turned her head, then clutched at the long scarlet skirt that she'd never worn before and ran away, all by herself, around the side of the barn. Larkspittle shook his head. The way that she looked at him now was just the way that she'd gazed at him with a warmth all of her own when they'd danced the last dance together, on the summer Green at the Blossom Moon. But now it was cold. The Moon of Blood was coming.

As their shadows grew longer, Riversong's hair grew stronger, and Larkspittle's chin grew a fuzz of fur and his voice dropped into his boots. Some days he hardly saw her at all - and Riversong found that some mornings she just wanted to sit by herself, all under the shade of the willow tree and puzzle out how her body was shaping and mellowing and where it would lead her and why. While Larkspittle ran with the boys-who-would-be-men and spent all the long day long bending branches and wrestling on the Green.

Now if they glimpsed each other in the shadow of the evening, Riversong and Larkspittle would gaze long and full and then they'd look away, look back to their companions and pretend that they had no memory of all the seasons they'd grown together and pretend they had no yearning for the years they knew would come. For now the boys grew whiskers and hung fox pelts from their shoulders and the girlen all wore scarlet skirts and braided ribbons through their hair. And each would watch each other and throw names at their childhood neighbours and taunt and chide and roll their eyes and streak their cheeks with clay.

And they'd play day-long games of Fox-and-Geese and Chainy-o, to try and catch each other then try and run away - with much falling down and laughter and fumbled mirth and tumbling while they watched the boys-become-men walk out in pairs with girlen who knew that they were full women grown - watched them walking side by side, elbow to elbow, waist to waist until they disappeared along the shady path that led to Sandy Holme.

At Sandy Holme the lazy stream flowed slowly under the arch of a cattle bridge and the flowers in the meadow grew bright and sweet and the birds flew up to the clear blue sky. And there a boy-who-would-be-man and a girlen-become-woman could lie down side by side in the long lush grass and watch the sun climbing high above them and feel its warmth in their arms till they walked on back home again past the old'uns who stood in their cottage doorways - some knowing, some disapproving, some too weary to care.

The Moon of Blood was coming, the first full moon after harvest. Riversong could feel its pull, tugging at her limbs till they danced without her bidding, tugging at her very veins as if they were rivers and streams, as if her body was the sea, dragged this way and that like the tide. She wrapped her red dress around her waist, just like all the other girlen. She tied her hair with ribbons bright and daubed a powder on her face to make it pale as the flowers which glowed in the wood and turned the colour of death.

Larkspittle watched her, but could not speak. He knew the words that he wanted to say, but knew they could not be spoken. He stretched his limbs like the branches of a tree as he felt the sap sluicing, flowing and forcing. The dance was coming, the Moon of Blood.

Far away in the Echo Field, they heard the Drummer beating. Heard him hammering out the rhythm, under the Fever Tree. But the pulse grew closer, as they heard him tracking in, all down the ditchways and the miry lanes, skirting round Oakum Marlroot's meadow, past Mottram Ironfield's stern-faced farm and Old Mother Tidgewallop's cottage, till he came at last to Mallenbrook Lane close by Pottam's Mill, calling the darkness down, each step closer he came. And as he approached, the boys took up the rhythm, beating sticks and stamping their boots. Some started chanting while others sang, and soon enough they all joined in:

"The Shuttle Stone stands tall and proud.
Hear our voices singing loud..."

While way out in the woods, Skyweaver took down his fiddle. He tightened the horsehair and rosined up his bow. He struck a chord, then another, then another before slamming shut his cottage door and stepping out into the darkness. But darkness was not darkness long as the full moon came rising high above the tree-tops, climbing through the sky till it hung huge and amber, lighting forest, lighting clearing. Lighting up the mossy hollow in the middle of Brunt Boggart's Green.

The girlen lit candles, while the old'uns and the wifen hung lanterns of paper, lanterns of gauze, lanterns of beeswax, lanterns twined of straw. Lanterns of feathers and butterfly wings - each of them gleaming, casting out redness, casting out scarlet, glowing rich as oxblood hung on poles, dangling from low branches all around the hollow, all around the Green, all along the avenue of trees that led away to a darkened grove at the edge of the waiting wood. While away and away, the other way, a path of tangled roots and scattered bones led along down to the Shuttle Stone which stood true and tall in the moonlight.

And then that moment they'd been waiting for, all this long season gone, when Skyweaver and Drummer met again, in the middle of the hollow in the Green. Skyweaver climbed a-top the platform of planks lashed together by hempen rope and Drummer sat cross-legged beside him and the rhythm beat on and the melody soared high. Though the two men never spoke, no more than a passing nod, their instruments spoke for them, the pounding of the drum-skin and the fiddle's searing shrill. Spoke more than words ever could. Spoke sunset and moonrise, night's raptures and rituals. Spoke sorrow and anguish, frenzy and desire. Spoke a language beyond singing, beyond chanting, beyond dancing. Spoke time beyond time, lost in the fire.

Caught up in the swirling crowd, caught up in the tug of the rhythm, Larkspittle rushed and stuttered along, looking out for his companions, Shadowit, Scarum, Scatterlegs and Longskull. But he could not see them. Could only see Oakum Marlroot and Mottram

Ironfield, drunk already, offering a fight to anyone who would take them. Larkspittle wheeled away. Saw the girlen in their ribbons, their red skirts swirling. Saw Duskeye, Silverwing, Dawnflower and Dewdream. And then the crowd scattered. The girlen shrieked and ducked away, and Larkspittle was standing, face to face with Riversong.

She looked at him.

He looked at her.

They both looked away.

Neither of them knew just what to say. Riversong smiled, her eyes open wide. Larkspittle's tongue trembled.

"Strong moon," he mumbled.

Riversong looked aloft. The moon was gone. It hid behind the clouds. She started to reply, but Silverwing grabbed her, seized her by the arm and steered her away, off with all the other girls. Larkspittle stood and watched her go. He raised his hand as if he was waving, but Riversong had gone, sucked into the crowd which rushed into the hollow where the drum was beating.

The Green was packed. From everywhere they had come, from far-flung farms, from broke-down cottages on Brunt Boggart's edge. Some even came from over the hills, from up river, from one day's walk down the Pedlar Man's Track. And the Pedlar Man himself was there, spreading out his wares on a stall at the verge of the Green - the ribbons and the trinkets and the glittery things. The revellers were tugged by Snuffwidget's wine and the howl of the wind and the surge of the rhythm and Skyweaver's fiddle and the blood in their veins sucked on by the moon in a raw red tide which they all could ride as the drum beat on.

But Riversong had gone.

Thunderhead hauled himself up onto the shaky wooden platform in the middle of the Green, his tall hat dark above his lime-daubed face. He raised one arm like a long white bone and pointed up to the bowl of the moon as it crept out from behind a cloud. The Drummer stopped, Skyweaver ceased and all the people on the Green fell silent.

"Let the Dance begin," Thunderhead intoned.

There was a shuffling and a shoving and a rushing and a pushing as women and men, girlen and boys took up partners, arm in arm. Skyweaver crouched and rosined his bow one final time, ready for the long night coming, while the Drummer tapped restlessly at the edge of his skins.

One beat. Two beats. Skyweaver unleashed his bow. Thunderhead leapt from the platform into the midst of the circling throng and wheeled away in a dervish dance, urging them on. Larkspittle glimpsed Riversong again, on the far side of the ring. He knew that if he waited, as the dance progressed, as each couple embraced and twirled, then she would come to him.

But first came Ravenhair, then Silverwing, then Dawnflower, then Moonpetal - and Larkspittle danced with each one of them. Each one of them took his hand, each one of them swirled him, each one of them twirled him and then each ducked under Larkspittle's outstretched arm and then the brief embrace as they swung one another around and Larkspittle sensed their clinging, their softness or their urgency, their distance or their delicacy, the kiss which followed moist and sweet or crisp and sharp, till the beat pulled their feet away and the dance wheeled on, driven by the rhythm, turn upon turn - till the next girl in the circle was Riversong.

And then she came to him, took him by the hand and they swirled and they twirled, same as ever before and Riversong ducked low, underneath his outstretched arm. And then they embraced. Uncertain at first. Riversong looked away. Looked away to the old'uns, clustered around the platform where the Drummer and Skyweaver played. Looked away to her companions, Silverwing and Dewdream. Looked away to the Moon of Blood, high above. Looked anywhere but at Larkspittle. But at the same time her hands gripped his waist, gripped him fast and close and hip upon hip, thigh against thigh, her body soft as the Hollow's moss and supple as a willow, they swirled and they span till the stars stood still though the beat of the drum rode on. And the dancers around were all waiting, waiting for Larkspittle and Riversong to part so that the circle could turn again and each take up new partners in a fresh embrace.

Skyweaver kept on playing, smiling as his foot tapped out the rhythm. And the Drummer's hands kept moving in a blur as fast as beeswings.

But while the dancers waited, Riversong cradled her arm about Larkspittle's neck. She pulled him close and closer still. The kiss was slow. The kiss was strong. Larkspittle trembled, every nerve-end awakened. He was lost in a darkness that was no darkness at all. Filled with light, filled with silence, in the midst of the row-de-dow. Then he felt a hand heavy on his shoulder. Other arms grabbed him round the waist, sturdy and muscular, prizing him from Riversong. He saw her led away amidst a circling throng of the wifen and the girlen and a clutch of grey-haired old'uns, all clad in red - red skirts, red scarves, red shawls and cowls, red poppies twined in their hair. They swirled her away, away from the dancing, the music and the rhythm. Away from Larkspittle who quivered, lost and confused, flanked by Crossdogs and Hamsparrow, Bullbreath and Shadowit, in the midst of the boys-who-would-be-men.

Away from the dance was the darkness. The rhythm beat on in Riversong's head as she was borne by the girlen, Ravenhair and Silverwing, Dawnflower and Duskeye. The wood was crow-dark and breathing. Their feet cracked on fallen twigs, brambles clawed at their skirts, their scarlet dresses. The trees loomed low and seemed to whisper, their branches beckoning sinuously.

The women carried Riversong down a gully of darkness, away from the eye of the moon. The floor was moist and slippery wet where the red leaves of autumn had fallen. Their hands pushed Riversong on, urgent and strong. Behind her, she heard the song:

"In the Red Grove our senses spin.
Look without and look within:
Girlen games no more to play -
Moon of Blood takes them away."

She looked for the women to follow her, for she needed their strength, their confidence, but suddenly she was alone. The Moon of Blood broke through from above, through the clouds, through the lattice of branches - and she could see that she was meshed in a tunnel of bramble thorn. She wanted to be back at the

Green, to be with Larkspittle, to hold him in her arms
and to kiss him once again - but she heard the women's
voices and she knew she must go on. As she pushed
between the bushes, sharp thorns snagged her arms,
jagged her fingers, ripped her legs. Her pulsing veins
were raked and torn and she tasted her blood pure red.

> "Wax and wane
> And kiss the pain.
> Share the pleasure,
> Turn again."

The song drove Riversong on, away from the clawing
thorns, and thrust her into a grove that was hid behind
the trees. Here were poppies, vivid red, alike the Echo
Field. Here were roses, blooming rich and rare. Here
were trees topped with plum red apples and berries of
darkest hawthorn. From away and away she heard the
voices of the women and all the other girlen, dressed in
scarlet petticoats, just as she wore now.

> "Girlen games no more to play,
> Moon of Blood takes them away.
> Look without and look within -
> In the Red Grove our senses spin."

Riversong looked around. Here was the Red Grove.
She was here now, this place the other girlen told her of
- that they sang about, whispered about all out on the
Green and all the way down by the edge of the wood.
She was here now. But now she was here, what should
she do? Under the light of the Moon of Blood,
Riversong could see everything and nothing at all. She

wanted to be back at the dance, she wanted to be here all alone.

And so she danced, she danced the Grove. Danced to embrace the apple tree, her scarlet skirt draped round its trunk. Danced to touch the hawthorn bush, its glistening teeth tormenting her. Danced to pluck the darkest rose, never mind that its thorns snagged at her wrists. She wiped her hands all down her dress. She wanted to let the blood run free. She wanted to let it flow.

She found the cup they'd told her of, back when they whispered in their huddles on the Green - found it caught in the roots of the tallest tree. She lifted it up to her lips and drank - and the wine was sweet, the wine was dark. The wine was laced with tang of salt and as she drank it spilled upon her dress. Riversong wiped the back of her hand across her mouth. Her head was clouded, her head was clear. And then she felt her body arch - and then she felt her body spin. All the trees about her were trembling within. Up above the Blood Moon swam. Outside the Red Grove, the women still sang.

She wanted to dance on, but was suddenly tired, as if she'd been dancing for years, though she knew that the dance she was dancing now had only just begun. And so she stood still, all alone in the Grove. Far off she could hear the fiddle and the drum, but here in the Red Grove, all was silent, nothing moved. A twig cracked. Riversong held her breath. Then Old Nanny Ninefingers stepped out of the shadows, holding up a lantern. Her gown was long and her head was shrouded in a shawl of faded scarlet. She held out her hand to Riversong.

"Now you have come to the Red Grove. Now you

have drunk from the Cup. Here is Death in Life and here is Life in Death. Guard the Red Grove well, for here is our place, the Sisteren. What you see here and what you learn, only you can tell."

Beyond the thicket of thorn bushes they could hear the voices of the girlen who were waiting to lead Riversong back to the Green.

"Here child, take this," the old woman said, before hurrying to join the others. She handed Riversong a small linen bag drawn at the corners by string. Riversong inhaled its strong aroma.

"Wait!" She called the old woman back. "Tell me what is here."

Ninefingers smiled.

"Rosemary, saffron, cinnamon and rue," she explained. "Keep it close when the moon comes full - it will be of comfort to you."

But what of Larkspittle? Where was he while Riversong was taken to the Grove? He too was dragged, by the boys-who-would-be-men, their shoulders hung with fox pelts, their faces daubed with clay, not smiling, not laughing, just fixed and determined as they bore him away. Larkspittle was coming with them, whether he wanted or no, whether he'd rather be back at the Dance, whether he'd rather be kissing Riversong still. Larkspittle was coming with them. And they were going to the Shuttle Stone, the tall rock which stood proud, naked and white in the shaft of light cast between the clouds.

All around the Stone were ashes and bones. The ground was charred with the scars of old fires. And the boys-who-would-be-men had piled a low pyre there, autumn's dead branches, fallen and broken, twisted and snapped. Bullbreath and Longskull seized Larkspittle fast, while Crossdogs and Hamsparrow busied themselves, setting a light to the nest of branches as Larkspittle watched, his limbs shaking. He knew of this, they all talked of this, the boys-who-would-be-men, as they wrestled and spat, as they strutted in their fox pelts, as they sang their ribald songs in the hollow on the Green. But now he knew this day was his, the day he longed for, the day he feared - while the flames caught and quickly spread as Crossdogs and Hamsparrow came back to stand by his side and silently tied the thin leather thongs, chafing at his ankles and his wrists.

And then the cry began. An intoned muttering at first, then louder and faster, faster and louder as the boys-who-would-be-men gripped the thongs and slipped them tight. Larkspittle fell to the ground. And then they were pulling him, drawing him along, through ashes, through brambles, across a clutter of old animal bones, towards the towering Shuttle Stone which rose tall and pale above him. Slowly at first, and then faster, then faster as the chant grew louder:

> "The Shuttle Stone stands tall and proud.
> Hear our voices singing loud.
> Touch the top with quivering hand,
> Never look down to the ground."

And then the heat. The heat of the fire as they reached the flames and the boys pulled the leather thongs tighter, jerking Larkspittle into the air. Then they ran, Crossdogs and Hamsparrow on one side, Bullbreath and Longskull on the other, running each side of the fire, running each side of the pyre which crackled and spat while Larkspittle passed through. Passed through heat, passed through flames, as he jerked, as he writhed, till he was out the other side, hurtling on towards the tall rock which waited, the white shaft of the Shuttle Stone standing proud in the darkness. And then Crossdogs and Hamsparrow, Bullbreath and Longskull all stopped. Crossdogs cried out, a cry like a beast in pain, in the pleasure of the rut, from the darkness in his gut. And he held the knife high, glinting in the moonlight. Down it plunged, cutting through the leather thongs which bound the young boy's wrists and ankles.

Larkspittle ran. Ran towards the Shuttle Stone, just as the chant began again:

> "First climb fast and then climb slow.
> The higher you reach, the further you go.
> Once you're there you'll never stop,
> Even though you're at the top."

Larkspittle gripped the Stone. Held it hard in both his hands. The chanting continued, behind him, all around him, the words beating in his head as he began to climb, hand over hand, hanging on to the toe-holds that had been worn into the stone by all the other boys-who-would-be-men who had climbed before him. He felt the blood surging in his head, urging him on.

"You have to reach the top before the chant is done." He knew what the boys had told him, in whispered huddles down by the water butt. He looked up. The pinnacle of the Stone seemed so far away and he could hear their song rising, louder and louder, but quicker

and faster, just when he wanted it to slow down. Slow down so that he could make each grip safely before he moved on. But he had to scramble, hand over hand, his feet slipping and sliding beneath him. He looked up. Beyond the Stone's white pinnacle he could see stars clear and brighter than bright, while the moon shone full. But he dare not look down. He could not go back. The ground was far below, and he could imagine the raised faces of Crossdogs and Hamsparrow, watching him, willing him, urging him. Goading him on.

"Never look down to the ground.
Touch the top with quivering hand.
Hear our voices singing loud.
The Shuttle Stone stands tall and proud."

The words spun on. He was nearly there. His hands touched the rim of the rock just below the pinnacle. He tried to grip, but his fingers were sliding. He cried out, just as a shaft of light from the moon spilled out to bathe the pinnacle in milky whiteness. He hauled himself up to the very top and for a moment so brief that it seemed never-ending, he could see the boys below, standing in a circle around the base of the Stone. Could see the dance continuing, back on Brunt Boggart's Green. Could see away off, deep in the wood, a stream of women dressed in scarlet petticoats, slipping away from a grove of trees, shimmering red with poppies, roses and berries.

And then just as he touched the Stone's pinnacle, he felt himself falling, spiraling through darkness to land in a pit thick with clay. He writhed and he thrashed, trying to pull himself free, but the more that he struggled, the deeper he sank, until the other boys tugged him out and he stood, smeared and shaken, his head spinning, his legs trembling, gazing up at the Shuttle Stone, up to its pinnacle. But he knew that he had been there, he knew that he had touched it, just as every boy-who-would-be-man who had come to the Stone before him.

They lofted him high, Crossdogs and Hamsparrow, Bullbreath and Longskull, daubed the dull clay across his face and carried him on their shoulders along the length of the Shuttle Stone's shadow, till at its end stood Thunderhead, his arms folded across his chest. He reached out and touched Larkspittle with the end of his stave.

"As a boy you learnt to climb. As boy-who-would-be-man you have learnt that you can fall. Now as a man you must learn that you can rise again."

Thunderhead beat his stave on the ground. The boys carried Larkspittle away from the shadow of the Stone and back to the dance that still raged on all around Brunt Boggart's Green. In the middle of the rhythm, the stamping feet, the wheeling arms, the gripping hands, they threw him. Larkspittle staggered, shaken and smeared, his legs wandering drunk from the fall.

"Dance," the boys shouted, clapping their hands.

"Dance!" shrieked the old'uns, milling around.

"Dance!" the girlen taunted as they bore Riversong towards him, her red skirts hitched high and her face glowing with wine.

They tipped her down and she stumbled into him. They held each other numbly, hardly knowing what to do, as the eyes of the onlookers burnt around them and the flames of the fire leapt higher and the rhythm of the

Drummer pulsed on.

Riversong looked back towards the Red Grove and Larkspittle released her. She stumbled slightly as she walked between the lines of watchers who parted to let her through. And Larkspittle was left standing, all alone in the middle of the crowd, who turned away as the fiddle played a slow lament and the Drummer's hands moved so quietly he scarcely touched the skins. Then they struck up again and the dance surged on, but Larkspittle walked away, out into the darkness as clouds drew over the moon, and cold was on the world.

Another day and another and the sun rose bright above the Green. The path to the Shuttle Stone was bruised with footprints and the path to the Red Grove strewn with fallen petals. But at the end of another path, Riversong met Larkspittle without ever saying a word, and they made their way to the stream which flowed, beside the meadow filled with pillows of grass, under the bridge at Sandy Holme.

ARNICA, CLOUDRUNNER AND THE WOLFSBANE

Let me tell you... Let me tell you about Arnica. Arnica was just a young girl, but her eyes glinted bright with the power of the sun which shone all day on Bare Stone Crag, where she lived all alone with her mother. Arnica would step from the house each day and stretch out her arms to greet the sky. Then she would run down to the rough of gorse and heather and stare out across the plain to the valley and the woods and the river. In the distance she could see Oakum Marlroot's fields, and just a little further over, she could see Brunt Boggart, with plumes of smoke rising from the chimney tops.

Arnica and her mother would keep each other company all through the day, washing and baking, sewing and cleaning, but Arnica was lonely. When she went out to play, she had nobody at all. And so she would sit at the top of the Crag and watch the clouds roll by. She'd pretend that each one was her friend and wish that she could fly out and touch them and run with them, all around the hill-top and back. But whenever she tried, when she spread her arms wide and she ran and she ran up and down the stony track, why she just fell over and her knees were all grazed.

When she grew tired of chasing the clouds and grazing her knees, Arnica would sit on a patch of scrubby grass betwixt the house and the mountain edge. And there she would gaze down at the river and the hills and the fields - and while she was sitting, staring far away and wishing for someone to play with on top of Bare Stone Crag, why then she thought that maybe somebody might come if she made a present for them. But what could she make, all up there on the bare crag with nothing but rocks and gorse and scrub? But then Arnica saw the wolfsbane flowering bright, opening its yolk-yellow blossom wide to the sun, just the way that she did when she stretched her arms each morning. She smelt their heady scent, so rich she felt she could drink it - and so she sat and rocked herself, bathing in the power of the wolfsbane.

Then she began to pick the flowers, slow and sure, one by one and two by two. Plaited and twisted their long green stems, making chains of wolfsbane to festoon around her. And she looked and she hoped and she watched and she wished that someone might climb to the steep crag's top so that she could drape the chains all around them and then they could play together, singing ring-songs and clapping all there in the sun.

But nobody came.

Then one day she looked down from the top of the crag and thought that she saw a great bird flying. A red bird, a yellow bird with blue feathers strung from the tail. From far away and far she saw it coming up the side of the Crag. But slowly, bobbing on and on, more like it was someone walking. And then it reached the meadow, the green meadow hung out like a pocket handkerchief, half the way up the Crag and half the way down. Until it flew. Flew up and towards her - and then she saw it was not a bird at all, but a kite. A great paper kite, yellow, red and blue. A great paper kite on a string. And it flurried and flapped and swooped up towards her. But then Arnica was not watching the paper bird anymore. Her eyes travelled down the line of the string pulled tight to see that there was a boy, tugging and reeling and twisting the line. Arnica called out to him.

"I love your kite!" she cried. "Bring it up here and show it to me."

But the boy did not hear. His eyes were fixed on the kite as it soared, as it swerved, as it flew. He was not listening for a girl's voice, lost in the wind on top of the crag. He only listened to the kite's string singing as it cut its way through the wind. And Arnica sighed as she watched him and wished he would come and play with her, for in truth she was more interested in meeting him and seeing his face and knowing his name and making wolfsbane chains for him and taking him to meet her mother than she was in the kite - be it ever so bright and yellow and red with blue feathers strung from its tail.

Day after day Arnica watched the boy, for he came every morning to the meadow where the wind was always high. Arnica knew which hour he would come - and every day she would call to him and hope that he would hear and throw his kite aside and climb to the top of the crag and come and play with her. But the boy never heard her, however loud she shouted - her words were always carried away by the same wind which tugged at his kite. In the end she decided that if the boy would not come to her, then she must go down to the boy. So early one morning, when the mist had scarcely lifted, she scrambled down to the meadow below where the boy came every day.

It was nearly the time when he would appear. Arnica felt excited. She raced around the meadow, flapping her arms as if she was the boy's great red and yellow kite. But he did not come. Arnica peered down over the edge of the ledge. She thought that she could see him far below, still crossing the plain all the way from Brunt Boggart. Arnica sat down. She combed her fingers through her hair. She spread her skirt around her on the grass. And then she grew restless and so she began picking at the wolfsbane blooming brightly all about - slowly at first, then quicker and quicker, gathering them into her lap. And then she made a wolfsbane chain, slitting the stems and twisting them till the chain was so long it fitted over her head and right round her shoulders and down to her waist. But still the boy did not come.

"He must be here soon," thought Arnica. She wanted to run and peer over the ledge, but her legs would not move and she stayed sitting there, with wolfsbane festooned through her long tumbling hair.

Then over the ridge at the edge of the meadow came a huge kite the shape of a bird, red and yellow with a tail of blue feathers. And beneath the kite was the boy, plodding slowly. He stopped, saw the girl sitting in the meadow that he came to every day. The meadow where he came, so alone and so free - only him and his kite and the wind. But now there was a girl here too, sitting making wolfsbane chains. He didn't know what to say and so he said nothing and did what he did every day. He ran with his kite until he could feel the wind tug it and pull it away, up and up, the feathers of its tail trailing out in the breeze.

Arnica didn't know what to say either. She had waited so long to meet this boy, to ask him to play - and now she didn't know what to say and so she bit her lip and turned away and counted the flowers in her lap again and again, as the boy rushed by, nearly as fast as the wind while the kite climbed higher in the bright morning sky.

Arnica shivered. The wind was cold. She hugged her bare arms and stood to stretch her legs, letting the flowers in her lap slither down to the ground. She turned around and there was the boy, almost on top of her, so busy with his running and tugging of the kite strings - it was as if he'd hardly seen her at all.

"Look out!" Arnica shouted and the boy swerved away, but then his foot seemed to catch on a tussock of grass and he fell. He fell to the ground while Arnica stood over him - and high in the sky the kite tugged away before he grabbed at the line and then pulled it back. But now he'd stopped running, the kite lost the wind and suddenly but slowly, downwards it came, a great red bird with yellow belly and blue tail - tumbling down, twisting and plummeting until it landed beside the boy where he lay on the grass.

He looked up at Arnica.

"Are you alright?" she asked.

The boy said nothing. He grabbed at the kite, checking it over, the thin gauze of its wings, the frame of light timber - to see that nothing was broken, nothing was snapped.

"Are you alright?" Arnica repeated.

The boy glared in front of him, then turned around suddenly.

"The kite is alright," he gruffly replied.

"Let me see," said Arnica.

Reluctantly, the boy showed her.

She ran her hands gently across its body, across its wings, stroking it almost as if it was a real bird. She let the long feathers of its tail play through her fingers.

"It's beautiful," she said.

"Careful," the boy muttered as he snatched the kite back. "It's just had a knock. You don't want to harm it."

Arnica smiled. "Of course not," she said. "Who made it?"

"Darkwind, my father," the boy replied. "He makes kites for all the boys in our village. Makes chairs and tables too."

"Why do you come here, all by yourself?" Arnica looked puzzled. "If Darkwind makes kites for all the boys, why don't you fly them together?"

The boy shrugged. He looked down. Down to the fields and the valley and the smoke of Brunt Boggart way across the plain.

"I like it here," he said. "You get the best wind. My father saves the best kites for me. Best kites need the best wind. And you can see so far. It's like being a bird. Seems like you could fly."

Arnica reached out to touch the kite again. This time the boy didn't pull it away. Arnica seized a fistful of wolfsbane chains and started to tie them to the kite's long blue tail. The boy smiled.

"What are you doing?" he asked.

Arnica grinned. "Nothing," she said. "I just wanted to see - wouldn't it be fun to fly wolfsbane in the sky? It would look just like stars coming out in the day!"

The boy grasped the kite and started to run, away from Arnica, away across the meadow. He ran and he ran, but the kite would not lift. When he got to the far side he ran back again, all the way to where Arnica was standing, her long dress billowing all around her in the wind. The boy shook his head and stopped to catch his breath.

"It's no good," he said. "The wolfsbane is too heavy."

Arnica sighed. "It would have been so beautiful to see it fly. I know," she cried, "come with me!"

She grabbed his hand.

"Where are we going?" The boy kept tight hold of his kite.

"To the top of the Crag. Follow me!"

Hand in hand they scrambled up the steep path of slippery shale, all the way to the top of Bare Stone Crag.

"Here!" Arnica shouted excitedly, her voice whipping away. "Here the wind is so high that the kite will fly with a tail of flowers as bright as the stars!"

The boy caught his breath and let go of her hand. Together they tied the wolfsbane to the kite's blue feathers again.

"Run!" the boy instructed and they ran, keeping pace with each other across the bumpy ground. At first the kite did not rise, but then they twisted around and ran back to meet the wind buffeting full in their faces as it rose from the flat plain below.

"Go!" cried the boy to the kite, as he let it drift away from them, up and up, tacking into the wind. Arnica stood beside him, hanging on to his arm as he played out the line. The kite rose higher, the great red bird with its yellow belly and tail of blue feathers pulling the line of wolfsbane that shone bright as stars up towards the sun. Up and up above the high crag top and Arnica's mother's house and the map of flat fields laid out far below. The kite dipped and soared and Arnica stood and watched the boy's face set in concentration as he guided its flight by the strings.

"Arnica!" her mother was calling her.

"I must go," she said, hurrying away to the house. And then she turned back. The boy was still standing, reeling in the kite.

"Wait!" she said. "You didn't tell me your name."

The boy paused. The line had become tangled.

"It's Cloudrunner," he told her.

"Arnica!" her mother called a second time.

"There - now you know mine," said the girl as she ran towards the door. "Come again, Cloudrunner. Come again."

And he did. The next day and the next. Arnica would watch for the red bird climbing up Bare Stone Crag, earlier each day as he seemed more eager to reach the top.

"For the wind," he said. "The best I've ever known."

And Arnica smiled.

But day by day the kites would change. Sometimes it was not a red bird she saw, trekking up the hillside. One day a giant eye, another a fish, and then a huge butterfly. And Cloudrunner would collect strange-shaped stones and dried sheep's bones as he scrambled up the path. One day he even brought a key and a tea-pot lid and a bag of shiny marbles that he found in the dark corner of his mother's cupboard back home.

And what did they do with them, Arnica and Cloudrunner, all up in the mist on the top of Bare Stone Crag? Why, they tried them and tied them to the tail of the kite, to see just how much weight each one would carry. And if one kite would not take the strain, why then next day Cloudrunner came back again with a bigger kite, a stronger kite - or sometimes even two!

"Look!" cried Cloudrunner, one blustery morning. "Look what I've brought." And he emptied a bag filled with old trinkets fished out of the stream. "Let's tie them up to this kite. It's the size of a haystack - the biggest my father's ever made!"

But Arnica looked away.

"That's all you ever bring," she told him. "Mean bits of metal to string from your kite. You bring nothing for me, no brooches, no baubles, nothing at all. And I stand here all day and watch you at play as you run with your kite. It's never me you come to see. Only Bare Stone Crag and the wind. I stand here in the cold and I may as well not be here at all!"

But Cloudrunner was away to catch the wind, to catch his kite the size of a haystack, to climb to the sky and rise. Arnica's words were borne away by the very same wind, across the valley and the fields of the plain, all the way to the river and over the sea.

Arnica shut the door of her house. She went inside to her mother. And all the next day the door stayed shut but Cloudrunner scarcely noticed when he came. He just shrugged when he saw that Arnica was not there and went on flying his kite, just the same as he ever had, just the way he had on the meadow lower down, before Arnica ever invited him to climb to the top.

And what of Arnica? She was so sad that Cloudrunner did not want her - only his kites and the Crag and the wind. So early next morning, while her mother was sleeping, Arnica rose and walked out through the door. She walked out across the scrub of grass where every day Cloudrunner flew his kite. She walked to the edge, where the cliff face dropped away. She stood and she gazed, out across the valley, out across the plain, out across the fields to where Brunt Boggart lay still slumbering in the morning mist. It was too early for Cloudrunner to have started his journey, though she looked for him still. And she looked and she stared and she strained her body forward till she could feel her flowing hair caught in the Crag's wild wind. As the wind tugged her hair she reached out towards it, reached with both her arms as her body stretched forward. As her body stretched forward, her arms flung out beyond her and as her arms spread outward, so her body followed. And she plunged and she span and she twisted. But then she did not fall. She did not fall - she flew. She flew as the wind caught her, caught her arms in its own and gently lifted her and turned her, till it bore her around the top of the Crag and there she stared down at the valley and the plain and the river far below. The wind took her and held her and filled her every pore. The wind became Arnica - and Arnica became the wind.

So that when Cloudrunner arrived, struggling up the track, carrying his kite, he finally began to wonder where Arnica had gone. She was not there to welcome him, to see his new kite and try how many trinkets they could fasten to the tail. Cloudrunner shrugged.

"Maybe she's still sleeping," he muttered to himself

and prepared his kite, all ready to fly.

But the kite would not fly, no matter how he tugged at it, all this way and that. No matter how fast he dragged at it, the kite lay on the ground, quite flat. The wind was on the far side of the Crag. The wind had become Arnica and Arnica had become the wind.

Cloudrunner shrugged again.

"Some days the wind comes, some days the wind goes. Some days the wind lies still, some days the wind blows."

But this day the wind did not blow at all, for Arnica did not come round the top of the Crag to play. But all his days flying kites, Cloudrunner had learnt to wait for the wind, so that's what he did now. He sat down on the ground, and there he spied one of Arnica's wolfsbane chains, which she'd made and discarded the evening before. While he sat waiting for the wind to return, Cloudrunner tied the wolfsbane to the tail of his kite, just the way they had the first day he ever came to Bare Stone Crag. As soon as it was tied, he tugged the line and he thought that he could feel it respond. It seemed to tug back, so he pulled it again. Then he picked up the kite and he ran it and ran it, then suddenly he flung it with all his strength up into the air.

He held his breath and played the string, for the wind was there, he could feel it. But the wind was far, the wind was hiding. He had to use all his skill to reel her in. And so she came. As the kite soared upwards, the wind returned. The wind which was Arnica. He could not see her, but he could hear her sing. Arnica was the wind.

And what did she sing? Why the song you can hear if you listen hard enough on any windy day:

"I am the Wind,
You cannot see me -
But you can feel me,
I am here.

      I am the Wind -
      Why do I cry?
      What have I seen?
      How far do I fly?

Let me touch your sorrow
And ease away your pain.
Let me take you round the world
And bring you back again.

      I am the Wind -
      How far do I fly?
      What have I seen?
      Why do I cry?

I am the Wind,
You cannot see me -
But you can feel me,
I am here."

Cloudrunner was so amazed to hear Arnica's voice singing to him that he forgot to play his line and the kite plunged down to the ground beside him. As he bent to pick it up, there was Arnica standing, right where the kite had fallen. She was standing, she was floating, she was hovering all around him. When he reached out to touch her, she seemed to slip away. He could hear her voice, from near, from far.

"Forget the kite," she said. "Forget the kite and come play with me, every day at the top of Bare Stone Crag."

Cloudrunner let go of his kite and it flew right away, right over the plain and over the woods, all back to Brunt Boggart where his father was waiting. Then Arnica took Cloudrunner's hand and they ran and they ran, all around the top of Bare Stone Crag. When they stopped, Arnica smiled, with her eyes open wide, reflecting the rays of the sun - and then she draped a chain of fresh wolfsbane, gently around Cloudrunner's shoulders.

FIREDANCER, TURNFEATHER AND THE LOOM OF NIGHT

Let me tell you... let me tell you - once there were three women - Silfren, Firedancer and Starwhisper. Now the first was Silfren and she had two daughters, name of Silverwing and Snowpetal. The second was Firedancer, who had one daughter only, name of Ravenhair. The third woman was Starwhisper and she had no daughter at all, nor no son neither.

Now Silfren had a husband name of Rattlehand and he lived all along with her and their two daughters, all up in their cottage by the edge of the Green. Firedancer had a husband name of Foxbriar, but Foxbriar was gone, lost him these long years ago to the darkness and the storm. And what of Starwhisper? Why Starwhisper had no husband. Never had no man at all - just spent all her time making dollies from straw. Some swore these dollies brought them luck with men - but however many dollies Starwhisper made for all the women of the village, they never seemed to bring her no luck that way.

But Silfren, Firedancer and Starwhisper, they had known each other all their lives long. They would sit out and gossip on the grass of the Green now that Silverwing and Ravenhair were all tall and grown and didn't need no mothers to follow them about. And though Snowpetal was still a little'un, the daughters could all do much as they wished, most of the day, long as they didn't go down by the wood.

"Let me tell you..." said Silfren to her daughters, and Ravenhair was listening too. "Let me tell you - once there was a mother, same as me, same as Firedancer. She lived all out in a cottage by the woods. Lived there with her daughters, very like the three of you. Now every day this mother would send her daughters out to play. And the very game they liked to play was picking berries in the wood. I know what you're asking, Snowpetal. I know what you want to say. Wasn't there a Fox living in the woods? Well maybe yes and maybe no - we will see what we will see. But anyways, in daylight the wood seemed safe enough. It was only with the darkness out under the frozen moon that they would hear howling and some said it was just the wind, but others said it was Fox for sure. So every afternoon the daughters would venture into the wood with their pinafores all pressed and clean. And they would tiptoe between the trees, gathering berries as they pleased to place in their baskets and take back to their mother who would set to and bake them all in a juicy berry pie.

"But this very afternoon, the girls stopped to look at the sky and saw the clouds scudding in and wondered if there might be rain as they skipped between the trees. They went on picking berries till their pinafores were stained with red, but then the eldest daughter felt the first rain on her head. And so they sheltered there and waited for the storm to pass, for as they peered up to the sky they were sure it would not last.

"Back home at the cottage their mother saw the rain and hoped that her young'uns were safe and would soon be home again. She set to mixing pastry and rolling it for the pie, while watching through the window to check the changing sky. She mixed the flour and water in her earthenware bowl, tipped it out and rolled it flat - then heard a knocking at the door. She shook the flour from her hair and wondered who this could be. At first she thought it was her daughters come home safe - but then she knew it could not be for they would have a key."

"Who is it, Mother? Tell us true." Little Snowpetal clutched her sister's hand and clung tight to Ravenhair's knee.

"Listen and I'll tell you," Silfren replied. She dropped her voice as low as low and whispered in their ears... "It was the Fox, my dears!"

Snowpetal jumped back, while Ravenhair caught Silverwing's eye and they exchanged knowing smiles.

"What should the mother do? Tell me, what would *you* do?" Silfren asked the girls.

Snowpetal covered her face with her hands.

"I'd run and hide!" she cried.

"What would you two do?" Silfren asked the older girlen.

Ravenhair and Silverwing smiled again and stroked each other's hair.

"All depends what he came for," Ravenhair replied.

"That's just what this mother thought," Silfren

continued. "This Fox did not seem a fierce fox, a hungry fox, such as she had heard. This Fox looked trim and handsome with a soft and winning smile.

"'Good woman,' the Fox said to her, ' - please let me come in for a while.'

"'For a while and a while,' the mother replied, '- but tell me what you want.'

"The Fox's eyes roved around the kitchen and spied the bowl on the table and the cups all set on the dresser.

"'Why, let me in, for I am thirsty and I crave a cup of hot nettle tea.'

"The mother combed her fingers through her hair and wiped away the flour she could feel tickling on her nose. She looked the Fox first up then down, then pulled the door full open wide.

"'Come inside,' she cried, for she was lonely these long days now, now that her husband was gone - and while her daughters were away in the woods she had no-one to talk to. The Fox smiled a winsome smile and stepped through the door, his long tail swishing across the floor. While the mother put the kettle on to start the brew, the Fox peered around the kitchen, preening his whiskers and picking up saucers and plates and cups, examining them carefully and putting them down again.

"The mother watched him curiously. 'It's very fine crockery,' she explained. 'My husband would buy me a piece each month when the Pedlar Man came along the track. Cup by saucer by plate we collected until we had all that we needed. Now I have a full set, but my husband he is gone. Only my daughters to eat with me and they use the earthenware bowls so none of the best china gets broken.'

"The Fox stroked the cup he was holding, then slowly put it down. He peered at the mother with enquiring eyes.

"'Then why do you keep a dinner set that no-one comes to use?'

"The mother poured the water from the kettle into the pot, patted her hair and smiled.

"'Why, you never know when a stranger might call, every once in a while.'

"The Fox smiled too and gazed at the mother and stroked his whiskers again.

"'Where are your children now?' he asked.

"'I sent them out to play in the wood,' the mother explained, ' - while I make pastry for the pie.'

"The Fox ran his paw round the bowl on the table.

"'So I see,' he said. 'Your children - will they be long?'

"'Who knows, who knows?' the mother exclaimed as she poured the steaming brew. 'But come along and sit with me and share a cup of tea.'

"The Fox sat down at the kitchen table and while his eyes roamed round the room, he blew gently across his cup of tea, then slowly put it down.

"'Your husband, tell me - what did he do?'

"The mother closed her eyes as if she was gazing into her dreams and memories.

"'He collected eggs,' she replied, then sighed. The Fox eyed her curiously, twirling his whiskers all the while. 'He collected eggs, oh so carefully. One here, one there - from blackbirds, robins, thrushes. Never enough to disturb the clutch, so the mother-bird wasn't scared off.'

"The Fox leaned forward.

"'Go on,' he said. 'What did he do with the eggs?'

"The mother closed her eyes again and clasped her hands at the thought.

"'Why, he painted them,' she explained. 'He would paint each one like a world in itself, with forests and villages, cities and mountains. Each one was like an eye that could see the world we could not see, stuck here in the village by the wood.'

"'How did he know of all these things?' The Fox sounded intrigued. He flicked his tongue across his lips.

"'Never knew for sure,' the mother pondered. 'Wasn't as if he was a travelling man. Sometimes he never set foot beyond this door from one moon's wane to the next. But he was a dream traveller, that's for sure. Could sail across oceans in his head, could fly through skies and climb far-off hills without ever leaving his bed.'

"The Fox took one more sip of his hot nettle tea, then wiped his lips again. Outside the rain drummed softly against the window pane.

"'These eggs,' he said, 'sound wonderful. Pray tell me, is it possible that I might view them, for I have never travelled far away from these woods, and I would like to see these eggs that can show me the world beyond.'

"The good mother hesitated. What could she do? What would you do?"

"I wouldn't show him the eggs at all," Snowpetal interrupted. "I would open the door that instant and send him on his way."

"You might be right. I'm sure you would - and I know that I would too. But that poor mother was lonely with her husband lost and gone. And so she reached inside her blouse and pulled out the key to the dresser.

"'Since you're so interested, I'll show you,' she said. 'But first I must explain.' She paused a moment, clutching the key. 'There are only six eggs left now. All the rest are gone. For my husband used to sell them - that's how he earned his keep. Some days there'd be a crowd all down the path waiting to see his latest batch. And most times when the Pedlar Man came by, why he would take some too and sell them on to the other villages, further down the track.'

"The mother turned and caught the Fox's eye. He was standing there staring at her in a strange and curious way, then he edged right up close to her and placed one paw on her arm.

"'Open the dresser,' he whispered, ' - and show me these marvellous eggs. Then perhaps you'll do me the favour of walking out with me. I can show you such beautiful dells, waterfalls and copses that no other creature ever will see, all hidden in the woods.'

"The mother hesitated. The Fox gently stroked her shaking hand which was clutching on to the key. She stepped away from him quickly and opened up the dresser. There beneath a linen cloth lay a clutch of painted eggs. The mother hurried away to the window and stared out at the woods while she considered what the Fox had said.

"'There are the eggs,' she told him. 'You may gaze at them as much as you wish, but please do not try and touch them, for they are very precious to me, so fragile and so frail.'

"But all the while she stared through the window and saw that the rain had stopped. She gazed across the lush damp grass to the tall green trees that were dripping still. How she longed to go there, to wander with the Fox, to visit the waterfalls, dells and copses which he had told her of. It was so long since she'd been out walking with her husband lost and gone. But her daughters three were playing there and she was waiting for them to come home. What could she do? What should she do? Then suddenly she heard a scrabbling behind her and turned to see the Fox, who had one of her husband's painted eggs gripped tightly in his jaw.

"'Stop!' cried the mother. 'What did I tell you? You can look all you want, but do not touch. Be off with you now!'

"She seized a broom and chased that Fox, sneaky and treacherous as he was, away out of her door."

"But what about the daughters?" Snowpetal asked as she wriggled away from Ravenhair and Silverwing who were trying to plait dandelions into her hair.

"I know what you're asking," Silfren replied. "What were her three daughters doing away out in the wood, where they had waited for the rain to stop? There they were standing under a tree, their pinafores all stained and red with the berries they had been picking, and their baskets filled to overflowing. The youngest had begun to eat the berries, for she was hungry and cold - and now her mouth was all smeared with the fruit and her cheeks were speckled and blotched.

"All of a sudden, her sisters turned with a start. There before them in the glade stood a slim and sinewy fox. No - I know what you're thinking, Snowpetal. Not the fox that had visited their mother's cottage while they were away in the woods. No, this fox was that cunning Fox's wife. But she seemed gentle and kindly to the sisters three.

"'Why, what are you doing shivering here all out in the rain?' she exclaimed. 'Come, come - come along this way with me. My cottage is close by, where you can get warm and dry.'

"The daughters looked at each other. They weren't sure what to do. But the youngest one pleaded, 'I'm hungry and cold.' Their own cottage where their mother was waiting was far away and far and so they followed the Fox's wife down an overgrown path beneath the tall dark trees. Her cottage was shadowy and small, but she kept it trim and neat. A row of gleaming pans hung all along the dresser and there were jars of sage and parsley neatly set in rows.

"'Come in - come in, my dears!' she cried. 'Take off your wet coats and set down your baskets of berries here. Why, I could bake you a delicious pie!'

"'Yes, *please*,' said the youngest, but her sisters kicked her.

"'Our mother is rolling out pastry right now to bake us a pie when we return.'

"The Fox-Wife paused for a moment.

"'So you have a mother, you say?'

"'Yes,' explained the youngest daughter. 'She lives in a cottage just beyond the wood, over that-a-way.'

"'I see, I see,' said the Fox-Wife as she pulled on her pinny and patted it down. 'And does she let you out roaming all alone in the woods?'

"'Oh yes,' cried the girls. 'She doesn't mind. She's told us which berries are safe to eat, which roots to pull, which flowers to pick.'

"'The woods can be dangerous still,' the Fox-Wife turned around, ' - but you're safe here with me. Now sit yourselves down and I'll pour you some milk. You must be hungry after walking so long and all soaking wet with the rain. I'll put on my pot and see what I can find to make us a hot warming stew.'

"'Yes please!' cried the youngest daughter, though her sisters frowned at her while the Fox-Wife clattered around, chopping up tatties, carrots and parsnips and rattling the pans. She popped all the vegetables into the pot and as soon as the kettle came to the boil she covered them over in bubbling water. The daughters three stared around the room as they slowly drank their milk.

"'Has it stopped raining yet?' the eldest asked, but it was very hard to see, for the windows were covered with curtains of net.

"'I'm cold and I'm hungry,' the second sister cried as the Fox-Wife raised the lid of the pot and sprinkled seasoning inside.

"'I'm so glad you found us,' smiled the youngest sister sleepily. 'And I can't wait to taste your stew. Will it be as delicious as Mother makes for us?'

"'Oh yes, I'm *sure* it will,' the Fox-Wife replied as she sidled up beside the youngest one and pinched her arm, just to keep her awake.

"The oldest daughter frowned and walked to the window, pulling the curtains aside.

"'The rain is easing,' she declared. 'And listen - ' She cupped a hand to her ear. 'You can hear the blackbirds sing.'

"'What's that you say?' asked the Fox-Wife sharply, setting down her cruet and her spoon.

"'Blackbirds, thrushes and starlings. Dozens of them. And pigeons too, all sitting on the branch of that tree.'

"Fox-Wife threw off her pinafore and was gone - out

through the door and over the grass, as quick as quick can be.

"'What's the matter?' asked the second daughter, staring at her older sister.

"The eldest daughter pointed to the stove.

"'Have you looked at the size of that pot?' she replied, as she lifted the lid. 'That's way too big for a handful of tatties, parsnips and carrots. What else is she planning to cook?'

"Outside was a commotion as Fox-Wife raced around the tree, barking and howling while the birds all clattered and rose up to the cloudy sky.

"'Maybe a pigeon. Mother does that,' the youngest sister reminded them.

"'*Maybe a pigeon*,' the eldest daughter shook her head. 'No pigeon is ever going to fill up this pot. This pot is big enough to take a ...'

"Just at that moment the Fox-Wife came back, her sharp teeth gripping a clutch of stray feathers - her eyes rolling wild.

"'Big enough to take...' the youngest sister trembled.

"'... take a Fox!' the second sister shouted as she leapt forward and threw her skirt and petticoat right over the Fox-Wife's head.

"The three sisters battled her and pummelled her and pulled her till in the end they tumbled her into the bubbling pot! Then they seized up their baskets all filled with juicy berries and they ran and they ran through the dripping woods and they did not stop till they came to their mother's cottage. They paused for breath before they reached the gate and as they did so the front door opened and out stepped the other Fox, quick as quick, still twirling his whiskers. At the end of the path the Fox slowed down, turned and blew a kiss towards their mother's front door. The sisters hid and watched as the Fox headed off to the wood.

"'Why would this fox blow a kiss to our mother dear?' the youngest wanted to know.

"'Shsh,' her sisters cautioned and they waited and they waited till the Fox was out of sight, then they ran up the path to the door.

"Their mother sat inside the kitchen. They expected her to welcome them with outstretched arms, just as she usually did, but instead she sat in the shadowy corner, staring at their father's painted eggs set out on the table before her. She stroked each one gently before turning around with a far-away look in her eyes.

"'Come in, come in, my little ones. Do you have berries ripe for me?'

"'Yes, we do Mother,' cried the sisters breathlessly, ' - but some of them got spilled as we had to come home so quickly.'

"'Yes, yes - I know,' the mother said. 'Come along now and step inside. You must be hungry, sit you down.'

"And while her daughters watched, she hauled her largest cooking pot up onto the top of the stove..."

Snowpetal gasped. Ravenhair and Silverwing giggled and pinched each other. But Firedancer interrupted:

"Why d'you plague our daughters with stories such as these? Ain't no Fox, ain't no Wolf neither, I can tell you. Nearest we got to Fox round here is when Pedlar Man comes round every moon. He be more Fox, I'm telling you - and you know how I know."

Starwhisper and Silfren nodded.

"We know, sure enough," smiled Silfren. "And know there's plenty more been that way too."

Firedancer spread her hands and sighed, then turned to Ravenhair and Silverwing who were still sitting listening, while Snowpetal had lost interest and trotted off to gather daisies.

"Be gone with you now. This ain't for your ears. This is grown woman talk."

"Ah, mother," Ravenhair protested, "we be near grown women ourselves now. Been down to the Red Grove and all, you know."

"I know, I know," Firedancer replied. "But little Snowpetal don't know nothing of that. Run along with you now and take her off with you. Take her over the Green this fine sunny day and run all your cares and worries away."

"Cares and worries!" Starwhisper echoed when the young'uns had gone. "When we were their age we never had none."

"Got them now," said Silfren.

"Got them now for sure," Firedancer continued. "Maybe that's what I meant to say - take all *our* cares and worries away."

Silfren laughed and Starwhisper too. Then they stopped and gazed up at the clouds. Stared down at the ground. Shuffled their feet.

"Be that time again soon. Season's moon. All that dancing and prodding and shoving," Starwhisper muttered.

"No good for me. I'm done with all that," Silfren sighed.

"Speak for yourself, gel. I'm glad of it still," Firedancer retorted.

"If anyone'll have you," Starwhisper chided.

Firedancer smiled a faraway smile. "I could still have whoever I choose."

"Got to find'em first," Starwhisper reminded her.

"Or they got to find me," Firedancer replied, with a toss of her hair and a glint in her eye.

Next day after next, and a few days after that, season's moon came and the cavorting and carousing all down on the Green. But then the next morning, early and bright, traders set up stalls where the dancing had been. There were petticoats and fancy shawls, sweetmeats and cakes and all kinds of trinkets such as no-one in Brunt Boggart could make. They came from far and wide - from over the hills and up the river, from the back of the wind and beyond. The Pedlar Man was there with his ribbons and his sack - and the horse traders washing their mares in the river, the bare-knuckle fighters in their make-shift rings and fortune-tellers hunched in their tents.

Quick and quick and slow as slow, the young'uns and the old'uns, the wifen and the girlen, the farmers and the Crow Dancers tumbled from their beds, never mind how late they been carousing, never mind some had never slept at all, never mind their fumbled heads - and stumbled down to the Green again where they had been just the night before - and traipsed around the market, stopping at every stall.

Starwhisper, Silfren and Firedancer met at the edge of the Green.

"What you minded to buy today, gel?"

"Don't rightly know."

"Depends what they got."

"Same as before, for sure, for sure."

"But always the chance you'll see summat new."

"That's why we come."

All three were agreed.

"How much you got?"

"Silver shillen."

Each one of them nodded. Each season's moon they each put by a silver shillen, specially for this day. Never less, never more - always the same, every time the market came.

"I'll go this way - you go that, and Starwhisper you go t'other. Then meet up back here in the middle of the market, in the middle of the Green at the middle of the day."

"And then we shall see..."

"... who's bought the best. Who's spent their shillen the wisest."

And they set out, Starwhisper, Silfren and Firedancer - to poke and to pry, to banter and haggle, to barter then buy.

Firedancer tried on bracelets and necklaces, pendants and ear-rings, but could find none that she wanted - none that made her feel more like herself than herself. But then she came to a stall where a tall man stood all draped with scarves - tied to his fingers, wound around his waist, twisted about his wrists, festooned across his shoulders and knotted into his long dark hair. Deep maroons and purples, moss-green and black, picked out in threads of shimmering silver, dazzling gold. Firedancer glanced at the man whose dark eyes seemed to be watching her without ever watching at all. She reached out and touched one of his scarves. The man smiled.

"My name is Turnfeather," he told her. "Try this scarf, I can see that you want to. It will suit your complexion so well."

Turnfeather let loose the scarf and draped it around Firedancer's neck. He took a step back and held up a mirror which glinted in the sun. The scarf was picked out with designs of creatures such as Firedancer had never seen before, as like they might be the wondrous eggs painted by the man who had lived in the cottage at the edge of the wood. Firedancer studied her reflection.

"It suits the sheen of your hair. It suits the tone of your skin. It suits the untamed child I see dancing in your eyes."

Firedancer gazed into Turnfeather's own eyes. They were deep, they were dark. For a moment she saw reflected, just as he said, the untamed child a-dancing there.

"How much is it? - for the scarf?" she asked.

"Two silver shillen," he replied.

Firedancer sighed.

"One shillen is all that I have," she declared.

Turnfeather stepped closer and took her to one side.

"For you - one shillen only," he whispered in her ear. "But do not tell the others."

Firedancer smiled, put her hand in her pocket and pulled out her purse, unbuttoned it slowly, then gave him the one coin that nestled there. Turnfeather took the money quickly and with a nod and a wink slipped it into a leather pouch tucked away under the scarves which festooned his waist. Firedancer hurried away. She felt the scarf around her neck caress her in a warm embrace.

While Firedancer was buying her scarf, Silfren flitted

from stall to stall. She felt hungry, but she couldn't decide what to eat. There were loaves, there were pies, there were fancy cakes - but hungry as she was, she just couldn't choose. She turned again to another stall, then another and another. The emptiness inside her led her on, but nothing that she saw was what she wanted. And she knew what she wanted, for every season it was the same, an old woman came to the market and with her she brought the most delicious sweetmeats you'd ever care to eat. Oozing with honey, all sumptuous and soft, yet crisp on the top.

"Have you seen her?" Silfren asked Moonpetal and Dewdream, but the girlen just shrugged and Silfren hurried on. Surely the old woman must be here - she always came and Silfren always spent her silver shillen on a bag of sweetmeats that tasted as golden as a summer's day - and Silfren felt just like a little'un again.

But not today. Not this market, not this season, not this moon. Silfren started to worry. Mayhap the old woman was sick. Mayhap she'd never come again - and then what would Silfren do? No-one could ever bake the sweetmeats the same. Silfren asked her once for the secret of the baking, but the old woman had smiled and looked away and said something Silfren couldn't quite catch about the colour of the sky and the bees. But mayhap she'd just run out of honey. Or mayhap, Silfren realised as she saw a familiar stooping figure setting down a basket and dusting off a table...

"Mayhap I just got caught up on the track!" The old woman greeted her with a smile and a kiss. "The way gets longer as each season passes. But what can I get you, my dear?"

Silfren watched excitedly as the old woman set out her wares.

"Oh - you know, you know. I don't have to tell you!"

And the old woman smiled and parcelled up a wrapper of sweetmeats from the tray on the table, then took Silfren's silver shillen and popped it in her pocket.

"A season's sweetness be there for you - eat them slowly now!"

But Silfren was away, lost in the crowd and already unpeeling the sticky wrapper as the sweet honey clung to her fingers and her lips, then danced on her tongue, as it slid down her throat to feed the hunger that she carried inside her from season's moon to season's moon.

While Silfren was eating her sweetmeats, Starwhisper moved slowly, picking at apples, pears and plums - weighing each one in the palm of her hand, then putting them back again. She was not hungry, just curious to test this season's crop. She passed the stall where Firedancer had bought her scarf, ran her fingers across the colours and textures, but then moved on. Her own clothes, which she made herself, were fine enough already. In her pocket was her silver shillen, but she was in no hurry to spend it. In her bag she carried the dolls of straw which she had made these last days gone. She was seeking out the Pedlar Man, for he always took some to carry with him to other villages, north of the river, south of the mountains. Starwhisper had never been blessed with children, nor even with a husband nor any other man - her dolls of straw were man enough and child enough for her. She spent her days gathering the straw for their bodies and the berries for their eyes, then twisting and plaiting the new dolls in her fingers. Now she wandered out to the edge of the market, away from the hubbub and noise, to where the grass was beaten flat from the dancing the night before and blackened circles marked where the bonfires had burned full bright. There stood the Pedlar Man with his pack upon his back. When he saw Starwhisper he swung it down and greeted her.

"Now then Starwhisper, what fine straw dollies have your nimble fingers shaped for me?"

Starwhisper emptied her bag and the straw dolls tumbled out and lay upon the grass. Their dried berry eyes stared up as the Pedlar Man prodded at them and turned them all about.

"Good as ever!" He clapped his hands. "I'll take them all," he cried as he poured a pile of silver shillen into Starwhisper's outstretched palm.

"Thank you," she said as she hurried away.

"Wait!" the Pedlar Man called after her. "Won't you stay and drink with me? I have good red berry wine all here in my flask."

Starwhisper stopped and shook her head.

"Not today, Pedlar Man. You have my dolls. I have your shillen. That's all we need to do. I've heard too many tales of what happens to young wifen who stop and drink with you."

The Pedlar Man shrugged and turned away, sat down on the grass and unscrewed the top of his flask. But Starwhisper hurried on, back to the bustle of the stalls where she caught sight of Firedancer parading her scarf and Silfren with her mouth crammed full of sweetmeats. The stalls were heaving with trinkets and baubles, but these were not for her. The racket of geese and swine filled the air as she strayed to the far end of the market where the farmers stood around - Oakum Marlroot, Mottram Ironfield and Redgut - running their eyes over the horses and goats which were tethered in a pound. And there on a table stood a line of open sacks, each filled with seed for the field - carrots, parsnips, turnips and beans.

"What can I have," Starwhisper asked the lad who stood at the stall, "if I give you this silver shillen?"

"Why, you can have a fistful of each of 'em," he replied - and quick as quick he weighed out the seeds into a wrap of sacking. Starwhisper thanked him and paid over her shillen as she tucked the wrap away into the pocket of her apron.

Firedancer stroked the scarf which clung around her shoulders. She liked the way it felt. She wished she had brought a hand-mirror with her so that she might see her face set off by the scarf. But then she realised she needed no mirror for as she walked around the market she could see how she looked in the eyes that followed her every step. Firedancer returned their gaze and smiled. She combed her fingers through her long tawny hair, letting it tumble loose down over the scarf. Then she sighed. For smile as she might, try as she might, the women only glanced in envy and then they looked away. And the men, why the men were nothing but a lunk-headed crowd who gawped at her stupidly. Each time she thought one might approach her, they took another draught from the glass in their hand and then turned the other way.

Firedancer stroked the scarf again. She pursed her lips and stared straight ahead. She found herself back at the stall where Turnfeather was still standing. He looked at her and smiled.

"The scarf suits you fine - it matches the glint in your eyes, the shine of your hair."

"Why thank you, so kind. Your words make me blush, almost as much as the touch of your scarf, which strokes my shoulders as I walk. It makes me feel so I want to be kissed."

"I'm sure that you will be," Turnfeather replied.

"Well none of these men folk have happened up yet," Firedancer sighed. "Do they think I'm a woman all alone? Or do they just think that I'm Foxbriar's wifen, though he be lost and gone? Or mayhap they just think of me as Ravenhair's mother? Or mayhap they just think that I'm Firedancer, that they've grown with and known, young'un and woman, all their lives long."

"They don't know what they're missing," Turnfeather replied. "I know when a fine woman wraps herself in a scarf of mine, then she's strong in need of a kissing!"

Firedancer blushed. "You know not what you say!" She took one step towards him, then another step away.

"Fine scarves! Step up! Fine scarves for all!" Turnfeather bawled, then turned to Firedancer once again and whispered quickly in her ear. "I will stay in Brunt Boggart awhile and awhile before I journey on. Old Granny Willowmist has lent me the key to the tumbledown cottage where one of her sons used to live. Come and see me there tonight and I will show you more scarves."

Firedancer cast her eyes to the ground, but then looked up again and smiled.

"I will," she said. "I will. But first you must tell me

how you come by your scarves, for they are handsome and fine and covered all over with such wondrous designs. Do you make them yourself? With your fingers so long and pale as the moon you could weave them deftly and strong - fine threads for fine women to caress their soft skin."

Turnfeather shook his head and smiled.

"My mother taught me how to weave in the years before she died, night after night as I stood by her side - shuttle and needle and loom - but she is the more skilful weaver still, although I've tried and tried."

In the middle of the market, in the middle of the Green at the middle of the day, Starwhisper, Silfren and Firedancer met again. They linked their arms each to each and gazed deep into one another's eyes.

"So how did we spend our silver shillen, this bright and splendid day?"

Firedancer tossed back her hair and stroked her scarf that was woven so fine with creatures from afar.

"Why, it's beautiful!" exclaimed Silfren. "Has it brought you some luck already?"

Firedancer smiled and looked away.

"Happen it has," she explained. "Happen a man has looked my way after all these lonely years. But what of you, Silfren? You seem happy too."

"I am, I am," Silfren replied. "You know I don't need to go looking for no man. I have Rattlehand my husband close at home, but I still have my own desire. The sweetmeats that tantalise my lips, then cling to my tongue and slip down my throat to feed the hunger I carry inside from season's moon to season's moon."

"They sound sweeter than a thousand kisses!"

Firedancer exclaimed. "I'd like to try one - have you saved any that you can share?"

Silfren hung her head and showed them the empty wrapper.

"I ate them all as quick as quick. As soon as the honey touches my lips I just want more, then more, then more. I ate them all an hour ago. There's nothing left to share."

"For shame, for shame," cried Starwhisper. "And I don't believe you care!"

"Maybe true I don't," grinned Silfren, licking her lips. "But a woman's got to have her pleasure. How about you, Starwhisper? How did you treat yourself today? Don't see no scarf, don't smell no honey. How did you spend your silver shillen?"

Starwhisper delved and scrabbled to the bottom of her bag and pulled out the wrapper of seeds. Silfren and Firedancer stared at her and laughed.

"How's that going to make you happy? Don't make you pretty. Don't keep you warm. Don't give no pleasure for your belly nor your tongue."

Starwhisper raised her hand.

"Give me pleasure soon enough," she said. "Maybe not now - maybe not tomorrow. Maybe not for a moon and another moon more. But some pleasures come quick and some pleasures come slow. My pleasure will come when these seeds grow."

That night Firedancer wrapped her new scarf around her shoulders to keep her warm in the chilly breeze as she made her way across the Green. She was shaking and shivering - though not from cold she told herself, as she knocked at the door of the empty cottage where

Old Granny Willowmist's son had once lived. She could see a light flickering inside, but there was no reply - so she knocked again. She heard a high voice singing, beautiful and pure. She heard a scuffling and a rustling, but no-one came to the door. She knocked again and called Turnfeather's name. The singing continued and Firedancer was puzzled, for it sounded like a woman's voice, sure and true.

She turned away. Who could it be? Mayhap Turnfeather had tricked her. Mayhap every woman who had bought a scarf that day had been invited to the cottage to meet with him. Surely not, she told herself. She paced up and down the overgrown path of the empty cottage, hugging the scarf around her shoulders and wishing its soft touch was Turnfeather himself. But if he had tricked her, why should she stay? Firedancer began to walk away, but when she reached the rusted gate she knew she had to return, drawn to the lighted window like a night-moth to a flame. She needed to see who her rival might be - who had got here before her. Firedancer paused. Dare she look? Did she truly want to know? What if it was Silfren or Starwhisper, her closest friends and true?

Firedancer shook her head. Surely it could not be. Silfren already had Rattlehand, her husband, who would not stray away. And Starwhisper, why Starwhisper had never taken no man at all. Maybe at last she found one. But why Turnfeather? Why now?

Firedancer heard the voice again, singing. She stood beside the window and tried to peer in through the glass. Maybe it was not Starwhisper at all. Maybe none of the women of the village. Maybe twas Turnfeather's sister come along with him. Maybe his mother, come to weave more fine scarves. But no, Firedancer remembered. Turnfeather had said his mother was dead. But at the window, plain as plain, she saw the shadow of an old woman sitting hunched over a small hand loom, rattling the shuttle this ways and that, all the while singing with a long dark scarf wrapped around her head.

Firedancer turned from the window and rapped sharply on the door. The singing stopped. There was a rustling and a shuffling. Firedancer pushed at the worm-raddled door. The cottage had been empty long years and long. The lintel was rotted and the hinges dull with rust. The door swung open as she pushed and there before her stood a figure in a shawl, threads hanging loose from pale fingers.

Firedancer stood rooted. Who was this person weaving in the night? New scarves lay littered across the dusty floor. The figure let out a cry and turned away, but not before Firedancer saw the face. It was Turnfeather - she knew it was him. But what was he doing wrapped up in a shawl and wearing a scarf that might be his mother's? Firedancer stood still. She could not step towards him, she could not run away. She wanted to go, she wanted to stay - for here was the man she had dreamed of all day.

"What are you doing?" she asked.

Turnfeather paused. What could he say?

"I need more scarves," he told her at last. "I need more scarves to take from village to village and town to town. My mother died these long years past - but she makes them for me still. I carry her loom on my journeys and so she is always with me. My mother wove her dreams for me into each of her scarves. Now

I dream her dreams for her and she continues with her weaving. I cannot leave her now and she will never leave me."

Turnfeather cried, the cry of a boy, the cry of a man, the cry of an old woman who has left her son to wander village to village, town to town, selling scarves that she can weave no more. Firedancer took him into her arms, this man who was boy, who was man, who was mother. Took him and rocked him till the crying was stopped, till the darkness was gone, till the morning sun slipped through the window to light the pile of silken scarves all strewn across the floor.

Next day as Firedancer walked down to the Green, she smiled a smile all to herself and stroked the scarf that was still wrapped around her shoulders. Stroked it smooth as a skin on her skin, but then she sighed. Silfren and Starwhisper looked into her eyes.

"Tell us..." they begged.

And she told them enough and she told them too much and she told them nothing at all. Silfren and Starwhisper looked at each other then stared back at Firedancer and her fine flowing scarf with a gaze as sharp as a blade in the dark.

Firedancer returned their glare.

"Why do you look at me this way? You chose to spend your shillen on sweetmeats and seeds. But I spent my shillen on a scarf." She tossed it quickly around her neck. "And my scarf will keep me warm. But more than that - my scarf has brought me Turnfeather and he will keep me warmer still."

Silfren shook her head.

"Don't want your man. I got me Rattlehand, my

husband true - and he is safe at home."

Starwhisper looked away.

"Never had a man yet and don't want one now. And sure as sure not one that's looked your way."

Firedancer stood.

"If you don't want my scarf and you don't want my man, then why do you look at me this way and this?"

And she walked away from the Green, wherever her feet would take her, all the way up to Langton Brow. But Firedancer was worried. Silfren and Starwhisper had been her friends ever since any of them could remember. Always shared everything they had, be it blackberries in a bowl, daisies to make chains or ribbons pretty as pretty to lace all in their hair. Firedancer, Silfren and Starwhisper went everywhere together, down Mallenbrook Lane tramping in all the puddles, wading in the water deep at Pottam's Mill or following the boys-who-would-be-men and the girlen-become-women all the way to Sandy Holme. Shared each other's brooches, necklaces and trinkets. Sometimes for the dance at season's moon they even swapped round their dresses. But now here they were sulking over Firedancer's scarf, the scarf all twined with creatures such as none had ever seen.

Firedancer sighed and gazed down at the village below. She knew Starwhisper and Silfren didn't want her man. But the man would soon be gone, Turnfeather had told her so. Soon as he had woven more scarves he'd be away to the next village and the next. Then Firedancer would be all alone again and more alone than alone for she'd have lost Silfren and Starwhisper too. And so Firedancer was decided - even though Silfren had spent her shillen on sweetmeats and

Starwhisper had chosen to buy seeds - they should both have one of Turnfeather's scarves just the same as her.

That night Firedancer came to Turnfeather's cottage and she stood beneath the moon with her shoulders bare and she knocked there slowly three times three. Turnfeather opened the door. This night he did not wear his mother's shawl and the loom was all packed away.

"Firedancer, Firedancer. You came to me first in the noise of the market, then you came to me again in the quiet of the night. Now here you are again in the silence of the moon - but where is the scarf that I sold you? Why do you not wear it now?"

Firedancer cast her eyes to the ground.

"I have lost the scarf," she said softly.

Turnfeather was saddened.

"I wove that scarf with my mother's skill. I am sorry to hear it is gone."

Firedancer clung to him.

"The scarf kept me warm, but I longed for your arms."

The moon rose high and the stars came and went. In the cold of the morning Firedancer stood at the cottage door, her shoulders bare, pale and shivering.

"Wait," Turnfeather called to her. "Careless as you were, I cannot let you go into the chill of the day without another scarf to wrap around your neck."

Firedancer took the scarf gladly and hurried off through the village. Before the blackbird sang, she happened upon her friend Silfren, trudging to the well to fetch water.

"Silfren, Silfren, I know that you're hungry for sweetmeats all dripping with honey. I cannot get you any of these, but I have a scarf as fine as mine to keep you warm."

Silfren looked into Firedancer's eyes. The scarf was embroidered with rainbows and clouds.

"Don't need no scarf to get me a man. I have my husband Rattlehand and he is true as true," Silfren paused and thought a while, "but this rich cloth is a handsome gift that will keep out the morning dew."

That night Firedancer went to the cottage again, knocked once, knocked twice on Turnfeather's door. Turnfeather opened it, same as before.

"Firedancer, Firedancer," he quickly exclaimed. "Where is the scarf that I gave you this morning? You lost the first scarf I sold you. Now you do not wear the next scarf I gave you, embroidered all over with rainbows and clouds."

Firedancer cast her eyes to the ground.

"I have lost the scarf," she replied.

Turnfeather had been saddened once. Now he was saddened again.

"I wove that scarf with my mother's skill. I am sorry to hear it is gone."

Firedancer clung to him once more.

"The scarf kept me warm, but I longed for your arms."

The moon rose high and the stars came and went, same as they had before. In the cold of the morning, Firedancer stood once more at the cottage door, her shoulders bare, pale and shivering.

"Wait," Turnfeather called to her. "Careless as you were, and careless as you have been again, I cannot let you go into the chill of the day without another scarf to keep you warm."

Firedancer took the scarf gladly and hurried off through the village. Before the cock crew she happened on her friend Starwhisper on her way to the field to gather stems of straw.

"Starwhisper, Starwhisper, I know that you wait on your seeds from the market, to see how tall they will grow. I cannot ease the waiting, but I have a scarf to make you look fine."

Starwhisper looked into Firedancer's eyes. The scarf was embroidered with rivers and mountains.

"Don't need no scarf to get me a man. Never had one before, don't need one now," Starwhisper paused and thought a while, "but this fine cloth will keep me cool out in the fields in the noonday sun."

Next day and next, Turnfeather happened from old Willowmist's cottage and down towards the Green. On his way he met Silfren, wearing a scarf sewed with rainbows and clouds and woven true with his mother's skill.

"That's a fine scarf you have there," he said, knowing full well he had given this scarf to Firedancer to replace the one she said she had lost.

"It serves me well," Silfren replied. "It keeps me warm in the morning dew."

"I could keep you warm," Turnfeather suggested, with a glint in his eye.

Silfren stepped away.

"I have my husband Rattlehand to keep me warm. I have no need for more," she replied.

Turnfeather walked on further as he headed towards the Green. On his way he met Starwhisper, wearing a scarf sewed with rivers and mountains and woven true with his mother's skill.

"That's a fine scarf you have there," he said, knowing full well that this scarf he had also given to Firedancer to replace the next she said she had lost.

"It suits me well," Starwhisper replied. "It covers me from the noon-day sun when I am out in the fields gathering stems of straw."

"I could cover your face," Turnfeather suggested, as he bent forward to kiss her.

Starwhisper pushed him away.

"Never had no man before - and I don't need one now."

Turnfeather walked on towards the Green. Soon enough and soon he happened upon Firedancer all wrapped up in a scarf of dancing creatures - the first scarf he had sold her back at the market.

"Good day, good day," he greeted her. "That's a very fine scarf you are wearing."

Firedancer blushed and pulled it tight around her shoulders.

"Thank you so much," she replied, though she felt a little flustered. "It suits me well to keep me warm while the dew's still on the ground. And later on it will keep me cool in the heat of the midday sun."

"Don't I keep you warm enough?" Turnfeather asked sadly. "You told me that this scarf was lost and yet I see you wearing it. I gave you two more yet I've seen them already, wrapped around the shoulders of two other women."

Firedancer hung her head.

"I gave them away," she said and stepped up close to Turnfeather to offer him a kiss. Turnfeather drew away.

"If you give away my scarves which I made with my mother's skill, then as true is false and as false is true, then I must give you away too."

And Turnfeather walked on, with his loom in a bag slung over his shoulder and a belt full of scarves flowing around his waist. He walked all down the main street then out by Mallenbrook Lane and up to Pottam's Mill till he set off up to Langton Brow, never to see Brunt Boggart again.

Back in the village the three women continued, each wearing their scarf for a different reason, each one watching the turning season. Silfren's belly was empty still as she craved the sweetmeats no other could bake. Firedancer gazed in the mirror each morning at the scarf that had brought her warmth but then left her colder than before. But what of Starwhisper, you ask. Did those seeds from the market ever grow?

Soon as she had bought them with her silver shillen, Starwhisper had squatted down and pressed them into the cold hard ground. Each day she tended them, kneaded them and sang to them, but no shoots appeared. Starwhisper was afraid that her seeds were dead, until one day a green blade slid from the ground and then another and another. Starwhisper was happy and watered them each day and even danced around them as she sang. But then the cold wind blew and the shoots turned black and blighted as she nursed them in her hands. The ground turned cold and hard again and soon all sign of the seeds had gone and Starwhisper knew her chance was lost to raise a crop. And so she turned her hand again to making dolls with the straw she picked in the fields.

Next season's moon Firedancer, Silfren and Starwhisper stood in the middle of the market in the middle of the Green, with a silver shillen jingling in each of their pockets. Firedancer was gazing this way and that, hoping Turnfeather would come with his scarves again - and Silfren was keeping a watchful eye for the old woman and her sweetmeat stall. But before either of them could go off looking, up came their daughters, Ravenhair and Silverwing, clamouring and pleading for a silver shillen each - for both had seen the very dresses they needed to turn the heads of the boys who had come to visit the fair. Before the two mothers could even think, they'd both parted with the money which they kept for themselves.

Now Starwhisper was the only one who still had a shillen left in her pocket. She had no daughters to distract her, or take the shillen from her, and so she wandered off from the other two and roamed up and down the stalls.

"Starwhisper, Starwhisper, what do you seek?" a familiar voice called out to her.

It was the Pedlar Man, newly come along his dusty track with his pack of shiny trinkets still slung across his back.

"I hear that last season you bought seeds. Tell me how did they grow?"

"Seeds grow quick and seeds grow slow and sometimes they do not grow at all," Starwhisper replied. "I have no time to wait, to water them and weed them. I have no time to watch them grow. I'd rather make my dolls of straw to bring people happiness."

Starwhisper looked up at the Pedlar Man.

"Let me come with you. I have a basket here of new straw dolls which we can take near and far. I will not drink from your flask of red wine and I will not sit by your side. But if you can take me away from here, then I can make new dolls for you to sell wherever you choose."

And so the Pedlar Man hoisted up his sack and set off again along the track with Starwhisper beside him. They walked and they walked down the dusty miles till they'd left the market far behind them.

When the season's moon came round again, the Pedlar Man returned. Firedancer and Silfren asked for news of Starwhisper their friend. And the Pedlar Man smiled and the Pedlar Man sighed and the Pedlar Man rolled his eyes - but then he opened up his sack again and hidden at the bottom was a brand new scarf such as Turnfeather made, woven with creatures from a-far. And when they unwrapped it there was a fresh-made dolly all nestling inside, and Firedancer took it into her arms and gazed deep into its dried berry eyes. But how the straw dolly and the silken scarf came to be all twined together, the Pedlar Man would not say.

SNOWPETAL, HA'PENNY ROSE AND THE STAR THAT FELL IN THE MEADOW

Let me tell you... let me tell you... Snowpetal was a little'un. In fact she was Silverwing's little sister, if you want to know. But Silverwing never wanted to know. She would never take Snowpetal with her, down to the hollow in the middle of the Green to sit with all the girlen. No - Silverwing always left her sister behind to stay in the cottage and play with her basket of twisted straw stars which Scallowflax made specially for her. And when Snowpetal was tired of the stars, she would talk to their grandmother, Ha'penny Rose, who sat all day in her great wooden chair with its great wooden wheels, which had been built for her by Darkwind, the man who made kites for all the boys in the village.

Ha'penny Rose would sit there, rocking and knitting while her grand-daughter played - until the time came for Snowpetal to wheel her, pushing the great wooden chair all down to the edge of the Green. And there Ha'penny Rose could watch them - Ravenhair, Silverwing, Duskeye and Dawnflower and all the other girlen, and remember when she had been a young'un, just like them. And even way back then, the young'uns had never let the little'uns play with them, so now nothing had changed - and Snowpetal whiled away all the day-long day, chasing after butterflies and singing to herself, all around the edge of the Green:

> "Find me a Star
> That will carry me far -
> Around the Moon and back.
>
> Find me a Star
> That will carry me far -
> And bring me all that I lack."

And when she'd done singing, Snowpetal would run over to her grandmother Ha'penny Rose and sit herself down beside her chair with her skirt all spread out around her on the grass and wait for her to start thinking back, the way she always did.

"Let me tell you..." said Ha'penny Rose. "When I was a little'un, just like you, I would go down to the meadow, just the way you do. I would go with all the others who were little'uns then - Ninefingers, Night-thorn, Nettleye and Willowmist. And we would play such games. We'd play Fox-and-Geese and Chainy-o and we'd dare each other to go to the wood, even though our mothers had told us to stay away, because that's where the Wolf lived - and you know what happens if the Wolf gets you, don't you?"

Snowpetal looked up at her Granny with big wide eyes and shrieked and giggled.

"Go on," she said. "Go on."

"Go on?" said her Granny. "What was I saying?" For Ha'penny Rose was very old, and sometimes she forgot what she had been telling you.

"Tell me about the Wolf," Snowpetal pleaded.

"Not so much to tell," said Ha'penny Rose, shaking her head. "You ever seen him?"

Snowpetal shook her head too, just the way her Granny did.

"Me neither," said Ha'penny Rose. "None of us ever did. Except Nettleye. She always told us she saw him once. But we reckon it weren't no wolf at all, just that bad lad Marlroot, you wouldn't know him, he was Oakum Marlroot's dad and was always trying to scare us. No - we never saw no wolf, but we did find a star once, down in the meadow."

Snowpetal sat up.

"What did it look like?"

"Why - twas a glittering thing, lying there in the grass, all white and shining. Willowmist saw it first and we all ran over - and the closer we got, the brighter it shone."

"What happened?" asked Snowpetal, her eyes shining like stars themselves.

"That was the strange thing," Ha'penny Rose told her. "Soon as we got right up to it, why then the star was gone."

"Where did it go?" asked Snowpetal.

"Nobody knows," said her grandmother. "We never saw it again, however hard we looked. I used to go out every night and gaze up at the stars and give them all names and wonder which one it was that came down to us in the meadow. But sometimes I think it never went away, because that star made us all feel special, the five of us who saw it - Ninefingers, Night-thorn, Nettleye, Willowmist and me. And whenever we got together, we'd smile and join hands like five points of a star - and when we were smiling we always felt happy. And when we felt happy, why then so many other wonderful things would happen."

"Such as what?" Snowpetal frowned, trying to hear her Nanny above the noise of Silverwing and her friends as they came racing by.

"Such as anything you wanted," Ha'penny Rose replied. "You should try it sometime. Ninefingers dug out a herb that would cure plagues and agues, pox and palsy. Night-thorn found a rounded jar to bottle her Morning Sunrise. Willowmist got her seven sons who grew to be farmers strong and true. Nettleye - what did she get? Why maybe she found a little crimson fish such as no-one had seen before..."

"And what about you?" Snowpetal asked.

Ha'penny Rose paused.

"What about me?"

"What did you get?"

"Why, I kept on smiling and a few years on and a few years after that, I met Scallum, your grandfather. And then I got Silfren, your very own mother. And she got Silverwing, your sister. And then in the end we all got *you*!"

Snowpetal stopped frowning and smiled as her grandmother tweaked her nose.

"That's better," said Ha'penny Rose. "Keep smiling and see what you get!"

"But first don't I have to find the star that fell in the meadow?" Snowpetal asked.

Her grandmother nodded.

"It's true," she said. "You do."

Snowpetal looked thoughtful.

"What are you puzzling on, little one?" her grandmother asked.

"I'm thinking about what to wish for when I find the shining star," Snowpetal replied.

"And what *will* you wish for?" quizzed Ha'penny Rose.

Snowpetal shook her head, but she knew that if she found the star, she would wish that her Granny was well again. For Ha'penny Rose was old and frail - and every day Snowpetal would push her in the great wooden chair that Darkwind made - trundling out of the cottage and across the grass, to sit at the edge of the Green. But sometimes when Snowpetal went to collect her, she'd find her grandmother just staring, as if she'd forgotten what she was doing there, as if she'd forgotten the names of all her friends.

"Tell me about the star again," Snowpetal asked her grandmother, as she rattled the chair slowly back towards the cottage.

"What star was that?" asked Ha'penny Rose.

"You know what star," Snowpetal replied, hoping her Granny was teasing, though she could never be sure these days. "The star you saw with Ninefingers, Nightthorn, Nettleye and Willowmist. What do they say about it now?"

Ha'penny Rose scratched her head.

"Don't say a lot," she said. "'Twas a long time ago. Long enough to forget what we wanted to remember and remember what we wanted to forget. Ninefingers says it weren't a star at all but a tree in blossom. Nightthorn says it was a sudden blow of snow. Willowmist says it was a sheep lost its way."

Ha'penny Rose paused.

"And Nettleye says twas a naked man running. But twas a star, sure enough. It was a star we saw, I know."

Snowpetal smoothed her grandmother's shawl and helped her out of the great wooden chair, into the shadows of the cottage.

That night, when her mother was busy tidying the kitchen and Silverwing was still out by the woods, where she knew she wasn't supposed to go - Snowpetal slipped away from the cottage and away across the Green, away from the straggle of lanterns that lit the back alleys, and the lights that shone from Brunt Boggart's windows. Darkness was creeping up out of the shadows, but the night was soft and warm. Snowpetal wore a daisy-chain that she'd made that day with Scallowflax all down in the meadow by the river. It swung from side to side as she ran breathless up the stony path that led to Langton Brow.

Snowpetal loved Langton Brow. By day she would come and sit here and listen to the blackbirds, the thrushes and the yellowhammers which would flit between the bushes with their trilling, chirruping songs. From the top she could see across the valley and the long river rolling on its way to the sea. She could see Pottam's Mill far down below, at the end of Mallenbrook Lane. She could see Oakum Marlroot's farm, the cattle and sheep dotted about the fields. She could see a plume of smoke rising from the cottage in the wood where Skyweaver lived.

But now darkness had fallen and Snowpetal climbed on, scrambling up the track, her feet slithering through a scree of pebbles, her hands grabbing out to clutch branches and brambles, hauling her upward towards the top. One more step, one more step - she was breathing heavily, then she reached the crest and a cry of joy burst from her. For Snowpetal could see every star in the sky. More stars than she could count on the fingers of her hand, or truth to tell on Silverwing's fingers and Ha'penny Rose and her mother as well. More stars than all the berries out in Pottam's wood. More stars than all the dewdrops on the meadow in the morning. At first each one seemed shimmering silver, bright and clear. But then when she looked, she could see as many more, floating into a milky haze.

When she closed her eyes then opened them again, Snowpetal could see the stars beyond the stars, more than she could ever name. And she felt as if she was floating high above Brunt Boggart's houses where they squatted far below, lurking in the darkness. Her head was spinning. She reached out her hands as if she could touch the stars, take them and scatter them through her hair, but all the time her feet were rooted firmly on the ground.

She wanted to run. She wanted to cry. She felt powerful and yet confused; lonely and lost, but loved. She wanted to tell her Grandmother Ha'penny Rose how she'd seen every star in the sky. But which was the special one, the star which had fallen into the meadow all those years ago - the star her grandmother had found? She wished that she could find it now and share in the secret that her grandmother shared with

Ninefingers, Night-thorn, Nettleye and Willowmist.

Snowpetal smiled and looked again. Which was her grandmother's special star? She didn't care. Each and every one of them was special to her now. She felt as if they were touching her, bathing her in light. She felt as if she was a child of the sky, floating through the night as she ran, ran and ran all the way home.

That night she dreamt of the stars. Dreamt she was flying through them, on and on, until she found the star which fell to the meadow - and there was her grandmother Ha'penny Rose with Ninefingers, Night-thorn, Nettleye and Willowmist. They were all as young as her sister was now, as young as they'd been that day in the meadow. They clustered around to greet her, then they linked their hands in the five points of a star and their voices joined together clear and high:

"Find me a Star
That will carry me far -
Around the Moon and back.

Find me a Star
That will carry me far -
And bring me all that I lack."

"Snowpetal, Snowpetal - what do you wish for?" they asked when the song was done.

Snowpetal felt confused. She knew the wish that she wanted to wish - that her grandmother would be well again. But here was Ha'penny Rose as young and as fresh as she could ever be.

"I wish that the stars didn't fade with the morning," Snowpetal whispered. "I wish they would shine all the day."

Ha'penny Rose smiled and so too did Ninefingers, Night-thorn, Nettleye and Willowmist. And then they dropped their hands and Snowpetal felt herself falling, falling down from the sky.

Next morning when she woke in the cottage at the end of the dusty lane, Snowpetal looked out of the windows to see if her wish had come true - but all the stars had gone. Last night there had been so many, but now there were none at all. Snowpetal rushed down the stairs, still in her nightshirt, and stood between the rutted puddles outside. Even though she could not see them, she knew that the stars must be there. She ducked under the sagging night-lanterns and set out towards Langton Brow.

But the sky was empty now. Even the sun had gone - hidden behind a dull grey cloud. Instead, drops of water fell, one by one, sparkling and fresh and clear. Snowpetal rushed on, holding out her hands, towards the path that led to the Brow. She didn't care that her nightshirt was soaked and her feet were muddied and cold. The raindrops fell as bright as the stars and Snowpetal tried to catch them, then splashed them over her face. The drops tasted sweet and sparkled clear, clear as the stars that shone in the night.

"The stars are falling, the stars are falling!" she cried to her mother, though her mother could not hear her - she was sleeping still, away back in their cottage.

Snowpetal ran on, scooping up the raindrops, scooping up the stars. Hundreds of stars, thousands of stars. Millions of stars. More than she could ever count, more than she could ever name - and they all came tumbling into her hands, all along the lane.

Snowpetal danced with the stars, as if they were sisters, as if they were girlen down on the Green. She danced although her feet were wet and her nightshirt soaked right through. But around her, where they had fallen, the stars lay dull in the puddles of mud. They had lost their sparkle, they had lost their shine. They ran into each other and lay weary and sad, tired and jaded by their journey from the sky.

Snowpetal began to cry.

"Where have the stars gone?" she wailed. "The stars I saw last night - more than I could count, more than I could name."

She trawled her way up and down the lane, picking at anything that seemed to glitter, dew-wet leaves or shining stones. But the stars had gone. They had melted away, lost in the puddles and the ditches and the ruts. Snowpetal shook her head and sneezed. Her nightshirt was soaked, her bare feet were muddied and she trudged her way wearily back to the cottage, just as the sun began to shine - to dry up the puddles just like her tears. When she got home, Snowpetal found her mother had risen from her bed and was pottering around the kitchen, preparing dough to bake a batch of bread.

"Where have the stars gone?" the little girl said.

Her mother wiped the flour from the end of her nose and peered out through the window.

"What stars are they?" she asked, checking the oven.

"The stars that fell down out of the sky, just like drops of rain," Snowpetal explained.

Her mother stopped and stared at her and tried to remember what her own mother had told her when she came asking questions - when she was a little'un, no bigger than Snowpetal.

"The sun has come to take them," she told her daughter quickly. "She scooped them up into her arms and carried them back to the sky."

But Snowpetal didn't believe her.

"I saw the stars. They came for me."

Before her mother could say anything, Snowpetal slipped back out of the door and ran and ran down the lane to Langton Brow.

"The stars are falling, the stars are falling," she said to herself, over and over again.

And then in the hedgerow she saw berries glistening - red and purple and shiny black.

"Now I know where the stars have gone." Snowpetal touched the elderberries, rain-kissed and shimmering bright.

"Now I know where the stars have gone!" she repeated in delight.

There were berries everywhere, festooned in the hedgerows, hanging high and hanging low. More than she could ever count, more than she could ever name. And Snowpetal picked just a handful. They tasted so sharp, they tasted so bright that she knew what she was eating. And soon her belly was filled with stars. She could feel them dancing - and as they danced, she started to laugh and as she laughed she wanted to tell her Grandmother Ha'penny Rose that she had eaten the stars. Maybe she had even eaten the special star which fell down to the meadow.

When she thought of that, she laughed even more and as she laughed she turned to run, all the way back to the cottage. She ran and ran, her bare feet hopping from stone to stone and over the fallen branches, all the way down the rutted track. When she reached the cottage she rushed inside, knocking over her basket of twisted straw stars which Scallowflax made specially for her. She dashed right into her Grandmother's room, and there was Ha'penny Rose sitting in her great wooden chair - waiting to go out. Her eyes were closed but a warm smile spread across her face.

Snowpetal shook her arm.

"Grandmother - look!" she cried. "Look at my belly, I've eaten all the stars." And she lifted her nightshirt to show her swollen tummy with all the stars inside.

Ha'penny Rose went on smiling, but did not open her eyes.

"Grandmother, I've found it - your special star. I can feel it in my tummy, dancing inside."

Her grandmother said nothing. Bright sunlight struck through the window, across the dresser at the side of the bed, as Silfren, Snowpetal's mother, quietly opened the door.

"Mother, Mother - why won't Grandma speak to me? I want to show her my belly all filled up with stars."

Snowpetal's mother took her arm.

"Hush now, little'un. Do not touch her. Your Grandmother is resting now. She is at peace."

Snowpetal twisted away. Then she turned again and looked at her mother standing there beside *her* mother, who sat so quiet and still. Snowpetal rubbed her belly again. She could feel the stars there, laughing and dancing. But then she knew. The special star was not there.

"I know where it is," she said to her mother who was looking away. "Grandmother has found it. The star that fell in the meadow has come for her at last."

And Silfren held Snowpetal tight in her arms, and sang to her in a voice soft and low:

> "Find me a Star
> That will carry me far -
> Around the Moon and back.
>
> Find me a Star
> That will carry me far -
> And bring me all that I lack."

SCALLOWFLAX AND TOM TATTIFER

Let me tell you... Let me tell you... there was a girl called Scallowflax who was all tongue-tied and gawkish. She used to hide in the shadows and watch while the others played Chainy-o and Farmer-in-the-Dell. Scallowflax would wander all by herself around the pigmires and trail her toes in the water pudge. She would sit all alone in the hollow in the middle of the Green and twist daisy chains all the day long to hang around her neck. And then she would wander out to the meadows and lie on her back to watch the skylarks rising and listen to their trilling song.

While Silverwing and Moonpetal would chase Hamsparrow and Bullbreath all around the alleyways, pretending they were playing hide-and-seek, then wait to be caught down by Pottam's Mill and kiss them when no-one was looking, Scallowflax would wander out to the woods and watch the squirrels skittering from branch to branch. And then she would tarry back, all along the edge of Oakum Marlroot's fields and there she would gather up scrags of corn and all the way down the path to her house she would twist them and plait them betwixt fingers and thumbs till there out of nothing at all, a straw doll would come, all twisted and braided with dried berries for eyes.

What did she do with them, these dolls made of straw? Why the old'uns would love them, would take them and cradle them and coddle them and coo, contented as pigeons with a pail full of grain. They would set them above their fireside hearths and over the lintels of their cottage doors. And the old'uns all swore that they kept the house clean, scurrying and tidying when no-one was looking. And Old Mother Tidgewallop said they kept the fever away and Old Nanny Nettleye lost all her warts as soon as she got one.

But Ravenhair's mother said to Scallowflax, "Give one to me. You know that they bring good luck with the men. Starwhisper, your mother's sister, made one of them dollies for me when Ravenhair's father came. And now that he's gone, why I sure need another to bring me more luck than any ribbon would."

Scallowflax blushed and looked away and handed Ravenhair's mother the straw doll that she'd made that day.

"I just make'em," she said. "Like to twist and tug and plait arms and legs. Poke berries in for eyes. I just like to make'em. Don't think about men."

And Scallowflax blushed again. But next day and next she made more straw dollies, long ones and short ones plaited this way and that. And she took them on a tray all down to the Green, down to the hollow where the girlen sat.

"What you got there Scallowflax?" Ravenhair asked her. "What you been doing down by the pigmires and out in the meadow all by yourself?"

"Never you mind," Scallowflax told her. "Just you look at these." And she pushed out the tray.

"What be these, Scallowflax?" Silverwing taunted. "Just scraggy old dolls stuck with dried berries. We don't play with dolls now, got better things to do."

Silverwing lowered her eyes and glanced over to the far side of the Green where Bullbreath and Hamsparrow were wrestling and tumbling, hitching up their britches and rolling their sleeves. Scallowflax followed her gaze.

"Don't you be looking there," Silverwing reproached her. "See that Bullbreath, he been waiting for me. He's boy-made-to-man now. He's climbed the Shuttle Stone these three moons ago. Look at you, Scallowflax. You ain't ready for the Red Grove yet, no way for sure."

Scallowflax bit her lip and she felt her cheeks flush.

"You think you know all, just 'cos you got a scarlet dress," she said. "But I been watching. Bullbreath don't look at you."

"Then who do he look at?" Silverwing sneered. "Don't look at you, that's for sure."

Scallowflax bunched her fists till her knuckles turned white.

"These straw men ain't no girlen dollies. Ravenhair's mother tell me that. Tell me you need'em to be lucky with men. They'll work a charm for you."

Silverwing laughed and pushed the dolls away.

"We got our own charms, Scallowflax. Charms you don't know about."

And she tipped the tray over and the girls ran away

to the boys-who-would-be-men and left Scallowflax to pick up her straw dolls from the grass of the Green. She gathered them together and laid them out on the tray, then went home to her mother's tumbledown cottage. Went home and stuck the straw men on top of the kitchen dresser. Climbed the rackety wooden steps up to the loft, to her bed. But when she'd pulled on her nightshirt and combed out her hair like a mess of wild straw, she looked at her bed so narrow and cold and looked at the moon that glowed outside her window and then crept quickly down the stairs.

"What are you doing back down again, Scallowflax?" she heard her mother call from the parlour where she sat rocking in her great wooden chair. "Child like you should be in bed already, not wandering round the house."

Scallowflax said nothing but climbed on a stool and reached up to where the straw dollies lay on the tray where she'd put them on top of the dresser. She scrabbled around, her fingers running over them, touching one then another until she found one that seemed to jump into her hand. She sprang from the stool all swiftly and quick and ran up the stairs before her mother could call her again. And there in the bed she placed the doll by her, alone on the pillow. She stroked its head gently as she lay there, its straw hair the colour of her own. She peered into its dry berry eyes, which did not look back at her, just gazed through the window at the cold white moon.

"You are Tom Tattifer," she told him, but the doll said nothing at all and Scallowflax fell to sleep.

Early next morning when Scallowflax woke, she could hear the birds scratting and squawking, scurrying and rustling through the straw on the roof. And when she turned over, to her surprise, she found herself staring into a pair of dried-berry eyes.

"Tom Tattifer!" she cried. "I had quite forgotten you."

She leapt straight out of the white linen bed and rushed to the mirror set beside the bowl of water and the jug on the dresser. She held up Tom Tattifer to let him see himself, but then to her alarm she looked at her neck and her shoulders and her arms. They were covered all over with mottled red rashes. At first she thought they must be sores, she thought she'd caught pond-fever or the night-sweating plague - but she did not feel ill, her eyes were clear, her tongue was pink. When she looked again at the rashes and sores she thought they seemed more like kisses and bites. She'd seen this before with the other girls, the ones who strayed to the wood with Longskull or Bullbreath. Tom Tattifer fell to the floor as she covered the marks with her hands.

Scallowflax looked around the room wide-eyed. The window hung half-open, the way she always kept it. Could someone have clambered up the guttering in the night? Could someone have climbed in and kissed her without her even knowing? She picked up Tom Tattifer from the floor and dusted him down and propped him on the dresser, up against the mirror.

Slowly and slowly she climbed down the stairs. Slowly and slowly she pushed open the kitchen door. Slowly and slowly she sat at the table where her mother was already sitting.

"Where have you been, child?" she chided, pushing across a bowl of porridge, already half-cold. "Been fussing about with your hair again, I reckon. I told you before - you don't need no fancy ribbons like all them other girlen. They just showing off. All's you need is a smart little bow to keep your hair back so it don't fall in your face when you're dusting and cleaning. And I can tell you now - there's plenty of that today."

Scallowflax prodded at the porridge with her spoon. It had gone hard and lumpy and she was minded to push it away, but knew she'd better not.

"Come on, eat up. What's to do with you child?" her mother began. But then she stared hard at her daughter.

"Why, you sloven. Here's me telling you not to waste your time on ribbons when you ain't got no ribbons or no bow at all. Look at you there with your hair all like that. You look like you been dragged through a haystack. What's to do with you? Pull it back, child, before it falls in your porridge."

Slowly and slowly, Scallowflax tugged back her hair. She could not look at her mother, and just squinnied down at her porridge bowl. But her mother stared at her. Stared at her arms and her shoulders and her neck. Stared at the red weals she saw there.

"Mercy, girl - what's all this? You coming down with some pox? How'm I going to clean the house now? I don't know, if it's not one thing it's another."

Scallowflax dangled the spoon in her bowl.

"Ain't pox, mother. Ain't pond fever or night sweats. I reckon it's just them old sheets. They rub me all night. You know how I told you they were all coarse and rough. They make my skin itch so I can hardly sleep and all night long I toss and turn."

Scallowflax's mother took hold of her arm and stared at it hard. She looked her in the eye and then she looked away.

"Could be you're right, child. Could be you're right. We'll have to get'em changed is all I can say. Eat up your porridge before it goes cold then get back upstairs to strip down your bed."

Scallowflax didn't want to say that her porridge was cold already. She scooped it down slowly, still squinting at the marks on her arms. She slopped her bowl into the kitchen sink, then clattered up the twisting stairs to the attic room where she slept. There she peeked at herself again in the mirror. The marks were still there right enough. And right enough, they didn't seem like sores at all, but like the kisses and the bites she'd seen on the other girls.

Scallowflax turned around and began to peel the sheets from her bed, while outside her half-open window she heard the birds all singing. But as she gathered up her sheets, she had the strangest feeling that someone was watching her across the room. Scallowflax turned around, expecting to see her mother standing there at the door, to make sure she stripped the bed as quickly as she could. She'd heard no footsteps on the stairs, and when she looked there was nobody there. But there on the dresser, beside the mirror, Tom Tattifer sat watching her. His dried berry eyes seemed to follow her every move, as Scallowflax closed her own eyes so that she couldn't see him while she bundled up the coarse dull sheets and threw them down the stairs like a billow of clouds full heavy with rain.

Her mother gathered them up and thrust them in a tub of suds and left them to soak the morning away, while Scallowflax brushed out the kitchen and scrubbed the scullery and beat the rush matting out in the backyard till her mother appeared with the basket of sheets and they wrung them and twisted them and hung them on the line to dry.

"Mother, mother, can I go now?" Scallowflax begged.

Her mother scowled and cast her eyes around to find more chores for her daughter. But they'd worked so hard, she could see nothing at all.

"Be gone with you, girl," she said. "Get out from under my feet. Just stay away from the corn fields. I want to see no more of your dollies made out of straw. Your Aunt Starwhisper used to make'em, and you know what happened to her."

Scallowflax gathered up her skirts and ran, ran down to the meadow where the other girls sat, playing a game of pit-a-pat, their hands held up in a ring, clapping and chanting:

"There was a girl who had a man,
His name it was Tom Tattifer.
There was a girl who had a man
And everybody laughed at her.

Tom Tattifer said he'd marry her
All on a winter's morn,
But when she came to meet with him,
Tom Tattifer had gone."

Scallowflax sat and watched them, waiting to see if they'd let her join in. She looked at her arms to check whether the kiss-marks and bite-marks had gone. She ran nervous fingers round her shoulders, round her neck, wondering if the tell-tale sores were still there.

But what tale would she tell if they asked her? For Scallowflax had no notion how they came to be there at all.

Silverwing turned and stared at her. Scallowflax smiled, hoping she'd invite her to sit in the circle and join in their game. But Silverwing turned away, raised her hands with her palms facing out and started the round again:

"There was a girl who had a man,
His name it was Tom Tattifer..."

Scallowflax watched the girls and wished she had dresses like them, cut full above the waist. She wished she had fancy ribbons from the Pedlar Man to tie through her tousle of straw-coloured hair. She wished she was not covered all about with strange red marks on her shoulders and neck. She looked up at the girls again, expecting to pinch herself with envy at their clear fresh complexions and their unblemished skin. But suddenly she noticed they all wore long sleeves and had bright silken scarves wrapped around their necks. Scallowflax wondered what they were hiding - for the weather was warm, a late summer lingering on into autumn, too fine for the girls to be covered this way.

"But when she came to meet with him,
Tom Tattifer had gone..."

The rhyme rattled on and on. Scallowflax gave up wondering if the girls would let her join in. She turned away and began to pick daisies, their petals like fingers of ice, their hearts as warm as the sun - till her lap was filled with flowers. And then she set to make a daisy chain, slitting her thumb-nail through the flowers' green stems, then linking them through, each one to the next, till she'd made a long necklace to hang round her neck. Then with what she had over she made bracelets and rings and a garland to twine around her head as she sat in the hazy sun.

The other girls had gone, scampering and skipping away through the lush grass of the meadow by the river. But Scallowflax didn't care. She had her necklace, her bracelet and her rings. She had a green garland to wear in her hair. And she'd done as her mother had told her, she'd not been down to the corn field, and she'd made no more straw dollies.

That night she slept a long deep sleep, as though she was diving deep into the river that wound through the meadow. When she woke she tossed her hair as if it might be straggled and wet. She climbed from her bed, her nightgown soaked, but then she realised she had been sweating, not floating in the dream river's darkness. She stood in front of the mirror and stared at her face. She looked at her arms, her shoulders and her neck. She was kissed again. Bitten and kissed. The marks were bright red. Scallowflax gasped. The chain of flowers still clung round her neck. When she looked back to her bed, the rings of wilted petals had slipped from her fingers and lay scattered across the pale rumpled sheets. Beneath the bracelets of twisted green stems, her skin was scarlet and raw. Scallowflax tore the flowers away, sure that they must have caused the sores.

She took a deep breath, ran her fingers through her straggly hair and sluiced cold water across her face from the earthenware bowl. Then she felt a sudden shiver, as if someone was watching, someone was with her, and looked up to see, on top of the dresser, there was Tom Tattifer staring down at her, sitting where she'd placed him before she went to sleep.

She stumbled downstairs, quicker than quick, quicker than that.

"Where have you been?" her mother chided. "The morning's half gone and your porridge is cold. And what are those sores that I see on your arms? Turn around, child - there's more on your shoulders and look what is this, right here on your neck?"

Scallowflax shook her head.

"It's my own fault mother. It's a rash from the flowers. I made a chain of daisy stems, all down by the river in the meadow. And now they have bit me, this way and that. I'll never go there again."

But each and every morning the strange marks came, florid and red, again and again.

"What is it child? Whatever's to do?" Even her mother was worried and puzzled. Scallowflax shook her head and stared down at the cold bare flagstones on the floor.

"It is the Night Fever, mother," she whispered under her breath.

"If it be Fever, then sure there's a cure," her mother declared. "Take you off to Old Nanny Ninefingers. She'll know what to do. Whatever anyone got, be it plague or ague, pox or palsy, she got the potion to cure you."

And Scallowflax went, all down Mallenbrook Lane, on the way to Pottam's Mill. There sat a cottage, grim-thatched and shadowing, but inside Old Nanny Ninefingers was singing as she busied around her pots and herbs, mixing this and that. Scallowflax peered in through the window and then she rapped on the door. At first Nanny Ninefingers didn't seem to hear her, because she was singing so loud. Scallowflax turned away. What could she say to her mother? How could she explain that she'd been all the way down to Nanny Ninefingers' cottage, all down Mallenbrook Lane, but Nanny Ninefingers couldn't hear her - and so she'd come home again? Scallowflax had her hand on the gate and was about to scurry down the rutted lane, when Old Nanny Ninefingers espied her through the musty glaze of her window.

"Wait child!" she called. "Was there something that you wanted?"

Scallowflax turned back. Nanny Ninefingers flung open the front door and ushered the young girl into her kitchen. Scallowflax stared wide-eyed at the pestles and bowls and crushing-hammers, the heavy wooden rolling pin and rows upon rows of bottles and jars.

"Sit down, sit down," Nanny Ninefingers fussed. "What be the trouble? Always is trouble when girlen your age come to me."

Scallowflax said nothing. She pointed at the sores, all up and down her arms, on her shoulders, on her neck. They were worse now, these few nights past. Nanny Ninefingers frowned and poked and prodded and walked all around the girl where she sat. Outside a jackdaw cawed, flapping through the branches.

"How long you had this?" Ninefingers demanded.

Scallowflax counted. "A week and a day and another week more."

Ninefingers chuckled and began to mix a potion of figwort and yarrow.

"But this be a rum do, I tellen you for sure. Seen plenty of these markens, these last few days and more. Look to me like bites... look to me like kissen. Someone been a-kissen you, Scallowflax my child?"

Scallowflax hung her head. Ninefingers sat astride another chair, leaning on the back.

"Come now, girlen. You can tell me. Ain't nothing Ninefingers don't know, else how my potions going to work? Be it Bullbreath or Hamsparrow, Scatterlegs or Scarum?"

Scallowflax shook her head. She bit her lip. Her cheeks flushed red.

"Ain't no-one kiss me. No-one at all. It be Night Fever, sure and true."

Old Nanny Ninefingers rose to her feet.

"If it be Night Fever, this'en'll do you, good as any other."

She shook the brown bottle, once to mix it, twice for luck and thrust it into Scallowflax's hand.

"Tell your mother she owes me a silver shillen, next time she pass this way."

Scallowflax ran. Ran up Mallenbrook Lane, the water-pudge spattering her long pale legs, till she reached the Green in the middle of the village. There the other girlen sat. Today they didn't ignore her. Today they reached out with their willowy arms and pulled her into their ring.

"What's this?" Silverwing demanded, snatching the bottle from Scallowflax's fingers.

Scallowflax said nothing. Silverwing prodded her and Moonpetal taunted:

There was a girl who had a man,
And everybody laughed at her..."

"What's this?" Silverwing asked again, twisting the bottle upside-down.

"Potion," Scallowflax said at last.

"What you want with potion?" Silverwing quizzed.

"Potion for Night Fever," Scallowflax explained defiantly.

"If you had Night Fever, you'd be lying sick a-bed, sweating and shivering."

"*This* be Night Fever," Scallowflax told her, and showed her the sores on her shoulders, arms and neck.

The other girls grinned and tugged at the scarves that each of them were wearing.

"You *sure* that be Night Fever, Scallowflax? Looks more like kissen." Silverwing puckered up her lips.

"Who want to kiss *you*?" Moonpetal mocked.

Scallowflax stood in the ring, angry and flushed.

"I know who want to kiss me," she said.

"So who is it, Scallowflax? Do tell us - who? Ain't Bullbreath or Hamsparrow or any of the lads. We know who they kiss and ain't you, that's for sure."

Scallowflax stared at the sky and then turned back and glared at the girlen.

"Why would I want to kiss any of *them*?"

"Who is it then? Tell us. Come on, tell us do!"

As Scallowflax clenched her hands tightly together, the marks on her arms stood out more lurid than wounds.

"I don't see who it is," she tried to explain. "He comes every night when my window is open. While I am asleep he holds me in his arms and kisses me before he steals away."

There was silence all around the ring. Far off in the forest the pigs were squealing. Then Silverwing giggled and Moonpetal joined in. They pulled off their scarves and rolled up their sleeves. All the girlen on the Green were covered with red weals on their shoulders, on their arms and on their necks. Weals that looked for all the world like bite-marks and kisses.

Scallowflax ran. She thought she had been the only one. Scallowflax ran. Though she did not know how it came to be, she thought the marks were for her alone. Scallowflax ran. All the way back to her mother's door, where she raced in and flung herself, breathless and flushed, into the chair by the kitchen table.

"What's to do, child?" her mother asked her. "Did you go to Nanny Ninefingers, just like I told you?"

Scallowflax nodded and held out the bottle. Her mother took it and shook it and sniffed it.

"What be this?" she asked.

"Figwort and Yarrow," Scallowflax told her.

"What she say you got, child?"

Scallowflax took a breath.

"Say I got Night Fever, maybe. But say it looks like kissens too. And when I got to the Green, all the other girlen there showed me - they got sores and marks, just the same as these."

Scallowflax's mother shut the door, and drew the bolts, one, two and three.

"I knew it, I knew it. Knew it all along. It's that boy Greychild. Nothing been the same since he came to Brunt Boggart, since Crossdogs found him all out in the woods. Now you ain't going near him no more. Now you ain't going down to the Green. You ain't going to the meadow, you ain't going by the river. And you ain't going near the wood no more, not now, not ever again!"

"Mother - I didn't," Scallowflax wailed. "Ain't nobody kissed me, though I wish they would."

Scallowflax's mother shook her head.

"If'n I believe you. If'n you say true. If it ain't

Greychild, then what Longskull says is true - maybe *he* weren't the Wolf after all. Real Wolf is still out there in the woods. Real Wolf still coming and breaking down fences and stealing all Snuffwidget's wine. Real Wolf been creeping around at night and climbing up into all the girlen's rooms."

She unlocked the door.

"You better go warn'em, Scallowflax my child. You better go tell'em to close their windows at night and don't stay out late all down by the wood."

Scallowflax raced away, though her legs were still shaking and she'd hardly gathered breath. The girlen were lolling around in the hollow, grinning and giggling and showing off their kiss-bites, bold and brazen as you like. Scallowflax leapt into the midst of them, gabbling wide-eyed:

"Stop! Stop all your jesting. My mother just told me. Ain't no Night Fever. The Wolf is come back. It be Wolf who comes to you, each night while you're sleeping."

The girls stopped for a moment and looked at each other. Silverwing tugged her dress up higher and showed off a new kiss mark, just above her knee.

Scallowflax stared.

"Who'd you think did this?" Silverwing asked her.

Scallowflax looked confused.

"Wolf," she said. "Like my mother told me."

Silverwing shook her head.

"Ain't no Wolf. I know who did this. I saw him sure and sure. Why - it was Bullbreath. Ain't no Night Fever. Ain't no Wolf. Ain't no flower rash or coarse sheets itching."

Then Moonpetal shook her hair back and pointed to

her shoulders.

"And *this* kiss was Scarum," she whispered with a smile.

"And this was Scatterlegs," Dewdream declared.

"Larkspittle did this one," Riversong told them, baring her neck.

One by one the girls showed where the boys had touched them and let loose their names. Then they turned to Scallowflax.

"So come on, Scallowflax - we asked you before. Who's been a-kissing you? Ain't no dream lover coming in the night, twitching at your curtains like you told us, that's for sure. Who want to kiss you, Scallowflax?"

"Ain't no-one you know, or likely to know," Scallowflax replied defiantly.

"Tell us," they pleaded.

"I been kissed by Tom Tattifer!" Scallowflax spat and turned away from the girlen in the hollow. "I been kissed by Tom Tattifer, for that is his name."

"Tom Tattifer? - Tom Tattifer!" the girls chanted after her, but Scallowflax said nothing and ran all the way home.

She rushed past her mother in the kitchen and right the way up the rickety stairs. She burst into her attic room and stared at the dresser beside her bed. The dresser was empty.

"Where is Tom Tattifer?" she said.

Scallowflax hunted hither and thither, peering under her bedstead and into the cupboard, pulling the dresser away from the wall to see if Tom Tattifer had tumbled down there.

"What's all that noise, child?" her mother called up

to her from the bottom of the stairs.

"Tom Tattifer, Tom Tattifer! Where is Tom Tattifer?!" Scallowflax shrieked in reply.

"Hush, child and come down here. Let me speak with you," her mother said.

Scallowflax rammed shut the drawers of the dresser and slammed her bedroom door before stamping down each step of the stairs.

"Sit there," her mother said sternly, pointing to a chair.

Scallowflax shook her head and remained standing where she was. Her mother turned away, turned her back on her daughter and stood gazing out of the window, across their tiny herb garden and out to Oakum Marlroot's fields.

"Where is Tom Tattifer?" Scallowflax demanded between gritted teeth.

"Let me tell you..." said her mother. "Tom Tattifer is gone. Gone where you'll never find him."

"But why?" Scallowflax cried. "He never did no harm."

"No telling what harm is, and when it's going to come," her mother said gently, turning back from the window. "I told you about your Aunt Starwhisper. She used to make them dolls."

"And the old'uns all loved them," Scallowflax protested. "They'd take them and cradle them and coddle them and coo, and set them above their fireside hearths and over the lintels of their cottage doors. Now they all tell me I can make dolls just like Starwhisper. Say I've got a gift for it, just like her."

Her mother paused and gazed at her daughter for a long time and long before she made any reply.

"So you have, child. So you have."

Scallowflax frowned. "Where did she go, Mother? - my Aunt Starwhisper. I only seen her when I was a little'un. How come I don't see her no more?"

Scallowflax's mother turned away again and gazed back out of the window, far away down the Pedlar Man's Track.

"Starwhisper is gone, child. Can't tell you where. But she ain't never coming back."

Scallowflax lay in bed that night and gazed around the room. The dresser seemed so empty now that Tom Tattifer was gone. The window stood half-open, letting in the light from the moon. Scallowflax tossed and turned awhile then finally fell to sleep between her clean linen sheets.

All night she dreamt of Aunt Starwhisper. Dreamt of the meadow and the flowers and the girlen as they all sat around in the hollow on the Green. Dreamt of their kiss-bites on their shoulders, arms and necks. Woke up sweating, but Scallowflax told herself that now that her mother had hidden Tom Tattifer away, she wouldn't find herself covered in sores ever again.

She climbed from her bed as dawn touched her window and she swung one foot onto the shivering floor. She tugged back the mass of tangled hair from her face and tiptoed over to the dresser. She rubbed her eyes and stretched as the curtains flapped round the window in the cool morning breeze. And then she peered into the mirror and saw that her arms, her shoulders and her neck were covered all over with kiss-bites bright red, same as they ever were before.

GREYCHILD, SCRITCH AND THE EYE OF THE GLASS

Let me tell you... Let me tell you about Old Granny Willowmist. Old Granny Willowmist lived in a cottage right by the Green in the middle of Brunt Boggart, the Green where the girlen would gather round the mossy hollow and the boys would come and sit and sing. The girlen would swap ribbons and the boys would wrestle and Granny Willowmist would watch them all the long day long. And she would remember her own sons and she would remember her daughters and wish they were still with her now. But they were gone off far away to other villages over the hills and around the bend of the slow running river, gone off with other girlen and boys.

So Granny Willowmist was all alone. She was happy enough chatting to Old Mother Tidgewallop, Old Nanny Nettleye and the rest. And helping round the village, drawing water and spinning and knitting. But at night her cottage was empty. The wind rattled at the window-frames and all she could do was stare at the moon. So when Crossdogs and Hamsparrow brought the WolfBoy home, it was Old Granny Willowmist who took him in. It was Old Granny Willowmist who taught him, patient as patient, how to sit at the table and eat all proper with knife and fork and a napkin tucked under his chin. It was Old Granny Willowmist who taught him, patient as patient, how to talk all proper, with 'please' and 'thank-you' and 'how-do-you-do'. And it was Granny Willowmist who gave him his name.

"I call you Greychild now. Ain't no WolfBoy. Never was. Just a poor boy lost, grown up in the woods. But now you got a home. My home is yours and you can live by me and fill up the empty room my own sons and daughters have left behind."

But in the end Greychild took to roaming again, all night under the moon, and never coming back till dawn, then lying a-bed half the day long until he took it into his head to get up and expect Granny Willowmist to fetch him his breakfast before he went out to wrestle with the boys and let the girlen ply him with kisses.

Till in the end Granny Willowmist said to him, "Greychild, this will not do. You eat more food than all my sons ever did all put together. You give me no help, you fill your room with spiders and frogspawn and twisted sticks and bits of stones. Time you did some work to pay for your keep."

So she took him by the ear and dragged him, howling and complaining, all the way down to the river that muddled its way around this middling village. Dull and sludgy and slow, it dragged its way in a great lazy bend all around the backs of the cottages. There was just one narrow hump-backed bridge to take you over this river - and by that bridge, Scritch sat. Scritch wore a coat the colour of dung and squatted all day by the sluggish stream. His eyes were sharp in his leathery face, darting quick, on the look-out for anything that glittered, glistening in the water, in the shallows by the bank. No matter what it was, be it fish or tin or silver, Scritch would have it, quick as a flash.

He would stare into the water, his eyes glinting with silence. The silence spread across the ripples, shimmering and steely, then darted down to the shingly pebbles that lay on the bed of the stream. The silence filled everything, like the silence that spreads beneath a heron's shadow as it sits and wills its prey to swim too close to the silver blade of its beak. And quick as a heron when it strikes, Scritch's hand would dart into the water and grab whatever he'd seen, grip it tight and pull it out. He would fling it onto the bank and clean it down and sluice it in a pail of fresh water. If it was fish he'd cook it and maybe he'd eat it for his supper or maybe he'd sell it to one of the wifen. And if it was tin or silver, why then he'd melt it down and smelt it and twist it into trinkets to trade with the Pedlar Man next time he came around.

Scritch would sit all day by the river, watching and waiting. He hardly spoke to anyone, but when he did, his voice was like a crow's - all dark and croaking. He knew the sky, he knew the clouds, he knew the water. That's all he needed to know. But now Granny Willowmist stood beside him, still grasping Greychild tight by the ear.

"What?" Scritch squawked. He was staring at Greychild. Greychild peered back at him, then tried to pull away.

"What?" Scritch uttered again, his eyes darting away

to the water. "What you want come troubling me?"

"Scritch," Granny Willowmist pleaded. "This be a good boy. He needs to work. Do you have anything for him? Anything he can do?"

Scritch said nothing. He stared at the water. He squinnied the sky. He hardly looked at Greychild. Then he nodded.

"See them pots."

Greychild looked over at a pile of broken earthenware. He looked back at the weather-eyed man, wondering what he meant.

"Clean'em," said Scritch.

Greychild turned to look at Granny Willowmist, to see what she would say. But Granny Willowmist had vanished. She'd already set out, back along the winding path that led right to her door. Greychild looked this way and that. He gazed towards the watchful wood, where his mother had left him. He looked at Scritch. Scritch looked at him, and then repeated.

"Clean'em."

And so Greychild began. All day, every day, down by the river, cleaning the broken pots which Scritch flung over to dry in a pile on the bank. Big bits, little bits, all of them shattered, all of them broken. Bits from old pots made long ago and tossed into the river.

"No good to me," Scritch told him. "Only want shiny things - fish, tin, or silver." His eyes glistened in the drizzle which was falling around them. Greychild wiped the back of his hand across his dribbling nose.

"Who made'em?" he ventured, pointing at the broken pots.

Scritch shrugged.

"Don't know. No-one knows. Older than the old'uns.

All broke now. All gone..."

Greychild swilled the mud from the broken pieces of dull red earthenware, but as he pieced them together he could see they were graven with patterns, all mazy and swirling, in shapes he'd never seen before.

"What do they mean?" he asked Scritch. But Scritch wasn't listening. He was gazing into the water again, as the dull rain ran down his back.

So day after day, Greychild washed and cleaned the broken pots. Then he pieced them together, trying to match the patterns. Bit by bit he'd stick the broken parts together with a gummy resin that Scritch showed him how to collect from the roots of the bluebells that grew in the woods. Then he'd put them in the window of the old wooden shed where he and Scritch would shelter when the rain got too bad. Sometimes the mothers and the old'uns would come and pore over them, and rake through the trinkets that Scritch had made from bits of tin and silver, the ones that the Pedlar Man hadn't taken, the ones that were crooked, twisted or misshapen. Scritch would sell them cheap. The women were happy enough with them, always bright and shiny. Then they'd look at the pots and pick them up and peer inside and put them back. Some days they'd buy one, but not very often.

"No good to me," Old Mother Tidgewallop told Greychild. "All cracked and broken. Tain't no good to look pretty on my mantle-ledge. And tain't no good for putting stuff in. All leak out the holes."

It was true. Greychild hardly ever found every piece for a full pot, so he would just patch two together, or leave them full of gaps for the wind to blow through. But he loved the patterns, the spiralling whorls and mazes, and always traced his finger round them, trying to figure out a meaning.

"Don't mean nothing," Scritch grunted. "Just old, that's all. Old and broken."

But Greychild waited till the Pedlar Man came next time around with his trays of ribbons and bright shiny knick-knacks which were no good for nothing except all the girlen wanted them. Greychild asked if he'd like to buy one of his pots. The Pedlar Man took a look. He fixed the pot with a crooked eye and turned it this way and that.

"This is a fine pot you have here," he mused.

Greychild was pleased.

"What will you give me for it?" he enquired.

The Pedlar Man turned the pot over.

"What do you want?" he asked.

Greychild wasn't sure.

"I want a ribbon," he blurted. "A long lilac ribbon to give to Dawnflower. She ties petals in my hair and slips me sweet kisses and sews together my clothes. At least I should give her a ribbon in return."

The Pedlar Man rapped at the top of the pot with his bony knuckles.

"This pot is cracked," he declared. "No way could I sell it in another village. Who wants cracked pots when I've got buttons and bows? Tell you what, you should keep it. It's a good pot, a sturdy pot. Just that it's cracked, that's all. Why not give it to Dawnflower instead of a ribbon? Then she can cook you a broth, so she'll not only clothe you and twine you with petals and give you sweet kisses - she'll feed you as well!"

Greychild scowled and the other boys laughed at him. He grabbed the pot back.

"Old Granny Willowmist already gives me food."

At the end of the day, when the sun began to dip, Greychild grew tired and started to find it hard to tell stones from mud from pieces of pot as he peered into the water. He started to think of food and Granny Willowmist's warm cottage and wondered if he might see Dawnflower again - and wondered if she might want to plait one of her ribbons through his hair and kiss him with one of her special kisses... Greychild trawled through the water one last time and pulled out one last mud-caked shard. He scrunnied it with his thumbs, just the way Scritch showed him. The mud flaked away, red and grey, but weren't no piece of earthen pot, the same as all the others which sat in a stack on a scrap of leather on the grass beside him. He scrunnied it again. Something shone. Greychild rinsed it in the water. Weren't no pot at all. Twas glass. It shone like a mirror.

Greychild twisted it this way and that, expecting to see himself - the boy with the tousled hair, the boy they'd called Greychild. Expected to see the clouds and the sky and everything around - the overhanging trees by the river edge, the swirling flocks of starlings. But instead saw nothing, heard a sound like whistling, and then he saw... markets selling treasures he'd never dreamt of - brought by ships sailing in from the ends of the world. And taverns and food and wine tasting sweeter than any potion that Snuffwidget ever brewed. Saw a far-off city.

"Must be Arleccra," Greychild mused, "just like the Pedlar Man told us. Must be where my mother has gone. If I go there, sure I'll find her."

Greychild turned the glass this way, that way as he peered over his shoulder. He thought that Scritch was watching him. But when he looked again, Scritch was sitting as he always sat, gazing into the water. Greychild slipped the eye of the glass in his pocket. He was hungry now. It was the end of the day. He cast another glance at Scritch, waiting to see what he'd say. Scritch took no notice at first, the way he always did, but then he looked up at the darkening sky. Rainclouds gathering behind them. Sun slowly sinking down.

"Time to pack up," he shrugged. "Soon be too dark to see anything here."

And the two of them got to their feet and scrambled back up the muddy bank, scraping and stamping their boots on the grass. Then Scritch opened up the door of the old wooden shed and chucked the small handful of tin he'd collected into a bucket in the corner.

"Lot of good that'll do," he muttered. "Won't make much more than a thimble from that."

That was what Scritch always said, good days or bad.

"How'd you do, lad?"

Greychild clattered past him and cast a motley collection of broken earthenware into a pile on the floor.

"No good to anyone," Scritch scowled. "You sure that's all you got? Not keeping nothing back?"

Greychild shook his head.

Scritch bolted the door, raised his eyes to the sky.

"Rain coming soon," he said. "Best be getting along." And without waiting for Greychild to reply, he tugged up his collar and set off away down the overgrown track to where he lived, a hand-built hut at the edge of the riverbank - half way from the village, half way to nowhere - a patchwork of planks and beams threaded together with wire and string. And out in the front where there might be a garden were all manner of bits and pieces and broken things.

Scritch would cook his fish outside, out on a tarnished griddle. When he'd eaten he'd sit in a battered old wicker chair and listen to the rooks away up in the woods. Then he'd stump inside and spend the night hunched by an oil-lamp, smelting and twisting all the metal he'd collected into trinkets for the Pedlar Man.

Greychild was skittering as quick as he could along the winding path that led back to Brunt Boggart. But not to go straight to Granny Willowmist's cottage, hungry as he might be, hungry as he was. No - for now he had the glass in his pocket, and as soon as he was out of Scritch's sight, he drew it out again and sat down under a tree in the spinney by the path. He looked all around and listened. Far away he could hear dogs barking in the village yards, and Oakum Marlroot calling in his cattle, out on his lonely fields.

Greychild thrust his hand in his pocket. What if he was just tired and hungry and the glass really was just a mirror? Or not even a mirror, but just another piece of broken pot? His fingers curled around it and he slowly drew it out. It was dull. It was nothing. Greychild shook his head. It was just as he feared. What should he do? Should he just chuck it over his shoulder, a useless piece of broken glass to lie in the bushes for the jackdaws to peck?

Greychild breathed on the eye of the glass and rubbed it with his sleeve. At first nothing seemed to happen. But then as he peered closer into its centre, he could see leaves. Leaves like the leaves all around him. Maybe was just a mirror after all. But then as he looked, the leaves turned to gold. He sat up and gazed around. Wasn't autumn. Was still summer, late summer, damp and wet. The leaves on the branches were dripping with green. But the leaves in the glass were burnished with gold. And then they faded away. Greychild could see hills. Hills that he knew, hills that he saw every morning from Granny Willowmist's top window - but he couldn't see now, here under the bushes. And then he saw the hills beyond the hills - the hills he only ever saw on a clear bright day, not when it was cloudy and dull, like now. The hills where no-one had ever been, only the Pedlar Man.

Greychild gasped and smiled. Now he could see far beyond the hills. He could see Arleccra, just as he had seen it before. He felt as if he was walking there, down the streets, through the alleys, past the markets down to the ramshackle warehouses where sharp-faced boys and grizzled old men unloaded barrels and bales hauled up from the harbour. Greychild gazed at the crowds, more people than he'd ever seen before.

And then at the edge of the throng, he thought he saw a woman. A woman waving to him. Greychild's heart beat faster. He was sure this must be his mother. He'd know her anywhere. He tried to call out, but his voice was lost, somewhere between the spinney and the Glass and Arleccra. But he was sure it was her. He ran towards her as she turned away, though she seemed to be beckoning still. But as he reached the spot where he'd seen her, she faded into the crowd. He was surrounded by faces he'd never seen before, and voices he didn't know. And then one voice that was familiar.

"Greychild, what are you doing?" He turned to see

Dawnflower sitting beside him in the spinney. She put one arm around him and kissed him on the cheek.

"What's this?" she asked and reached into his lap for the fragment of glass. Greychild pulled it away and sat up straight.

"It's just a bit of glass - nothing to do with you."

"Let me see," Dawnflower teased. "You know I like trinkets and sparkly things. Is it something you found down there in the river? Let me see - I won't break it."

Greychild shrugged and handed her the glass.

"It's dull and scratched," she said. "Not pretty at all. What you bother fishing this out for? Why you bother keeping it? It's just a dirty old bottle, broken in the stream."

"Look again," Greychild told her. "Here - breathe on the glass. Polish it with your sleeve."

Dawnflower blew on the glass, as if she was kissing his lips. She rubbed at it with the hem of her dress.

"What can you see?" asked Greychild.

"Can't see nothing at all," she said. "Just looks like a great sad tear."

She held it up to the sky. A drop of water splattered onto the glass. Greychild looked at Dawnflower, afraid that she might be crying.

"Scritch said it would rain," he remembered as he grabbed Dawnflower's hand and pulled her to her feet. She tugged her coat around her shoulders, and gave him back the piece of glass which he shoved into his pocket while they sheltered under the trees. The rain kept on falling, rattling the leaves, soaking into the grass around their feet, pelting the river's dull surface as it wound around the bend. Dawnflower sneezed. Greychild rubbed his rumbling stomach.

"I'm hungry," he said.

Suddenly all he could think about was Granny Willowmist's kitchen and the steaming hot supper that he knew she'd have waiting for him. And so they ran hand-in-hand, up the narrow winding track, all through the water-pudge, mud splattering up their legs. They ran past the pigmires and the turnip-stooks. They ran past the middens and the scratted patches of parsnips and turnips till they reached Granny Willowmist's cottage.

She was standing there in the doorway waiting. When Dawnflower saw her, she stopped abruptly, planted one last kiss on Greychild's cheek and skidded away suddenly through the mud, her hair plastered to her face, her dress clinging wetly around her as she slithered and slipped away to her own mother's cottage, the other side of the Green.

Granny Willowmist looked at Greychild sternly.

"Get inside at once. Look at the state of you! Where have you been?"

Greychild stood dripping in the middle of the kitchen, eyeing the bubbling pan on the stove.

"Take off your jacket, you're drenched, child."

Greychild sneezed.

"What's for supper?" he asked.

"Never mind what's for supper. There's no supper for you till you tell me what you've been up to."

"Been working," said Greychild. "Been working with Scritch, down by the river, same as I do every day."

"But what you been doing with Dawnflower? I don't trust that one."

Greychild put his hand in his pocket and touched the

glass.

"Nothing," he said. "Been doing nothing. Just met Dawnflower out on the path in the spinney where I been sheltering under the trees when the rain came. And we waited together a little while to see if the rain would ease off - and then we came home."

He stopped.

Granny Willowmist was still staring at him, this strange lost child who came from the woods, who could speak no words at first but only sing one song, who stood dripping wet in front of her in the middle of her kitchen floor.

Greychild looked at the pans again.

"I'm hungry," he said. "What's for supper?"

Willowmist smiled.

"Come on, get your clothes off. You'd better sit down - you'll catch your death of cold."

Greychild sneezed and wrinkled his nose.

"It's bacon and tatties and dandelion leaves," Willowmist reassured him, taking his coat. Greychild laughed. He couldn't wait to scoop out a bowlful.

"Don't worry 'bout me," he said. "Seen worse rain than this when I lived in the woods."

"I know, I know," said Willowmist, rattling the pan and the ladle. "Just stay away from that Dawnflower, that's all. You never met no-one like her when you was alone in the woods. She's just like them girlen from across the river and over the hill who took my sons away. Most times never see them now, too busy tending their cattle and digging of their fields. She's just like them. I know what she's after, she'll take you away. And it's too soon for you, my Greychild. Too soon by far..."

Greychild was tired. Soon after supper he took off to bed and wrapped himself tight in the blankets. He fell into a sleep that felt deeper than sleep and dreamed a dream that felt more real than waking, that he was there in Arleccra again, could hear music and dancing and his mother was near calling his name, again and again.

Greychild sat up. The voice was in the room. He stared around, suddenly awake. A soft milky light bathed the walls. He could hear Granny Willowmist across the way, snoring. Then the voice came again.

"Greychild... Greychild..."

Not Mother now. Not in the room, but somewhere outside. He climbed out of bed and tiptoed through the moonlight which flooded the floor. Eased the casement slowly open so its creaking wouldn't wake old Willowmist. He looked down and peered around.

"Greychild..."

He heard the voice again. Then out of the shadow of the chestnut tree on the edge of the Green stepped Dawnflower. She was about to call his name again when she looked up and saw that he was there.

"Dawnflower, what are you doing?" he asked.

"I don't know, I don't know. I lay in my bed and twined this way and that, but I just couldn't sleep. I wanted to see you. The rain has stopped and the moon is so bright. Come down to me..."

Greychild looked down at Dawnflower, standing under the moon. He looked back inside at the four stone walls of Granny Willowmist's room. He looked away to the woods, where he'd once roamed so free.

He looked to the road that wound out of town.

"Meet me down at the bridge by the river," he said. "I'll be with you there soon as I can."

Dawnflower caught her breath with delight and blew him a kiss and ran on away. Greychild grabbed up a bag and stuffed it with all that he had, his jacket, spare britches, a fistful of ribbons, one from each of the girls. He crept down the stairs and then in the kitchen he wrapped up a loaf of bread and a round of cheese from Granny Willowmist's pantry. He checked that the Glass was still in his pocket, then lifted the latch and closed the door quietly and padded softly out into the night. He darted around the bends of the track that led him to the river. There was Dawnflower waiting, her white dress glowing in the moonlight. As soon as she saw him she rushed towards him, and threw her arms around his neck.

"Oh Greychild, Greychild, I'm so glad you've come! And what's this you have here?"

She poked at the bag slung over his shoulder.

"Oh Greychild! What are you doing?" she cried. "Have you packed a bag to leave home? Are you running away from Granny Willowmist? Will you come with me now to stay with me in my mother's cottage? - I can dress your hair every day and keep you warm every night."

Dawnflower's eyes were shining. Greychild gazed at her face. What could he say? His hand slipped deep in his pocket and stroked the glass that lay there.

"Dawnflower," he said. "I can't stay here. Four walls don't suit me, be it Granny Willowmist's or your mother's. I have to leave. I wanted to see you one last time. I'm going over the bridge and down the Pedlar Man's Track. I need to go where my mother has gone, to the city of Arleccra, far over the hills."

Greychild took Dawnflower in his arms and held her

for a moment, so gentle and warm. But then he turned and walked away over the hump-backed bridge, while Dawnflower stood and watched him go as her eyes filled with tears, just like the tears that she'd seen in the Glass.

OAKUM MARLROOT AND THE LUMPEN STONE

Let me tell you... Let me tell you about Oakum Marlroot. Oakum Marlroot was miserable and miserly and melancholy, anyone would tell you that. Always had been, always would be.

Oakum Marlroot's fields were a rough dry scrat of wheat and barley and weeds. And a clutch of old cattle that wandered around, in and out the mire; too skinny for meat, too shrivelled for milk, but Oakum Marlroot kept them all the same. All the day long he would work his fields, whatever the weather: sleet, sun or rain, it made no matter. Oakum Marlroot would go, with his hoe, or his shovel, or his hammer, harrying out weeds, filling in fox-holes and waiting for the crops to ripen before he could hack them down.

Oakum Marlroot was a big man, big hands and broad shoulders. He worked all day by himself. He liked it that way, he said. No-one to bother him, no-one to get in the way. But few would work with Oakum anyway.

Those that had never lasted long. Young lads from the village, he near worked them to death, carrying great heavy loads. Up every morning before it was light and never leaving the fields until it grew dark. But it was only what Oakum did himself. May as well do it all by himself - that's what he said. Nobody else to get in the way.

Oakum Marlroot lived all by himself in a brooding house on the edge of his farm, out on the edge of Brunt Boggart. Rooks came and nested in the chimney tops, and the gutters needed fixing. Each time it rained, the water would sluice down and fill up the barrels and overflow across the yard in a slurry of stench from the pigs and the chickens that scavenged and pecked all day long.

Oakum Marlroot lived all by himself, but it hadn't always been that way. Used to have wife. Big woman, just like him. Big and proud. Used to brew bitter wine from the darkest of berries and make succulent pie out of lambs' brains and squirrel gut. But Oakum Marlroot's wife never gave him a son. Never gave him a daughter neither. Never gave him nothing, some folks said. Then she died strange one day when the thunder came, out in the fields alone with Oakum Marlroot, both of them shouting and carrying on. And then she was dead. Alone with Oakum Marlroot, no-one else to see.

And Oakum scooped her up in his arms, big as she was, heavy as she was, and carried her like a sack of tatties all the way across the fields, back to the farm, his hard boots tramping on through the mud as sheets of rain came lashing down. Buried her quick, soon as he could, out in the burying ground. Thunderhead put on his tall hat, black and battered - and said the words he always said. And then Oakum Marlroot dropped her in the cold hard ground. Nobody else came. None of the wifen. None of them dared.

The wind blew hard and the wind blew black as Oakum Marlroot strode back to the farm, all by himself. Been all by himself ever since, saddened not to have no son, for there had always been Marlroots on this farm, ever since Brunt Boggart began. Now at night he walks to the tavern and there he slakes his thirst alongside Mottram Ironfield and Redgut and all the other men who work the farms. Don't say nothing much then, neither. Not till he's drank his fill of ale, and then no-one can shut him up. He rants and he curses all the night long and stomps round the village kicking on doors and smashing down fences. Then come noon-time next day he'll be back in his fields again, grunting and glowering, alone with the rooks.

It was one of those very days when Oakum Marlroot went a-digging, all out by Black Meadow, with nobody with him but the sky. And he thrust his shovel deep in the ground and felt it strike something hard. Just another stone, Oakum reckoned and hacked all around to try and lift it out. And lift it out he did, all grimy and lumpen and as big as two fists. He was about to pitch it away when he rubbed off some of the mud with the end of his thumb and saw that the stone was glistening.

"What could it be?" Oakum Marlroot wondered. He put down his shovel and scrunnied the stone with his hard horny hands, sloughing off the mud to show that underneath was all the same - glittering and shining in the dull midday sun. Oakum turned it and twisted it. Hadn't ever seen anything like it before. All lumpen and glinting, no shape at all.

Oakum looked up. "Maybe it fell from the sky."

He stuck the stone in his pocket. It hung heavy in his coat as he trudged across the brackish mud to wash it under the water pump in the middle of his yard. It was shiny, sure enough. It glistened in his hard horny hands that worked in any weather, but now held something bright, something pretty. Oakum turned it this way and that. It sparkled, sure enough. Was pretty, sure enough. Pretty like his wife would have liked before she turned sad and sour. But she was gone now, gone to the thunder, gone to the cold dark ground. Oakum Marlroot shrugged. The stone was no good to him. Couldn't plant it, couldn't eat it - and he had no-one to give it to. So that night he took it with him, down to the tavern - and when the drink had started flowing, he took the stone from his pocket and showed it to Mottram Ironfield and all the other farmers sitting round.

"What you got there?" they asked.

"Not sure," he replied. "Thought you might tell me. Ever seen anything like this before?"

Mottram Ironfield took the stone in his hands, held it up to the lantern light, squinnied hard at it this way and that, then rolled it around in his palms.

"Don't know what you got here. It's pretty right enough. But what good's pretty to the likes of us?"

The other farmers laughed.

"Tain't no good to plant seeds," Mottram Ironfield went on. "Ain't never going to grow. Tain't no good to sharpen knives, it's all knobbled and lumpen. Tain't no good for nothing at all, Oakum Marlroot. I'd have pitched it in the pond. What good's traipsing it down here?"

Oakum Marlroot shook his head and watched while the other farmers passed the stone around.

"Tain't worth nothing to us," they said. "Why not take it to the Pedlar Man - see if he can make some trinkets out of it? That's all it's good for."

So Oakum Marlroot stuffed the stone back in his pocket and pulled out a handful of coppers to buy himself another drink. But next time he saw the Pedlar Man coming over the hills, Oakum put down his hoe and went hurrying over. The Pedlar Man looked up at the great burly farmer blocking his path.

"Now then?!" he exclaimed, gripping tight his sack in case this was another ruffian come to try and rob him.

"Now then," Oakum grunted in reply and thrust his hand into his pocket. The Pedlar Man paused, fearing he would pull out a weapon. But Oakum Marlroot drew out the stone, wrapped up in a rag of cloth, and shoved it under the Pedlar Man's nose.

"What be this?"

The stone sparkled in the midday sun, rainbow hues and other colours too, such as neither of them had ever seen.

"What be this?" Oakum Marlroot asked again. "Be it gold?"

The Pedlar Man shook his head.

"Ain't gold," he said, weighing it carefully in his palms. "Ain't silver neither. Ain't any sort of precious stone that I've ever seen."

Oakum snatched it back.

"Will you buy it?" he asked.

The Pedlar Man shrugged.

"I've got no money," he said hurriedly. "I can give you rings and ribbons."

"What good's rings and ribbons to me?" Oakum Marlroot demanded. "Got no wife. Got no girlen. Got no women wants to catch my eye - I leave that to the likes of you. Can't you give me silver? Can't you give me shillen?"

Oakum pushed his face up close to the Pedlar's.

"Give me shillen, then I can buy more seed to plant the fields for next year."

The Pedlar Man shook his head.

"I tell you plain," he said. "I don't know what this stone is. Never seen nothing like it before. If I had any shillen I wouldn't know what to give you. If it be gold or precious stone - I can't afford it. If it be worthless glittery thing, then there's no point me giving you anything!"

Oakum Marlroot trudged back to his farm, across the dull stooped fields. Each bush that he passed, each ditch, each pond, the stone itched in his hand and he wanted to pitch it there. But something in his head told him - no, he should keep it. So when he got home he took the stone from his pocket and laid it in a drawer in the dresser in his room, under the crisp linen sheets which had never been moved since his wifen died.

Oakum Marlroot was weary, but that night he could not sleep. He found himself wondering, what if they were wrong - Mottram Ironfield, Redgut and the Pedlar Man. What if the stone really was worth something? Longskull or Crossdogs, they might try and steal it. Ravenhair or Silverwing might charm it away from him. The stone would not be safe lying there in the dresser while he was out at work in the fields. And so at first light he clattered down the stairs and took his longest shovel from the barn in the backyard and set out to Black Meadow where the dark water gathered and ran down through the claggy mud to the ditch, right at the edge of his farm.

There he struck his shovel into the earth and he dug and he dug, all the while glancing over his shoulder, this way and that, to be sure that nobody saw him. When he'd dug so deep that he nearly struck rock, he placed the stone right there at the bottom and climbed from the hole and shovelled back the mud. He trod it all down till it was firm and hard so that no-one would know that his stone was hidden there, right out under the towering sky.

Every morning and every night, Oakum Marlroot passed by Black Meadow, right where the stone was buried. He would check for footprints leading that way. He would check for signs of digging in the dull dark earth. But no-one came. Oakum's stone was safe where he'd buried it, deep down under his field. And Oakum Marlroot toiled on, ploughing and sowing, hoeing and weeding, same as Mottram Ironfield and all the other farmers. But when summer came and his crops should be high, Oakum Marlroot looked at the dark barren ground.

Back in the tavern, Mottram Ironfield and the other farmers shook their heads and tugged their beards. "Dunno what it is to be sure. There's wheat in our fields, springing high as ever. You must have got a bad batch of seed."

But then in the midden, all his cows fell dead. One by one, one after next. Just keeled over and dropped. And Oakum hauled them down to the burying pit. The wind blew hard and the rain fell weary and Oakum Marlroot stopped going to the tavern at all so he couldn't hear Mottram Ironfield and all the other farmers bragging and gloating how their barns were stuffed with corn.

He strode across his empty fields. Dusk was coming. Hedges were ragged, middens were clogged, the slurry pits overflowed, but Oakum had no mind to tend to any of them.

"Tis the stone," he said. "Ain't worth nothing to no-one and I've gone and kept it and now it's blighted my land."

He fetched his long shovel and went out to Black Meadow and he dug and he dug, that way and this, till at last his shovel struck something hard, something shining. He gripped at it with both his hands and scrunnied away the mud with his thumbs. Would it be changed? Would it be broken? But it glowed still as bright as ever before, all the colours of the rainbow, and other colours too, such as no-one had ever seen.

At first Oakum Marlroot clutched it, almost happy to see it again, though he blamed the stone for all of his troubles. He turned it slowly, back and forth, and watched the colours glint in the light of the dying sun. But then it felt as if the stone was burning him, searing his hands. He felt the blood beating hard in his head and threw the stone down. As it lay on the cold hard ground he raised his shovel high in the air and brought it down with a crack. He stepped back and wiped his palms. The stone was not broken, but when he looked at his shovel, the handle and the blade were split from end to end.

Oakum Marlroot picked up the stone and put it in his pocket, just as he had the day he first found it. He trekked across the flat dreck fields, his coat hanging heavy with the weight of the stone. He trudged on down

Brunt Boggart's main street as stray dogs rattled at his feet and kept right on until at the far end he came to the Blacksmith's yard. A fire was roaring and sparks flew from the anvil as Oakum Marlroot stepped inside. The Blacksmith nodded and swung his hammer one last time, then stopped and mopped his brow.

"Now then, Oakum Marlroot. What brings you here? There's still three silver shillen to reckon with me since last time I shoed your horse."

Oakum Marlroot folded his arms. "Don't have no cause for no horse now, not since wifen died. She only used it to take fruit to market. Don't do no fruit now, neither. So I ain't got no silver shillen."

The Blacksmith hoisted his hammer. Oakum Marlroot raised his hand.

"Never mind about shillen. Time enough for that. I got something special to show you. Worth more than silver or gold."

The Blacksmith stood back. Oakum thrust his hand in his pocket and pulled out the glowing stone. The Blacksmith stared at it, then tapped it with the handle of his hammer.

"What be this then?"

"Don't rightly know," Oakum Marlroot replied. "Nobody does."

He threw the stone on the anvil.

"There. Just one blow from your hammer and the stone will shatter. Who knows what might be inside. Could make you richer than three silver shillen."

But as the Blacksmith gripped his hammer and glared through the swirling smoke, all he could see was the young lads Oakum Marlroot had taunted and maimed with driving them hard on the farm. One had been his own brother's son. And then he saw Oakum's wifen who'd died that night, out in the fields, in the thunder. Wasn't right, they said. Wasn't right at all. The Blacksmith hauled up his hammer and swung it into the air. The hammer seemed to hover as it arced towards Oakum Marlroot's head.

But as it whistled down, the Blacksmith changed his aim. Just glancing away from Oakum Marlroot's brow, he struck the stone instead. Oakum felt the force of the swirling hammer as it scythed right past his face. Now he watched as it hit the lumpen stone. He heard the crack as the metal struck, then watched as the hammer shattered into a thousand tiny pieces and the stone still lay on the anvil, exactly where he had placed it.

Oakum Marlroot seized the stone and held it high above his head. He ran back out of the Blacksmith's yard, away from the village and towards the bridge where Scritch would sit every day, looking for glittering things in the stream. And when he reached the bridge, he hurled the stone in the water.

There was a mighty splash and then the river seemed to swirl around and suck the stone right down. Oakum Marlroot turned and strode away, never looking back. He kept on walking down Brunt Boggart's high street, ignoring the dogs and the young'uns at play. He kept on walking until he reached his farm. He slammed the door and stamped inside. The stone had gone, the lumpen stone, the stone which brought him so much sorrow. He sat down at his table by the window and stared out at his black bare fields. Next day, Oakum Marlroot told himself, he would set out with his hoe and his plough and prepare the ground again, ready to plant new seed, ready to see it grow.

Next day, Scritch came down to the river, same as he did every morning and squatted alone by the sluggish stream. He sat and fixed his gaze on the water and then he rubbed his eyes. The river was filled with glittery things. He leapt to his feet, ready to grab them. But then when he looked again, he saw that they were fish. Scritch thought he had seen his supper for this night and the next night and many nights to come. He thought he had seen enough fish to sell to every wifen in the village. But the fish were floating slowly, belly-up in the water. Their wide eyes mirrored the rainy sky. All of the fish were dead.

Scritch stepped back and sniffed the air. A smell hung heavy as lead, burnt and sour and brackish. Scritch shook his head. He would not touch these fish. He was not sure if he should touch this water which brought him his livelihood, this stream which stank now, heavy and black. Scritch watched till the sun stood high in the sky and all the fish had floated by and the water ran clear again. Scritch studied the stones at the bottom, on the watch for anything that glittered, just as he did every day. And then he saw it - the lumpen stone, the stone which glowed all the colours of the rainbow and other colours too, such as Scritch had never seen.

Scritch paused. He squinnied long and hard. And then he grabbed it. He held it tight in his leathery hands, weighing it carefully, figuring how many trinkets he could make from this grumous mass if he took it to his hut at the edge of the riverbank halfway to nowhere. That night he thrust the stone in his fire to smelt it, then he waited and he watched to see it turn red and then white, same as all the other bits of metal that he collected always did. But the stone just glowed dark in the middle of the fire. Scritch seized his tongs and hauled it out again. He spat on the stone but it did not sizzle. He touched it with his calloused fingers, but it was not even warm.

"This ain't no good to me," muttered Scritch. "Can't melt it, can't smelt it. Can't break it. No good to me and no good to no-one."

Scritch took the stone out into the darkness, and he walked and he walked right past the village till he came to the edge of Oakum Marlroot's fields. He came to Black Meadow, and there he threw it, hard as he could. Then Scritch turned and strode away, never looking back. He kept on walking all the way to his hut by the bridge by the bend in the river.

Next day after that day, Oakum Marlroot came out into the fields, with his shovel and his hoe, poking and prodding. When he got to the middle of Black Meadow, he stopped and stared down at the ground. There was the stone, the lumpen stone, the stone which glowed all the colours of the rainbow. Oakum Marlroot let out a cry. A cry which turned into a howl that nearly cracked the sky. What could he do with this stone which had blighted his crops and caused all his cattle to die, which his shovel couldn't break and the Blacksmith couldn't smash, which he'd thrown deep in the river - and still it came back here?

Oakum Marlroot seized the stone which had brought him so much sorrow and he walked and he walked till he reached the Burying Ground. And there he came to his wifen's grave and he stood above it, legs astride, and then he spoke:

"You gave me nothing. No son, no daughter neither. You gave me nothing - only sorrow." Oakum Marlroot cast the stone where his wifen lay. "Now here is my sorrow for you."

But before he had time to walk away, came the thunder again, just as it had the night that she died, rolling out of the darkening sky. Oakum Marlroot stood. He couldn't move if even he had wanted to. And the lightning flashed. And the whole sky cracked. And the stone cracked too, the lumpen stone, the stone of sorrow. It cracked to a hundred thousand pieces, till it was no more than dust.

And as the stone was gone, Oakum Marlroot's sorrow seemed gone as well. That autumn, all season he tended his fields till they were ready to plant in the spring. Mottram Ironfield and Redgut and all the other farmers were so glad to see Oakum happy again that they all lent him a share of their grain till he had enough to plant his fields. And the fields grew full high with wheat. But anyone who saw him, out in his fields alone, said Oakum Marlroot was talking, the way he never did before, unless the drink had got him late at night in the tavern. Oakum Marlroot was ranting, ranting and cursing. Oakum Marlroot was talking to no-one at all. Oakum Marlroot was talking to himself.

But what they never saw, these people that told this, was the shadow that was moving, walking at his side. And who was that shadow? I knew that you'd be asking. Why that was Oakum Marlroot's wifen, who still walked there beside him, sharing the sunshine and the storm clouds, same as they had every day.

OLD MOTHER TIDGEWALLOP AND THE WELL

Let me tell you... Let me tell you... Old Mother Tidgewallop lived in a cottage of low squinty windows and damp sodden thatch littered all through with thistles and weeds. All day she knitted and all night she sewed. She knitted a waistcoat all brindley and snap - yellow and orange with scarlet red patches and pockets for berries gathered up from the hedges. She knitted it for her wayward son Larkum who left the cottage one long year ago.

Each and every morning Old Mother Tidgewallop went out to look for him. She'd call his name beside the ponds and all around the wallowing pigmires. Sometimes she thought she saw the print of his boot in the churned-up mud but she knew it was only her own clodhoppers where she'd been wandering the day before.

Then she would go back to her cottage and sadly gather her needles again and carry on knitting, picking out patterns, the brightest she could imagine, to lure her lost son home. But at night when the moon rose, she'd set down her tatting and take up her sewing. Every night, Old Mother Tidgewallop drew together a great cloak of darkness, picked out all over with stars. She made the stars from anything shiny that she could find - a glow-worm's tear, a droplet of dew, the lost sparkle of hoar frost. Now all she needed was just one more star to sew onto the shoulder of the cloak.

Every day she would visit the well in the yard behind her cottage. At the bottom of that well lived Snizzleslide, who took the shape of a troublesome snake. Every day she'd go talk to him, and tell him all about Larkum, her long-lost son.

"He woke one day and told me he'd dreamt of a girl called Grizzlegrin who lives beyond the far mountains. He said she sits and cries at the moon every time that it waxes full. He had to go and find her and then her tears would stop. He went away to look for her and he's never come home again..."

Snizzleslide would lie and listen, coiled in the murky darkness at the bottom of the deep dank well. When Old Mother Tidgewallop had done with her talking, Snizzleslide would simper and say how sad he was to hear about her missing son. But then he would hiss and beg her to bring him his breakfast of mice and dead bats' wings, spiders, slugs and snails. And Old Mother Tidgewallop would scrabble away to find what she could find at the back of her broken-down barn. She'd bring them in a bag to the rim of the well and toss them down slowly, one by one. Snizzleslide would swallow them with a great grinning gulp and then writhe slyly round and round.

"Guess what I have here," Snizzleslide would hiss. "Guess what I keep in a bottle all tucked away in the shadows."

Old Mother Tidgewallop scratched at her chin as she replied.

"Is it a thimble of song lark's tears? Is it a spoonful of the silence that gathers just before dawn? Is it an egg that isn't hatched yet filled with the dew of the moon?"

"No, no," hissed Snizzleslide. "It is far more precious to you than any of these. Deep in the darkness of the well, I've been hiding a star which fell from the sky. I keep it in a bottle here to stop it flying back. Now... you tell me you are seeking one last star to stitch on the shoulder of your cloak. Climb down here into the well - and surely it will be yours."

Old Mother Tidgewallop shook her head.

"I'm not climbing down a slippery well to be bitten by a great long snake."

"Mother Tidgewallop," Snizzleslide wheedled sadly, "whatever would I want to do that for? You are my friend, my provider. Who else would bring me my breakfast of mice and dead bats' wings? And besides, you know that you need this one last star so that you can finish your cloak."

Old Mother Tidgewallop tugged her shawl around her shoulders and stamped back into her cottage. But sew as she might, by day and by night, she could find nothing that was bright enough to fill the space that was waiting for the cloak's last shiny star. In the end she set the cloak aside and trudged through the meadows and over the hills, calling out for Larkum, her long-lost son. All she could hear was the wind, but then the wind seemed to sing with his voice.

"Larkum, Larkum, where are you?" she cried.

"I'm over the mountains and far and wide."

"Are you safe my boy, my only child?"

"I'm as safe as the tall oaks, and safe as the stones."

"And have you found Grizzlegrin, Larkum, my son? - have you found Grizzlegrin, the girl who cries at the moon?"

"She is here beside me, Mother dear."

"Larkum, Larkum - I'm happy to hear it. Now that you've found her, won't you bring her home?"

"How can I bring her, Mother dear, when we have no clothes to greet you in?"

Old Mother Tidgewallop shook her head.

"Larkum, Larkum, Larkum... all day long I knit and at night I sew and I have made you a fine waistcoat all brindley and snap - yellow and orange with scarlet red patches and pockets for berries gathered up from the hedges."

"I have no need to walk the hedges, Mother, collecting sweet berries, for when I'm with Grizzlegrin, we feed on the light in each other's eyes."

"Bring young Grizzlegrin home to me," his mother replied, "and she shall be your wifen."

"But what can she wear?" wailed Larkum, his voice fading further away.

"I have made her a cloak stitched with bright shining stars..." Old Mother Tidgewallop told him, then listened for the wind, to catch her son's reply.

But his voice blew over the mountains and down to the sea as Old Mother Tidgewallop picked up her skirts and ran all the way home, across muddy fields and down twisting lanes, until she came back to her very own cottage.

"Snizzleslide, Snizzleslide - are you awake?"

She scrambled over the wall of the well and lowered herself slowly with her back pressed hard against the slippery stones and her hands and her feet clinging on tight. Water trickled down her neck and the moss grew slimy beneath the soles of her boots, but hand over hand and foot over foot, Old Mother Tidgewallop slithered and slid all the way down to the bottom of the well. It was cold, it was dark, and when she looked up, all that she could see was a tiny blue circle of sky. Under her feet the sweet water trickled, though the stones all around were slippery and dank.

"Snizzleslide, Snizzleslide, where is the bottle? Where is the bottle in which you hide the fallen star?"

Old Mother Tidgewallop waited while her eyes grew used to the darkness. She peered into the shadows, feeling sure that the bottle would be easy to find, as it would glow with the brightness of the fallen star. And she was sure that she would see Snizzleslide too, with his eyes all gleaming as he coiled among the pebbles at the bottom of the stream. But Snizzleslide was not there. Snizzleslide had gone. While Old Mother Tidgewallop was sliding down, Snizzleslide had wriggled his way up, slithering past her in the darkness.

Old Mother Tidgewallop groped around in the gloom, her frozen hands splashing in the cold running water. And then her fingers wrapped around a shiny green bottle lodged under a stone.

She picked it up quickly and struggled with the stopper, her hands trying to grip the slippery neck. She struggled and she grunted and she nearly flung it back, but the stopper flew out. Old Mother Tidgewallop shook the bottle. She held out her hand, but nothing fell into it. She raised the bottle up to her eye and peered right into the darkness inside, but try as she might she could see nothing there that looked in any way like a star. She threw the bottle back into the water that was lapping around her boots. Up above, from the circle of cloud and sky, she was sure she could hear Snizzleslide shaking with laughter as he slid quickly away.

Old Mother Tidgewallop clambered out of the well. She rushed across the yard and into her cottage, then raced up the stairs, two steps at a time. Then she flung up her hands to cover her eyes. Her neat tidy bedroom had been ransacked. While she had been down the well, someone had climbed up here and pulled open cupboards and rummaged through drawers and strewn everything around. Her sewing baskets had been turned upside-down and her threads were tangled all about while her knitting needles lay scattered across the floor.

"Oh no! Oh no!..." Old Mother Tidgewallop wailed. At first she could see nothing missing, but then she realised that the waistcoat was gone - the yellow and orange waistcoat with scarlet red patches all brindley and snap that had been hanging behind the door. And so too was the long dark cloak.

"Snizzleslide, Snizzleslide - I know it must be you. Why else did you trick me to go down into the well? Why else did you tell me that I'd find my very last star when all that was down there was an empty bottle?"

All that night Mother Tidgewallop sat in her chair and wept. Her frenzied fingers could scarcely stay still. They had spent so long sewing and knitting but now they had nothing to do. Then early next morning, just as soon as dawn rose, she got up and set out straight away, down to the woods. There she hunted through the thicket and under the trees for any sign of Snizzleslide, the waistcoat with scarlet patches or the cloak of stars which she'd taken so long to make. And all the while she still called out to Larkum her son and Grizzlegrin his wifen-to-be, in case they appeared suddenly between the rustling trees.

But no sign of anything could Old Mother Tidgewallop find. She sat herself on a mossy tussock and hung her head and wept. Just then she heard a shuffling and a slithering. She saw a flash of yellow and orange patched about with scarlet red. She saw a cloak of darkest black, picked out with a welkin of stars.

She did not see Snizzleslide wearing the waistcoat. She did not see an old dead branch which he dragged along beside him, draped over with the cloak of stars. She could only see Larkum, her long lost son and Grizzlegrin, his wifen-to-be.

Suddenly sunlight flooded the clearing. Old Mother Tidgewallop rushed towards them, her arms flung open wide. She embraced her son. She ran her fingers through his tangled hair. She gripped the knots of his great strong arms. She danced around him, caper-skelter, as he stood proudly in the clearing, sporting his waistcoat all brindley and snap...

Then she wrapped her arms about Grizzlegrin's waist and rocked her and hugged her and greeted her like a lost daughter new-found.

But they were all too busy crying and laughing to hear the sound of a slithering, scurrying away. The sound of a dead branch, dragged across the ground.

"Larkum, Larkum, come back to the cottage," the old mother exclaimed. "Grizzlegrin, Grizzlegrin, make our home your own."

And so every day they lived as happily as they could, chopping wood and tending the fowl and drawing water from the bottom of the well. And Grizzlegrin made Larkum as contented as could be, even though every time the moon was full she would sit and cry and wail for her home back over the mountain. But when the moon was gone she would smile again and walk with Larkum under the trees. And Old Mother Tidgewallop would watch them, and she would smile too.

Then one day when Larkum was out by himself tending to the pigs in the wood, Old Mother Tidgewallop and Grizzlegrin sat down together to drink a cup of fennel tea and watch the leaves drifting down from the top of the tallest tree.

"Tell me, how do you do it?" the old woman asked the girl. "What is it you have that makes my son so glad? Is it your smile? Is it your eyes? Is it the touch of your soft tender hands?"

Grizzlegrin looked away, uncertain what to say.

"Why, Mother Tidgewallop, it's surely none of these, but the power of this long black cloak, sewed with a skyful of stars."

She opened up a cupboard and showed it hanging there.

"I don't know how it came to me, and I'll never know who made it, but I do know that I found it one day when I was out walking on the mountainside, crying at the moon. But as soon as I put it on, the warmth of the cloak wrapped around me. And it's that warmth I share with your son. This is what I give him when I want to make him happy. And when he feels the warmth, then he's kind and gentle and then he comes and talks to me and tells me that I make him happy. What he likes most of all is to nestle his head onto the shoulder of the cloak in the only place where there's one space left between the stars."

Old Mother Tidgewallop smiled as she heard her son Larkum coming back from the wood. She took Grizzlegrin's hand between her crooked fingers.

"I could not find the last star," she said, "but I have found my wayward son Larkum again, and now he has found you."

LARKUM, GRIZZLEGRIN AND THE
COTTAGE SAD WITH DUST

Let me tell you... Let me tell you... the grey wind blew
and rain scattered sudden down Brunt Boggart's sullen
streets. Thunderhead put on his tall hat and his cloak of
many feathers and he led the wifen and the daughters
and the boys-who-would-be-men and the men who
wished they were boys and the Crow Dancers and the
farmers, he led them all through the Sorrowing Field
and down to the Burying Ground. And there they
waited while the Drummer played and the dark birds
whirled in the air. Then Thunderhead said the words he
always said, the words to the sky, the words to the river,
the words to the earth.

Then Old Mother Tidgewallop was lowered down
and Larkum her son scattered the first dirt upon her,
then handed on the great iron shovel to Grizzlegrin his
wife, and then on and on, Old Nanny Nettleye and
Oakum Marlroot and Nanny Ninefingers till Old
Mother Tidgewallop was covered all over, snug as

snug, under the ground, under the sky. And then they sang; sang on while the Drummer played, and then they trudged their ways all back to their houses while Larkum and Grizzlegrin returned to the cottage, the cottage on the edge of the village where Old Mother Tidgewallop had lived all her long years long, ever since she was a girl. But now it seemed so empty without her.

The cottage had always been tidy and bright. The other wifen would come around and say Old Mother Tidgewallop's was the neatest in all of Brunt Boggart. And they'd ruffle the hair of her tousle-maned son and watch as he played all out in the back yard. But when he left home, that's when Old Mother Tidgewallop's cottage grew sad with dust, until Larkum returned with Grizzlegrin. But by then Mother Tidgewallop was old and old and there was dust on top of the dust and however much she brushed, she could never brush it away. Until one day she just gave up.

"Let the wind come," she said. "Let the wind blow. Wind and rain will come and go, but the dust is here to stay."

But the dust did not stay for long. Larkum and Grizzlegrin fell to cleaning and brushing, polishing and scrubbing.

"Now that your mother's gone," said Grizzlegrin, "we can make the cottage just the way we want it."

In the days that came they brought down all of Old Mother Tidgewallop's trinkets and rings and glittery things. They brought down her needles that had knitted a waistcoat all brindly and snap and sewed the cloak of darkness, picked out all over with stars.

But now Grizzlegrin forgot to wear the cloak. She

was too busy scrubbing at the cottage floors and whitewashing the walls and clearing out everything Old Mother Tidgewallop had stored away so safely in drawers and dressers. And when she went down to the village, none of the other wifen wore a cloak all covered in stars. They wore dresses and stockings and smocks and so that's what Grizzlegrin wore too, for she was new to Brunt Boggart - she came from over the mountain and far and wide.

Back in the cottage she'd sweep and she'd dust, she'd mop and she'd wash and she changed all the linen, all the curtains and hearthrugs, because this was her cottage now - the cottage she shared with Larkum, the man who made her happy. But Larkum didn't seem so happy any more. He remembered the cottage the way it had always been, the way it had been since he was a boy, when he'd play in the yard in the sun and the rain and throw shiny pebbles down into the well and hold his breath and count till he heard them hit the bottom.

Now Larkum spent all day out in the fields and tended to the pigs in the wood, while Grizzlegrin was dusting and cleaning the cottage. When he came back he was tired - and just sat all evening in his chair, the chair that had once been his mother's chair all the years he'd lived there. He couldn't believe she was gone. And he couldn't bear to see Grizzlegrin changing this and changing that, clearing and sprucing and putting things about.

"Stop all your fidgeting and fussing," he grumbled. "You never said nothing was wrong with the cottage all the time my mother was here."

"I do not like this musty house," Grizzlegrin told him. "It's full of cobwebs, dust and damp. I want to make a new home for us. I want to clear out your mother's clutter and make room for the children we'll have."

But Larkum was sad, and his sadness spread till Grizzlegrin fell sad as well. Every month she cried at the moon and every other night too. The sadder she felt the more she decided that now this was her cottage, she wanted to make it all sparkly and new. She packed Old Mother Tidgewallop's trinkets into a box - all her rings and her scarves, her plates and her cups, her cruets and her bowls, and the needles that she'd used to knit the waistcoat and to sew the cloak of darkness all picked out in stars.

That evening Larkum came home, tired and aching from working the fields and stinking of the pigs in the wood. He looked at the box that was blocking the door.

"What's all this?" he exclaimed.

"It's your mother's old nonsense," Grizzlegrin told him. "I've no use for it all. Take it down to the village and see if you can sell it for shillen and coppers, then we can buy curtains, all bright, new and clean - then the house will feel like our own, and we'll be happy again."

Larkum just looked even sadder, but all he had was Grizzlegrin now and he wanted to make her happy - so next day he took the box away, packed with his mother's trinkets. He took them down to the hollow in the Green, right in the middle of Brunt Boggart, and there he tried to sell them to anyone who would have them - Old Nanny Nettleye, Nanny Ninefingers and old Granny Willowmist poking and prodding over his mother's treasures.

"These be Tidgewallop's," all of them said. "Can't take them off you, they were hers. They were all of her own precious things."

Larkum didn't know what to do. He packed his mother's trinkets back into the box and trudged slowly, a long way and long, to his home. When he got to the cottage, there stood Grizzlegrin.

"What took you so long?" she demanded. "And why you been dallying all down by your mother's well in the yard?"

Larkum wiped the back of his hand across his dusty brow.

"Been a long walk all back from the village," he explained. "I just stopped off beside the old well to get me a drink of fresh water."

Larkum paused. He stopped and saw she was standing there with fistfuls of flowers strewn all around - the daisies and valerian which Old Mother Tidgewallop had tended all her life.

"What's this?" Larkum exclaimed.

"It's more of your mother's old nonsense," Grizzlegrin told him. "I want the garden to look tidy and neat, not covered in brambles and choked up with weeds. I want you to pave it all over, just the way Wife Pottam has it."

What could Larkum do? He wanted Grizzlegrin to be happy. What point was there in more sadness? So he followed her wishes and covered the garden with great heavy flagstones - the garden where his mother had tended her flowers, the garden where he used to play. When he'd finished, toiling all day in the back-breaking sun, Grizzlegrin came to look at his work. At first she smiled.

"Why - it's beautiful," she told him. "Just like I wanted. Just the way Wife Pottam has it."

But then she fell sad again.

"The flagstones look too grey."

"Of course they look grey," Larkum replied. "Everything looks grey now the flowers have gone."

"I don't like flowers," Grizzlegrin told him. "The colours are so bright that they blind me and the pollen makes me sneeze. But the garden looks bare now. Go down to Scritch's hut, down by the river and see if you can get me some of those windmills and butterflies he twists from the metal that he finds in the stream."

And so Larkum went out again, and with their last few coppers bought a whole basketful of Scritch's shiny trinkets. He placed them all around the garden in front of the cottage to cover the grey of the stone. But the harder he worked to make Grizzlegrin happy, the sadder she became. And that made Larkum sad too.

"What else do you want me to do?" he asked. "I've lost my mother, now all her precious things are gone, her knick-knacks and her needles, her garden and her flowers."

Grizzlegrin strode into the house and returned a few moments later.

"You can take away this old cloak too," she said. "I don't wear it any more. None of the wifen in the village ever wear a cloak like this. They all wear dresses and stockings and smocks."

And Grizzlegrin gave him the cloak that Old Mother Tidgewallop had sewed for her. Larkum scurried off with it and in a while and another while he came scurrying back again.

"Oh, Grizzlegrin, are you happy now? What else do you want me to do?"

"What else do I want you to do?" Grizzlegrin cried.

"Next you must cover the well, that old well at the bottom of the yard. The bricks are broken and the water's too deep and your mother told me that Snizzleslide the troublesome snake used to coil up at the bottom. You must cover it over before he comes again. I couldn't stand him slithering round, not when we've got the house so neat and the garden so trim."

Larkum sighed and did what she said. He nailed planks of wood across the top of the well where Old Mother Tidgewallop had drawn water every day. When he had finished, Grizzlegrin came to look.

"I'm thirsty," she said. "Make me a brew of good nettle tea."

"I'm thirsty too," Larkum replied. "It's dry work hammering and nailing. But we've got no water now I've covered the well."

Grizzlegrin scowled. "You'll just have to go down to the village and fetch a fresh bucket from the well by the Green, same as all the rest of 'em do."

So every morning before he could start his work in the fields and tending of the pigs in the wood, Larkum would trudge to the well in the village, with a bucket on each arm. The more water he brought, the more Grizzlegrin needed, for she kept the cottage clean as clean to drive away the dust which made her so sad. Every day she would wash the new curtains and hang them to dry and scrub the floor of the kitchen till it was worn near away and as soon as she'd brought in the curtains from the line she'd be back again at the tub, rubbing and scrubbing the blankets and pillow cases and all of the table-cloths and napkins as well. But still she was never happy.

"I don't know why I bother to fetch water," Larkum

remarked. "You spill enough tears to fill both of these buckets."

Soon Larkum was so tired from trudging with those buckets that he would fall asleep in the fields. And while he was sleeping, the weeds began to grow and the black crows flew down and pecked up all his seed and the pigs ran amuck in the woods. So when harvest time came, Larkum had no grain to sell and the pigs had all strayed and Grizzlegrin just sat in the cottage all day staring at the walls which she kept on painting first cream, then pink, then lilac, then green, then cream again - and crying and wailing because whichever colour she painted them, they didn't seem to suit her.

Then one morning, dull and misty, Grizzlegrin was sitting in the kitchen, waiting for Larkum to bring the water for her first brew of nettle tea. When Larkum struggled in through the door he dropped the buckets onto the floor.

"Put on the kettle!" cried Grizzlegrin, without even looking up. "Put on the kettle, I'm mardy dry."

Larkum banged at the buckets with his boot.

"Tain't no use," he wailed. "Brunt Boggart well's run dry. There's been no rain for many a moon. Ain't no water for the chickens, ain't no water for the swill, ain't no water for the washing and sure as sure, there ain't no water for your brew of nettle tea."

Grizzlegrin burst out sobbing.

"Whatever shall we do?"

"Ain't no use crying," Larkum replied. "Your tears ain't no good. Not lest you're going to cry them into this empty bucket and go on crying till you've wept enough to mop the floor."

So Grizzlegrin stopped.

"You'll have to go down to the river," she said. "Go down to the bridge where Scritch always sits and draw me some water from there."

So Larkum went to the river, bucket in hand. On his way he met Granny Willowmist and Wife Pottam and Oakum Marlroot, all clattering along with their pails and their kettles and their watering cans. And little'uns with bowls and cups and Pickapple with a sieve. And they clanked and they clacked and chatted and worried, all the way down to the river. And there sat Scritch with his back to them all, glaring out at the cracked dry mud where the water should be. But the water was gone. Just puddles of sludge. Old Granny Willowmist tucked up her skirts and trudged out into the silt and tried to fill her bucket with sullage. But it was no good, no good at all.

"Can't drink it," she cried. "Tain't no good for washing. Tain't no good for nothing."

And Pickapple sat with his sieve on his head and stuffed mud in his mouth and cried. Larkum looked at them, looked at them all - the old'uns, the farmers, the wifen, the girlen, the boys-who-would-be-men, the Crow Dancers and Thunderhead - all staring at the sky, with their tongues dark and dry, waiting for the rain.

Larkum ran home and picked up his axe.

"Where are you going?" Grizzlegrin cried. "Was there water at the river? Can you brew me up my strong nettle tea? - I need a cup before I start my washing!"

"There's no water at the river," Larkum told her. "I'm going to my mother's well, the well we boarded over."

"Our well's a curse," Grizzlegrin snapped. "Snizzleslide comes there and I don't want him back. I couldn't stand him slithering around - not when we've got the house so neat and the garden so trim."

"What good's a neat house and a garden where nothing grows?" Larkum sighed. "And what good's a well that's all boarded over when there's no water down in the village? Never mind your nettle tea, never mind your washing. There's all of Brunt Boggart sitting down there with their tongues drying out. Oakum Marlroot can't water his fields and poor Snuffwidget doesn't know what to do for he can't brew none of his wine."

And before Grizzlegrin could stop him, Larkum threw his axe across his shoulder and marched down to the end of Old Mother Tidgewallop's yard. He swung his axe once, he swung his axe twice, till the boards on the well were smashed to smithereens. Then he flung the axe aside and clambered down the slippery walls, hand over hand. When he reached the bottom, he heard a slithering and a sliding - and there was Snizzleslide the trickster in the guise of a troublesome snake, all wound around a box that was sitting in the water. For yes, there was water, there in Old Mother Tidgewallop's well, flowing strong and clear.

"I knew it," cried Larkum. "I knew I'd be right. Old Mother Tidgewallop's well is deeper than Brunt Boggart's, for it taps straight into a sweet clear stream flowing down from high in the hills."

Snizzleslide raised his head.

"So," he hissed. "You have returned."

"Yes, I've come," said Larkum, "just as I said I would. Is the box safe?"

"For sure, for sure. I would not let it wash away. Old Mother Tidgewallop was good to me. She brought me my breakfast every day of mice and dead bats' wings, spiders, slugs and snails. I was so sorry to hear she'd been taken off to the Burying Ground. The least I could do was keep my word to you and guard the box where you'd locked all the trinkets."

Larkum seized the box that lay in the water, the box where he'd placed all his mother's precious things which Grizzlegrin had asked him to sell. But he hadn't sold them at all. He'd packed them up tight in the box and taken them to the well at the bottom of the yard on his way back home to the cottage.

Snizzleslide smiled and Larkum thanked him, when from the top of the well he heard Grizzlegrin calling.

"Larkum, Larkum, come quickly. There's a great crowd of people here, knocking at the door."

Larkum scrambled quickly out of the well, dragging the box behind him. There at the cottage gate was Snuffwidget carrying two great pails. And behind him was Wife Pottam and Old Granny Willowmist and the rest of Brunt Boggart, all waiting down the track with their buckets and kettles and watering cans. And Pickapple stood at the back with his sieve still jammed on his head.

"Larkum," they cried, "you're our only hope. We heard you say you were going back home to open your well again."

"Come in, come in," Larkum replied. "Our well is deeper than Brunt Boggart's well. There's water a-plenty. You're welcome one and all."

Before Grizzlegrin could say anything, the villagers tramped in through the cottage, scattering mud from their boots all over her neat clean floor. Grizzlegrin looked ready to burst into tears, but Larkum took her aside.

"Don't cry," he said. "Look what I have here." And he opened up the box, still dripping the well's deep water. And there inside were necklaces, bracelets and rings. Grizzlegrin gasped when she saw them all.

"They're beautiful!" she cried. "Wherever did you get them?"

She picked out one of the bracelets and slid it over her wrist.

"Don't you recognise them?" Larkum asked her. "They all belonged to my mother. You wanted to be rid of them, but I knew that they were precious to her, as you are precious to me - and so these should be precious to you."

Grizzlegrin blinked and looked again. "Larkum, they're beautiful. I just never fully looked at them when first I cleared the rooms. Now here they are all shiny and bright. But I thought you took them away. I thought you took them down to the Green and sold them."

Larkum shook his head.

"I polished them up and packed them in the box, but nobody wanted to buy them - so I hid them away at the bottom of the well."

Grizzlegrin was puzzled.

"But where did you get all the silver shillen to buy new curtains for the windows, shiny trinkets for the garden and whitewash for the walls?"

"I wanted to see you happy," Larkum explained. "I always kept a few shillen stashed away, in case hard times came. But now hard times have come anyway, with the crops all failing and the pigs gone missing and the well in Brunt Boggart run dry."

But Grizzlegrin was hardly listening, she was too

overjoyed. As she gathered up the trinkets, the needles and the rings, she saw something shining beneath them all and plunged her hands deeper, down into the box. There at the bottom lay the cloak that Old Mother Tidgewallop had made her, the cloak of darkness sewed all over with stars.

"Put it on," Larkum told her, and so she did - and as soon as its warmth wrapped around her shoulders, why then she felt happy again.

"Oh, Larkum, Larkum - you know I always loved this cloak. I only stopped wearing it because none of the other wifen in Brunt Boggart ever wore one, and I wanted to dress in stockings and a smock just the same as them."

But then there came a clanking and a rattling as Snuffwidget clattered in from the yard, spilling water from his buckets all over the floor. He set them down and out tipped more, but Grizzlegrin didn't say anything, she only stood and smiled. Snuffwidget wiped his forehead, then thrust his hand into his pocket and brought out a bottle of his celebrated potion - Nana Corbin Night-thorn's Morning Sunrise.

"Here - this is for you. Now that I have water I can start to brew again."

And so it went on. Granny Willowmist brought them a pie to eat that she'd been saving in her pantry. Nanny Ninefingers gave them a linen bag, packed with Herb Robert and Golden Rod - and Pickapple gave them his sieve.

As Grizzlegrin stood in her cloak of stars a broad smile spread across her face.

"Thank you all for your gifts," she said. "And thank you Larkum, for bringing Mother Tidgewallop's cloak

of darkness safely back to me. And now, husband, I
have a gift for you."

Larkum stared at his wife to see what she had to give
him. She stood and she smiled and placed his hand on
her belly.

"We're going to have a child..."

THUNDERHEAD AND THE FIVE CURES

Let me tell you... let me tell you... Ramshadow House was built before Brunt Boggart came to be. Now it sat at the edge of the village like an old man slumped by his fire. Half the roof was missing and weeds and herbs pressed up through the floor. Wind blew down the chimneys as sharp-eyed crows hopped in and out as if it was their home.

Shattered pots lay all around, made of dull red earthenware, graven with patterns, mazy and swirling. The old stone walls crumbled while its carvings and statues were so weather-worn you could scarce see their faces - and who they were and what they had done, no-one knew nor cared.

Thunderhead lived there now, waking each morning, sometimes in one room, sometimes in another. He would lie and listen to the crows' raucous call from the chimney tops. And he would call back, a throat-racking screech, before scratching and stretching, his long limbs striding, his shirt a-tatters, his face daubed with clay the same as the Crow Dancers as he loped all out to the garden that grew around Ramshadow House, a tangle of briars and thorns. Then Thunderhead poked and prodded and pulled until he'd gathered up a handful of sagebrush and hawkbit, silverweed and Knotty Brake - which he carried back into the smoke-blackened kitchen where he set a pan of fresh water to simmer on the stove.

Soon as the bubbles were breaking, Thunderhead plunged in the herbs then dragged his long fingers through his straggling hair and reached for his hat, his black hat, his tall hat which hung on the wall. Its rim was festooned with feathers and bones and weasel skulls all whitened in the wind. The talismans and trinkets rattled and shook as Thunderhead began his dance. Slow as slow, his strong limbs shadowing, his long arms reaching up, calling sunlight and rain, whirlwind and hail, calling snow and ice, blizzard and gale - while far away, from across the flat meadows, he could hear the sound of the Drummer a-beating, out by the Fever Tree, at the end of the Echo Field.

Thunderhead danced till light filled his eyes - light of watching, light of dawning, light of sun and moon and stars. And then he stopped. Pulled on a shirt, a raggedy shirt, hung all about with tassels and patches. He sat on a wooden bench, lifted the pan from the stove and poured his herb brew into a bowl. He settled there and cradled it between his sinewy fingers, then he breathed in the aroma, his head wreathed in steam. It tasted of pasture, of woodland, of birdsong. Tasted of mountain and river and Wolf. Was stronger than anything Nanny Ninefingers would brew for the village, or anything

Snuffwidget served up from his cellar. This was Thunderhead's potion that he brewed for himself.

He wiped the back of his hand across his mouth and reached down his cloak of straggling feathers - eagle and raven, kestrel and hawk - and hung it around his shoulders. Then he stood and let out the crow cry again and strode into the morning.

He walked down to the village to tend to anyone who had some sickness, some sadness of spirit that couldn't be cured by Nanny Ninefingers' potions. He'd talk all gentle and soft, or curse and chant, his crow voice shrieking. Or he'd dance and rattle his bone-sticks, his long stave shaking to his foot's stomping rhythm. And sometimes he'd shiver till his limbs lost control and his eyes would fix far on lost suns and moons. He would writhe on the ground, he would wail, he would moan. And then he'd lie silent. But the sick'un he was curing - from head-pains, from darkness, from fever, from sorrow - would stand there all smiling, and their pain would be gone.

Thunderhead would rise from the ground where he'd fallen and he'd gaze at them strangely and then take their hand. They'd pass him a shillen, or what they could give and then they'd slip quietly away, their heart lightened, their head clear, their limbs moving true, while Thunderhead turned to spew bile in a hole.

At the top of the house a bedchamber sloped between the broken walls, hung with bunches of ribbons, all the colours of the sun. In the corner was a chest filled with white dresses, shining clear as the moon. There slept Jonquil with her face so serene. She would walk round the house in the morning, fussing at dishes and baking sweet bread and trying on brooches enamelled with patterns, mazy and swirling.

But no-one who passed the house ever seemed to know of her, or saw her step out into the woods that grew tangled and dark right up to the door. But some said they saw Snizzleslide, the trickster who took the shape of a troublesome snake, slithering through the tall grass, right up to Thunderhead's door. Then he would look this way and he would look that and then he would slip in through the gap beneath the door. Soon as he was on the other side, all Thunderhead saw was Jonquil, who soothed his sore head and poured him his potion and took him to bed till the morning.

One night Jonquil woke and heard a dog barking, heard it scratching at doors, whimpering and howling.

"Thunderhead!" she shook him. "Whose is that dog?"

Thunderhead turned over and opened one eye.

"There is no dog," he said.

And sure enough, Jonquil knew she never saw it, just heard it scratting outside. And other times when she came she heard foxes prowling and one night thought she heard a Wolf at the door.

"Thunderhead!" she cried as she woke him. "Wolf be here for sure."

Thunderhead shrugged.

"Ain't no Wolf," he said. "And if'n there is, then dog will see him off."

Jonquil shivered.

"I thought you told me there was no dog," she said as she sat upright in the old creaking bed. Then she heard a baying, a howling and a rapping of claws on the great oaken door. Jonquil clung tightly to Thunderhead's shoulders. He was sleeping again, but in a moment and another moment, all the commotion was still. Wolf was gone. Dog was gone. Only Thunderhead now. But when he woke in the morning, Jonquil was gone too.

Thunderhead rushed to the door, quick as quick but no-one was there. He was too late to see Snizzleslide sneaking away through the thicket and all down to Brunt Boggart to find what he could.

Snizzleslide was gone all the long day long and all the next night too. Thunderhead was alone in Ramshadow House, stretched out under the broken roofs, staring up at the stars as they wheeled across the patch of sky. He traced out their paths with his toe in the dust that covered the uneven flagstones of Ramshadow's floor, then lay down to sleep beside this chart he had drawn of the sky.

Next day when he woke, he heard the Drummer, out by the Fever Tree. Heard him moving, closer and close as he came across the fields, till the Drummer was there, outside his door, beating a rhythm through the overgrown garden. Thunderhead flung the door open and brought him inside - and as the Drummer played on, Thunderhead danced, trip and step, along the lines of the chart he had drawn on the floor. Thunderhead knew, for others had told him, that when he danced, someone might fall sick, and someone might get well. Or sometimes nothing would happen at all. But Thunderhead did not dance to cause sickness, nor dance to bring a cure. He danced for the sake of the dance. He danced to map out the stars. Not the stars in the sky, nor the stars on the floor but the stars and the galaxies and the planets far away that he could feel turning inside him - in his limbs, in his body, in his head - as he danced and he danced until he could dance no more.

Then the Drummer wiped the back of his hand across his sweating brow and Thunderhead sat awhile and then set the pan on the stove in the old blackened kitchen to brew up a potion of herbs. Then they fell to talking, Thunderhead and the Drummer. Talked of rivers and mountains and storms before time. And come the late afternoon, they played again - Thunderhead pulling a flute from his pocket which he blew till the notes rose wistfully above the Drummer's beat. And way off and away, down in Brunt Boggart, Snizzleslide heard the flute, sensed its silver voice tremble through his slithering body, and he set off home again, back to Ramshadow House to show Thunderhead all that he had found.

By the time Snizzleslide reached the house, the Drummer was gone - and when Thunderhead opened the door, the snake was gone too and there stood Jonquil, all smiling and fresh.

"What have you brought me?" Thunderhead asked, never minding where she'd been as she emptied her basket filled with trinkets and shiny things. Thunderhead pored through them, grabbing at baubles and handfuls of geejaws. A fistful of spoons, lost rings, tarnished thimbles. He rushed through to the floor strewn with dust, strewn with sand, where the lines of the stars had been traced by the soles of his feet. At each point where a star would shine in through the broken roof, he placed one of the glittering things to mark it on the floor, till the whole room was lit by their glinting, reflecting the last rays of the setting sun striking in through the rafters.

Back in the kitchen, Jonquil kindled the stove and set

up a brew, for the road from Brunt Boggart was dusty and dry - then wandered back to see whether Thunderhead had finished his chart.

"One star more!" he pointed excitedly.

Jonquil smiled.

"One star more," she responded. "You always ask for one star more. But then when I bring it, you need another and another. Always one star more. And I go out and find it, but you're never satisfied. Each night you gaze up and see a new star in the sky."

Thunderhead ran his fingers through his grizzled hair, all hung with tarnished glitter.

"This time, tis true," he declared. "I need one more star to draw them together. One star more to lay over here."

Jonquil followed his finger to where there was one space more for one more star at the point which would join all the lines, for once, for all.

"Fetch me my star," Thunderhead pleaded.

Snizzleslide sped away from the house, slithering through the undergrowth, the long grass whispering.

"I know this chart," he hissed. "Seen it all before. Seen the cloak that Old Mother Tidgewallop sewed, a cloak as dark as night, stitched all over with sparkling things, same as this chart that Thunderhead's made. And the cloak had one star missing too. One star in the corner she never could find. And I told her that I had that star, that I hid it in the well. I tricked her then - I tricked her false, I tricked her true."

Snizzleslide paused, his quick tongue licking his lips as he remembered. "But can't trick Thunderhead. No-one tricks Thunderhead. Thunderhead must have his star, and Snizzleslide must find it."

Snizzleslide came to Brunt Boggart and soon as they saw him people turned away, hid their coins and their keys full deep in their pockets as he slid by. Snizzleslide watched with eyes sly as sly.

He tried to look in Snuffwidget's house, but Snuffwidget sent him away. He tried to slip in through Willowmist's window while she was out for the day. But the locks were all bolted and he hurried on, while mistrustful eyes seemed to follow him, glinting as keen as the star he was seeking. But where? This crawling through dust on his belly made his throat parched and dry. Snizzleslide headed on to Mother Tidgewallop's old cottage, to slake his thirst in the well just as he'd always done.

He slithered down the slippery walls, then he drank and he drank of the clear icy water before climbing back up to the yard. There he stared and he stared at the cottage, the sun glinting bright off the windows. He knew that Old Mother Tidgewallop was gone. Larkum her wayward son lived there now with Grizzlegrin his wife, who cried at the moon - and their baby daughter Lovage who was the one crying now, up in the bedroom, wailing for milk.

Snizzleslide slipped in through the door, same as he ever had before. Slipped up the stairs quick as quick. Larkum was away in the woods, tending the pigs - Snizzleslide knew that. And Grizzlegrin was too busy with baby Lovage, so no-one noticed Snizzleslide as he slipped up to the dresser. No-one noticed Snizzleslide as he opened up the drawer. No-one noticed Snizzleslide as he seized the cloak as dark as night and dragged it off behind him, away across the floor.

"What's this?" grunted Thunderhead. Jonquil stood before him and spread out the dark black cloak.

"It is a chart," she replied. "A chart of stars. There are many stars here, many shiny things. I reasoned any one of them could be your missing star."

Thunderhead pushed back his battered black hat and twisted a strand of hair.

"You reasoned wrong," he said.

Jonquil looked disappointed. Thunderhead led her to the room of dust with the trail of stars laid out on the floor.

"Look," Thunderhead pointed, spreading out the cloak. "These charts are the same. The stars on the cloak are lined up the same as the stars on the floor. Both map the path of the planets. Both have one star missing. See, there…"

He placed a hand on Jonquil's shoulder and pointed. Sure enough, in just the same place was a space, a darkness.

Jonquil shook her head.

"The cloak is no use to me," Thunderhead told her as she gazed at the chart of stars on the floor. "Fine as it may be, handsome as it is, it is not my cloak," Thunderhead continued. "Belongs to another. Belongs to Grizzlegrin, made for her by Mother Tidgewallop, fine woman and true. I laid her in the Burying Ground and spoke the words to the sky. This cloak is no use to me. Take it back to Grizzlegrin."

And early next morning, Grizzlegrin was woken in her bed, just as the birds were singing, by a rustling, a scurrying, a dragging and a slithering.

"Larkum! Wake up!" she cried.

Larkum sat up slowly and rubbed his bleary eyes. Daughter Lovage began to weep at their side.

"Listen!" whispered Grizzlegrin.

"Can't hear nothing," grumbled Larkum. "Must be the wind and the morning birds. Go back to sleep now, will you - or tend to Daughter Lovage."

Just as Grizzlegrin took the child on her arm, they heard the sound of a rattling door. Larkum leapt from the bed and rushed down the stairs, but nothing could he see, anywhere around.

"Snizzleslide! Snizzleslide been here, sure as sure. It was him took the cloak of darkness that Grizzlegrin wore to comfort me. Snizzleslide took it, he must have done. What's he taken now?"

Larkum poked around in the half-light of the kitchen, but nothing seemed to be missing. Not a key nor a needle, not a kettle lid nor a thimble - not any of his mother's old keepsakes and trinkets. None of the things Snizzleslide usually came for.

"Nothing's gone," he said and scratched his head. "Too early to get up yet. Too late to go back to bed."

Larkum trudged up the stairs and set his eyes on the spare room door, hanging half open.

"Strange," he said. "I shut that last night."

He looked inside. The drawer of the dresser was open too, same as the door. Larkum went to check.

"Snizzleslide, Snizzleslide... now let's see what he's took."

He pulled the drawer full open and then he saw - Snizzleslide had taken nothing at all, but there - just where it should be - was the cloak of darkness all covered in stars, a little rumpled, a little crumpled, a little dusty where it had been dragged down the track.

A little stained where it had slithered through the grass and the mud, all the way back from Ramshadow House. But now it had returned.

"Grizzlegrin!" Larkum shouted to his wife as she held Daughter Lovage to her breast. "Look here - no need to cry now, the cloak of stars is come back!"

"Go! Go and don't come back. If you cannot bring the star to me - then what good are you here?"

Thunderhead's words still rang in Snizzleslide's head as he slipped away, not wanting to hear the voice again, but saddened to have failed. So he curled himself at the bottom of Old Mother Tidgewallop's well, to hide away and watch the sky, watch the clouds and sun and moon as they passed above his head.

Back in Ramshadow House, Thunderhead lay sick. He called for Jonquil, but she came no more. His voice echoed around the empty walls and up through the rotted rafters to rise through the broken roof and send the crows that sat there clattering to the sky. His head was heavy, his mind was fevered, his limbs they would not move. He lay a-bed and watched the stars, wishing he could reach out and pluck one down. Take it in his trembling hands and place it in the empty space that waited on the dusty floor.

The Drummer did not come any more. Thunderhead could hear his rhythms out by the Fever Tree where he played each day to the Crow Dancers. He did not come to Ramshadow House, for Thunderhead was too sick to mix his own potion and it was for the potion that the Drummer came, as much as it was to talk with Thunderhead or to beat out a rhythm for his dancing and his flute. So Thunderhead lay for days, counting the moons as they turned. He had no victuals, no water passed his cracked parched lips. Some days he heard a knocking, a knocking at the door - but it was not the Drummer and was not Jonquil. He knew by the voices calling him that it was the sick'uns come for a cure, though now he was more sick than them. He heard them talking, muttering, in the garden overgrown with weeds.

"Where is Thunderhead?... No-one seen him... He can't be here... This cough sits on my chest worse than a bear in a fog. How'm I going to fix it now if Thunderhead is gone?"

"Go to Nanny Ninefingers, same as me. She got the potions to fix you up..."

"Go to Ninefingers, that's for sure. She can cure you right as day..."

And Thunderhead lay in his fever bed and heard the voices pass away.

"Ninefingers, Ninefingers..." he repeated to himself.

But he would not go to her. All down the years, Old Nanny Ninefingers and Thunderhead would watch each other, eyes askance, pulling the same roots, picking the same herbs and flower heads, treating the same sick'uns who would come clamouring to see them. But Ninefingers would give'em one cure and Thunderhead would give'em another. And they both might work in their different ways, or they might not work at all. But Ninefingers and Thunderhead they never worked together, and if they could help it, they never spoke to each other. But who else was there? Who else to cure Thunderhead now he couldn't cure himself?

First cure was getting up. He looked at the walls. He gazed at the sky. He could do that, and rose up shaky on his long spindled legs. Second cure was getting dressed. He looked at his feathered cloak laying there and his tall battered hat. He could do that, though his hands were trembling as he pulled them on. Then he walked to the earthenware pot in the corner and daubed some clay in blotches and streaks, all down his cheeks, across his forehead and up his arms. Third cure was going out. Thunderhead pushed open the door. It creaked on its rusted hinges. Thunderhead took one step outside. He could do that. He blinked awhile and peered around, listening out for far-off sounds coming down the lane - voices raised and children squealing and the long wind rushing, hithering and thithering in between the trees. Thunderhead took one step more, then another and another, all the time listening as he went - hoping he might hear Jonquil yet, coming back to him. But she was gone. Thunderhead knew it.

So he walked on, on past Pottam's Mill and down Mallenbrook Lane, threading through the ruts and the standing puddles until he came to Old Nanny Ninefingers' cottage. And there he rapped upon the door. Rapped once, rapped twice, as loud as loud. Nanny Ninefingers was pouring powdered silverweed into a vial and she near spilt it all, he knocked so loud. But she kept on pouring until she was all finished and done - and then she swept the powder she'd spilt, all careful back into the jar. Then she rubbed her hands together and went and opened the door.

There stood Thunderhead. She looked him up and down.

"Why do you come here knocking? You never come to this door before. What is it you want?"

Thunderhead's hands were shaking. His limbs were

weak. He opened his mouth but could not speak. Old Nanny Ninefingers squinnied his eyes.

"You have a sickness, I can see." Her voice was gentle now. "Come in, come in."

Thunderhead took one step inside. This was the fourth cure. Now he was here. Now he was here, but what could he say? Ninefingers gestured to the kitchen chair.

"Sit down," she said.

Thunderhead sat, removed his tall battered hat and dragged his long fingers through his matted hair.

"Take your time," Ninefingers murmured. "You took time enough to come here all these years, that's for sure."

"All these years," said Thunderhead slowly. "All these years I never needed you. All these years you never needed me, though maybe one day you will. But today I come to ask you, Ninefingers... Don't come for no potion - I can make potion of my own..."

"I heard about your potions, Thunderhead..." Ninefingers began to admonish him gently, but Thunderhead raised his hand.

"Don't need no potion, Ninefingers - though I see you got plenty here and more." His eye roamed around the kitchen, the bottles and jars, the vials and pitchers racked along the shelves and cupboards that covered every wall.

"Don't need no potion, I just come to ask you..." Thunderhead paused.

Ninefingers watched him. She was listening. Outside in the treetops the jackdaws clattered. Thunderhead looked down. He stared at the floor as if he was tracing the chart again, that was marked in the dust back at

Ramshadow House. He pointed, his long finger quivering. He pointed to a spot where the sunlight fell in through Nanny Ninefingers' window, but that was not what he saw. He saw the star.

"What is it?" asked Ninefingers.

"The star!" he roared suddenly. Then was quiet again. Quiet as a child.

"The star that I seek." His shoulders were hunched beneath his cloak of feathers. He was sobbing almost.

Ninefingers shook her head.

"You do not seek it. This is a craving. This is a sickness."

Thunderhead nodded.

"Can you give me a potion?"

Ninefingers stood up and looked away.

"Thought you didn't want a potion, Thunderhead. And no potion of mine could help you, even if you did. If you want the star so bad, you got to find it yourself."

"But where?" he begged.

"Ain't in no tawdry shiny things," Ninefingers explained. "Ain't in Brunt Boggart, ain't in the fields. Ain't in the river, nor the sea. Not even in the sky. Ain't nowhere you been looking, nor anywhere you might go and look."

Thunderhead was shaking. He stretched his arms. His hands were trembling, his fingers shivering. He cupped them about as if they might be filled with a ball of bright light - but nothing was there but the dust in the air. Thunderhead slumped back in Ninefingers' kitchen chair. The old woman shook her head.

"There are no stars to guide you. You must find the star inside you," she said.

Thunderhead sat still, as quiet as quiet. Quieter than

you are now. Ninefingers reached for a piece of chalk and drew on the floor a five-pointed star.

"Go to the top of Langton Brow when the night is dark and the stars full bright. Lay yourself out beneath the sky with your four limbs stretched to the four points of the star."

"And where is the fifth point?" Thunderhead asked, knowing this must be the fifth cure at last.

Ninefingers looked at him.

"You must close your eyes. The fifth point is where you find the power of the star inside you."

Thunderhead strode to the top of Langton Brow. As he lay on his back he breathed gently, breathed slowly, drew the whole of the sky deep into his lungs. He felt himself bathed in the light of a hundred stars, a thousand stars. A thousand, thousand stars, and a thousand more - the stars beyond the stars.

Thunderhead cupped his hands and raised them. It seemed to him they were filled with an energy which he could not see, but he could feel as he drew it like a glowing ball towards him. As the power surged through him he let out a great cry - then leapt to his feet and ran. He ran all the way down Langton Brow, down the rutted lane towards Brunt Boggart. When he reached the meadow he paused, for the darkness was filled with a sudden light as if a star had fallen, not now but a long while ago. He shook his head. Not a star at all but a bush in early blossom. He looked again. Not a bush but a sheep, wandering lost back to its field. He looked again. Not a sheep but a fall of sudden snow. And then he ran on. Ran on across the meadow and through Brunt Boggart's sleeping streets, way past the Blacksmith's forge and beyond until he reached Ramshadow House.

With his hands still cupped, he shouldered open the door, still clutching the power, the energy of the star. The chart of planets lay traced in the dust on the floor, marked by a myriad of meaningless trinkets, geejaws and baubles, lockets and pendants, brooches, bracelets and keys. Thunderhead leapt to the shadowy space which waited for the final star. He unlocked the cup of his hands and let the glow of the energy seep into the space. As he did so, he heard a familiar rhythm as the Drummer set out from the Echo Field. Thunderhead began to move. His long limbs swayed, his hair shook free. As the Drummer arrived through the open door, Thunderhead clapped his hands. And then the dance began.

A turning dance, a burning dance. A dance of all he'd ever learned. A dance of stars as the planets were joined all across the chart. But as they joined, the stars in the dark of the sky above Ramshadow's broken roof began to wheel as if the whole universe was revolving. Thunderhead let out another cry, so loud that down in Brunt Boggart, everyone must have heard it and they stumbled sleepy from their beds, out into the streets to see what the matter might be. And there above them they saw the stars spinning across the endless sky.

As the sky gyrated, so just for an instant Brunt Boggart was gone and they stood in a place they did not know - a teaming city crowded with more people than they had ever seen before. Down on the waterfront drums were beating and trumpets braying. Beside the quayside stood a sagging collection of tents, painted bright colours. A fire-eater leaned back with his hands on his hips, breathing flames that shimmered and twisted while a one-legged juggler tossed wooden discs into the air and caught them as they fell. All around there were stalls ladened down with pies and loaves and sweetmeats. A grizzled brown bear, its legs in chains, capered sluggishly on top of a barrel.

And as the drum beat, the people of Brunt Boggart danced, twining and kissing the same as they might at the season's moon when Skyweaver would come and play his fiddle all out on the Green. But tonight it was only the Drummer who played, though where he was, nobody knew. They could only hear his echo, be it from Ramshadow House or down on the city's waterfront.

Ravenhair was there, with all the other girlen, and she found herself holding Crossdogs' hand and peering up to the sky. Her head was spinning, she felt fearful yet happy. She felt as if she was dancing although she was standing quite still as Crossdogs took her in his arms. She looked up.

"The stars have stopped turning," she whispered.

Crossdogs followed her gaze. It was true. And when they looked back, the city had gone - the stalls and the minstrel troupe and the crush of the throng. The drumming had stopped and all the people of Brunt Boggart stood out on the Green, bemused and shivering in their nightshirts and gowns. They shook their heads and shuffled back to their beds, back in their own familiar cottages.

Back at Ramshadow House, the Drummer slipped away. Behind him lay Thunderhead, collapsed on the floor in the midst of his chart of the stars. And from beneath his prone body a strong smoke rose in a shadow all around him, rose through the timbers of the broken rooftop and out towards the echoing sky.

THE PEDLAR MAN'S TRACK

SAFFRON

Let me tell you... Let me tell you... the mist hung low over the meadows and the air tasted sharp with the soil's sodden blackness, as Greychild woke on a day much like today, nuzzled in the warmth of his coat beneath a canopy of twigs. In the distance he could hear a rising lark, while close by a dead branch snapped. Could be fox, could be badger. Greychild rolled over, shivering in the cold of the morning. He could feel damp dew flowing through his veins and kissing his bones.

Brunt Boggart was behind him now. All the day before, in the hedgerows and the gorse bushes, the dunnocks had chirruped and yellowhammers too, wagtails, goldfinches and little tippet wrens, all calling him and leading him, dipping and weaving as he walked.

Greychild rose and shook himself. Through the trees he saw a patch of blue, the very same colour, the very same hue as the dress he knew his mother wore, whenever she came to visit him. He followed it through scagging briars, followed it through nettle bite, followed it through mud and mire - but walk as he did and try as he might, the blue dress stayed ahead of him, leading him on, till Greychild pushed the branches aside, sure that he must find her. He saw the blue of her dress shimmering before him, but when he rushed out to touch it again, to bury his face in its folds, he knew it was only the blue of the sky. Greychild gave a sigh, then let loose a howling cry. All around him soft leaves fell and he held out his hands to touch them as if these were his mother's tears and she was weeping now that she'd lost him. But not lost him at all for she'd found him again as he felt the sweet sunshine warm his face just as his mother's smile had done.

A skein of geese flew across the sky, leading Greychild on again, slow as quick, quick as slow, only his coat on his back, his pockets empty as they'd ever been, till he came stumbling down the side of a hill where chaffinches rose twittering and the long grass swayed in the wind. There sitting on a stile was a girl with a wide friendly smile. As Greychild drew closer, she ran her long fingers through her dark flowing hair and spread her skirts around her like the petals of a flower.

"Come sit with me," she said and smoothed her hand along the fence beside her. Greychild scrambled up. He was glad to settle awhile, for he was weary from walking all the morning.

"Tell me your name," the girl implored, stroking Greychild's face the while, her fingers light as any feather.

"I'll tell you mine when I know yours," Greychild replied.

"They call me Saffron," said the girl, and when Greychild told her the name that Old Granny Willowmist had given him, why then she said, "I can see you're grey from the dirt of the road. Do you think that the dust is water to wash your face and clothes?"

Greychild grinned.

"I know that dust is dust. But I am thirsty now. Tell me Saffron, you have asked me to sit with you - can you offer me a drink?"

Saffron laughed and tossed back her hair.

"I can give you a drink here, I can give you a drink there."

Then she took off her shoe and gave it to Greychild.

"But this is a shoe," he protested, "and an empty shoe besides."

Saffron frowned and shook her head.

"Tis nary a shoe, but a fine drinking cup!"

Greychild glanced at her nut brown face, all grinning and laughing in the midday sun, and thought that he would play along with her game. He raised the shoe to his lips and took a draught full long and true. The taste was sweet, the taste was clear, as pure as any water. And when he stopped his drinking, for sure his thirst was quenched. He passed the shoe back to Saffron who bent down low, her hair all tumbling, to slip it back on her foot.

"Thank you," he said to her, "for offering me your cup."

Saffron smiled and took his hand.

"Are you warm from your journey?" she asked.

Greychild nodded and pointed up.

"The sun is full high," he exclaimed.

But Saffron shook her head.

"That is not the sun," she said. "The sun would never shine by day. Why no, good Greychild, I know not who taught you but here we call that the moon."

Greychild was puzzled. He looked into Saffron's eyes to see if she was teasing him, like the girlen in Brunt Boggart when they played with him on the Green.

"If that is the moon," he reasoned, "then what is that great white plate that climbs in the sky at night?"

"Why that," cried Saffron, as she leapt from the stile and spread her skirts wide on the grass. "Why that, good Greychild, that be the sun, as anyone round here will tell you."

Greychild scratched his head as he gazed down at the merriment in Saffron's eyes. He could never be sure about words - he'd learnt them all as quick as quick at Old Granny Willowmist's table when she'd taken him in from the woods, but sometimes he mixed them about. Saffron laughed at the puzzlement on Greychild's face and reached up to pull him down beside her on the grass.

"Lie with me awhile," she begged. "Awhile and another while more."

Greychild didn't know what to say. His limbs were tired and aching and he would be pleased to rest, but he needed to continue his journey before the end of the day and anyway, he mused, what did Saffron mean?

"If the sun be the moon and the moon be the sun when you ask me to stay, do you mean *Go away*?"

Saffron laughed and plucked up a buttercup to tickle him under his chin.

"That's for me to know and you to find out. Come

and sit closer now."

In her lap lay an orange between the folds of her skirt. Greychild reached out to take it, but she pushed his hand away.

"I'm sorry," he said, hanging his head. "My belly is growling with hunger. I have not eaten all morning and I love the sweet flesh of an orange and the tang of the juice on my fingers."

Saffron looked at him and frowned.

"This is no orange," she said, "but a fine speckled egg, laid freshly at dawn in my own father's barn."

Greychild scratched his head.

"Nothing here is what it seems to be," he said. "If the sun be the moon and your shoe be a cup... and now an orange is an egg, why how can I be sure that you're even a girl at all?"

Saffron shook out her hair and ruffled her skirts. Then she stood up of a sudden and the orange rolled down to the ground. As it lay on the grass between them she flung her arms up into the air as if they might be wings.

"You have guessed true," she declared. "I am no girl, but a goose!"

Greychild grew afraid, for this goose girl looked so suddenly fierce.

"The sun is the moon," he shouted, "and the moon is the sun," agreeing with all she had told him. "Your shoe is a cup and the orange is an egg!"

He picked up the fruit and its skin seemed brittle and speckled, as like an egg might be, and as he did, the girl's arms beat down then beat upwards again with a flap and a clatter, and she rose up before him then flew away over the trees and the hills. As Greychild watched the great bird go, the trees were no longer trees, but flowers and the hills had all sunk down into valleys. The sky was darkened, it was day no more, but deep in the pitch of the night. Greychild shivered. He felt he should sleep, but his belly told him it was still only afternoon. And so he walked on down the Pedlar Man's Track, though it seemed more like a sparkling stream than any road he knew. The wheat in the fields around him stood frozen with frost. Rainbows arched into bridges of stone across the dark sea of the sky. Birds crawled about him as if they were spiders while a leather backed beetle perched on his shoulder and sang like a nightingale.

Greychild felt as though he'd been turned inside out. His tongue hung dry and parched even though he'd just slaked his thirst. His belly growled empty again as soon as he had eaten. He cried salty tears even when he felt happy and when that made him sad he couldn't stop himself from laughing. He stood at the top of a high hill with the wind roaring round in his head. Below lay dark fields scattered over with flowers whose petals glowed purple and beckoned like fingers. But how could he be sure if this hill was a hill, or was he deep down in a vale?

"Moon is moon!" Greychild threw back his head and shouted. "Moon is moon and sun is sun. I am Greychild and you are Saffron. Orange is orange and egg is egg. Your shoe is a shoe and no cup anymore!"

He closed his eyes, then slowly opened them again, hoping that all would be changed. But he still stood on top of a high hill, the wind blowing wild through his tangle of hair and the dark fields below calling his name. And so he followed, down and down. Down a track of pebbles that glistened like eyes. Down a gully of shadows brighter than sunlight. Down to a thicket of soft velvet bushes and there he heard a girl crying. He pushed on through and there she sat, the girl who told him moon was sun. The girl who told him sun was moon.

"Greychild!" she called to him, and held out her hand. An orange still rolled in the lap of her skirt. She lifted the fruit and begged him to take it, to stroke its soft skin, to suck of its juice. But Greychild refused.

"You are not Saffron, true." His voice was firm and steady. "For in this place where night is day and day is night, then if you seem to me to be a girl, then I know you true to be a goose."

And so she was. Her arms raised up to beat again and she was gone. But as she left him, sun became moon again and moon became sun, and Greychild came stumbling down the hill where chaffinches rose twittering and the long grass swayed in the wind. He found himself standing back at the stile, his belly growling with hunger and his tongue dry with thirst and his feet sore and weary at the end of a long morning's walk. But in the long grass, by the side of the fence, lay the segments of an orange, all freshly peeled.

THE WAKING SLEEPERS

Let me tell you... let me tell you how Greychild came rattling at the cold metal knocker on the great oaken door of the house that stood at the end of the wood. Not a sound could he hear from within and so he knocked again. Knocked once, knocked twice, but with the second knock the door swung open. There inside was a passageway heavy with dust which clung to the carvings of the low heavy beams.

As Greychild tiptoed forward to shelter from the night's chill wind, the door creaked shut behind him. He stood awhile, letting his eyes grow used to the smothering darkness. Then he thought he heard a rustling, a low gentle moaning, a muttering and a calling from somewhere up the long narrow staircase which he could just make out before him.

"Who's there?" Greychild cried, but the voices continued their mumbling like as if they were talking to each other in a dream, like as if they had not heard

Greychild's knocking at all, or the heavy thud of the door.

Greychild paused at the foot of the stairs. He could smell a smell such as he had never known before. More potent than any of Nanny Ninefingers' potions: orange and clove, cinnamon and comfrey. But something else. It was the smell of death, but not death at all. It was the smell of sleep, but not sleep at all - it was the smell of dreams.

Greychild moved forward slowly, his hands groping in the darkness. He brushed against a table, and from it rolled something cold, something metal. It clattered to the floor, echoing eerily along the passages of the house. From above the voices rose, a curious muttering at being so rudely disturbed. Greychild paused. Who would come? Who would come shuffling down the stairs to confront him? But the voices quietened and Greychild crept forward again, his foot knocking up against whatever had fallen. It rolled and rattled away from him, but he bent to pick it up. His hands ran over the length of its smooth cold surface until he came to a design all mazy and swirling. Greychild realised he was holding a long metal horn and without thinking raised the instrument to his lips and gently blew, then harder. One ringing note seared through the dust, the cobwebs and the gloom. Greychild caught his breath, for the sound was louder than ever he'd imagined. It echoed and ran along the deserted passageway, was swallowed up into the empty rooms, then welled out and around again.

He dropped the horn clanging to the floor, louder than ever before. Greychild froze. What should he do? The echo trailed away. He turned to run towards the door, but his legs would not move as up above his head he heard footsteps drawn towards him, shuffling and groaning as the muttering grew louder. Then a slithering and a shuddering came trundling down the stairs, juddering along the corridor from the rooms up a-top.

Then light. Light of lanterns, light of candles. And faces pressing close to him. Greychild gasped. These creatures seemed same age as him, their skin was smooth, their limbs long and supple. But in the light of the lanterns' flicker, their eyes stared ancient and rheumy and their hair hung matted and straggled in snow-white locks.

A girlen pressed her face up close to his and peered into his eyes. Prodded at him with an icy finger.

"I am Ashblossom," she whispered.

Her voice was thin and reedy, like as if it was here, but not here at all. Her dress was long and blue as sky and her fingernails they were painted each one with a glittering dragonfly.

"Who are you?" she asked.

"I am Greychild," he said, his eyes darting back and forth as the figures pressed around him, pushing and poking as if they could not see him.

"Greychild..." Ashblossom's voice shivered. "Why did you come here? Why did you wake us? Who taught you to blow the horn?"

Greychild shook his head.

"No-one taught me - I just blew it. And no-one was sleeping - I could hear you all talking up the stairs."

Ashblossom squinnied hard through her olden eyes.

"We sleep," she said. "We sleep till the darkness. And then we walk. Walk room to room. But you have called us with the horn."

Then she reached up and kissed him - and her lips were soft and moist. Her lips were warm, not cold and frail like her voice.

"Come with us," Ashblossom said and took his hand in hers as she guided him up the stairs. The waking sleepers followed them, their voices brighter now and chattering. She led Greychild from room to room, lighting lanterns as she went to chase away the shadows that massed within as dark night gathered beyond the blackness of the windows. The last room was draped out all in white, a gauze of curtains and hangings. A linen cloth covered a wooden table, and on it set dishes and bowls. Greychild picked one up and stared at the design. Ashblossom watched as he ran his fingers around the pattern. A whorl of swirling mazes such as were graven on the shaft of the horn - such as he remembered from the broken pots in the stream beside the hump-backed bridge back at Brunt Boggart.

"What is this?" he asked.

"Let me tell you..." she replied. "Let me tell you of the old times, of the time before this time, of time beside time - of time beyond, a-like when you stare into the embers of a fire and see other worlds all dancing there."

She held up the bowl and pointed to the spiralling maze of patterns. She took his hand in her long smooth fingers.

"See as it circles. We are here. But not here, for while we are here - we are also *there*."

Greychild stared at Ashblossom. The fine skin of a girlen, topped with an old'un's long white tresses. She kissed him again and then held him in a slow embrace, which reminded him so of the soft moist stillness of the woods back by Brunt Boggart's green - where he would walk with Dawnflower. He stepped back from her and gazed at the whorls of the bowl again.

"Tis the same," he exclaimed. "Tis true the same as the pattern on the crockery I fished from the stream. But more - tis the same as the patterns on the wall of Ramshadow House where Thunderhead lives."

Ashblossom nodded and took his hand again.

"Ramshadow was home," she said. "Time before this time. We lived there and played there, shaped pots and sang, made music on harps and on horns such as the one you found in the hallway. Let me tell you..."

But Greychild held up his hand.

"Stop," he said. "My head is spinning like a sky full of stars. Let me eat."

And so they ate, a meal like as Greychild had never tasted before - dark berries that laid bitter-sweet on his tongue, bread as fulsome as furrowed fields, wine strong and rich, brewed from nettles and honey that made him heavy with sleep while at once wide awake.

Ashblossom explained, "Before we all recline, we set out a meal to eat when we wake. For who knows how long we will sleep? - sometimes a day, sometimes two. Sometimes a moon passes by and more... seasons and years slip away all the same. Sometimes we wake and the food is gone, nibbled and gnawed by beetles and mice. The berries are shrivelled and the bread turned to mould. Other times like this, it is waiting fresh as fresh."

All around them the waking sleepers gorged on the food, their voices dark whispers that rose to shrill screams.

"We dream we are in Ramshadow still, playing our music and dancing in the halls. But all is gone now. Our harp-frames warped and fell out of tune. The horns grew rusty and their notes cracked and flawed. Ramshadow's roof caved in, till all we could do was lie there and gaze at the stars through the broken rafters. We fell sick with the sleeping. But one night we could live without music no more and so we left Ramshadow for the last time, scrambling out along the paths that wove through the woods. Set out to find new clay to make new pots. Set out to cut boughs from sweet cherry trees to mend the frames of our harps. But nothing brought back the music that used to sound out from Ramshadow's halls. We wandered and wandered till the seasons turned round and then turned round again - until we came here."

Greychild gazed around the room. Gazed at Ashblossom's companions, who were moving now, slowly, latched in each other's arms, dancing to the rhythm of a music which only they could hear.

"This place seems fine enough," he said.

Ashblossom shook her head.

"Tis not the same. Here when we fire the clay it is pale and brittle and we have dredged all there is from the pits."

She took him in her arms again and as she pressed him close, Greychild heard the music too, as if from a far-off room. He looked once more into her eyes and then he turned away to stare at the ceiling and the walls. The whorls and mazes were scrolling there, same as before, and yet not the same. The patterns were swirling, plunging this way and that, misshapen and crooked. Greychild span around. He did not know which way to turn. In the room all the heavy-lidded eyes were staring at him as the sleepers moved closer, shuffling and muttering.

"Come with me, come," said Ashblossom. She took his arm again and their feet rattled light down the stairway and on to the end of the hall - but when they reached the door, two watching sleepers were there waiting for them.

"Nobody leaves," they intoned. "Nobody leaves once you have eaten."

But Ashblossom leaned close to each of them and whispered in their ear, then she touched their cheeks with her lips and they fell fast to sleep again. And so they left the house, Greychild and Ashblossom, past the shadow of the clay-pits in the darkness outside, until they found themselves on a path all damp and oozing with leaf-mulch. The sky was dark but the moon was high and shone down on Ashblossom's robe, so it seemed as if she lit the way as she led him in between the trees. An owl watched them with eyes as bright as two burning stars, while its wings beat slowly between the dead branches. They ran on and on until they came to an orange grove where the fruit shone like very suns.

Greychild stood shivering, his limbs trembling with excitement and fear. Ashblossom held him like she was a torch of flame that would burn, would consume him all. He gazed into her eyes again, so ageless old, so wondrous young. Same eyes as he remembered when his mother came, back in the dark wood outside of Brunt Boggart. Greychild was shaking and confused. He wanted to push Ashblossom away, wanted to hold her close. Was not his mother but seemed more like her than any girlen he'd met before. She shook her hair and stepped away. Stepped to stand beside an orange tree. There she reached out to pluck from the bough the ripest fruit that she could find. As she stretched, Greychild gazed on her arms, her face, her neck, all milky white in the moonlight. Ashblossom held out the orange, glowing bright as gold. She smiled a smile so old, so young, as her tongue licked soft about her lips.

"Eat with me and then we sleep. In your sleep, why then we dream. You can dream who you want to be with. You can dream where you want to go."

Ashblossom stared into Greychild's eyes. He felt himself growing sleepier.

"*Nobody leaves once you have eaten...*" He remembered the words of the Watchers, waiting at the door of the house. His eyes blinked. The clearing all around him seemed to swim. He blinked again. Ashblossom was standing in front of him, holding the orange in her outstretched hand.

"Who do you want to be with?" she asked. "Where do you want to go?"

Greychild said nothing. He knew who he wanted to be with. He wanted to be with his mother. But he wanted to be with Dawnflower too, the girlen he'd left behind beside the bridge in Brunt Boggart.

"Take," said Ashblossom. "Take and eat with me."

The fruit glowed still brighter as Greychild stepped forward. But as he did, so Ashblossom's face changed. He swore twas as if Dawnflower was standing there, her tresses hanging long.

"Do not eat the fruit," she said.

Greychild shook his head. Had he heard his friend's words true? He took a step back, then stood root still. Dawnflower had gone. Ashblossom was still smiling at him, holding out the fruit. From far away and far he heard an owl calling. But then he heard Dawnflower's voice again.

"Do not eat the fruit," she repeated. "Do not eat the fruit."

A twig snapped as Ashblossom stepped full close to him. She took his hand in hers and stood before him, holding the shining orange as if it was kissing his lips. The blue dragonflies flashed on her painted fingernails. Greychild turned his head away.

"I know who I want to be with..." he repeated, shaking his head as he did so to drive the sleep from his eyes. "...I know where I want to go. I want to travel the Pedlar Man's Track that will take me to Arleccra where I'll find my mother waiting for me, all in the market square."

Ashblossom touched him on the cheek, but Greychild pushed her away.

"You are not my mother," he said "nor even Dawnflower neither."

"Eat the orange," Ashblossom whispered, kissing the fruit. "Eat the orange and sleep. Then your dreams will take you wherever you choose."

"But the dream will be only a dream," Greychild retorted. "When I wake it will be gone and I will have travelled no further."

Ashblossom paused and looked down.

> "One bite to taste," she whispered under her breath –
>> "One bite to taste
> Of the fruit on the tree.
>> One bite to taste

And you stay here with me."

Her voice was so low that Greychild could not hear, and so she sang on -

> "You stay with me here
>   To sleep down the years -
> If I trick you to keep you,
>   You'll drown in your tears."

The first light of dawn touched the leaves of the trees around the grove. In their branches, blackbirds scrambled, their voices urging the rising sun to climb the sky. Ashblossom's eyes widened in panic as she watched the darkness slide away.

> "One bite with me
>   Is all I crave.
> One bite with me
>   Before break of day."

She held up the orange till it glowed between their hungering lips.

"Eat with me," she begged, as a tear of ancient salt trickled down her smooth young cheek.

Greychild felt himself sway, as if he slept on his feet. He felt hungry. He felt thirsty. The fruit was close and tempting. He opened his mouth, that his teeth might tear into the flesh of the orange, same as Ashblossom was about to do. But then he heard his mother's voice, close at hand yet far away.

"Do not eat the fruit," she said. "Do not eat the fruit. *Nobody leaves once you have eaten...*"

Greychild stopped and drew away, but now Ashblossom's teeth gripped the fruit's glowing skin.

"Eat with me..." she begged again as her eyelids hung heavy and her limbs grew limp. The sun rose full above the horizon. Dawn had broken and as the light touched her cheek, Ashblossom fell fast asleep and the half-bitten orange rolled from her fingers across the dew-laden grass.

Greychild stared. He felt as though his mother was there, standing with him in the grove. Then not his mother but Dawnflower, calling him back to the Green. Then he looked again at Ashblossom's face, so old and so young, yet both at once. He wanted to kiss her, he wanted to embrace her. As the blackbirds' voices trailed away, Greychild bent down and gathered her into his arms. Step by step he carried her back along the path, back past the clay-pits, brim full of glistening water, back to the sleeping house. All there had fallen into a slumber again, even the Watchers who had stood at the door.

"Nobody leaves..." mumbled the first. "... once you have eaten," the other replied.

Greychild carried Ashblossom upstairs and placed her gently on the waiting bed. Her lips parted softly into a pleasured smile, but she was full asleep and Greychild knew she would wake no more, not for a night, nor a season long until a hunter came again from out of the woods to blow one ringing note on the horn.

THE DAUGHTER OF THE WIND

Let me tell you... Let me tell you how Greychild came from the dark woods and found a spring tumbling out of the rock. As he bent to quench his thirst he thought he felt someone sit down beside him - but when he turned round there was nobody there. He waited a while then heard a voice singing:

> "You see me when the clouds ride by,
> You see me when the brown leaves fall -
> But when the sun climbs full and high
> You scarce see me at all."

"Who is there?" Greychild asked, as sinewy fingers ran through his hair. But no-one replied.

"Who is there?" he asked again, as the voice seemed to drift further away. But then it was as though it was beside him again.

"Who is there?" Greychild asked a third time.

"I am Mystra, the Daughter of the Wind," said she:

"You see me when the tall boughs crack,
You feel me throw you on your back -
But if you shelter by the wall,
Why then you'll scarce see me at all."

Greychild turned and could just make out a wraith figure sitting beside him, laughing and giggling, though her eyes seemed deep and sad.

"My father was the Wind," she explained. "And my mother lived on the farm, just a little over yonder. Some days I do my father's work and some days I do my mother's... Watch!" she said, then vanished again, but Greychild could see where she went as she flew around the clearing rattling all the leaves. Then the clouds above seemed to rush and scud. Greychild rose to his feet in amazement and thought that she was gone, but then felt her back beside him again, teasing at his scarf and tugging his hair.

"Where are you now?" he cried and held out his hand to trap her.

"You cannot catch the wind," Mystra replied as she swung from the branch of the nearest tree.

Greychild laughed. "Why would I want to catch *you*," he said, "when it's much more fun to let you catch *me*!"

Then Greychild slipped off into the thicket and crept round the bushes and slithered through gorse and covered himself all over in bramble thorns. They played seek-and-hide till the sun slid from sight, then he smiled as he watched the wind-child ride by, ruffling up the grass. But soon enough she found him out and stroked his cheek and tickled his neck till his skin was covered in goose bumps and the hair tangled wild round his head.

Greychild stopped and caught her hand.

"Where do you live?" he asked.

"Oh, I live here and I live there. But the Daughter of the Wind truly lives nowhere, for wherever I am, I must be gone, and wherever I fly, I'll be back before long."

"Take me with you," Greychild begged. "I'm tired of my travelling and would rather stay here and play."

Mystra frowned and took his hand.

"I do not play," she said. "I blow the seeds to plant new trees and fill the sails for the tall ships to ride that they may plough the tide. Then I rattle the windows and wail through the locks to remind good folk they should all be in bed."

"But that's your father's work," Greychild reasoned. "What do you do when you follow your mother?"

"My mother is gone," Mystra explained. "She pined away for want of my father. But some mornings you see me milking the cows and long afternoons tending the fields. Then night after night weaving the yarn as if to bind myself close to the farm. But I always break free when I hear my father's voice and I follow where he leads me as if I have no choice."

"Take me with you..." Greychild begged again and Mystra held his hand tighter and drew him into the sky.

They flew above hills and hovered over fields. They clung to the tops of chimney pots and sang in low voices which were moaning and wild. They flew till they came to Geddum Leatherbarrow's farm. Now let me tell you about Geddum Leatherbarrow. He had grown from a boy to a man and then taken on his father's farm. He ploughed the fields and sowed the seeds and come harvest time he cut the corn. But best of all he gathered the apples that grew in the orchard along by the lane. He heaped them into baskets, then he took them down to the market where the wifen and the girlen clustered around, for Geddum brought the sweetest fruit of any farmer in the vale.

So Geddum was happy, but not happy at all, toiling in his fields from dawn till dusk with no wifen to come home to. But one day, sure as sure, down in the market, one of them girlen caught his eye and soon enough became his wife. And wifen fell with child and she swelled plump and ripe just as the apples in Geddum's own orchard. And Geddum he was glad, for soon they would have a little'un who would grow to help around the farm. But when the birthing came, his wife fell pale and the thunder rolled and the rain lashed down in a lightning flash - then both were taken, wifen and child-to-be, and Geddum Leatherbarrow was left all alone again, working on his fields.

As each moon turned, every apple in the orchard ripened to black and they tasted of darkness and nightmares and bile. Geddum toiled hard to be rid of this crop, carting them away and ploughing them deep so that they might never grow again. Next spring when the blossom came, he watched and he waited till the fruit grew full and ripened russet and gold. But Geddum felt a great weariness upon him, for he missed his young wife so much he had not the strength to visit the orchard and gather the apples, and the weeds grew long in the nether meadow and the ditches were all choked with silt.

At night the rain came and slaked the slates from his

roof, till Geddum would lie and stare at the starless sky and dream of his wifen dead and their child who was never born. Then when he slept, another child came, the one I told you of, the Daughter of the Wind. She wailed around his house like a creature in pain, till Geddum woke again and went out to see what the howling was, but he knew well as well 'twas only the wind - and returned to his bed to rest at last. But he slept so deep that the day slipped away, and as he slept, so Mystra came and snatched every apple from every tree in his orchard and dashed them to the ground, while Greychild watched in dismay.

"Why do you do this?" he asked, but Mystra only smiled.

"It is what the Wind, my father, does - and so I do it too."

And before he could stop her, Mystra ran on, hither and thither all about the farm, knocking down fences and ripping off guttering, like as if she was a terrible storm. Greychild didn't know what to do. What would you do if you were caught up by the wind? Would you try to fix her harrying? Greychild watched as the farm door swung open and there stood Geddum Leatherbarrow, looking on in despair.

"Stop!" cried Greychild. "Enough is enough."

But Mystra had grown tired from all the damage she had done, and settled down lightly at Greychild's shoulder.

"Watch now," she whispered into his ear, "and see what Geddum Leatherbarrow will do."

Geddum Leatherbarrow shook his head and surveyed the damage done.

"Worse as it is and worse as it gets, then just gets

worsen again," he moaned as he stared at the broken-down fences and his apple orchard's branches stripped bare. But then he jutted his jaw and clenched his fists.

"Wifen and child are taken away and will never come back no more. But fallen fruit and broken fence - these I can fix for sure."

He rolled up his sleeves and set to work and soon every apple was gathered in and stowed away in baskets. And then he fetched his mallet and set to mending the fences.

"What now?" asked Greychild. "Do we wait here and watch him? I need to make my way back to the track."

But Mystra was standing, suddenly taller, and not afraid to be seen.

"Come away," pleaded Greychild, "come away with me. Your work here is done. You've set Geddum Leatherbarrow back on his feet, and he has mended his farm."

But Mystra shook her head.

"Oh no," she said, "my work here has hardly begun."

That night as Greychild watched, she blew in through Geddum Leatherbarrow's broken roof and whispered soft in his ear.

"Who's there?" cried Geddum, suddenly waking.

Look as he tried and look as he might, he could see no-one at all. But he could feel the Wind's daughter close by his side as soft and gentle as the very night when he first took his wifen as his bride.

"*You see me when the clouds ride by...*" Mystra murmured in his ear. "*You see me when the brown leaves fall - but when the sun climbs full and high, you scarce see me at all.*"

And they lay together, Geddum Leatherbarrow and

the Daughter of the Wind, as she whispered soft and true.

"Don't ask me now who I might be - but I know you need someone to help you - mending barns and tending the fields. This work I can do, and if you'll take me, then I am my mother's daughter and I'm the woman for you."

But what of Greychild? - I know what you're asking. He stayed around the farm for a while and a while, almost a wraith himself. He watched while Mystra worked the fields, same as her mother had done. He watched while sometimes she would straighten her back and peer up into the sky. And then he thought she might fly again, just as she had done when she brought him here. But no, she seemed content to return to her work, with Geddum Leatherbarrow close by her side.

At last one night Greychild caught her, as she made her way back from the orchard.

"What of me?" he pleaded. "What am I to do, now that you have brought me here? Won't you take me back to the Pedlar Man's Track?"

Mystra looked up. At first she smiled a smile, as if she was about to fly through the trees and the bramble thorns, playing hide and seek again. But then she shook her head and turned her eyes away.

"My work is here now," she said. "My days of mischief are done. I cannot play catch with you anymore. You must continue your journey alone."

LUDDITCH AND SCRUNT

Let me tell you... Let me tell you... Crossdogs peered through the overhanging trees as the stars began to beckon. Where had he come to now? A day's walk from Brunt Boggart was all that he could reckon as he followed Greychild down the Pedlar Man's Track. The sun was gone, the moon was rising. His feet were blistered, his limbs shaking, as a cold wind blew from the distant mountains. Crossdogs heard the night come whispering through the shadows of the wood. Where could he shelter? Where could he sleep? His belly was empty, his legs were aching.

He sat in the middle of a thicket. Darkness flooded his eyes and soon he was asleep. But no sooner asleep than Crossdogs woke again, shivering. He gazed around the clearing. Damp grass and brambles etched sharp and grey in the moonlight. The owl that he had heard before clattered closer now as he felt his teeth chattering in the breeze. Crossdogs wished he was back at home in his mother's cottage, wrapped up warm in his blankets.

A slender birch bent to brush his cheek and he felt as though it was the soft touch of Ravenhair's hand. He thought he heard her voice again, begging him to return. Felt her arms twine around him, supple as the birch tree's branches. Felt her kiss slip across his lips as she tugged at him, leading him back to the path which led to Sandy Holme - where she told everyone he gave her a root all twisted and gnarled, like as if it was a Wolf's Claw, though he knew full well she found the root herself and all he'd ever given her was a daisy and a rose. Crossdogs stared at the pale moon's ghost spilling through the clouds, as he stroked the branch of silver birch till the light flooded through him soft as milk and the dark wind came howling out of the trees. But Crossdogs slipped into a sweet deep sleep as he heard the voice of Ravenhair and all the other girlen calling through the trees -

"Come home, Crossdogs, come home."

As soon as dawn broke, Crossdogs rose quickly. He was shivering and cold as he stood there shaking, the dark wood behind him. He bunched his fists and clenched his teeth. He scanned all around, like a kestrel, like a fox. Suddenly saw a plume of smoke rising.

"Where there's smoke," Crossdogs reasoned, "there's fire. And where there's fire there's warmth. Might even be food."

And it was food he wanted most as he blundered off down a narrow stony path. Food for his belly which gripped like a fist and twisted at his guts. He struggled on towards the smoke which seemed to grow more distant with every step he took. Then just as his guts had become so hungry he felt sure they might eat him whole, a shadow fell across the path and a lad stood there in front of him - as tall as Crossdogs and taller and yet not as tall at all.

"Now then," the newcomer challenged him.

"Now then," Crossdogs returned.

They bared their teeth in wary smiles.

"Where been going?" the lad enquired.

Crossdogs pointed towards the plume of smoke rising away in the distance.

"Nowt there," said the lad. "Where been come from?"

Crossdogs pointed back towards the Pedlar Man's Track.

"Brunt Boggart," he told him.

The lad spat on the muddy path and muttered something under his breath which Crossdogs could not catch. The two boys stared at each other. Crossdogs' stomach growled inside him, begging him to ask for food. But Crossdogs would ask for nothing. He looked the lad up and down.

"What been name?" he asked.

"Sapwood," the lad replied.

Crossdogs offered his hand in greeting as the men in Brunt Boggart always did. But Sapwood ignored him. Perhaps here, by this village, they greeted different, Crossdogs considered. Sapwood stepped towards him. Crossdogs held his ground.

"This is Ludditch, not Brunt Boggart. You don't belong here. What you come for? Can you fight?" Sapwood demanded as he took another step closer, staring at Crossdogs.

Crossdogs stared back. Sapwood looked strong as him and stronger, yet not so strong at all. He was lithe, but scrawny and thin. His eyes flicked quick as a rat's.

"Can fight," Crossdogs countered evenly. "Can fight Bullbreath and Hamsparrow and Longskull. Could fight Oakum Marlroot if'n I had to."

"Don't know none of 'em," Sapwood said and took one step closer. They stood there now, toe to toe. They breathed each other's breath. Could sense each other's sinews tensing. A lone dog howled away in the trees by the smoke where the village must be.

"Don't know none of 'em," Sapwood repeated. "But I know someone'd fight you." He stepped away. Crossdogs followed, curious, not a-feared, but hungry true and true. Followed Sapwood through a gap in the trees where the path wandered blindly, grown thick with nettles and scagging brambles. Sapwood pushed back a low-hanging branch. The leaves blocked Crossdogs' view for a moment, but then he stepped out into a straggle of cottages more near like huts stood in a squint-eyed circle around a green which was not green at all but a rut of dull mud.

"This been Ludditch," Sapwood told him.

The houses were squat and scowling. Roofs hung thick with moss and the eaves leered low while out from each window peered eyes that had never seen Crossdogs before. Skinny urchins stepped forward to stand in the doorways and behind them old crones glowered from the shadows. From around sunless corners and out of dank gullies, tall men shuffled with fists big as hams. All of them staring at Crossdogs as he stood beside Sapwood - staring as if he was Wolf or some other wild creature fetched in from the woods.

Crossdogs stared back and stood his ground, clenching his fists the way his stomach was clutching from lack of food and trying not to let any of them see the way his legs were shaking, not with fear but through hunger and cold.

"Who be this?" One old'un stepped forward, poking at Crossdogs with a finger long and bony.

"Be Crossdogs," Sapwood explained. "Found him out there, up by the Pedlar Man's Track. Says he's a fighter."

"So why don't you fight him then, Sapwood my lad?"

"Says he's a great fighter. Fought plenty and more, back in Brunt Boggart."

Another of the old'uns spat on the ground at the mention of the name.

"Didn't want to spoil the sport," Sapwood continued. "Thought as should be Scrunt who fights him. Same as he's fought all the great fighters before."

The old'uns nodded. There was a hush and then a mutter ran through the crowd, repeating the name again and again.

"Scrunt... Scrunt... *Scrunt*!" till the sound became a chant and then a thunderous roar.

Crossdogs' eyes darted round. He tensed his muscles, clenched his fists. Where was this champion they were calling for? The crowd gathered round, in their broken hats and skanky coats, old'uns drawing tatted shawls around their shoulders, grinning and whistling through blackened teeth. Crossdogs was alone in the middle now, his boots slithering and sliding in the slippery mud. But where was Scrunt? Crossdogs peered around again, dizzied by the surge of faces.

And there he was, Scrunt. Not tall as he'd imagined. Not lithe and firm of muscle, but a squat old man with a gap in his teeth and a squint in his eye, stripped to the waist and circling Crossdogs around and around. Crossdogs made to shake his hand but Scrunt slapped it aside, spat on the ground and lunged. Crossdogs' breath was knocked from his guts. The old man was stronger than he expected and stronger still again.

They locked arms as Crossdogs dug in his heels, the hunger and the weariness forgotten now as he felt his limbs filled with the fire of the fight. Scrunt shoved, heavy and stubborn as a boar. Crossdogs shut his eyes, determined, as his feet wrestled to fix in the slip of the mud. Scrunt grunted and groaned. Crossdogs looked down. Not a man at all but was a boar, sure as sure. Crossdogs felt the hot breath, the rasp of his tusks - and sprang back. But the boar had gone. Crossdogs switched around. Must be man again. He could take him now. Soon he would tire, soon as soon. Was an old man after all and Crossdogs was young. But where had he gone?

The crowd were chanting on. Their voices grew louder as dark rain lashed down.

"Scrunt... Scrunt... *Scrunt...*"

The mud was sliding under his feet. But Scrunt, he had gone. In his place stood a fox. Crossdogs sprang forward. Had fought fox before, out in the woods. Grabbed at the shivering body, the brush of the tail. But Scrunt was gone again.

"Who'm I fighting now?" Crossdogs brayed, clenching his fists and staring up to the sky as the rain raked his face and the voices of the crowd roared on.

"Scrunt, Scrunt, Scrunt, Scrunt..." like as if they

were pigs.

Crossdogs caught sight of Sapwood, the lad who had brought him here, watching from the shadows, cunning and sly. Crossdogs wished he could drag him out, pitch against *him* in this ring. Least be a fair fight. Same height and age. Not this old man who was not man at all but kept on changing. What was he now? Crossdogs turned round.

There stood a young man he knew and did not know at all. Not Sapwood - he was still slinking behind the old'uns round the edges of the crowd. No - this one's hair was matted, his shirt ripped and torn, his boots bent and broken, just as Crossdogs' own. Crossdogs latched on to him, scuffling and scurrying.

"Got you now," he said. "You'll not move this time. You'll not shape-shift and fly. Now I find who you truly are, I can hold you and match you. We'll see now who'll win!"

They locked hard and tight like two brothers in battle who'd grown up together and hated and loved the same as the same. Their faces pressed close as they wrestled and slithered, their dark eyes staring wildly, one into the other.

"Scrunt!" the crowd exclaimed.

Crossdogs pulled back.

"Don't believe'em no more. Just tell me your name."

The other pulled back the same, shaking and breathless. He pushed the hair away from his face so Crossdogs could see him.

"You know me," he whispered. "I'm Crossdogs. Same as you."

What could Crossdogs do? He matched himself strength for strength, grip for grip. Every move he made he already knew. When the other Crossdogs stumbled, then so did he. When the other Crossdogs tripped, then he tripped too. He could not win. He could not lose. What to do?

Crossdogs drew breath. His leg bent beneath him, same as it always did. Never let anyone know when he was fighting, but his left leg was his weak leg. Always had been since he fell from the branch of an apple tree where he'd been scrumping when he was a boy. Bullbreath had nearly beat him once when he'd kicked him there, but Crossdogs had fought back. Now he fought back again in the slip of the rain. Caught the other Crossdogs full force on *his* left leg. Knew that if he be Crossdogs true, then he would surely fall. But other Crossdogs just shook it off. Now Crossdogs knew, this could never be him.

"Tell me true," Crossdogs gnawed the words into the other's ear. "What be your name?"

But Crossdogs stepped back as Crossdogs stepped back and then slowly grinned and offered a hand, and as they shook, Crossdogs felt his own hand in his own, but then was not a hand, was fox and then was no fox but boar, breath hot as hot, then was Scrunt and the crowd was cheering. Crossdogs drew himself up as tall as tall and Scrunt embraced him again. Could taste his breath, could feel the pain of the fight as the hunger coursed back and his knee felt to buckle, to fold into the mud. But he held on to Scrunt, as Scrunt grinned up at him.

Then was not Scrunt no more but other Crossdogs again. And this other Crossdogs cast him down to the ground as the crowd roared and cheered. *"Scrunt... Scrunt..."* calling his name. Crossdogs looked up from the mud. He had lost. He knew that. First fight in his life. He shook his head and watched as the villagers carried their champion away. Was not Scrunt had defeated him, he reckoned. Scrunt could not do it. Boar could not do it. Fox could not do it. Only Crossdogs. None but himself. How could he win? How could he lose?

His eyes wheeled wildly around, picking out Sapwood standing there. The scrawny lad nodded.

"You said you could fight," he accused.

"Should have said *I want food*," Crossdogs replied, scraping lank hair from his face as he glanced this way and that over his shoulder.

"Could have won if I wasn't so hungry!"

"We can give you food," Sapwood told him. "Eat, drink - then I take you to the Track. But no going back. Put Brunt Boggart behind you. Scrunt guards the place where the paths cross. He'll not let you return."

Crossdogs shook his head and drank deep from the bottle which one of the old'uns held out to him. His head was spinning but he could hear voices far off. Greychild was calling him and Ravenhair too. He could hear them on the wind. As Sapwood led him away up the path through the trees, Crossdogs turned once to look back at Ludditch, at the ring of squat cottages. In the centre of the circle of dull trodden mud stood a young man with lank hair, his shirt torn from fighting, watching him go.

THE SISTER IN THE WATER

Let me tell you... Let me tell you about Aylsa. Her hair was dark as Ravenhair's - remember now I've told you. Aylsa lived alone and alone in a cottage all huddled up under the hills. Each morning she would wake and walk among the briar bushes, gathering the strands of wool that she found snagged on the teeth of the thorns. At night she would wash this wool in a bucket, rinse it and swill it in the cool clear water, comb it and twist it betwixt her long fingers. Then she'd sit by the light of the lingering moon, hunched over her spinning wheel and reel out fine lines of plaited wool.

And the lines she would twist onto tall wooden cones and wait for the women to come from the cottages all around to buy what wool she could sell them - that they might weave and knit the garments they needed for their daughters and sons to keep them warm as they worked in the fields or followed the sheep up over the hills.

Who taught her to spin? Why, Aylsa had a sister tall, born full ten years before her. And this sister taught her to gather, this sister taught her to spin. This sister would travel over hilltops far and wide to bring the snagged wool in. But one day, when Aylsa was still only a young'un small, this sister went down to the river to bathe, took off her dress that was mossy green and sewn all over with silver stars - slipped into the water and swam. She swam out into the river, but she never came back again.

Now day by day in the late afternoon, when the morning's gathering was done, Aylsa would pull on her sister's dress, all mossy green and sewn with stars - and walk where her sister had walked before, all down to the river and the bridge's cold stone. There she would sit alone in the shadow, gazing into the deep, dark water, and this is the song that she sang:

"Spin me a song,
Oh sister dear -
Spin me a sister's song.

　　The willows hang dark
　　And the willows hang low
　　Down by the bank
　　Where the tall rushes grow.

Spin me a song,
Oh sister dear -
Spin me a sister's song.

　　The willows hang dark
　　And the willows hang low,

262

For the nights they are long
And the days are so slow -
Oh spin me a sister's song."

When she'd done with her singing, Aylsa stared deep into the water. There she saw her sister's face gazing back at her. Now you know and I know, this must have been her own face reflected by the sun. But Aylsa could not guess this, for she lived all alone and had not looked on her own face since the day her sister left. Ten years had passed since that day and Aylsa had grown to look like her sister in each and every way. But she would gaze at her sister's face watching from the water and wish as strong as the sky was clear that she could swim there with her. But she knew that she could not and she knew that she should not, for much as she longed to plunge into her sister's arms, she knew that the river might take her.

But had the river taken her sister, or did she just swim away? No-one ever found her, though Aylsa had asked all the old'uns who came to buy her wool and she'd asked all the young men who came there fishing, but never a glimpse had they seen. Mayhap she'd grown tired of the spinning, or mayhap she'd found her a sweetheart, beyond the far bend of the river. So Aylsa stared at the water and she watched and she waited and she wondered.

But day by day as she sat under the echo of the bridge, Aylsa came to realise that there was a young man there watching her. And who was this young man? - you might well ask. Listen, and I'll tell you. This young man's name was Scillow and he lived up over the hill. And what did he do, all the day till the night?

Why, he followed the sheep if they strayed out of sight. His dog Callum ran to his whistles and calls, scrambling up through the bracken and down to the fields, nuzzling and nipping at the laggers and strays till Scillow's small flock was safe in the pen.

From the top of the hill, Scillow would watch come late afternoon as Aylsa walked down to the bridge to sit there peering at her sister's face that she thought she saw in the water. Scillow would watch her and then he would listen, as she raised her voice high in song:

> "The willows hang dark
> And the willows hang low,
> For the nights they are long
> And the days are so slow -
> Oh spin me a sister's song."

Each day Scillow sat and listened as her singing echoed up to the top of the hill. For Scillow he was lonely too - he had lost his brothers three all up in the mists of the mountain when the cold wind came calling. He longed to run down and sit there beside her, to take her hand in his and join her in her song. But the sky held him back, and the sheep's call and the gorse brambles - and his dog Callum, who sat beside him and watched with an eye cocked to every move he made. But then one day he left his sheep behind him, and with his heart bursting and bounding he sped sliding and scrambling all down the long dirt track.

Dog Callum followed after, in one mind and two, yapping around his master and racing up to the sheep and back, till in the end they were too far away and grazing contented at the top of the hill. And so Callum stuck close by Scillow's side as they came down to the path to the bridge where Aylsa sat singing.

Scillow paused. He was breathless and his brow full beaded with sweat. What could he say now he'd come all this way? He looked at the girl, hoping she'd see him, hoping she'd turn and ask his name. But Aylsa did nothing, said nothing at all, just stared down more closely at the face in the water and muted her song till she sang in a whisper, all under the shadow of the bridge. And Scillow, what did he do? Scillow did nothing, but just sat and waited and watched.

"When she is finished singing," he muttered to Callum, "that's when I'll walk right up and speak to her."

Callum pricked his ears and listened for the bleat of the sheep on the hillside. Scillow patted his head and waited and waited, but under the bridge, Aylsa sang on. Softer and lower, but still she kept singing. And she did not look up, and she did not turn round, till the sheep called louder from the top of the mountain and dog Callum nipped at his master's ankles and led him away and away up the track.

What of Aylsa? Did she not feel pleased that a young man would climb all down from the hill just to listen to her song? Did she not wish that he would talk to her and ask her to walk along with him? You know that she wished this and you know that she did not, for she thought she never could look so fine as her sister who watched her each day from the water. And so she hid herself away under the echo of the bridge.

The days went by as the tall clouds drifted across the sky and mist rolled over the crags of the mountains. Did Scillow come again to listen to the singing? You know that he did. You know that he left his sheep far behind at the top of the hill - and in the end his dog Callum no longer followed but lay flat-bellied in a hollow, guarding the flock. And did Aylsa wait, wishing that he would come? You know that she did, and you know that she did not. She longed to look as pretty as her sister in the water, so that she might step out boldly in a fine dress to meet him. But some days even her sister did not come. In days of rain when the clouds were grey, she would stay hidden in the dull muddy water, and Aylsa would sing to entice her out from the shadows of the reeds:

"Spin me a song, oh sister dear - Spin me a sister's song."

One fine day when the sun sparkled across the river, the sister in the water came to greet her. Aylsa smiled and her sister smiled too and held out her open arms. As Aylsa leaned forward, her long hair skimmed the surface and then dipped under. She felt as though her sister was tugging her, and so Aylsa lowered her head still further, and began to wash her hair where she knelt. It was as if her sister's long fingers were kneading her scalp, combing out her tresses and stroking her neck, just the way she used to. Aylsa sang, her lips close to the water, as if she was breathing her sister's breath.

Then Aylsa straightened and her hair swung back in an arc of sparkling droplets. She span around, her arms reaching skywards as she pulled her dress up over her head. She folded it carefully and placed it in the shadow under the bridge, before turning and diving into the water. As her arms reached out, so too did her sister's, drawing her in and drawing her down, holding her in a cold embrace - and yet she felt warm as the water caressed her skin. Down she swam and down, deep into darkness, searching for her sister there in the water, wanting to be with her, wanting to become her. Wishing that she could step out of the water looking just as she looked - then she could wait on the bank for Scillow to come down from the hills and listen to her song.

She swam on and on with the current, diving and bobbing with her sister, as if at last she had become her and found her true self there. As she swam she sang, further from the bridge and further, around the bend in the river, until at last she was out of sight. And just at that moment, who should happen along? A girl whose hair was dark as dark. Was not Aylsa, for she was in the water. Was not Aylsa's sister, for she was gone these ten years long. Why no, twas Ravenhair herself, happening along the way.

She rested under the shadow of the bridge and dangled her feet in the cool clear water - and then she spied a dress all folded in the corner, just where Aylsa left it. Ravenhair ran her hands across the cloth, all mossy green and patterned with stars shining silvery bright - finer by far than her own drab smock which hung dull and dusty from her journey. She picked it up and held it to her, swinging it first this way and then again the other.

"Who could have gone off and left such a fine dress behind?" Ravenhair pondered as she glanced about to left and to right. Nobody else was anywhere in sight and so Ravenhair slipped from her own garment and left it bundled up in the corner while she bathed herself in the river. When she was done, she took a fancy to pull on the dress of moss green and silver that Aylsa had left there. The dress felt fresh, the dress felt fine and

Ravenhair knew she could walk a road and another road more before the moon began to shine.

But what of Aylsa? Aylsa was swimming alone in the river, singing to the sun and the skylarks and the willows as though she was her very sister that she had always wanted to be. Soon enough and soon she began to feel hungry, and she ducked and she swept through the cool clear current all the way back to the bridge. There she hauled herself up onto the bank and stood as water trickled in rivulets from the strands of her long black hair.

Aylsa looked this way and Aylsa looked that, but the fine long dress of mossy green was nowhere to be seen. And then at last she spied Ravenhair's smock, all dull and dusty and crumpled in a bundle underneath the shadow of the bridge. Aylsa gasped as her song trailed away. This weary garment was not hers at all, but her own dress was gone and she had nothing else to wear - and so she shook the droplets from her body and pulled Ravenhair's dusty smock up and over her head.

The cloth was coarse. It hung heavy and awkward and she could feel the weight of the miles it had walked dragging her shoulders down.

"Whose dress could this be?" Aylsa wondered, though she had little choice but to wear it - and set off along the path to the house where she lived with her spinning wheel all alone.

All alone and alone, Ravenhair wandered on along the track, wearing Aylsa's dress sewn with silver and green. Before too long she met a man who stood in the dust at the side of the road, watching every step she took as she came closer to him. Soon enough and soon she was stood by his side. Ravenhair smiled at him, for she was wont to smile at anyone she met along the way.

Scillow, for I know that you know it was him, looked surprised, for the girl with the long dark hair that he knew, who wore a dress all mossy green, had never smiled at him before. At first he stood and gawped at her, but then he returned her smile.

"How do you fare?" Ravenhair enquired, and was puzzled when Scillow just stared - for how could she know that he'd waited so long for a girl in this very dress to walk by this way. And now here she stood, all close by his side speaking to him as plain as the day - and his mouth opened wide, but no words could he find for this girlen he took to be Aylsa.

Ravenhair laughed and shook her head and then Scillow laughed too.

"What is your name?" asked Ravenhair. "And tell me - what do you do?"

"I'm Scillow," his tongue stumbled. "And I keep sheep - there up on the hill so high."

He pointed, and Ravenhair looked, up to where the sky met the peaks of the hills, with a flock of white clouds all sat at the top.

"Why, your sheep are so big they block out the sun!" Ravenhair exclaimed and laughed again and Scillow laughed too and told her everything he knew about Callum his dog and how to read the wind and the way that his flock would get lost and then find themselves again, all up in the mist and the dew.

Ravenhair smiled and listened.

"And tell me," Scillow asked her, "what do you do? For I see you each day there under the bridge, all alone and alone."

Ravenhair frowned.

"I'm travelling to Arleccra to find Greychild," she told him, "all along the Pedlar Man's Track. I have never come to this bridge before."

Scillow scratched his head. "How could this be?" he wondered.

"Sing me," he said, "the song you always sing, when I see you each day there beside the water."

Ravenhair frowned again.

"I know many songs," she said. "I know the song that Greychild taught us, that his mother sang to him:

> Coddle me, coddle me,
> My darling son.
> I'm leaving you here
> Till the crying is done..."

Scillow listened but then shook his head.

"No - that's not the one," he said.

Ravenhair's eyes lit up and she flipped her fingers as she sang:

> "Tie me a ribbon -
> I'll wear it so well;
> It will whisper me secrets
> That I'll never tell..."

Scillow rubbed his eyes. Ravenhair's voice was hushed to a whisper. But then he shook his head.

"No - that's not the one," he said. "The song I remember is a sister's song, where the willows hang low - down by the bank where the tall rushes grow."

Ravenhair shrugged and then she turned away.

"I have no sister," she said. "And I must take me now to Arleccra, for the way is long and long."

"Won't you stay and sing me just one more song?" Scillow pleaded with her, hoping she would remember what Aylsa sang, though he could hear his dog Callum calling for him, high up on the hill.

Ravenhair tossed her long dark tresses and threw back her head and sang -

*"There was a girl who had a man, his name it was Tom Tattifer...*but I do not know the song you crave - and now I must truly go before darkness falls."

"When will I see you again?" Scillow asked.

"The road is fickle and the road is strange," Ravenhair replied. "Who ever knows who any of us will meet all along the way?"

She smiled and kissed Scillow lightly on the side of his face and then was gone around the bend in the track. Scillow stood puzzled, staring after her. For so long he had waited for the girl in the green dress sewed with silver stars to speak one word to him. Now all at once she had tarried with him, had laughed with him, had sung for him - though ne'ery the song that he'd heard her sing so often. Scillow touched his cheek. She had kissed him. He could still feel the soft moist breath of her lips - but the girl herself had gone.

Scillow trudged slowly back up the hill, gazing down at the fields spread out below, and way in the distance a river winding on its journey to the sea. He scrambled through bracken and the coarse grip of gorse, his boots knocking loose small flurries of stones, until he reached the top. Dog Callum came running, yapping at his ankles, leaping up in greeting and then lying flat, belly low to the ground. Scillow followed where the dog's nose pointed, across the bare hilltop to the towering sky.

"Where are my sheep?" Scillow asked as Callum ran off and then tracked back, tacking through the heather to be sure Scillow followed him. But the sheep were gone. "What have I done?" Scillow moaned. "Been spending all my days waiting for this girl - now this very day she's kissed me soft upon my cheek - why this is the same day I've lost her and all my sheep are gone as well!"

Scillow sat on the hilltop with dog Callum close beside him. Down below on a bend in the road, far away and far, there he spied a girl in a green dress walking, but all around him on the windswept hills his sheep were nowhere to be seen.

Ravenhair walked on and on until she came to a leafy lane. There, standing at the corner as if she had been waiting, stood Aylsa wearing a dull and dusty smock. Each girlen stopped and looked at the other, both with their hair all shiny and black - remember how I told you?

Aylsa stared at the green robe sewed with silver stars that was draped over Ravenhair's shoulders. Ravenhair paused. What could she say? What should she say? She knew that this dress was not her own, but belonged to this other girl standing before her. She wanted to see what the stranger would say. Would she throw out a challenge or call her 'Thief!'? - though Ravenhair did not steal the dress but only find it true, lying where Aylsa had left it under the shadow of the bridge.

But instead Aylsa said nothing of this. Her eyes

opened wide with wonder.

"Oh my sister!" she cried. "You have come back to me after ten long years. Where have you been? Did you not hear me singing every afternoon? –

> Spin me a song,
> Oh sister dear -
> Spin me a sister's song.

>> The willows hang dark
>> And the willows hang low
>> Down by the bank
>> Where the tall rushes grow -
>> Oh spin me a sister's song."

Ravenhair shook her head.

"I am not your sister, but a traveller down from the hills. My smock, that you wear now, was ragged, bedraggled and torn. Under the shadow of the bridge, I took up this dress all moss green and silver - though I meant to do no harm. But I am Ravenhair, come from Brunt Boggart - I can never be your sister who is gone."

The girlen stared at each other. Aylsa embraced Ravenhair and wept - then they exchanged their garments again before Ravenhair journeyed on.

But what of Scillow's sheep? I know what you're asking. They were lost on the hillside, no matter how long he searched. On he trudged and on with dog Callum running before him as he called each one by name. Scillow's eyes were weary, but still he kept calling, until at last he saw them, way off on another hillside. So on he walked and on again until he came close up to them. And then he saw was not his sheep at all but only wisps of cloud blowing ghostly across the heather. Then Callum howled a wretched howl from deep inside his belly and ran on headlong towards the cloud while Scillow followed after. As he drew close and closer still he saw it was not clouds at all but his brothers three who were lost up on the mountain when the cold winds came wailing. Now they were walking towards him, their faces wreathed in smiles of greeting. Scillow flung his arms out wide as he was about to embrace them and Callum barked and shook his tail and chased on all around them. But then the mist swirled and Scillow blinked and was just cloud again. Only cloud, not even sheep - and he lay down weary in a hollow on the hilltop and there he fell to sleep.

In the morning he was woken early by something soft and warm licking around his face. He opened up his eyes full wide and there stood dog Callum panting above him, whimpering and calling, running this way and that. Scillow sat up and watched where his dog was fetching. He followed him, stumbling on through mountain dew, up a track and down a track until he heard what Callum had heard right from the morning's dawning - the call of his sheep all lost and bedraggled, clustered about in the shelter of a gully.

And then he ran and then he sang and called them all by name. He flung his arms about them, buried his nose in the wet smell of their fleeces - then ran his frozen fingers through their greasy matted coats in the cold biting wind. The sheep stuck close by him all the next day as their shadows grew short then lengthened again. They clustered around him through the frets of pale mist, then trailed his sure steps through sunshine and rain.

So that when another day and another day on, Scillow found himself all down by the track, then his sheep were gathered with him and dog Callum too. But in the distance Scillow saw a girlen in a green dress all picked out in silver, walking towards him. Scillow scratched his head, for he thought this girl had gone, but now here she was come back again and stepping towards him down the dust of the track, picking bright-eyed buttercups as she tripped this way and that.

Scillow approached her with a spring in his step, knowing that now he had spoken once with this girl, why then he had the courage to speak with her again.

"Good day!" he cried. "How do you fare?"

He stepped up to greet her, leaving his sheep by the side of the road, though dog Callum was with him, close at his heels.

Aylsa, for of course it was her - Aylsa looked startled and turned her head away, but Scillow just laughed as if she played a game.

"Come, you remember me," he said. "Are you footsore and weary and come back again?"

He danced around her, but the girl turned away and Callum began barking. Scillow reached out and touched Aylsa on the hand.

"Soft," he chided, comforting. "I did not mean no harm. But sing me again those songs you sang before... 'Coddle Me, Coddle Me', 'Tie me a ribbon' and 'Tom Tattifer' - the one that I liked best of all."

Aylsa looked puzzled.

"I know only one song," she said. "And I know that you know it too - for I see you listening every afternoon."

"Then sing it to me now," Scillow begged her, and Aylsa began:

> "Spin me a song,
> Oh sister dear -
> Spin me a sister's song.
>
> > The willows hang dark
> > And the willows hang low
> > Down by the bank
> > Where the tall rushes grow -
> > Oh spin me a sister's song."

As Aylsa's voice soared higher, Scillow took her by the hand and they walked away from the river and the bridge, up the winding path that led them to the hills, where Aylsa could gather all the wool that she liked, just as her sister had done before, while dog Callum and his flock of sheep followed on close behind.

But soon as they had gone so far up into the hills that they were only specks as small as flowers up among the lowering cloud, then beneath the echo of the bridge came a ripple in the water - and out stepped the figure of a woman who had been swimming there, her dark hair plastered wet all down around her shoulders. And so she walked away, singing sweet and long:

> "Spin me a song,
> Oh sister dear -
> Spin me a sister's song..."

And all around the corner, who there did she meet but three brothers lost, come down from the mountain

where the cold winds blew - and they sang there
together till the sun began to set:

> "The willows hang dark
> And the willows hang low
> Down by the bank
> Where the tall rushes grow...."

THE HOUSE OF THE SEA

Let me tell you... Let me tell you... Ravenhair's shoes were broken and worn with walking all the way from Brunt Boggart. She pulled them off and set them down on the grass beside her. There to her surprise, she saw another pair under a stone. They were covered all over with gold brocade and laced with crimson flowers. She looked around, but there was no-one else in sight. Not even a house, nor a cottage, nor a farm anywhere that she could see - only the strong copper beech trees and a carpet of moss that lay soft and neat.

Ravenhair wriggled her toes and rubbed the soles of her aching feet - then she slipped her old shoes under the stone and looked around again. There was still nobody else in sight and so she slid the golden shoes with the crimson flowers onto her own weary feet. The shoes were soft, the shoes were light, not like any shoes she'd ever seen before. Ravenhair stood up and straight away her feet were walking on air. She felt as if she had no cares as she took a step and a trip and a skip and found herself dancing around and around, prancing so lightly she scarce touched the ground.

As the shoes danced, Ravenhair danced with them. They took her this way, they took her that, leading her along a winding track through the trees to where the grass was a cushion of tussocks, soft beneath her feet. The shoes skipped and turned as if they tripped to a music whirling round them in the wind. Ravenhair clapped her hands, keeping time to the rhythm.

When she opened her eyes again, she was standing at the door of a house, but not a house at all, more like the hulk of a huge rotting boat, thrown here miles from the sea. Ravenhair looked up. Where the chimney might be rose a mast and rigging. Her legs were weary and she wanted to rest, but the golden shoes kept on dancing, right there at the door. She grasped at the knocker and lifted it up, then brought it down like a hammer upon an anvil.

There was a clatter of birds from the rigging above as they scattered off into the trees. As Ravenhair looked down, her feet danced on and she could feel a trembling in her knees. She grasped the knocker again and brought it down once more. On her third stroke there was a creaking, and the door opened just a crack. Ravenhair reached out to grip the wall, but the shoes danced faster and faster still as the door swung open and there before her stood a tall stooped man. His eyes stared out before him, but he seemed to gaze beyond Ravenhair, as if he was searching the sky.

"Who is there?" he asked. His voice was as dark as the waters where the House of the Sea must have sailed. As he turned to reach towards her, his hand brushed against her hair.

"Your tangled tresses are longer now. Are you come back again?"

Ravenhair hesitated.

"Come to me," he commanded, in a voice both kind and strong. "You know me true - I am Karroc. I am here always, I am always here. This is my ship though I sail no more. This is my cradle, my house, my shroud. Dance with me and tell me your dreams."

Karroc held her, softly, gently. He stilled the rhythm of her frantic feet, till she could feel the pulse of the ocean as they danced like birds who skim the water, barely touching as they wheeled and turned. They swirled and they whirled all outside the door and in. Into the shadows, into the belly of the ship which was heavy with mould and rust. Ravenhair clung dizzily as Karroc danced, her head spinning as they swung waist-to-waist, hip-to-hip.

And then they stopped. Karroc led her step by step and Ravenhair walked close by his side as the shoes had finished their dancing. Inside, the walls were moss-covered planks, lined with pitch but dark and damp. From hooks and nails hung robes and shawls, woven with pictures of cities and deserts such as Ravenhair had never seen. On shelves and cabinets stood treasures and trinkets all corked up in bottles. Karroc reached to touch one.

"Tell me what you see," he instructed.

Ravenhair took the bottle. "I see a mountain with a tongue of fire. I see a tree whose fruit burns bright as lanterns. I see flowers dancing in hidden caverns, their petals twined tight with desire."

Karroc was thrilled and held Ravenhair closer.

"I need your eyes," he said. "Today you see more clearly than ever." He shook his head, as if suddenly not certain who Ravenhair was after all. "It is as though you had never seen these treasures before, these relics I brought from far-off lands when I sailed out from Arleccra."

"How far to Arleccra?" Ravenhair asked.

Karroc pointed vaguely.

"Arleccra is beyond and beyond, and then beyond again. From there I have sailed for a hundred days and a hundred days more, through storm and wind and hail, until I came to a shore where creatures sported such as no man had ever seen before. Their eyes glowed bright as burning coals, their backs were hard as polished horn, yet their bellies were smooth as babies' milk and their long tongues licked soft as a mother's breast.

"I have been to where the bear was born who dances now on Arleccra's quay - to caves to the north of the west wind's mouth, in a land of ice and blood, where pale birds circle the sullen sky as they sing with voices pure as snow.

"I have danced with girls in forests dark who were not girls at all but the daughters of sinuous serpents, writhing to the rhythm of the sea. This is the dance which they taught me - hold closer and follow my steps."

And so Ravenhair held close and they danced again - but this time it was Karroc's lead she followed, and not the golden shoes. They danced through a chamber of wind and rain that came from a far-off land. They danced through a chamber of scorching sun that beat down onto burning sand. And then they stood in a room of blue light which was filled with a lapping sound and the call of wheeling gulls. Karroc reached out and touched a finger to Ravenhair's lips, and then he kissed her, sweet as cinnamon, gentle as jasmine and wild as wine. She could feel the dark fingers of the ocean knotting and unknotting inside her and then she crumpled down onto an embroidered cushion and fell into a long deep sleep.

As she slept, the shoes danced on, all the way across hill and stream until she came to Arleccra. And there she saw the market stalls with silken scarves and hand-sewn shawls. There she saw the dancing bear and pale-faced girls slipping through the shadows of the alley ways. She flitted quick from stall to stall, touching, tasting, trying. And following her all the way was Karroc, indulging her in dresses and ear-rings, shifts and skirts and a purple scarf all edged with silver to wrap around her hair. Whatever she asked for, he would buy, even though she knew that he could see none of them. But each time she reached up to kiss him, to show her gratitude, then Karroc turned away. And yet whatever she wanted, he bought her - and still she asked for more, until she had so much she could not carry it all. She looked around for Karroc then, to beg him to help her to bear all his gifts, but he was nowhere to be seen. Ravenhair dropped the pile of treasures in a useless heap between the stalls. Where had Karroc gone? She chased his shadow through the throng, but none of them seemed to see her as she ran, as she stumbled, as she fell...

...as she woke in the room of blue light, lying on the cushion where Karroc had left her. She looked around eagerly, knowing that he must be here. But no, though she searched through every room, Karroc had gone. She felt the shoes of gold brocade tugging at her feet again. Ravenhair let them lead her, just as they had before, hoping they would help her to find the man who had bought her so many gifts, and yet no gifts at all.

She danced and danced from the House of the Sea out into a shadowy garden, dark as the ocean and darker still. There she circled, step and toe, around black roses with silvered thorns, across the tide of a moonlit lawn. Ravenhair caught her breath as she whirled, as she twirled. She could hear a voice singing, soft and low.

"If I am you and you are me,
Where is the man that makes us three?"

The sound came from far away. Where was the girl who sang so sweet? Ravenhair peered all around. Was she behind the apple tree whose fruit glistened pale in the darkness?

"If you are me and I am you,
Where is the man that makes us two?"

As Ravenhair grew closer, the voice flitted off, deep into the bushes of blood-red berries.

"If yours is the voice that is singing my song,
Where is the man that makes us one?"

Ravenhair dragged the brambles aside, expecting to find a girl. But no-one was there, the singing had gone - then it returned, closer than ever before, as if the voice was singing inside her head. Her tongue moved without bidding, carrying the tune, extending the melody, searching out new harmonies. Ravenhair stopped, and the song stopped too, but then came again and this time the other girl stepped out into the moonlight from under a yew tree's brooding shadow. Ravenhair gasped and gazed at her ragged dress, her pale bare feet all twisted and blistered.

"Who are you?" Ravenhair asked, but the girl gave no reply, save to sing the song again:

> "If I am you and you are me,
> Where is the man that makes us three?
>
> If you are me and I am you,
> Where is the man that makes us two?
>
> If yours is the voice that is singing my song,
> Where is the man that makes us one?"

Ravenhair tried to join in, but no sound would come from her own lips all the while the girl was singing. When the song was done, the two girls stood facing each other. But the other girl said nothing, only stared at her, and began her song again. And as she sang, the golden shoes on Ravenhair's feet shuffled and span, dancing once more in twisting spirals, closer to the girl and closer still, all around her and around as she sang on and on. They danced so close their hair was twined and their arms were wrapped around each other as they whirled faster and faster still, until in a swirling blur they flew - and far below was the garden which spread dark around the House of the Sea. And there on the step stood Karroc. He was peering blindly up towards the stars through the eye of a tarnished brass telescope, as if he might be watching the girls as they flew away and away.

They flew beyond the trees and back along the path which led to the Pedlar Man's Track. As they drifted down slowly, Ravenhair felt the girl's body shivering and cold. They landed soft beside the stone where Ravenhair had found the shoes.

She wrapped her coat around the girl's shoulders. The girl met her eyes, then looked away - and there she saw, beneath the stone, the shoes which Ravenhair had discarded. Ravenhair bent down and let her long dark tresses spill around the girl's twisted blistered feet. She smoothed and rubbed and caressed, as if she was washing them in a darkness of milk. The girl stood up and smiled, then suddenly grabbed at the old shoes which were still lying there, seeming pleased of anything to wear. Ravenhair felt glad to have made a gift to this stranger, but then the gold brocade slippers on her feet started to quiver and twitch.

"Stop!" she cried to the girl, who had begun to walk away. "Are these *your* shoes?"

The girl turned around.

"Those shoes you are wearing are mine," Ravenhair explained. "Broken as they might be, they have brought me here, all the way from Brunt Boggart."

Ravenhair pulled off the gold slippers before they could start to dance again.

"*These* shoes are soft and beautiful, but they will take me nowhere at all - except dancing away from the Track. I must walk to Arleccra in my own old shoes, every step of the way."

She unlaced the slippers of crimson and gold and held them out to the girl.

"*These* are the shoes that will take you home - back to the House of the Sea."

Ravenhair tugged on her own worn-out shoes while the girl tucked her feet into the slippers of gold brocade, which started dancing right away. She waved to Ravenhair as she twirled to the bend in the track that led all the way back to the House. But as she did, her tattered dress turned to sinuous snakeskin as she writhed to the rhythm of the sea. And there by her side stood Karroc, with his telescope under his arm. He seemed younger now than he had before, and fixed Ravenhair with a curious stare as he danced away with the girl.

THE BLUE CROW

Let me tell you... let me tell you how Crossdogs heard the sound of a baby crying as he walked on down the lane. He turned the corner and another corner and there he saw a girlen walking towards him, pushing a hand-cart cluttered with baubles and gaudied all over with painted flowers.

Crossdogs came closer and peered at the mother who bent down to coo and to fuss at the bundle in the cart who kept crying louder than ever. The girlen smiled at Crossdogs, her face all flustered - and he stepped in to look close at the child to see what the crying was for. He was about to tell the mother how fine her baby looked, for he knew that the girlen liked that all back in Brunt Boggart - but as he leant in, to his surprise twas not a child at all but a sharp-beaked crow, its feathers a rich shade of blue.

Crossdogs stepped back, not sure what to say. The mother, whose name was Downfeathers, stared straight at him in a most puzzlesome way. But then before either of them could speak, the blue crow flapped its wings with a clatter and flew clean away. Downfeathers wept and wailed for her child, who sat squat on the branch of a tree, stropping its beak and cawing raucously.

"What am I to do?" she cried. "What am I to do? - I have lost my only child."

Crossdogs scratched his head.

"Wait there," he said - and left Downfeathers alone in the lane, clutching the handle of the bright-coloured cart. He ran to the tree and gripped and grappled at the hollowed out knots until he hauled himself near to the top. The crow sat and watched him as he clambered to the end of the branch. As he reached out to grab at the bird, the crow tilted back its head, crying like a child. And then it spread its wings and with one slow flap, flew away.

Crossdogs scrambled back down and set off at a run, tacking and twisting across the fields as he followed the bird. He could hear its cry, the cry of a child, echoing back to him. Crossdogs paused and bent down to catch his breath. His head was spinning but he could still see Downfeathers in the lane with her hand-cart gaudied with flowers. He stood up. There was the bird, strutting before him as if it was waiting. Crossdogs reached out but again the bird was away, and Crossdogs after it, stumbling across the uneven stubble until he came to the side of a pond.

The water was brackish and covered in weed. The blue crow sat waiting on a branch on the opposite side, still whimpering and wailing like a baby. Crossdogs set off carefully, bending brambles and branches before him as he crept till he was closer than an arm's-length to the bird. The crow turned its head the other way as Crossdogs reached out, not sudden but slow, then quicker than quick as he grabbed true and firm and gathered the bird into his arms. There it lay whimpering and staring up at him, like as if it was a baby true and not a fowl at all.

Crossdogs carried the bundle gently back over the fields and the criss-crossing tracks till he came to the lane where he'd first met Downfeathers. He thought she'd be waiting there with her hand-cart, but when Crossdogs turned the bend, she was nowhere in sight. He called out, thinking she'd gone on to seek the bird herself - but he heard no reply. She couldn't be far if she still had the cart - but search as he did, Crossdogs could see no sign of her.

As he continued down the lane, the blue crow cried louder, cried out for its mother. Crossdogs cradled it and rocked it and cooed, just as he'd seen his own mother do. But the crying continued, louder and louder till the poor bird was sobbing as true as a child.

"Child wants its mother, not me," he said to himself. "And if I cannot find her, sure it'll find her itself."

He stopped cradling the bird and flung it on upwards, that it might fly free. But the blue crow wheeled round, lost and bewildered, still whimpering and sobbing, till it fluttered back again into Crossdogs' arms.

"What am I to do now?" Crossdogs beseeched the bird. "Got to get to Arleccra. Got to find Greychild. Can't spend all my time minding you. Don't even know what kind of beast you be. Be you crow or be you babe, don't know how to feed you. Fly on! Find your mother or feed yourself!"

But the crow just lay there and gazed up at him till its

lids became heavy soon enough and soon, and then it was sleeping in the crook of Crossdogs' arm.

Crossdogs scraped a nest of straw and placed his new charge to rest there. He peered up and down, watching the bird and watching the road and the fields all around, listening out for any sound. Each time he heard a rustling his ears pricked up, hoping it might be Downfeathers returning, or worried it might be a fox or a stoat come to steal the blue crow away. But as night came, Crossdogs could stay awake no more. He curled himself around the bird and there they slept, wrapped one with other while Crossdogs dreamt of his own mother who fed him porridge from a spoon.

But the blue crow woke him, pecking and nuzzling. At first Crossdogs rolled over but the babe gave him no peace and he had to stumble about in the moon-blighted darkness to find a handful of berries to give his charge to eat. Crow gobbled them all then looked up at him and seemed to smile with contented eyes before slipping into sleep again. But just as Crossdogs fell to sleeping too, the crow was wide awake once more, pecking at Crossdogs to harry him out and collect up a leaf full of early dew. When morning came with the rising sun, Crossdogs felt as though he should be sleeping on, but the crow was awake already, hopping all around him.

"What am I to do with you?" Crossdogs bewailed. Then he set his head all down the road.

"This is the way I have to go," he told the blue crow, who was burbling happily now. "Mayhap your mother has travelled this way too. Mayhap soon we'll catch up with her and I can give you back."

The blue crow squawked and nodded and hopped up on to Crossdogs' shoulder. And so Crossdogs trudged on in the gentle heat of the morning sun. Every now and then he called out after Downfeathers.

"Helloooo," he bellowed lustily. Then *"Helloooo"* sounded back from the hills around.

Twas only the echo of his own voice, but Crossdogs liked to hear it and soon began to sing that song that Ravenhair had sung to him when they'd sat out together, under the stars:

> "... whisper of rivers
> That shine in the sun,
> Carrying tears to the ocean
> When the long day is done."

The blue crow squawked and pecked at Crossdogs' chin. Crossdogs wasn't sure if it was trying to stop him or doing its best to join in.

> "... whisper of mountains
> That rise to the clouds
> And gather the silence
> While the wind blows so loud..." he sang on.

But then from far and far:

> "... *whisper me my true love*
> *Who I've never met...*" came back to him.

Crossdogs stopped and listened. It wasn't the sound of his own voice he heard. The echo had never been that clear. He listened again and the refrain continued:

> "...*But he'll bring me sweet happiness*

I'll never forget..."

pitched higher than his voice and higher.

The crow let out a raucous caw. Crossdogs pinched its beak.
"Hush," he muttered.
The crow looked abashed and shuffled silently on Crossdogs' shoulder.

> *"Tie me a ribbon,*
> *I'll wear it so well..."*

The refrain came again, still closer.
"I know that voice," Crossdogs exclaimed. "Tain't your mother, sure - though where she is I do not know. Your mother would nary know this song. Tis a song from back in Brunt Boggart and only one girlen would ever sing it...

> ... Let me tie you a ribbon,
> You'll wear it so well..."

he sang out full and true.

> *"It will whisper me secrets*
> *That I'll never tell!"*

came back the response.

"Ravenhair!" cried Crossdogs as the girlen from Brunt Boggart with the dark flowing tresses stepped round a bend in the track. The crow flapped its wings and clattered above them.
"Ravenhair!" he cried again and they stood side by

side once more.

Ravenhair's eyes were gleaming, though her feet were sore and weary and her dress turned the colour of dust. They stared at each other a moment long, their minds swept away. Both started to speak together, then stopped, then waited, each catching their breath.

"Went following Greychild," Crossdogs gasped, in answer to a question that had not been asked.

"Came following you!" Ravenhair smiled and they stood awkwardly laughing until they embraced, same as they ever had, under the shadow of the tall trees by the edge of Brunt Boggart's wood. But as they held each other close, Ravenhair felt something scrabbling and pecking between them.

"What's this?" she cried, as Crossdogs eased out the blue crow that had nestled back snugly under his coat.

The bird blinked and opened its beak.

"Ain't never seen a crow so blue before," Ravenhair exclaimed.

Crossdogs shook his head.

"Ain't even no crow, be it blue or no. This be baby, sure."

Ravenhair stepped back.

"Tain't no babe, Crossdogs. Think you been out wandering these roads too long."

But then the crow let out a wail, full-lunged as any baby.

"Oh Crossdogs! You tell true! It *is* a child."

Ravenhair stepped closer and stroked the bird's head.

"Tis child, sure and sure," Crossdogs nodded. "Could be our child Ravenhair, such as we always dreamed."

Ravenhair frowned.

"Don't remember no dream like *that*, Crossdogs my

lad. We be too young for childern. Whatever put that idea in your head? And anyway, this babe must have a mother of its own. How did you find it? Where has she gone?"

"Who knows where she's gone," Crossdogs replied. "Reckon we must find her. Reckon we must tend to this blue crow child best we can until we do."

Ravenhair smiled and stroked the baby's head.

"Best we go then," she said.

"Best we do," Crossdogs agreed.

They trudged on and on, singing the songs they knew from the Green and swapping snatches of tales about all they had done and where they had been.

"Look there!" Crossdogs suddenly exclaimed as over the brow of the hill a figure came straggling.

"Is that her?" said Ravenhair. "Is that the mother of this troublesome crow that pecks at my face and frets at my dress?"

Crossdogs called to the figure who came stumbling and tumbling down over the hill. But there came no reply. Crossdogs shook his head.

"Tis not her, to be sure."

To be sure, the figure approaching was no girlen at all but a man tall as short and short as tall, all dressed up in motley and beating the air with a sheep's bladder tied to the end of a stick. He tumbled right up to them and sprang into their path with a somersault and a bow.

"I walk alone, but not alone. Others follow after me, by one, by two, by three."

Ravenhair looked around, but could see no-one else, just a slack wind whining across the flat muddied fields.

"Where are they?" she asked.

"Look at me and who do you see? You see me - see

Homminy!" The bedraggled figure flapped his hand. His face was caked with flaking paint.

"Yes - but where are the others?" Ravenhair was curious.

"They are here, they are there. We wander in the air like seeds. We scatter and we fall. We crawl through mud like slugs. But we will all rise up again when the hurdy-gurdy plays. Listen, can you hear it now?"

Ravenhair looked away. She could hear nothing more than the wind she heard before. Homminy beat his sheep's bladder on the ground and let out a wail, which woke the blue crow who had fallen asleep, who then let out a scream like a baby. Homminy rushed up to him, pushing his face full close to the creature's head.

"Hush now, little one - don't you cry. There's clouds in the well and flowers in the sky."

Homminy pulled a face and tweaked his ears, but all this just made the crow cry more - until Ravenhair gathered the bird to her and pushed Homminy away.

"Stay back," she said. "Don't you come here all sudden, bothering this child."

"Tain't no bother to me," Homminy replied. "No bother at all. Just bring it to our show tonight, when the stars shine bright in the sky."

Crossdogs eyed Homminy curiously.

"Where will the show be?" he asked.

Homminy rolled his eyes and then flipped over on his back till he stood upon his head.

"Don't rightly know yet," he said. "Have to see what tune we play."

He pulled another face at the blue crow babe and this time the child stopped its wailing and began to chuckle and chortle. Ravenhair turned around, and there over the brow of the hill came a huge brown bear, led on a chain by a short-necked man with a gap-toothed grin.

Homminy spun around on the ground.

"Tis Lumbucket and Hobknockle - the bear and his keeper."

The bear flopped down and laid himself flat on the grass. Ravenhair stepped up closer.

"Can he dance?" she asked.

"Can't dance now," Hobknockle replied. "Been walking all day. In the old days Lumbucket only danced when Marsh Brunning played his hurdy-gurdy."

"Why doesn't he play now?" Ravenhair asked.

Homminy and Hobknockle looked at each other.

"Lost him," Homminy shrugged. "One night after the show our tent burnt down. Nothing left but ashes and dreams. Marsh Brunning walked off into the rain. Never seen him since."

Hobknockle nodded. "We keep on without him. Each time we meet up we wish one and all that this will be the night he'll come back and play again."

Homminy cocked his head.

Ravenhair listened. She could hear nothing. Only the sigh of the wind, a fox way off in the distance and then the raucous cry of the blue crow that she was cradling. Homminy glared at the bird.

"Stop that squawling," he snarled under his breath, but when he saw that Ravenhair was staring at him, he broke into a broad grin and beat his sheep's bladder on the ground, then spun around and turned three handstands.

"Don't cry, little one," he cooed. "Don't cry."

The bear let out a drowsy growl and opened one eye as it lay stretched on the ground.

"Be still," Hobknockle instructed - but more to Homminy than Lumbucket the Bear. "Time enough for cavorting when Marsh Brunning comes. The sky was filled with falling stars last night. Soon enough now, I can feel it. Soon enough."

Ravenhair shivered. She was comforting the crow.

"Let's walk on," she said.

Crossdogs looked at her, wondering whether she was making an excuse to escape from their new companions.

"I'm cold," she explained. "And the baby needs feeding."

But as she walked, they all followed on - Homminy dragging his sheep's bladder along the ground as Hobknockle and Lumbucket lumbered behind, clanking their chain, while on top of the hill in the distance the broken sails of a windmill creaked around and around. A dark flock of birds wheeled above them from beyond the flat horizon.

Then by the side of a tumble-down wall they saw Whisper, his face as pale as ash, his belt hung with kindling sticks and a dull metal tinder-box dangling on a string near down to his knees. He struck the flint, then struck it again. Nothing came but a tiny spark which would not light the wad of oily rag wound tight about a stick which he clenched in his fist.

"Curse this wind," he muttered, his voice rasping and hoarse, his nostrils twitching, discoloured with snuff. "Curse this wind. Never blew like this when Marsh Brunning played his tune."

Lumbucket cocked his ear to one side, as if he was listening, but no sound came. Not any wind and not no hurdy-gurdy either. They gathered themselves together, grunting and muttering, with Crossdogs, Ravenhair and the blue crow babe tagging on behind.

They came in a while to a bend in the road, where leaned a shack with its roof staved in. There stood Slipriver - all willowy and tall on only one leg, tossing painted wooden discs slowly up in the air. First one by one, by two, by three, by four and five. But she dropped them all and they rolled this way and that. She leant down awkwardly, trying to keep her balance.

"Never used to happen," she said, "when Marsh Brunning stood beside me, urging me on with his tune."

She gathered up the discs one by one and slipped them in the pocket of her great black coat.

Then as the moon rose the dishevelled troupe halted in a dark rooted hollow. Slowly, in cracked and broken voices, each began to sing:

> "Which way is the wind
> Who runs with the sun?
> Soon as you find her,
> You know that she's gone.

> Soon as you find her,
> She turns to a stone
> That shrivels to dust
> When the long day is done."

Crossdogs and Ravenhair watched while the blue crow babe slept. There was much fussing and flurrying as a dull crumpled canvas was pegged out on the ground and a flutter of faded banners strung between the trees. Hobknockle began to beat his drum in a steady rhythm while Lumbucket rattled his chain and howled mournfully, as out of the bushes came a scramble of childern, old'uns and mothers who must have heard the commotion from a village nearby. They fell to clapping, singing and laughing while Homminy rolled over and over, tumbling and stumbling, leering at them all with his wild-eyed grin before chasing the childern all about the hollow. They screamed and shrieked as they ran away, wheeling past Ravenhair and almost knocking her over.

"Don't wake the babe!" she protested.

One by one, the troupe stepped forward. Whisper carried a star of twisted twigs, which he placed in the centre of the clearing. Then Slipriver followed, with a star carved from stone which she laid down carefully beside it. Hobknockle pulled a star hammered out of metal from deep in his pocket. And finally Homminy waved a star of plaited rushes and flung it to land beside all the others. As the last notes of the song faded, the crowd of waiting children applauded them, then sat to wait expectantly. The ring of performers looked at each other.

They closed their eyes, listening for the sound of the hurdy-gurdy, listening for the crack of a footstep in the woods. But all they heard was the restless complaining of the waiting children which rose to a hubbub, cursing and calling. "Now he will come," Whisper rasped hoarsely. "The stars are joined."

Slipriver shook her head.

"Not all joined yet. Downfeathers is missing. Marsh Brunning won't come till she is here."

Whisper stepped forward, brandishing his unlit torches, trying in vain to light them again in the breeze which swirled around the clearing. Then he sat down and Slipriver rose, standing elegant and tall on her one slender leg. Out of her hat tipped a cascade of oranges which she began to juggle, tossing them higher, up into the air. But as first she dropped one and then missed another, the children dived forward, seizing them eagerly, tearing off the peel and cramming the juicy segments into their mouths.

Ravenhair clung fast to the blue crow babe who was still asleep on her shoulder, while Lumbucket the Bear rocked this way and that, all the while mauling at the air with his paws, a desolate roar trapped deep in his throat while Hobknockle beat on his drum - but still Marsh Brunning did not come. In between and all around, Homminy roamed with his foolery, beating his bladder-stick upon the ground and bawling lewd jokes in the girlen's ears as he tweaked the little'uns under the chin before blundering away again.

Then they stopped. Ravenhair looked around. The ragged troupe stood in a line and joined hands, as if to take a bow, just as they always had done at the end of any show. But the childern and the old'uns gathered on the mossy bank at the side of the hollow pelted them with the oranges, with turnips and rotten apples.

Lumbucket lunged forward as Hobknockle held him back.

"None of this ever happened back in Marsh Brunning's day," Slipriver whispered.

But then a silence fell as out of the darkness between the trees at the far side of the hollow, there came a woman, young as old, who carried a star that shone so bright it seemed twas made of pure light. She placed the star in the centre of the ring while her companions capered around her. She held out a hand and all were hushed as she began to sing:

"Where is the shadow
That follows the wind?
Who knows where she goes to,
Who sees where she's been?

Soon as you find her
She turns to the sun
Which holds you so tightly
When you are alone."

One by one the troupe joined in, spinning around and around, their voices both harmonious and hoarse, while Lumbucket shuffled and bellowed and Hobknockle took up the rhythm on his drum. Soon as they stopped, a hush fell on the grove. One of the little'uns let out a cough, but his sister clapped a hand across his mouth.

Then out of the dark woods came flurries of moths, a cloud - thicker and thicker, flying all around. The moths turned to butterflies then bright coloured birds all singing, flying faster and faster till they changed to a snow-storm, a blizzard. A blizzard of fire, of thunder, of ice. Then the ice was as swans, their wings spread and wheeling, their long necks pulling as they sped. Ravenhair gasped as they sailed straight towards her, becoming boats with white sails drifting down from the sky. And from the vessels stepped pale-faced children all clapping their hands, though their faces did not smile. They stepped into the hollow that was woodland no more but a quayside and harbour - and there they danced to Hobknockle's drum.

And then they were gone. The blue crow babe in

Ravenhair's arms, who had slept through all the rumpus and commotion, woke up and looked about with a bright beady eye and then opened its beak and let out a cry which was not babe true and not crow neither and the sound it grew louder while the woman in the centre of the ring held out her arms. The bird flew to her and nestled there close at her breast and Crossdogs looked and looked again and saw twas Downfeathers, with her painted cart waiting at the edge of the clearing.

The bird was blue crow no more, but true a babe, crying as only a babe can cry, then chortling and cooing contentedly, nestled in its mother's arms. The childern of the village looked around, wide eyed and puzzled. A rattle of applause rippled around the grove and then they straggled away, leaving Ravenhair and Crossdogs sitting together, watching as the tired troupe gathered up their props and bags, then picked up their stars: the star of twisted twigs, the star hewn out of stone, the star of hammered metal and the star of plaited rushes.

Ravenhair sat beside Downfeathers as she held the star of pure light carefully in her hands.

"Where did you find it?" Ravenhair asked.

"I went back to the field where our tent burnt down, back to where we left our dreams. There on the ground I found this star, burning fierce enough to start a fire. It cooled each day as I kept it, as I carried it, bright enough to light my way. Ever since that day, I had this star - but don't have Marsh Brunning, sure and sure."

"But you have your babe now," Ravenhair said.

Downfeathers frowned, fussing and fidgeting at the bird's flustered feathers.

"Got him right enough," she shrugged. "But still ain't got Marsh Brunning. That's who we wait for. Wait for him to come again. Wait for him to play."

"What happens when he plays?" Ravenhair asked.

Downfeathers squinnied up at her.

"You have to be there," she said. "You have to wait and see."

Then she lay the blue crow babe in the cart of gaudy flowers and pushed him away after the others as they slipped into the silence of the woods.

Ravenhair walked slowly back to Crossdogs and they sat alone underneath the glimmer of the moon.

"The babe is gone," Crossdogs sighed.

"Twas never our babe," Ravenhair reminded him.

"Felt lost when it came," Crossdogs mused. "Didn't know how to tend it. Didn't know what to do... now feel more lost without it, wailing and pecking and wanting its food."

Next day they woke and looked about the hollow. The ground was all trampled and a litter of orange peel strewn all around. Crossdogs rubbed his eyes.

"Come on," he muttered. "There's nothing here now. Need to find our way back to the Track."

But Ravenhair stopped. There at the centre of the clearing five stars were burnt into the grass.

"Come on," Crossdogs called again as he set out to follow a path through the trees.

But Ravenhair paused and bent to pick up one stray blue feather. She stood alone in the centre of the hollow, and then began to sing, as if she could hear a hurdy-gurdy, playing beyond the hills:

> "Which way is the sorrow
> That dwells in the shade?

THE PEDLAR MAN'S TRACK

Who knows where she comes from,
Who sees where she strays?

Soon as you find her,
She laughs like the wind
And hides in the days
Where no-one has been."

THE EDGE OF THE WORLD

Let me tell you. Let me tell you how Crossdogs left
Ravenhair back on the Track and met a man all stooped
and squat with squinnied eyes and his forehead
frowning. On his shoulders he bore a great wooden
yoke and balanced up on top of the yoke was a rickety
chair. In the chair sat a scrawny old woman who called
out every step of the way in a voice that rasped out
harsh as a crow:

"Go this way, go that! Go faster, go slow!"

The man traipsed on, dusty and weary, his brow wet
with sweat from the sun's raging heat. He tottered and
staggered with the weight of the woman and all the
while, beside her cursing voice was the clatter of pans
that she carried in a basket and the racket of the
chickens that sat in the pans. A clucking and squawking
and a laying of eggs that toppled from the pans to
splatter all around the man as he walked.

"Now then!" Crossdogs sang out in greeting as the

man sank to his knees. "Which way are you going and why do you carry that old woman that way?"

"This woman's my mother," the man replied. "Carry her this way and carry her that." He gasped for breath as his fingers dug deep into the damp green grass that grew at the side of the road. But before Crossdogs could say more the mother shrieked out -

"What have we stopped for? Get up, carry on, you lazy good-for-nothing. We have to be there before long and long!"

But the man did not move, he was straight out of breath.

"Have to be where?" Crossdogs asked him, offering a drink from the flask of water that he kept on a strap at his waist. The man slaked his thirst gratefully and wiped his mouth with the back of his hand, ignoring his mother sitting above him as she continued to chide and to curse.

"Have to go here," he said. "Have to go there. Have to go on till we find a new home for mother and me - for our house it burned down three long moon ago."

"But sure twould be easy enough to set up a new home," Crossdogs said. "I seen empty shacks a-plenty as I've passed along this road. Slept in 'em too, for one night or more. Could fix one up easy to make a new home."

"What have we stopped for?" the mother called again. "I don't like it here. Go on - go on!"

The man shook his head. "You hear what she tells me. Wherever I find, be it ever so fine, she has to move on. Says nowhere's as good as the house that burnt down."

"Why, where did you live?" Crossdogs asked him,

ignoring the eggs that came raining down and the clatter of pans and the mother's shrieking whine.

"Twas a house such as you have never seen," the man explained, "with twisted turrets and winding stairs and windows tinted the colour of petals. In every room a music box played, each one of them a different tune. And if you climbed to the top of the house, right to the topper-most turret, why there was a little round room. And the windows were as clear as day and if you looked out of them, any way you chose - why then you could see to the edge of the world!"

"What's all that talking?" his mother exclaimed. "And why aren't we moving? Got a long way to travel if we're to get there by nightfall!"

There was a flurry of eggs which splattered to the ground and a rattle of pans which echoed all around. The cockerel started to crow and the hens chattered on, picking and pecking at the sides of the basket.

"Move!" The mother lurched, swaying in her chair. "Move on! Move on! Did I rear you to sit on your haunches all day, you lazy good-for-nothing son?!"

The man winced and brushed away the sweat from his brow as it mingled with the tears that ran down his cheeks. Crossdogs gazed upon him.

"I'm sure I could help you," he said. "I'm young and I'm strong. Let me carry your load for you a little way down the road and then you can set your back straight."

No sooner had Crossdogs suggested this than the man began unstrapping the harness that fastened the yoke. Easy and steady he lowered the chair till the whole caboodle was set around Crossdogs' broad shoulders. As soon as he was done, the man straightened up. Crossdogs took the strain and raised the yoke and chair, mother and chickens, pots and pans, teetering and tottering up into the air. He braced his knees and took a step, then another and another until he had gauged the weight and the height of his load and they trundled on slowly all down the road.

"Which way are we headed?" he called to the man. There came no reply, so he asked him again -

"Which way shall I go?"

"On and on! On and on!" the mother's voice shrieked. "On and on till you find me a house with a turret so that I may see to the edge of the world!"

Crossdogs squinnied round as far as he could. He looked for the man whose mother he carried. Peered this way and that and called out again - but there was no-one in sight. The man had gone. The moment that Crossdogs had taken his burden, the man had put foot for foot towards the horizon.

"On and on!" shrieked the mother, high up above him. "On and on!"

On and on they trudged, mile upon mile. Crossdogs staggered and stumbled. The knee that he'd crocked all back in Brunt Boggart when he fell from the apple tree - why it buckled and bent. But still he kept on, for what could he do? The mother kept screeching, like as if he was her son - for how could she know, up there in the sky, who was carrying her at all? And the sun it beat down, then the rain it came falling and Crossdogs' face was all matted with sweat and the trickle of eggs slithering down with every step he trod.

A cluster of crows came cawing around and a raddle of ferrets stalked after the eggs. Across the fields a lone fox bayed just as the day began to fade. Far away Crossdogs spied a light glinting. He bunched his fists and straightened his back and strode on towards it.

"On and on!" the mother cried, for she had seen the light too - and soon enough they were upon it. It was a house fine and strong. Not a big house, not a small house but a middling sort of house and though it had no turret on top, the rays of the fading sun were glimmering on two huge windows.

Crossdogs lowered his burden and unfastened the harness. The mother clambered crookedly all down to the ground and straightened her back with a crack. What did she say when she saw Crossdogs there and not her own son at all? Why, this woman said nothing, just stared at the house.

"What's this place you have brought me to? Looks worse than all the others you've shown me. Got no petal-tinted windows. Got not turret on top. Now how'm I going to see to the edge of the world?"

Crossdogs shook his head wearily.

"Mother," he said, for he knew of no other name to call her. "Mother, be it tall or small, this house is all that we're going to find today, for I am full weary and can travel no further - so let us go in and see what we can see."

"See what we see," the mother retorted. "See what we see... See everything, see anything, see nothing at all."

But Crossdogs ignored her, and the racket of chickens and rattle of pans, and set his shoulder firm to the door. Inside was a carpet of warm grey dust and spider webs hanging from the ceiling. But Crossdogs was more weary than he'd ever been before and even his new-found mother, who was no mother at all, seemed thankful to find a place to shelter from the night. They set to, closing the curtains and brushing away the dust while the chickens squawked and cackled in and out the rooms, their long legs strutting, pecking and scratting at anything they could find. But wasn't much to find at all - only a table and some chairs and an old blackened cooker huddled in the kitchen. Soon enough the mother gathered eggs from the chickens and cracked them into a pan.

"Eggs for tea again, m'dear," she cried in a voice that was almost kind. "Hope you ain't sick of eggs, but it's all we got, is all I can say, though I know we eat'em every day."

Crossdogs shook his head. No good trying to tell her that he was not her son at all, that her own son had gone, over the hills and away. At least here was sheltered and out of the wind and up the top of the rickety stairs he found two beds where they could rest for the night while the chickens were roosting all down in the kitchen.

"On and on!" the mother called. "On and on! Your eggs are done. Come and get'em while they're hot."

They sat side by side at the old kitchen table as if they'd sat that way all their lives. The mother sucked and gobbled at her eggs then wiped her hand across her mouth.

"Why are we sitting here, staring at curtains? Pull'em aside, son - let's watch the sun setting."

Crossdogs tugged at the length of grey curtain. Dust billowed everywhere as he slowly drew it open. There was the eye of the glowing sun - there beyond rivers, beyond forests, beyond ocean, sinking down blood red and fierce. Crossdogs had never seen so far before.

"It's the edge of the world," he whispered, hoping the

mother would believe him and then she'd cease her searching and he could leave her here and continue his journey, knowing at last she was happy.

He looked over at her, to see what she was thinking, but all of a sudden the mother was sleeping, her head nodding down and her gap-toothed mouth drooling. Crossdogs stared again through the window. Could he truly see to the edge of the world? He stared on as long as he could and then he stared some more till he swore he could see all the way to Brunt Boggart, see Hamsparrow and Bullbreath wrestling on the Green and Riversong and Larkspittle kissing down by the woods. Could hear their voices calling and old songs on the wind. But was this truly the edge of the world, or just his mind dreaming, weary from walking all this day long with a yolk on his shoulders and a chair balanced there, carrying this mother who was sleeping now? But then she awoke. Awoke with a start.

"Been dreaming," she said, rubbing her eyes.

"What did you see?" Crossdogs enquired.

The mother glared at the darkness that had gathered outside the window.

"Seen the edge of the world," she said, "just like before."

"Who did you see there?" Crossdogs asked her.

The mother rubbed her eyes again and gazed around the room.

"Seen my son," she said thoughtfully - then stared at Crossdogs, as if for the first time. "You ain't my son!" she suddenly cried. "You been trying to trick me? Where is my son?"

Crossdogs sighed.

"I ain't your son, though was no good to tell you, for

you took me to be him. But I ain't trying to trick you for I brought you here true as true when your own good son ran off and left you stranded by the side of the road."

"Least he's not stranded now," said the mother. "I always told him he should leave and find him a good woman and true. Seems like he's gone and done that now, for back in my dream, when I saw him standing at the edge of the world, he was kissing a girl whose hair was long and shining and as black as any crow."

"Know only one girl who looks like this," Crossdogs cried, and before the mother could say any more he sprang to his feet and rushed out the room.

"Ravenhair! Ravenhair!" he called all down the night. He wandered long and lonely over crags and through the mires - for he could not bear the notion that this man who he had helped by taking up his burden might be out there at the edge of the world kissing the girlen he'd known since they were children.

He cried her name to the dawning. And then in the early morning light he heard feet running towards him. Could this be her? - he asked himself, as his heart beat fast and pounding. But over the brow of the brooding hill came no girlen but the man who'd deserted him to his mother and the chickens. The man was running, wild-eyed and breathless. Crossdogs looked behind him, looked to left and right to see if Ravenhair was following out of the shadow of the night. But no-one was there, only the wind - and the man was alone and alone. His breath was seized in silent sobs and he was scarce able to speak.

But Crossdogs had no truck with the man who had tricked him so.

"Where is the girlen?" he demanded. "What have you done with her?"

"What have *I* done with *her*? You should rather ask what has she done with *me*?"

The man lay gasping at Crossdogs' feet, his shirt ripped to tatters and his back all covered in scratches.

"How did this happen?" Crossdogs asked.

The man sat up and took a deep breath.

"My mother always told me I should go out and get a girl. She told me to do it, but she never let me go. So when you took up the yolk and the chair, I ran and I ran out over the hill, under the clear blue sky. And there I espied a charming girl with her hair all long and black. Before I could speak she seized me and flung me on my back. She ripped my shirt and kissed my lips so hard that they're bruised and blue. And then she rolled me swift and sure into a bed of thorns."

"Was this rage or was it loving?" Crossdogs clenched his fists.

The man raised his hand.

"To tell the truth, I would not know. Happened so fast that it seemed both the same."

"Did she tell you her name?"

"Didn't stop long enough to ask, for I felt so ashamed and knew that I must find my mother again."

The man looked around.

"Where have you left her?" he asked suddenly, gazing out across the deserted moor.

Crossdogs nodded away to the distance, to where dawn broke slowly up over the hills.

"She is safe enough. I found her a cottage. Can see there for miles - and she dreamed she seen to the edge of the world. Dreamed she saw you there kissing

Ravenhair."

The man shook his head.

"Didn't know what her name was - she had no time to tell me. But all the while as she kissed me and rolled me in the briars, she called but one name."

"What she callen?"

"Called for Crossdogs," the man replied, and then he looked down.

"Twas Crossdogs," he repeated, but when he raised his eyes again, Crossdogs was gone. In the distance, shrill and clear, his mother's voice echoed:

"On and on!" she shrieked. "On and on!"

GRINFICKLE, CHAINDAISY AND THE WHEEL

Let me tell you... let me tell you... Grinfickle's hair hung lank and straggled, matted by rain, the salt of his sweat and the dust. His shirt was weary-ragged and his limbs dangled gangly-loose as he toiled in the shadow of the wheel which stood as high as he was tall and then as high again. Each day the wheel dragged deeper into the mire as Grinfickle traipsed along his route across the dark flat fields. Its rim was rusted and its spokes loose and rotted as it clattered and it rattled along the rut that it had worn.

Grinfickle trailed on, hauling his burden from homestead to village to town. Along the way he gathered anything he could find in the hedgerows or by the roadside - tattered rags and shrivelled flowers, shards of glass and tarnished bones. He knitted them and twisted them with bits of wire and lengths of string, till he made them into dream spindles to hang from the spokes of his wheel. Who did he make them for? - I know what you're asking. Why, at first he made them for the girlen-soon-to-be-women and the wifen-without-men he might find along his way. They would wait wide-eyed outside their cottages when they saw him come trundling over the hill.

"What do you have for me?" each one asked and Grinfickle presented his latest spindle which the girlen clutched and twirled before planting a kiss on his cheek.

"If you hang the spindle about your neck before you go to sleep," Grinfickle dropped his voice so no-one else could hear, "then whatever you dream of in the night you will see before you when you wake."

And one might dream of bright-eyed daisies and another might dream of rainbows - and sure enough next day they would find them. But soon the spindle would fade, its berries would wither, its petals would droop and the girlen and the women would each grow tired of him - and so Grinfickle set off again, his shoulder to the wheel. And the women would forget and forget they had forgotten until he came back round again when a moon and another moon had been and gone.

One night a wifen dreamt of mountains when she wore Grinfickle's spindle, but the next day when she woke all she found was dust. And another dreamt of necklaces and another dreamt of rings, but all they saw in the morning were turnips rotting on the floor and nettles with no sting.

"Grinfickle, Grinfickle - not another spindle," first one said then another. "Once they brought dreams of nightingales and primroses blooming fresh all out in the fields. But now the only dreams the spindles bring is rain and bleak wind as it blows through your wheel."

What could Grinfickle do? All he knew these long years gone was how to make dream-spindles and push the great wheel. And so he kept toiling, decking out spindles to sell to the mothers to give to the childern at each cluster of cottages. But never no more did he offer them to the wifen-without-husband or the girlen-come-to-be-women, for they would only push him away.

"That great wheel become a shackle," Grinfickle muttered, "and these dreams been no dreams for me at all. The harder I push the wheel, the quicker it brings me back to the place where I started. On and on and back again, through sunshine, wind and storm."

So Grinfickle journeyed across the flat marshlands, over rattling bridges and ford of stream, past stooks of hay that rotted in the shallow fields, until he came to a broken-down hut in the middle of a mire of brackish mud. Grinfickle clung to the wheel and heaved and hawed until the sweat on his forehead stung his eyes. The mulch sucked his boots, tugging him down - but at last he gained the door of the hut and pushed it open on its rusted hinge.

Inside by the flickering lamplight Grinfickle could see the Pedlar Man sitting, his nimble fingers threading beads onto a line of spindles. In the corner leant his sack, waiting to be filled with all the scarves and trinkets he'd take with him next time he set out along the Track. But as Grinfickle stood in the doorway, the Pedlar Man hardly looked up at all.

"See you come back," he grunted as he bit off a length of thread with his broken blackened teeth.

"Always come back," Grinfickle replied. "Can't go nowhere else 'cept to follow the track of this cursed wheel."

The Pedlar Man sat up and fixed him with a beady eye. A lantern flickered, hung from one hook in the cobwebbed roof.

"Wheel ain't no curse," he said. "I told you that yearen ago. The wheel is your own dream. Take you wherever you choose."

Grinfickle sat down on the edge of a bench cluttered all over with trinkets and geejaws.

"Wanted to go over the hills to find me wifen in every village and give each one of them a dream."

The Pedlar Man studied the spindle he'd made, glittering with insects' wings and specks of shell from a song thrush's egg. He brushed it down with his sinewy fingers and tossed it into a box.

"Grinfickle, Grinfickle," he said. "When will you ever learn? One dream is enough, don't need no more. Too many dreams make a man muddle-headed."

Grinfickle sighed and nodded.

"None of my spindles bring pleasure no more. Making'ems a chore. None of the wifen wait for them - and the childern I sell'em to, why they just play with them for a day then throw them away."

The Pedlar Man looked at him.

"Grinfickle - what did I tell you when I showed you how to make your first spindle?"

Grinfickle shrugged and gazed around the shadowy shack.

"Told me every spindle should be the best I ever made - whether it be of shiny berries or sparkling cobwebs or bits of broken old glass."

The Pedlar Man winked at him.

"You know that," he said.

Grinfickle got to his feet and opened the creaking door. He trekked all by himself until he came to a scrub of ferns and ran his fingers beneath their fronds to touch the golden spore which lay hidden there. He gathered up a thimbleful which he placed into his pocket, then made his way back to the Pedlar Man's shack where he worked all night silently on just one spindle made of mulberry leaves and primrose petals. When he finished he paused, just as the dawn light crept under the door, then he took up the spindle between finger and thumb and sprinkled it all about with the golden dust of the spore.

Now let me tell you about Chaindaisy, who lived in the midst of a hawthorn thicket - its branches heavy with pale white blossom and peppered with yellow lichen. Whichever way she went, whichever way she turned, the thorns would rip and rake her limbs, so that every day she was scratched and bleeding - until this was all she knew. At night the dark-winged Shrike would come - the butcher bird with its hooded head and hooked black beak - and hang its catch upon the thorns. Lizards, beetles, mice and frogs all dangled in the sallow moonlight till Chaindaisy stole out and gorged them under the shivering stars.

She sighed as she stared at the gashes and scars that laced across her hands and breast until she fell asleep with her head in the crook of her arm and a lick of blood on her lips that tasted of salt and iron. When morning came she woke again, still trapped in the cage of thorns. She plunged into the bushes, determined to break free - but the more she struggled, the more the briars held her close. She thrashed and writhed, but the thorns tore her flesh and fresh blood stained her dress again. She clenched her fists in despair and wrenched the brambles from her tangled hair. She made one last lunge, but in vain and so she dragged herself back to the thicket's heart and sat there listening to the song thrush which sang beyond the thorns.

The thrush's song was filled with joy, but Chaindaisy changed it to a mournful refrain:

> "Death is living all around,
> In the sky and underground.
>
> Underground and in the sky,
> While owls swim and fishes fly.
>
> Life is dying as we breathe -
> As soon we come, so soon we leave."

Then from far distant she heard a rattling and a clanking, closer and closer until it came to a stop just beyond the thicket. Chaindaisy sprang to her feet.

"Help me!" she implored. "Free me from the thorns."

Beyond the bushes, Grinfickle stood and leaned upon his wheel. He heard Chaindaisy calling to him.

"Free me," she cried. "Each night I dream I walk the roads and journey to lands that are far and strange, but instead I wake to find myself trapped in this bed of thorns."

Grinfickle shook his head.

"Each night I dream that I can lay down my wheel and rest, but each morning I wake to find that I must journey on along these endless roads."

"Can you not help me at all?" Chaindaisy wailed.

Grinfickle looked all about. The thorns were long, the thorns were sharp and the branches which bore them were thick and strong.

"I have no axe to hack them down. I have no fire to burn them. But catch this spindle, true as true and see what dreams it brings to you."

With that, Grinfickle seized the spindle of mulberry leaves and primrose petals and began to grapple his way up the spokes of the wheel. But as he climbed, the wheel started turning and Grinfickle flung the spindle straight over the top of the thorns to catch in the brambles on the other side.

Chaindaisy saw the spindle covered all over with golden spore and scrambled up to reach it, never minding no more that the thorns tore her dress, raked at her flesh and scratched her eyes. She clambered until she was just a fingertip away, then she stretched out as far as she could reach, grabbed hold of the spindle and jerked it away from the thorns. As she did so, she fell toppling down to land on the mossy turf on the floor of the thicket.

And so there they were, Chaindaisy on one side of the thorns and Grinfickle on the other.

"What to do now?" asked Chaindaisy, clutching the dream spindle between her trembling fingers.

"You must hang the spindle about your neck before you go to sleep," Grinfickle instructed. "Whatever you dream of in the night, you will see before you when you wake."

As darkness fell, a thin moon rose and Chaindaisy lay down to rest. Grinfickle sat beside his wheel on the other side of the briars and watched while the butcher bird came and left its catch of mice and lizards impaled on the thorns.

When dawn was just breaking, Chaindaisy stretched.

"I dreamed a dream the thorns were gone and a tall man came a-kissing me!"

As she spoke, Grinfickle rose and looked about. The mass of tangled thorns fell withered to the ground and through the branches thin and bare he could see Chaindaisy sitting all alone in the heart of the thicket. And so he left his wheel and pushed his way through the branches to stand beside her.

"Sit with me a while," said Chaindaisy. "Sit with me a while and a while and kiss me full and sure."

Grinfickle sat beside her. He had played this game many times and more with the girlen he met on his journey. But when he gazed upon her face, he saw her cheeks were ripped and scratched and even her lips were covered about in scabs.

"Why will you not kiss me?" Chaindaisy demanded.

"I thought you wanted to escape this place. No time to dally with kisses."

But Chaindaisy moved closer.

"Why will you not kiss me? Plenty of time for running away - I have been here so long, one moment more will not hurt."

"But you are hurt enough," Grinfickle declared. "I do not want to hurt you more."

"How can you hurt me?" Chaindaisy chided as her finger stroked his cheek. "Your mouth is soft and tender. You will not rip me like the tangling thorns. Here - put your arms around me."

Grinfickle closed his eyes as Chaindaisy kissed him long and true. But when he opened them again and looked upon her face, the cuts and wealds and scars were gone - and her skin was smooth as milk. So they kissed again both full and long until they heard a thrush's song.

"The scars are gone and the thorns which brought them!" Chaindaisy exclaimed. "Now I am free to walk with you. Now I can go wherever I choose."

Grinfickle shook his head.

"If you walk with me you cannot choose but to follow the rut of that wheel."

He pointed to where it stood, propped against the branches of the bushes.

Chaindaisy clapped her hands.

"But just to walk and feel the air! I'll follow you and will not care. I can help you bear the weight of the wheel."

She ran across and tried her shoulder against its rim. Then her eyes lighted on the spindles dangling from its spokes and she ran her fingers through the array of beads and trinkets.

"And I can help you to make these!" she cried. "I can pick berries from the hedgerows and collect dew from spider webs. I can help you to make spindles such as you have never seen!"

But Grinfickle hung his head and sighed.

"You are welcome to the wheel. I am too weary to push it any more. You are welcome to make spindles and follow where the wheel might take you."

"What will *you* do?" Chaindaisy asked.

Grinfickle shrugged and sat down on the grass.

"I will rest here," he said. "Now that the thorns are gone, this place feels peaceful and warm. You can take the road alone."

And so Chaindaisy shouldered the wheel. She could

feel its weight as she pushed and heaved until it rolled slowly on its way and then she trundled on behind, treading the rut that Grinfickle had trodden for so many years, on across the dark flat fields.

At first she felt happy, at first she felt free, now that the thorns had withered away. She could smell the rain on the wind. She could hear the call of the flocks of birds who followed her on her way. But then as darkness began to fall, she approached her first steep hill. She heaved and she groaned, she shoved and she moaned, but the wheel would not move.

Chaindaisy tore at her hair and wailed. The wind blew wild all around her and grey rain began to fall. As she stood back to take a breath, the great wheel slowly toppled to shatter on the stony ground. Chaindaisy stood and stared at the sad spindles which Grinfickle had spent so many hours in the making which now lay tattered and forlorn. As the rain beat hard upon her, she felt her arms begin to itch as if the wealds of the thorns might suddenly now return. Quick as she could, she gathered up the spindles, grabbing and scrabbling as if they might protect her. She plunged them in her pocket and then she ran, leaving the wreckage of the wheel, its spokes splintered and broken across the cold hard stones.

She ran and she ran all back to the thicket where the branches were still bare and the thorns were all gone. There she found Grinfickle sitting and waiting. As she ran towards him, he took her in his arms and while the thrush hopped around them, so they sang together -

"Life is living all around,

In the sky and underground.
Underground and in the sky
While flowers dance and shadows fly.
Life is living as we breathe
In every spindle that we weave."

GRANNOCK

Let me tell you - let me tell you... Greychild followed the track till it was no more than a scrat of flint high up in the hills. As he reached the top he rested beside a cairn of stones, but beyond him in the valley he spied a rising storm. Its voice howled in anger as it rode towards him, pushing him back then dragging him on. Greychild clenched his fists as he wrestled with the wind which filled his coat and turned it all about, clawing at his face and ripping away his hair.

It swept him up and knocked him down and when he landed on the ground his legs were buckled and his back was bent. His eyes stared through a bleary mist until he saw a cleft in the hillside and a path leading on to a small stone croft.

He struggled on as if his legs did not belong to him until he came to the croft's wooden door and beat upon it with a fist that seemed bigger than his own two hands. The door swung open as if he was expected and there inside a kitchen, three children played with a handful of stones.

"Father...!" they cried, jumping up to greet him.

Greychild swung them round in delight and found himself calling each of them by name in a rasping voice which he had never heard before. Then the children fell silent. Behind them stood a woman with her back to them all, stirring a thick stew in a large copper pot.

"So you're home," she said in a dull leaden voice. She turned around and looked at him. Greychild held out his arms to greet her, thinking that if the children knew him then she must know him too. But she flinched away and her eyes looked down more like a frightened creature. Greychild reached out to touch her but she turned back to stirring the pot.

An anger turned in his gut that she might mistrust him this way. A darkness gathered in his head bleak as the clouds rolling in from the hills. A thunder rose in his throat until he heard a voice roaring and bellowing off the smoke-scorched walls that was not his voice at all.

He turned and saw the children, who had greeted him so gladly, scatter away to hide behind the dresser in the corner of the croft. His fists bunched up and then fell loose again, tightening and clenching as he fought with words he did not recognise and felt the silence of the woman at the stove with her back turned mute against him. The silence gouged inside him into a knot of pain which he could not untie, could not wrench away, until he strode once more out through the door and shook his fists at the sky and let out one long and terrible cry which echoed to the hills and back again. When it died away, he heard the voices of the children, singing in the kitchen:

"Here are stones,
One, two and three.
Feel the stones -
What do you see?

One for you
And two for we.
Feel the stones -
What do you see?

Two for you
And one for we.
Three for you
And none for we.

Feel the stones,
What do you see?
None for you
And three for we.

Here are stones
All set around.
See them lying
On the ground.

Feel the stones,
What do you see?
Here are stones,
One, two and three."

Greychild wanted to rush and join their game, but soon as his hand touched the latch, the singing stopped and he heard them scuttling away. He knew he was Greychild no more but the crofter, who had lived here all his life, trudging the hills in search of lost sheep and coaxing a lean crop of bitter roots from out of the shallow soil raked around the door. And as he stood outside, alone and chill, the wind swirled in from the hill and he heard the crofter's voice inside his head.

"Grannock's eyes are blind," it said. "Grannock cannot see. He wanders the mountain, howling silently. Grannock cannot see, and yet he sees inside our eyes, sees the fear that we see - fear of slash of wind, fear of lashing rain. Fear we will never leave here. Fear that the childern will grow hobbled, crippled, lame. Fear that the hill will crush us, though it is the hill which gives us home. Grannock sees all this in his blindness. Grannock feeds on fear. When he is sated, Grannock will sleep. But Grannock never sleeps. He wakes again to roam again in crack of lightning, sluice of rain. He is the tears which never fall. He is the knot of aching hunger. He is the fear which binds us here. He is thunder. He is blizzard. He is pain."

Greychild slept strange that night, dreaming another man's dreams of mist fret and lightning strikes and a cold wind blasting through shattered trees. And he dreamt of Grannock who roamed these hills, formed of mist and formed of sorrow. Each day the crofter would stalk this creature, though it was his own fear that he followed. Dreamt that he must tame him and dreamt that he should ride him, across the sky and away from the mountain where the rain lashed down and the dark mists harried.

At dawn Greychild woke while the others were still asleep and scraped out a thin gruel of oats from the bottom of a blackened pot. And then he set out, following steps he did not know and yet familiar and sure, searching for Grannock in the skirl of the hills.

On one side rose craggy mountains, on the other a rolling waste of brush and heather. Greychild hung his head. His belly sank empty already, feeding on churlish anger. A veil of rain fell all about him, until he could see the hills no more, only the darkness of the crofter's dreams. But then he wiped a hand across his face and felt the rain had ceased. Greychild stood on top of the crag.

He felt Grannock coming, felt him at his back. Turned to face him, though he could not see him - and then Grannock was all around. Grannock seized him in a wheel of wind that near took his breath away. Grannock's voice was raging in his ears, but loud as Grannock roared, Greychild summoned up his strength, strength of tree-root, strength of wing-beat, and Greychild let loose his own voice into the force of Grannock's gale. The wind continued, but Greychild's lungs were strong, and as he sang, another voice joined him. It was the voice of the crofter, the man he had become. And their voices rang together as they sang, till soon there was a third voice which stood with them true - and Greychild knew the voice, had known it all along, that within their own voices lay Grannock himself. And so they shouted long, three voices joined in one. Shouted down the thunder, the hailstorm and the rain. Shouted down the hunger, the darkness and the pain.

And then Grannock was gone and Greychild was all alone as he hurried back to the croft, his feet racing before him and his shadow chasing behind. When he came to the door it seemed to fall open and the cold dark room was filled with light. The crofter's wifen greeted him with arms outstretched and the children danced around him, each one holding a smooth white stone in the cup of their hands.

> "Here are stones,
> One, two and three.
> Feel the stones -
> What do you see?"

The children sang as they capered and tumbled, calling him to join them.

> "One for you
> And two for we.
> Feel the stones -
> What do you see?"

Greychild took the stone from the eldest's outstretched hand.

> "Two for you
> And one for we..."

- the chant continued as Greychild took the second stone.

> "Three for you
> And none for we..."

- the chant concluded. Greychild took the third stone.
"Don't be afraid," he told them. "Grannock is wind

and Grannock is darkness - but only this and nothing more. If you do not fear him, then there is nothing to fear at all."

Then Greychild seized the stones and thrust them in his pocket and raced away and away again, back along the path that would take him to the cairn where he had first seen the croft. He placed the three stones carefully around the others in the stack. He felt the rhythm of the hill, moving slow beneath him.

He looked up and shook his head. There was nothing at all, only the roar of the wind. But then he saw the crofter, standing before him, his weathered face all lined and smiling. He offered Greychild a drink from a leather bottle. Greychild drank deep of the cool fresh water, but when he looked again there was nobody there, only a swirl of mist. He stood on the hillside's green moss and peered into the distance, but no path could he see and no croft. He slung his pack upon his back as he set off along the track. Above him a glimmer of light struck through the cloud as from far away he could hear the voices of the children, all singing:

> "Here are stones
> All set around.
> See them lying
> On the ground.
>
> Feel the stones,
> What do you see?
> Here are stones,
> One, two and three."

JESSIMER

Let me tell you... let me tell you, in the dark garden the flowers glowed bright as the sun and butterflies flew as large as Greychild's hand, their wings all sparkling with turquoise and azure. Between gleaming rocks flowed glistening streams that rippled beneath low hanging trees whose fruit shone full as lanterns. Here on a rock was a girlen whose dress hung long and golden. Greychild sat down beside her and saw that in her lap she held a basket.

The girlen smiled with sparkling eyes.

"My name is Jessimer," she told him.

"What do you keep there in your basket?" Greychild asked.

"It is a basket of desires," Jessimer replied.

"What do you desire?" Greychild asked as she lifted the corner of the linen cloth which covered the top of the basket.

"Here let me show you," Jessimer smiled as

Greychild slipped his hand under the cloth. Inside the basket was warm as new laid eggs. He felt a fluttering of wings, like the feathers of a baby thrush soft against his fingers. He felt flowers which thrust as soft as silk. And then from beneath the linen of Jessimer's basket, Greychild pulled out a peach. Its flesh was firm and golden and he knew it would taste sweet.

Jessimer smiled and gazed at him.

"I can see that you are thirsty. I can see that you wish to eat." Then she snatched the fruit away. "But you must wait another day."

Greychild tugged his jacket around his shoulders and went on his way until he came to another garden, where all around bloomed purple flowers whose thorns gleamed sharp as silver knives. As the last light faded, the flowers became black shadows and through them trailed an old woman, her skin as pale as the moon. As she moved she did not speak, but seemed to be singing a high wordless harmony, although her lips did not move. She smiled as she glided between the flowers, beneath the skeletons of trees. Greychild sighed and breathed in the sweet perfume that the flowers breathed out.

"Tell me, what do you keep in that jar you are carrying?" Greychild asked the old woman.

"It is a jar of memories," she replied.

"What do you remember?" Greychild asked, as the old woman opened the jar.

"Here, put in your hand," she smiled.

Inside the jar was cooler than shadows. Greychild felt a blind moth's wings brush against his fingers. He felt shrivelled leaves which turned to dust and a trace of forgotten tears. And then he drew out an apple, its skin all withered and weather-worn.

"This was the first apple that I ever tasted," the old woman explained. "I've carried it with me through sunshine and rain, but I know I'll never eat it. Here - you may keep it."

Greychild took the fruit curiously, though he wished it was the peach which Jessimer had shown him.

He thanked the old woman and bade her farewell then set off once more along the Pedlar Man's Track until he came to a third garden where mirrors hung from the boughs of the trees and span slowly around. Everywhere he looked he saw reflections of the sky, and every mirror was painted with an eye which watched his every move.

From behind a bush he heard a mother's laughter. Could it be his own mother, come to find him again?

"I can see you!" she cried and then dashed out, but before Greychild caught sight of her face, she hid again. Greychild knew this must be a game and so he knelt behind a tree.

"Mother, mother, I'm here," he called. "You can't catch me."

As soon as he heard her coming he called again and ran and she ran too, until at last Greychild knew that game was enough and stepped out into the sun to find himself staring into the face of a woman he had never seen before.

"My child!" she cried as she ran towards him.

Greychild stood still, waiting to be embraced.

"I thought I'd never find you," she scolded, then rubbed her eyes and gazed at Greychild.

"I thought you were some-one else," she said.

Greychild nodded. "I thought you were too."

335

He looked at her slowly.

"What do you keep in your apron?" he asked.

"It is filled with regrets," the mother replied.

"What do you regret?" Greychild asked again.

"Here, put in your hand," she told him.

Inside the apron was a twine of string, a pitcher of milk and a wooden spoon. Then Greychild drew out a damson. Its flesh was firm though its skin seemed drawn.

"Tis a damson I keep and mean to eat," said the mother, "but I never have the time. You look as though you must be hungry. You may take it with you on your journey."

Greychild smiled and put the fruit in his pocket where it nestled beside the withered apple that the old woman had given to him. But as he set off along his way, he still dreamt of the peach which Jessimer had shown him.

Soon enough and soon he came upon a house nestled under the trees. The door frames and windows were buckled and botched and the chimney so twisted the smoke coiled out crooked as a corkscrew. As Greychild watched, the old woman who had given him the shrivelled apple came hobbling up the path. She drew a key from the jar that she carried and unlocked the door, then quick as slow, she slipped inside. He was just about to set off again when he heard footsteps approaching and the rustling of a long golden dress. Greychild held his breath, for it was Jessimer sure as sure, who brushed past him in the twilight, pulled a key from out of her basket, unlocked the door and went inside.

Now Greychild he was curious, for he longed to see Jessimer again and so he hid behind a tree to watch this house where she must live. Before too long he heard the mother coming, still calling out for the boy she could not see. She took out a key from her apron pocket, opened up the door to the house and then she too vanished inside.

Greychild settled down to sleep, still dreaming of the peach which Jessimer had shown him. In the morning, just as the first birds began to sing, Greychild woke to see the door of the house swing open. Who should come out but the old woman and she went tottering off all down the path, carrying her jar with her. Before too long the door opened again and out came the mother, still wearing her apron and calling for her long lost son.

Now that they were gone, Greychild knew that Jessimer must be in the house alone - and so he stepped up and rapped on the door. There was no reply and so he knocked again, but then to his surprise he saw that the door was not fully closed. As he pushed it open, there inside was a passageway leading to the foot of the stairs. He called out full loud, "Jessimer!"

He heard the sound of starlings rattling and scratching up on the roof - and then his voice echoed back to him, all turned around and twisted. Greychild tiptoed up the stairs, expecting that he would find three rooms - one for the old woman, one for the mother and one for Jessimer herself. But to his surprise, there was only one door standing ajar. Greychild peered inside, thinking he would find Jessimer sleeping there, but all that he saw was a freshly made bed, a jug and a bowl on the dresser and a vase of faded flowers on the shelf.

He called out again, but came no reply, only the

gentle patter of rain against the window pane. Greychild scratched his head.

"If three women come in and only two go out, then where can Jessimer be?"

He knocked upon cupboards and searched for secret doors, even lifted the lid of the linen chest, but twisted and crooked as this house might be, he could find no hidden corners where Jessimer might be hiding. Greychild sat himself down at the table in the kitchen, for he was hungry now after all of his searching. He plunged his hands into his pocket to find the damson and the shrivelled apple that still nestled there. He switched them about and about on the scrubbed wooden table top.

"Which should I eat?" he pondered.

First he tried the apple that the old woman had given him. Though it seemed shrivelled and worn, he found that inside the fruit was sweet. But soon as the juice touched his tongue, why then he spat it out, for it had turned sour again. Then he tried the mother's damson, for though its skin was weary he could feel its flesh was firm. But when he tore it open, he found the stone was blackened and so he pushed it aside. Greychild was more hungry now than ever before and wished that he could eat the golden peach which Jessimer had shown to him before she snatched it away.

Just then he heard a footstep on the stair and the door swung slowly open. Who did he see standing there? I know what you are thinking - wherever she had hidden herself, could only be Jessimer now - for he had seen the other two women leave the house as soon as dawn had broken.

Greychild blinked. Twas not Jessimer at all, with her

golden peach beneath the linen of her basket - and not the old woman nor the mother neither. Twas a little girl who was standing there.

"What is your name?" Greychild asked.

The girl turned around and smiled.

"My name is Jessimer," she said.

Greychild scratched his head.

"Then who is the girlen with the golden dress and where is the old woman who carries a jar and the mother who calls for a boy she cannot see?"

Jessimer turned round twice again and stared at Greychild as she winked and smiled.

"Nobody lives here," she said. "Nobody else but me."

She reached out and took Greychild by the hand.

"Come with me and you'll see!"

She led him in a spinning dance, all up the stairs and down, through the kitchen, in the hall, out the house and in again. They twirled so fast as Jessimer laughed all through that twisty house, they sent it whirling round and round till suddenly it vanished.

Greychild stood, catching his breath. The house was gone and the fruit gone too which he'd left upon the table. The old woman was gone and the mother and the girlen, who had all been Jessimer all along. Greychild was standing alone on a bridge and beneath its shadow the water flowed as quick as slow.

Across the bridge was an island where the trees were smothered all over in blossom, and out of the shadows stepped Jessimer, the girlen in the golden dress. She smiled and she beckoned, calling Greychild to cross the bridge and join her, singing:

> "Bury me in earth,
> Drown me in water,
> Burn me in fire,
> Spin me through air."

But as soon as he set his foot on the boards, the leaves of the trees turned golden and fell, and he saw the girlen grow older, until soon she became Jessimer the mother, singing:

> "Bury me in water,
> Drown me in fire,
> Burn me in air,
> Spin me through earth."

Jessimer the mother was belly-full, swollen as a pod about to burst. As Greychild watched she squatted down and gave birth there to a babe. When he looked again the mother was gone and the babe was left alone and alone, but as she stretched she grew and grew, just as the tree broke into bud - and she became Jessimer the child again, running here and running there and calling Greychild to chase her, singing:

> "Bury me in fire,
> Drown me in air,
> Burn me in earth,
> Spin me through water."

But Greychild did not move, for fear that she might trick him - and for sure, soon as she disappeared behind a tree, just as the branches turned frozen and bare, she stepped out again as Jessimer, the old woman, singing:

"Bury me in air,
Drown me in earth,
Burn me in water,
Spin me through fire."

Greychild blinked and watched her there as she grew older and frailer more, until she lay full still. Greychild waited to see whether she would move and then took one step forward to help her. But as he trod upon the bridge, the tree snapped and broke and fell to the ground. The old woman was gone, the mother and the girlen too - returned to the gardens where Greychild had found them: the garden of darkness lit with desires, the garden of thorns all sharp with memories and the garden of mirrors filled with regret. Greychild stood a moment and wondered, then turned around and there he saw Jessimer the child again - an apple, a damson and a peach cradled safe in the cup of her hands.

ARLECCRA

MILKTHISTLE

Let me tell you... let me tell you - on the horizon Greychild spied a cottage no bigger than the tip of his thumb. But though it was far away, this cottage glowed warm and welcoming. He could see the firelight glinting in the windows and a plume of smoke rising from the chimney. But walk as he might, the cottage grew no closer, and every time he looked, it still seemed no bigger than the tip of his thumb. And then as he turned a bend in the lane, the cottage was gone, lost behind the trees. Greychild sighed, for he was weary hungry and would like to reach there before nightfall. He walked this way and that, following the winding track, scrambling through ditches, scaling fences and gates. Every now and then he spied the cottage again, but still it grew no closer as twilight crept around him.

Darkness fell, the darkness of a night that has seen no moon, but Greychild walked on - and then of a sudden the moon appeared from behind a cloud and there was the cottage standing before him. Greychild pushed open the door to find not a kitchen but steps leading down to a dimly-lit shop, all dingy and dark. He stumbled forward blinking, till his eyes could see through the gloom. Before him was a wooden counter, all laid out with painted eggs, each one a world in itself - of forests and villages, cities and mountains. Behind them sat a line of straggling straw dollies, watching him with bright berry eyes.

Then his hand chanced upon a scarf of maroons and purples, moss green and black, all picked out in threads of silver and gold. He let its silk run through his fingers as the curtain at the back of the shop slowly opened and there stood a woman. Greychild held his breath. In the dim light she looked so like his mother as he remembered her, stepping through the shadow of the trees in the forest, come to bring him food.

He could not speak, did not know what to say. His hands were shaking. But as the woman stepped forward he saw that this was not his mother at all, though her face smiled kindly out of the shadows.

"I am Milkthistle," she said.

Her long dress was pale, as pale as her face, like as if the sunlight never reached her. Outside Greychild heard the rattle of carts across cobbles, the call of skirling gulls as they twisted and harried, a surge of harsh voices hurrying by and from away and away the creak of tall masts moored at a quayside.

"Where am I?" he asked.

"This is Arleccra," Milkthistle replied. "Have you come alone?"

Greychild nodded, still trailing the silk of the scarf through his fingers.

"I need this," he said, "to give to my mother. I've come here to find her."

Milkthistle smiled.

"That costs a silver shillen," she told him.

Greychild shuffled his feet.

"Got no shillen," he said. "Got no pennies neither. Never had no need of 'em. Been living out in the hills and the ditches and sleeping under the sky."

Milkthistle eyed him.

"Mayhap I can help you. Come with me and you can have any scarf that you choose."

Greychild followed through a maze of narrow streets, back alleys and courtyards where the sun could never reach. Each overhanging row of tenements housed more people than ever lived in Brunt Boggart. They piled on top of each other, door on door, window above window - and down in the dank dirty basements below. Crying in the dark and shivering. Hunting for slops and whimpering. Trawling the gutter for scraps as he had once rooted through the woods for fallen fruit and hidden truffles. But their eyes stared wildly. They had seen no trees, they had heard no song birds, buried deep in their own sullen shadows.

Milkthistle led him on and on until at last they came to an unlit house standing tall and dark where she fumbled with a bunch of keys.

"Come in," she cried. "Come in," and ushered him into a shadowy hall. There they climbed the creaking stairs until it seemed they must be at the very top. She unlocked another door and led him into an attic room where the ceiling sloped so low that they both had to stoop.

"Sit down," she said.

Greychild looked around, then perched on the edge of a narrow bed. As Milkthistle paced up and down the centre of the room, Greychild wondered where were the scarves that she had promised him. But then she threw open a wardrobe door and a cascade of fine clothes slithered onto the floor. She snatched up britches, a tunic and a cape, all of them cut from the smoothest brushed velvet.

"Put them on," she instructed.

Greychild looked away. He was used to girlen plaiting ribbons in his hair, but had never seen such finery as this before.

"Come," Milkthistle smiled, her eyes all glowing as she wrenched the shirt from Greychild's back. Slowly by the light of the moon that stole through the attic window, Greychild stripped away his travel-weary clothes and pulled on the britches, the tunic and the cape.

"Stand!" Milkthistle commanded.

Greychild rose to his feet, ducking his head as he did so, to avoid the low beam of the ceiling.

"Turn!" she cried, grabbing at his elbow and spinning him about, this way and that.

"Now you are *my* boy," she said. "Come with me."

And she brought him back down to the street again, where she led him around like a dog on a lead through the hustle and shove of the night market where the stalls were a-glitter with all manner of frippery, lit by low hanging lanterns and the flare of flaming torches. All eyes turned to watch him as they peeked and they peered, they laughed and they sneered till Greychild felt like as though he was WolfBoy again, newly come to Brunt Boggart.

They came to a narrow alleyway lined from one end to another with stalls loaded down with all manner of sweetmeats and pies. Greychild's mouth started to water for he was sore hungry, but Milkthistle dragged him away.

"This is not for you. You will eat soon enough, back in your room."

Back in his room, Milkthistle closed the door on him. He heard her keys jangle on the other side. Greychild looked about. There was no food. Perhaps she was preparing a meal in the kitchen downstairs, he told himself. Sure enough, he soon heard the rattling of pans and the smell of a hot rich stew drifted up the stairwell.

Greychild sat on his bed and waited. Outside he could hear the braying of the hawkers and from the half-open door of a tavern the wheeze of a hurdy-gurdy and the rhythm of a drum. Greychild pressed his face to the window, but all he could see was row after row of chimneys and roofs stretching away to the masts of the boats on the harbour. He felt the hunger knotting in his stomach. Downstairs he could hear the rattle of pans as Milkthistle ladled out a bowlful of stew. Greychild sat upright, waiting for the sound of her foot on the stairs. He trembled inside, just as he always had when he lay in the wood and waited for his mother. But same as night after night his mother would not come, so Milkthistle did not come now. Instead he could hear the scrape of a spoon on the side of her bowl downstairs in the kitchen and he could almost taste each mouthful of the stew as she ate.

Greychild paced up and down, like a WolfBoy true, trapped in a cage. He rattled the handle of the door, but the lock held tight. He tried to pick at the catch on the window, but that was shut fast. He let out a wail, a long howling cry and flung himself back on the bed. There came a knocking under the floor as Milkthistle beat the ceiling of the kitchen beneath him with the handle of a broom.

"Be quiet up there," she cried. "Now you are my boy, you'll do what you're told!"

"Not your boy," muttered Greychild. "Not no-one's boy at all."

And he ripped off the tunic, the britches and the cape and pulled back on his travelling clothes all caked and matted with mud.

The door flew open.

"Ungrateful boy! How dare you? - I made these clothes for you!"

Greychild said nothing but sat in the darkness as the blows from her broom rained down about his head. And then she was gone. The door was closed again, bolted and locked. Outside the window Arleccra was silent and all he could see was a small patch of stars. Same stars as he'd watched in the wood at Brunt Boggart. Same stars as he'd trailed down the Pedlar Man's Track. But now even the stars were dark as the clouds rolled across, heavy with smoke. Mist swathed the city and Greychild slept.

He woke in the half-dawn and there in the corner of the room he saw something move, something shift beside the curtain. Lurid and white, the size of a rat, its body was soft but covered in a hard horny shell. Two pincers groped blindly then it scuttled away, leaving a trace of its stench behind.

The door scraped slowly open. Milkthistle stood there, dark-eyed and scowling. Greychild pointed.

"There was a creature - there in the corner."

Milkthistle shook her head.

"There was, I saw it," Greychild insisted. He showed

her where it had sat, described how it scurried away.

"Wicked boy!" Milkthistle retorted. "There are no scabbindgers here. This is a clean house. I scrub it myself on my hands and knees. The scabbindgers stay away. They do not come here. They go to other houses. The moon draws them out from the wainscots, out from the gutters. They come from the sewers, but they do not come here. There are no scabbindgers in this house!"

Greychild stared past her. The scabbindger had returned. It was sitting in the corner watching them, as if it might suck out their very thoughts. Milkthistle turned. Greychild looked at her face. It was as if she could see the creature, and yet not see it at all.

"There are no scabbindgers here," she repeated as she turned from the room, slamming the door.

Greychild sat on the bed for a while till finally the scabbindger scuttled away. The shadows of carts sailed across the ceiling carrying bales of fine cloth up from the docks. Then he noticed the door. The door stood half-open. Milkthistle had not locked it when she left him before. Slowly Greychild crept out onto the landing. A floorboard creaked. He heard scuttling and scurrying in the walls, under the floor. Another scabbindger shot out of the darkness and vanished through a crack in the floor. Then came another and another one, two. These did not vanish but followed each other into a room.

The door hung ajar. Greychild peered inside. There on the bed lay Milkthistle. Her ashen dress was rumpled and her hair tangled wild. She stared past him with fevered eyes as her flesh crawled with scabbindgers, her arms and her legs, crawling and scuttling to settle on her neck. Greychild stared into her eyes, but she gazed straight past him as she writhed on the bed, a pale smile on her lips.

Greychild ran down the stairs, to find the heavy front door bolted and locked. He beat his fists at the panels, scrabbled with his fingers - but he was trapped. He turned and saw Milkthistle waiting for him, rattling her keys at the top of the stairs.

"You can't get away," she told him.

And then she smiled and led him back to his room. All of the scabbindgers had gone. Sun shone through the window. She fed him eggs and oatcakes seasoned with herbs and spices such as he had never tasted before. She sang to him as she washed him down with warm soapy water from a bowl, then dressed him again in the tunic and britches and sat down beside him on the bed.

"There," she said. "Now you are my boy. You would not want to run away. You would not want to run, for if you did - Gobbeth would get you."

"Who is Gobbeth?" Greychild asked, peering out of the window.

Milkthistle shivered. A shadow of panic passed through her eyes.

"You would not want to meet Gobbeth," she said. "Gobbeth roams these streets day and night. He never sleeps. His face is hidden by a mask of leather set all about with jagged wire and thorns. If he kisses you, your lips will be torn, your cheeks ripped and scarred and your eyes gouged out."

The next day Milkthistle dressed Greychild again, this time in new clothes, a green velvet cloak and a hat with a peacock feather. She led him out about the streets, waving to one and all and bidding Greychild to doff his hat to every lady who passed them by. Greychild did this with a surly scowl until she cuffed him about the head.

"*Smile* when my friends smile at you. Do what I say!"

And Greychild smiled. He smiled until his face was aching and then he smiled some more again and swept his hat so low that the feather trailed in the dust.

"Pick it up!" Milkthistle hissed. "Not like that!"

Greychild sighed and followed on behind her. The streets were not so busy now. They passed empty warehouses, the windows barred and boarded. A gang of sailors jostled beside them, singing raucous songs.

"Stay close by me," Milkthistle snapped. "And watch out for Gobbeth, he roams this way. He goes wherever he pleases, for he is wild and free."

Greychild closed his eyes. He remembered a wood by a middling village at the foot of a tall misty mountain, at the back of the river next to the meadows where the grey geese gathered. He remembered Crossdogs and Ravenhair and wished they were with him now.

Milkthistle grabbed him suddenly.

"Stay close by me," she pleaded.

There before them stood Gobbeth, his face a mass of thorns and wire, razorblades dangling from each ear. He did not move. Greychild stared. Milkthistle's screams echoed back along the deserted street as she ran, leaving Greychild to face Gobbeth alone. Greychild stood his ground, then dropped into a squat, his palms spread open.

Gobbeth lunged towards him. Greychild sidestepped and turned. Gobbeth towered over him. Greychild wished now Crossdogs was here, to protect him the way he always had back in Brunt Boggart.

Gobbeth laughed. Greychild paused. The laugh sounded familiar to him, like warm wind rippling through swaying trees. Gobbeth pounced. His breath close and heavy behind the mask of wire and thorns.

Then he pulled the mask away and there was only laughter, filling the street as the two boys wrestled in a swirl of joy, bearing each other down to the dust. They laughed and laughed and laughed full more until their very jaws were sore.

"Crossdogs!" Greychild exclaimed beneath his breath. "Crossdogs... what are you doing here? You've not turned to Gobbeth - the boy they're all afeared of?"

Crossdogs laughed again.

"Nothing to be afeared of there. First day I came here Gobbeth leapt at me out of an alleyway. But he was no match for a Brunt Boggart lad. Weak as a puppy, soon as I gripped him. Ripped the mask right off his face. He was all pale and trembling beneath. Looked in need of a meal. So I put on his mask and watched how everyone stayed out of his way... what of you?"

Greychild explained how Milkthistle had trapped him and promised him a scarf.

"But she ran off soon as she saw you. She's frit scared of Gobbeth."

"Here," said Crossdogs, fastening the mask around Greychild's face. "You're Gobbeth now."

"I'm Gobbeth now!" Greychild cried and before Crossdogs could stop him he raced away.

As he dashed down crowded streets, women and young children cowered in doorways and watched him go by, until he made his way back to Milkthistle's door. There he beat both full and loud.

"Gobbeth - what do you want with me?" Milkthistle begged, wide-eyed.

"Give me the scarf which you promised to Greychild." The voice growled hoarsely from behind the mask. "He wants it for his mother."

"Do not kiss me, Gobbeth," Milkthistle begged as the wire and thorns brushed close against her cheek. "I will give you anything if only you leave me alone."

She closed the door quickly and Greychild heard her running up the stairs then scrambling back again. She threw the door open and stood there, a long silken scarf in her hand. She smiled as she twined it round his neck then slowly looked him up and down.

"Take off your mask," she said. "For I see by your cloak of green velvet that you're not Gobbeth at all."

Greychild lowered the mass of wire, thorns and leather.

"True - I am not Gobbeth. But Gobbeth sent me here. Gobbeth said you must give me the scarf, and I must return this cloak and this hat, for I am Greychild, born in the woods and not your boy to lock in a room."

"Then you must come in," whispered Milkthistle, "for your clothes lie on the bed where you left them."

Greychild stepped forward.

"Wait," she said, raising a hand. "Leave Gobbeth's mask here. I don't want that fearsome thing under my roof."

Greychild hung the mask on the handle of the door, before following her again to the room at the top of the house.

"Here are your old clothes," she smiled. "I will leave you a while to change."

But soon as she had gone, Greychild heard her key

twisting in the door. He was trapped in the attic room again.

"You are my boy once more," Milkthistle cried.

Crossdogs roamed the streets, watching how people stared at him now he was not Gobbeth no more but a boy from Brunt Boggart lost in Arleccra. He wandered the shanty town down by the harbour, built of the wreckage of boats and boxes washed up on the shore. Here lonely wifen sat waiting for their sailor-men to come home from the sea, seagulls scratted and grey pigeons pecked as ravens looked on with cold dark eyes while rats scurried between puddles of stagnant water. Soon enough he tracked up through the alleys until he came to a tall house. A mask of leather hung outside, all studded with wire and thorns. He seized it up and put it on and beat upon the door.

Milkthistle stood before him and screamed.

"I am Gobbeth, true as true," Crossdogs roared. "Release the boy you are holding here."

Milkthistle pulled the key from her skirt and ran to the top of the house to return with Greychild behind her, dressed in his travelling clothes again, while draped about his neck was a scarf of maroons and purples, moss green and black, all picked out in threads of silver and gold.

Then she turned to Crossdogs, who watched through the eyes of the mask.

"I have no boy now," she sighed. "You are all that's left to me, Gobbeth. Do not leave me all alone."

Before Crossdogs could stop her, she kissed him. She kissed the mask of wire and thorns - and as she pulled away, her lips were torn, her pale cheeks ripped and her eyes ringed round with blood.

SCUMKNUCKLE

Let me tell you... Let me tell you... Greychild delved deep in his pocket for the Eye of Glass, hoping it might show him his mother again, just as it had before - standing here in this very market where now he leaned against a peeling pillar. A knife-grinder pressed dull blades to a wheel, sending sparks flying high in the air while Greychild wiped the dust from the Glass and glimpsed two shadowy figures. One was Scritch, standing at the edge of the stream by the hump-backed bridge, squinnying for anything that glistened. And the boy beside him was Greychild himself, scooping down hopefully into the water to pull out the very Glass which he now held in his hand.

Greychild looked up and stared about the market, and there was Scritch himself, as real as real, squat and scowling in the shadows where the bone men scratted for rips of paper, tattered rags and scrags of cloth. Scritch watched and waited till a woman came by all decked out in necklaces, bracelets and rings. He hurried quickly towards her then stumbled and tripped right into her, not enough to knock her over, not enough to do any harm. The woman stood startled then brushed down her dress as Scritch smiled and apologised before sauntering away. As soon as he turned the corner he began to move faster as he heard the woman let out a cry, "Where is my ear-ring, my bracelets and my jewels?"

A while later, and a while later more, Scritch stood again on the far side of the market while the wifen pawed over the baubles laid out on the tray which he hung around his neck.

"Only the best," he nodded and winked. "Only the best. Anything that glistens, anything that shines."

"This shines," exclaimed a woman in a turquoise gown. "Shines like the necklace I was wearing yesterday."

She glared at Scritch accusingly, but Scritch only shrugged.

"How can it be? If it was your necklace true, why then it would be round your neck and not here on my tray."

Greychild watched as the woman flounced away. Soon as she'd gone, he pushed forward.

"Scritch - don't you know me?" he said.

Scritch gazed at him quizzically.

"Ain't no streams here, boy. Go away."

Greychild went away.

"In this city nothing is ever what it seems," he pondered. "Maybe wasn't really Scritch after all but some other old'un come to trick and deceive."

He pushed his hand in his pocket, just to touch the smooth surface of the Glass which had brought him here. But his pocket was empty.

"Scritch," he muttered. "You old trickster. You got the Glass quick as quick. Never showed it you when first I found it, but now you got it after all."

Next day Greychild headed back to the market. Scritch was there again, the dull sun glinting off the baubles and trinkets laid out on his tray. A ring, a bracelet, a string of beads... but no Glass was to be seen. Greychild flitted back and forth so Scritch didn't see him. Then Scritch slipped his hand in his pocket. The sun glinted on something shining. Scritch gazed around then slid the dull polished crystal into the centre of his tray.

Greychild sidled up to him as a small crowd jostled round.

"How much you want for this?"

He nodded at the Glass.

Scritch peered at him.

"How much you want to give?"

"Two silver shillen," Greychild replied.

Scritch raised an eyebrow in surprise.

"If'n you think this glass is so precious that you would give me this much - then other folks round here be sure to give me four. And if someone offer four, why then another would give me six."

Greychild shook his head.

"Ain't got six," he said. "Tell the truth, ain't even got two."

He turned sadly away and stood and watched the crowd of wifen milling around, pawing over the geejaws that glittered on Scritch's tray. Each time one of them plucked up the Glass, Greychild closed his eyes.

"If she bought it," he thought, "why then I could snatch it back again..."

But no-one did. Bought rings and bracelets, necklaces and combs till all that was left on the tray was the Glass.

"No-one wants it anyway," Greychild muttered. "I'll give you two silver shillen, just like I said before."

Scritch shook his head.

"You told me you didn't have the two."

Greychild grinned.

"Told you false. Told you true..."

He felt his skin tingle. His breath came short and fast. Then quick as a flash he made a grab. He made a grab, but Scritch was faster, same as he'd always been. He pulled the tray away and slipped the Glass back in his pocket before Greychild had hardly moved.

Scritch eyed the boy and winked knowingly.

"Greychild, my lad, I know you true - and you know I was always faster than you. Was then. Still am. If'n you want this glass so bad, come back when you find me not two silver shillen, not four, not six - but ten."

"Ten silver shillen, ten silver shillen..." Greychild muttered, lost in the crush of the crowd. A woman jostled past him, a bag filled with everything and anything and nothing at all dangling from her shoulder. Greychild stepped in close to her and tried to hoist the bag. He felt it strain and slip, then slither to the floor. The woman stood and looked at him accusingly. Greychild felt a hot sweat pass over him, but did not run. He stood his ground. Bent and picked up the bag.

Gathered the trinkets which had scattered all about, then handed them to the woman who frowned and then smiled.

"Why, thank you young man," she said, before setting off briskly in the opposite direction.

Greychild paused and looked back at Scritch. Was he watching him? He could never be sure. He seemed intent on his own business - showing off the baubles for sale on his tray. Greychild gazed long enough to be sure that the Eye of Glass was still there.

"Ten silver shillen... ten silver shillen..."

Greychild saw a leather purse hanging loosely from a belt and snatched sudden, snatched quick, just as Scritch had taught him. But the buckle held fast. Greychild had no time to run as he found himself staring into a pair of heavy-lidded eyes.

"What's your game, young'un?"

Greychild was hauled clean off his heels by a sluggish shaven-headed figure.

"I'm Scumknuckle," breathed a rasping whisper. "Don't you know who I am? Don't you know what I do?"

Greychild shook his head, his legs rattling as Scumknuckle dropped him suddenly.

"I keep an eye out for little scrunts like you, thieving from the market. Don't like to see no-one trying to steal, so I specially don't like to find no-one trying to steal from me!... You understand?"

Greychild understood. Greychild understood that Scumknuckle had gripped him again before he even had time to think if he could flee. Greychild understood that Scumknuckle was dragging him out through the market, past the corner where Scritch stood unblinking.

Dragged him down past the water pump and a line of barrows filled with stinking waste. Down to the steps that led him to a dimly-lit basement. Greychild blinked and looked around. In the gloom he could see a shadowy figure sitting before him.

"Who have we here?" a velvet voice hissed.

"Snizzleslide!" Greychild exclaimed.

For sure enough, sitting deep in the damp dripping darkness was Snizzleslide, the trickster. Before him on a table he placed three upturned cups, then produced a pure white shell, edged a delicate pink.

"See the shell," hissed Snizzleslide.

Greychild nodded.

"I place it under a cup."

Greychild watched.

Snizzleslide swapped the cups about and about, faster and faster. Then stopped.

"Where is it now?"

Greychild shrugged.

"Pick one," Snizzleslide wheedled.

Greychild guessed. Snizzleslide turned the cup over. There was no shell. He smiled and turned up the cup on the end of the row.

"It is here," he grinned. "Now watch again. Watch carefully."

Greychild watched the cup where Snizzleslide had hidden the shell. He kept his eye fixed as Snizzleslide wove them in and out, about and about.

"Now which one?"

Greychild rubbed his head. Paused awhile and pointed. Snizzleslide turned the cup over slowly. There underneath was the shell, gleaming white.

"See - it is easy. Now play again. But this time we

put some money on the table. Put down one shillen. If you find the shell, why then - I'll give you three. Think what you could buy with three silver shillen. What do you desire?"

Greychild paused. He knew what he desired.

"Come on, come on," Snizzleslide hissed. "Why wait? Let's play. Put a shillen on the table and you could win three. But if you don't find the shell, why then I keep your money. I stand to lose far more than you."

Greychild hesitated then reached in his pocket for the one silver shillen he had. Immediately Snizzleslide spread three shining coins on the other side.

"Take the shell," he said. "Place it under one of the cups."

Greychild paused. The shell lay cool and hard in his palm. He reached out towards the cup at the end, but then changed his mind. He put the shell under the cup in the middle. Snizzleslide seized the containers, mixing them and swirling them about and about.

"Do you see it?" he cried. "Are you watching?" as Greychild kept his eyes fixed on the cup where he'd placed the shell. But the cups were a blur and Greychild's head was a blur as Snizzleslide fixed him with a glittering eye.

> "Under one cup the shell is cast,
> Be it first or be it last.
> Watch the cups and you will see -
> Do you give me one shillen,
> Or do I give you three?"

Snizzleslide stopped. He gazed at Greychild, his

tongue flicking quickly about his lips.

"Pick one," he invited casually.

Greychild was sweating. He looked at his shillen. He looked at Snizzleslide's three. He had long since lost track of the cup he had been following. Which could it be now? A glimmer of light from a lantern flickered across the porcelain.

"... do you give me one shillen, or do I give you three?" Snizzleslide mused.

Greychild gritted his teeth. He closed his eyes. He thought of the Eye of Glass lying out on Scritch's tray. He reached and lifted one cup, slow and slow. Felt sure he could glimpse the shell nestling there. But as he tipped it over, was nothing. It was gone. And quick as quick, Greychild's shillen was gone too as Snizzleslide scooped it up, along with the other three.

Greychild hung his head in his hands.

"What can I do? I have no money now."

Snizzleslide patted him on the shoulder.

"Not to worry," he said. "Come with me."

As they climbed the basement's uneven steps, Greychild was aware of Scumknuckle's heavy-lidded eyes glaring after him.

Snizzleslide slithered and scurried through the streets.

"See! See!" he cried.

There on the corner was a boy dressed in velvet britches and a waistcoat, crying -

"Watch the cups and you will see -

Do you give me one shillen,

Or do I give you three?" as he glanced nervously this way and that.

Before him on a table he had set three cups and in

between them lay a pink-edged shell.

"Watch this." Snizzleslide dragged Greychild back into the shadows.

Soon enough, a small crowd gathered - and just as Snizzleslide had done before, the boy twirled the cups around and about, and just as before the shell seemed to vanish. Snizzleslide licked his lips as he watched the boy rake in piles of silver shillen. Then watched a while and a while more until the crowd had vanished - and then he slithered out. The boy looked up, startled.

"Snizzleslide!" he cried.

"Snizzleslide, indeed," purred the trickster. "What do you have for me?"

"Please," begged the boy. "Give me a while more. I ain't had time to make the settle I owe you. Give me a while more. Sundown you said. Sundown you come."

The shadows were lengthening.

"Sundown will soon be here, my boy," Snizzleslide hissed. "I been watching you. Made my settle twice over and more. I hope you're not holding out on me."

The boy shivered nervously. Greychild could see his pockets were bulging with shillen. A squat, short-legged dog appeared out of an entry. It gave a growl. The boy stood helpless.

"Please Snizzleslide, I meant no harm, but my sister is sick. She needs a potion. She needs me to fetch her Corbin Night-thorn's Morning Sunrise from where Snuffwidget brews it down on the dockside. Let me get it for her tonight and I'll pay you double tomorrow."

The dog growled again as it moved closer.

"What do I care of tomorrow, boy?" Snizzleslide whispered. "Settles must be paid each day by sunset. And sunset it is now."

The boy cringed back as the dog sprang at him, but not a dog. Scumknuckle stood before him, his glowering hulk towering. He picked the boy off his feet. The table and the cups clattered to the floor and silver shillen scattered all about.

Snizzleslide slid after them.

"Just as I thought. Here's my settle and more... Greychild, don't just stand there. Help me pick it up."

Greychild stooped then looked up again to see Scumknuckle drag the hapless lad away and trample the table and cups under heavy studded boots. He turned back to find Snizzleslide watching him with a fixed and glittering smile.

"So what do you say?"

Greychild said nothing.

Snizzleslide edged closer.

"So what do you say?" he hissed again. "Think you could do it? Think you could run a game for me?"

Greychild shrugged his shoulders.

"Think what you could do," Snizzleslide wheedled. "You could make enough in a day or two to buy anything you want."

Greychild shuffled his feet and thought of the Eye of Glass still lying on Scritch's tray.

"Or put it another way," Snizzleslide cajoled. "You have seen Scumknuckle. You have seen what he can do. You have seen that he can come to you any way he chooses. Some days he's a dog, other days he's a raven. He can come as a rat, he can come as a shadow - he can come as a flitting bat with wings of flame. And for sure he will find you. And for sure he will remember. He will remember you already for trying to dip his pocket."

The next day Greychild stood under the eaves of a merchant house. Pigeons and crows rattled above him, their droppings scattered all around. He set out his table and carefully placed the cups in a line. Then he slipped the white shell from his pocket.

"Under one cup the shell is cast," he cried. "Be it first or be it last..."

He began to stir the cups about, just as Snizzleslide had shown him. The crowd were jostling round him, wifen and girlen and market boys, their eyes hard and sharp. Greychild was sweating, his fingers slippery as he clutched the cups. Round and round. Round and about. He let out a shout.

"... do you give me one shillen, or do I give you three?"

Everyone pointed to the cup in the middle. Greychild winced. He knew sure as they did that the shell was there. He tipped the cup slowly, hoping that it wasn't, but there it lay glistening in the sun. A clamour of hands thrust forward, clutching for their money. Greychild paid them reluctantly. Now half the float that Snizzleslide gave him had gone. To settle up by sunset he would have to win every game for the rest of the day - or else Scumknuckle would come.

As the shadows lengthened, Greychild played on, his greasy palms slipping as he twisted the cups. He lost again, again and again - but then he watched the glad faces of the wifen and children as they hurried away. Some to buy dresses and trinkets, but others hobbling off crying, "Now I can buy the potion I need."

On the edge of the crowd stood a tall man who stroked a thin moustache and leant upon a cane. He watched the game attentively, hissing gently to himself, for it was Snizzleslide true as true, who in the end stepped up to play. He watched as Greychild switched the cups, he watched as he shifted them and shuffled them about.

"Watch the cups..." Greychild stuttered. Then he stopped. Snizzleslide stared straight into his eyes, but Greychild did not recognise him.

"Well, sir," he said, lifting the cup. "It seems you have won... let me pay you..."

Snizzleslide pocketed three of the silver shillen that he had given Greychild that morning, then slid back into the shadows to watch the game in play.

"Let me win," a small boy pleaded. "I need to buy new teeth for my grandmother."

"My father needs a wheel for his cart," another wailed, "else he cannot go to work."

"My sister needs strong medicine to cure her from crying each time the full moon comes..."

Greychild smiled at them all.

"My master Snizzleslide is wise and kind. He likes to see people play. He likes to see people win. He wants everyone to be happy!"

Snizzleslide slid away, slithering up the sides of buildings, along windowsills, clinging to gutters, all the time squinnying for baubles that might glitter like stars. When he returned to the basement he called Scumknuckle to him.

"Fetch me the new boy," he hissed. "Fetch me Greychild. He is standing in the market square giving away all our shillen."

Scumknuckle snarled and lumbered to the door.

"*Quickly*," Snizzleslide urged.

Scumknuckle nodded and in a trice was a dog again, then a hump-backed rat scurrying through the gutters till he came to the market. It was sunset. There stood Greychild, rummaging frantically through his empty pockets. He glanced about, but there was no-one in sight. He did not see the rat scuttling behind him, trailing him down the alleyways, then suddenly cutting in front of him and appearing as a dog.

Greychild smiled. He was used to dogs and patted this creature on the head, even though it bared its teeth and snarled. Greychild stroked its matted fur.

"Are you hungry, lad? Come with me. My master Snizzleslide is generous. Come home with me and I'm sure that he will feed you."

At this Scumknuckle rose to his full height, a man again and more. He pressed his face up close to Greychild.

"Your master Snizzleslide is angry at your generosity and wants to see you right away."

Snizzleslide was waiting at the end of the wharf. A small boat bobbed in the water, rising and falling with the swell of the river.

"Get in," he hissed as Scumknuckle pushed Greychild roughly into the craft which rocked alarmingly, shipping a slop of dull grey water.

Snizzleslide scrambled in as Scumknuckle seized the oars, hauling them out right to the very middle of the river. Greychild's eyes were closed tight. He felt sure they meant to bind his arms and legs and tip him over the side. He gazed back to see the dying sun glinting off the windows of Arleccra.

Scumknuckle paused and rested on his oars.

Snizzleslide shot him a glance.

"Keep going," he urged.

Scumknuckle guided them through the swell and suck of the water. Soon enough they slipped under the shadows of the trees that edged the shore on the far side of the river. Scumknuckle lashed the boat to a mooring post and Snizzleslide led them up a winding path onto an esplanade lined with silver trees.

"Who lives here?" Greychild asked.

"Who lives here?" Snizzleslide hissed. "Who lives here? - Let me tell you. I don't live here, and Scumknuckle don't neither. Where do we live? In a cold damp basement at the back end of an alleyway on the other side of the river. We've come a long way, you and me, Greychild my lad. Come from Brunt Boggart, down along the Pedlar Man's Track. Come a long way - but we don't live *here*. Why don't we live here?"

Greychild squinted sideways at Snizzleslide.

"We ain't got no shillen," he replied.

"Quite right," said Snizzleslide. "We ain't got no shillen. And what little we got, we trick and steal. I make no secret of that. Always have done, always will. Trick and steal - it's what I do. But what do these folk do?"

Greychild shrugged.

"What do they do?"

"Let me tell you," Snizzleslide confided. "They trick and steal - same as me and you. These folk own the workrooms where girlen go to toil in the darkness. And when they go to collect their pay, these folk tell them they have spent it all in the slop kitchen buying soup and crusts to keep up their strength through the long working day. They own the mulch-sheds where they squeeze the grease from cargoes of nuts to feed to those who can afford nothing more. And down on the dockside they run the taverns where sailors come and drink their wage. When the men are drunk they lock them up and send them off to sea again before they've ever made it home to see their wifen and childern.

"Never mind no game of cup and shell. These folk are the real winners. These folk trick the money out of poor'uns who can't afford to lose it."

A high gate swung open and a large man confronted them, his pot belly barely concealed by a silken robe. His long tongue lolled lazily, dull purple with salt lick and red ruby wine. His gut rolled and rumbled, uneasy with sweetmeats and sourmilk, heavy with offal and undercooked veal.

"What are you doing here?" he demanded. "Be off with you."

But Snizzleslide smiled.

"We have come to do you a favour," he said.

Lollingtongue frowned as he stared down his nose at the troublesome snake and his two companions.

"What favour can *you* do *me*?" he sneered.

"What favour do you wish for?" Snizzleslide replied.

"My head is seized with dreams," Lollingtongue sighed, "of all that I have, and yet all those things I cannot buy. What I dream is beyond my reach..."

"We are here to help you," Snizzleslide smiled as he pulled out three cups and a pink-edged shell.

Then to Greychild's amazement, he pulled out the Eye of Glass and held it up for Lollingtongue to see.

"This glass," he hissed, "is worth more than all your wishes. This glass will let you see the one thing you truly desire."

Lollingtongue made a grab for it, but Snizzleslide quickly pulled the glass away.

"Put down a shillen," he said. "If you find the shell, the Glass is yours."

Lollingtongue rolled his eyes.

"Don't carry no shillen in these pockets. But if this Glass is worth winning, then win it I must..."

And from his ample robe he poured fistfuls of gold, a diamond-studded pin and an emerald ring. Greychild blinked and looked on as Snizzleslide cried -

"Under one cup the shell is cast, be it first or be it last..."

He switched the cups around and about, as slickly as he ever did. Lollingtongue rubbed the back of his neck. He was sweating now as his hand hovered above first one cup and then another. Then picked up the third. Snizzleslide paused and looked him in the eye.

"Are you sure?" he asked.

Lollingtongue nodded slowly.

Snizzleslide raised the sup.

The shell was gone.

Quick as a flash, Snizzleslide flipped over the far cup to show the shell, and as he did so, Scumknuckle seized up their winnings before Lollingtongue could protest and the three of them bundled away down the path to the waiting boat.

Back on the other side of the river, Snizzleslide set up the game again. It was night now, but the waterfront was alive with flame dancers, fire eaters, knife throwers, jugglers, beggars and gangs of roaming girlen whose pale faces were painted with blood red smiles.

"You play," Snizzleslide hissed, pushing Greychild

forward. "You still owe me your settle. I'll give you till dawn."

Greychild stood nervously beside the table, watching as Snizzleslide and Scumknuckle stood and watched him from the shadow of a doorway.

"...watch the cups and you will see - do you give me one shillen, or do I give you three?" he called out half-heartedly.

A shillen lost, a shillen won as people came and went, more eager to see the dancing bear who was roaring inside a small striped tent. Snizzleslide sidled up beside him.

"Listen boy," he said. "Let me give you a tip. If you think your player has found the shell, just cry - *With your shillen three, tell me what do you see? Close your eyes and dream of your prize*. You won't believe how many will shut their eyes just for a moment... and then you switch the cups again."

Snizzleslide winked and slipped back to Scumknuckle who was devouring a hot meat pie from one of the stalls.

"Under the cup the shell is cast..." Greychild called again. And then before him at the table stood a young woman. She looked lost and alone, her eyes rimmed with crying and her hand clutching her belly.

"I am hungry. I am thirsty," she whispered.

Greychild stopped and stared at her face, half lit by the flickering shadows. Could it be? At last this was his mother, lost in the city, same as he remembered her lost in the woods. In his head he heard the words turning, "*Coddle me, coddle me, my darling son...*" The woman moved closer. Greychild held out his hand, hoping to feel the warmth he remembered, her hair soft as leaves draped all around him, her lips sweet as berries as she kissed him, her body warm as sun-baked earth as she held him, her tongue sharp as thorns when she scolded him. But as their fingers touched, all he could sense was numbness and cold.

His head was spinning. Was this his mother? He could not be sure. He peered at her again in the half light and then looked down at the cups on the table. He knew Snizzleslide was watching him.

"Do you have a shillen?" he asked.

"Yes sir, I do."

Greychild hesitated.

"Well don't give it to me," he whispered under his breath. "Take your shillen with you and buy a bowl of hot soup."

The woman shook her head.

"If I win this game," she said, "then I won't have only one shillen, why then I will have three!"

Greychild glanced at Snizzleslide. Snizzleslide nodded and Greychild took the money. The woman watched, sucking one finger and gazing with eyes that were tired beyond hunger as Greychild slowly shuffled the cups. He stopped. The woman stroked her belly and pointed slowly. Then Greychild heard Snizzleslide hiss from the shadows.

"Switch the cups like I showed you," he urged. "Switch the cups."

Greychild's heart was heavy. Here was his mother who had fed him. Whether she knew him or not, he had to feed her. He had to let her win. But Snizzleslide needed his settle and Scumknuckle began to grow restless.

"Close your eyes and dream of your prize....."

Greychild intoned.

The face of the woman who stood shivering before him was suddenly lit by a flare of flame from the fire-eater's torch. Her features were blotched and scarred. She coughed and bit her lip as she closed her eyes. Greychild turned away. It was not his mother at all. He was about to switch the cups when Snizzleslide slid from the shadows and stayed his hand.

"Leave it be," he insisted. "Leave it be."

Greychild raised the cup. There was the shell. The woman's tired face spread into a smile.

"I've won," she cried dreamily.

"Yes, you have won," Snizzleslide declared and gestured to Scumknuckle who stepped forward from the doorway. Snizzleslide nodded.

"Here is your prize."

Scumknuckle handed the trembling woman the bag that they had taken from Lollingtongue back across the river. The bag that was filled with fistfuls of gold, the diamond-studded pin and the emerald ring. The young woman ran off, not even daring to open it to see what was inside. Snizzleslide met Greychild's puzzled expression.

"Sometimes to win is to lose," he said. "And sometimes to lose is to win."

"But where is the Glass?" Greychild asked. "And how did you come by it?"

Snizzleslide shrugged. "Scritch is quick, but I am quicker."

Scumknuckle jerked it out from his pocket.

"And I am quicker again!" Greychild cried as he made a grab. Snizzleslide struck too, but both of them missed as the Eye spiralled upwards then fell to the ground where it shattered into splinters.

Greychild turned and walked away. Now he knew that if his mother was in this city at all, he would have to find her all by himself, for the Glass would help him no more.

When dawn broke, and all the flame dancers and fire eaters and knife throwers were gone, who should appear but Scritch, who scooped up the fragments of glass as they glistened on the cold damp cobbles like so many stars, and laid them all out on his tray.

THE WOMAN IN BLUE

Let me tell you... let me tell you how Ravenhair woke on a cold narrow bed wound in threadbare sheets at the back of a rackety boarding house. From along the dank grey corridor she could hear dull voices grumbling and wheezing, the swill of water and the cracked rattle of cups. Ravenhair dressed quickly, pulled her shawl round her shoulders and clambered down the wooden steps that led to the alley outside.

The market traders were setting up their stalls, a tarnished array of trinkets and baubles, while a one-eyed cat scurried out of the gully. Ravenhair called it over, but the cat arched its back and bared its claws before slinking away.

Ravenhair followed the cobbled streets that slid slow and slippery down to the river where overloaded boats plied back and forth. Ramshackle warehouses rose high around her, where sharp-faced boys and grizzled old men unloaded barrels and bales hauled up from the harbour. Beside the quay stood a sagging collection of tents, painted bright colours but faded and torn. A crowd of finely-dressed women drifted in and out, trailing children in silk brocade. Their faces seemed to shine although their skin was so thin it was almost transparent, as if they had never seen the sun. As Ravenhair watched she felt a hand touch her shoulder and turned to see one of the women standing before her smiling a stern chill smile. She wore a long blue dress and her face was as pale as the morning. High above them lost gulls swirled, skimming along the harbour front, while smoke billowed from a brazier outside the gaudy tent.

"Come with me," the woman said suddenly, and before she could reply, Ravenhair found herself tugged away from the river, through a swirl of winding streets, past pot-swills and lantern-gardens, dimly-lit taverns and money-lenders' stalls.

"Stop!" gasped Ravenhair. "Where are we going?"

She tried to slip from the woman's grip, but the woman held fast and strong. They paused by a courtyard of tailors' shops where bundles of silks and taffetas spilled out on the uneven flagstones. Ravenhair stared at the woman's face. She had no idea how old she might be. Her skin was so pale, as pale as the snow, but her eyes seemed a little warmer now.

"Come quickly," she said and dragged Ravenhair on through a bewildering maze of alleys and gullies, past flower-sellers and hawkers, knife-sharpeners and beggars. Suddenly they stopped in front of a tall house on a narrow street. Two worn steps led up to a shabby front door, its grimy windows curtained with a mesh of dull drapes.

Ravenhair was trembling. The sky above was heavy with smoke, shading out the sun. As the woman let go of her hand, Ravenhair looked this way and that, wondering which way to run, but the street was as long to the left as it was to the right.

"Follow me," the woman said, holding out her long slender hand. Ravenhair stood quite still in the hallway, staring up at the high marbled ceiling and the chandelier which hung above them, glittering like ice. Before them a wide white staircase swept up to the floor above.

The woman smiled.

"Don't be surprised, my child," she said. "Nothing is ever what it seems. Not here, not anywhere."

And she led her on along a corridor hung with a hundred mirrors. Ravenhair peered into them as they hurried by and she saw herself side by side with this woman and then not a woman at all. In the next mirror she was running with a deer and then a tall white mare and then a wolf and a fox and an eagle. Each mirror reflected in the mirror that hung on the opposite wall until Ravenhair found herself lost in a forest of reflections with a dance of creatures spinning around her.

"Stop! Stop!" she cried and they stopped. The woman stood beside her again. She was smiling kindly now and her hand felt soft and warm. They both stood breathless and laughing and the woman's laughter was happy and full. For a moment she held Ravenhair close in a sudden embrace.

"But who are you?" Ravenhair wanted to know. "And what is this place?"

The woman gazed into Ravenhair's eyes.

"I am Ashblossom," she replied as she pressed one

finger against Ravenhair's lips and led her out into a courtyard with a high glass ceiling. It was warmer than a summer's day and everywhere orchids flowered, vivid reds and purples and yellows. All around echoed the cries of a hundred exotic birds, their wings even brighter than the flowers.

Ashblossom sat down on a low stone wall which surrounded a pool in the centre of the courtyard where a fountain flowed, sending cascades of water in ever-changing patterns. Ravenhair dipped a hand in the water. It was warm and luxurious. Ashblossom bent over and let her long silvery hair fall forward. The nape of her neck was slender and white as she lowered her head and slowly began to wash her flowing tresses. Ravenhair watched in fascination as Ashblossom raised her head, her face sparkling with rivulets of water.

"Why don't you join me?" she asked.

Ravenhair unfastened the ribbon from her locks, the ribbon dark as night which her Grandmother Ghostmantle had given her. She hung it carefully over the wall of the pool then bent her head forward as Ashblossom had done. The water was soft as milk to her touch and she let it soak gently into her scalp, rubbing her fingers in circular movements. She rinsed her hair and shook it as she rose to her feet so that a shower of silver droplets flew through the air and the birds in the trees rose with a flap and a clatter of wings, clamouring and squawking to the higher branches.

Ravenhair felt full of life as she ran around the courtyard, letting her long wet hair flow free while Ashblossom watched and smiled, cupping water through her hands as she sat at the edge of the pool.

"Come," she said and led Ravenhair again, back

along the corridor of mirrors. This time they walked slowly, chatting intently about anything they thought of and nothing at all, so that Ravenhair hardly noticed that when she glanced at the mirrors, all that she saw was a woman and a girl. The deer and the mare, the wolf, the fox and the eagle had gone. Instead, just a corridor, serene and white, and the sound of one harp playing which seemed to come from everywhere and anywhere, but nowhere that Ravenhair could see.

They arrived in a spacious dining hall where a meal was set on the table. Ashblossom gestured Ravenhair to be seated. Ravenhair lifted the cover from her plate and was surprised to find her favourite meal of dumplings, chicken and thinly sliced parsnips.

Ravenhair looked over at her companion's plate. It was piled high with fruits and fancies so brightly coloured and giving off an aroma which she'd never smelt anywhere before. When the meal was over, Ashblossom patted her lips delicately with a starched white napkin.

"Now," she said to Ravenhair, "I'll show you to your room."

She led her up the marble stairs, along another corridor and into a small white room. As soon as Ravenhair was inside, Ashblossom kissed her once on the forehead.

"Sleep well," she said and closed the door.

Ravenhair stood and gazed around. The bed was low and narrow but looked soft and comfortable and was covered all over with a silver eiderdown. Ravenhair stretched and ran her fingers through her long dark hair which was nearly dry now - so she decided to tie it up again, ready for the night. She reached into her pocket for her long black ribbon, but the ribbon wasn't there. She searched her other pocket - and then she remembered that she had left it hanging over the wall of the fountain.

Ravenhair stood up again.

"I'm sure Ashblossom won't mind if I just go down and get it," she said to herself, but when she tried the handle of the door she found it would not open. She twisted it this way and that and realised the door was locked. She crossed the room to the window. It was covered by long black curtains, already drawn, so that Ravenhair had no notion whether it was dark outside or daylight still, or maybe was just turning dusk. She tugged at the curtains and they parted gently, but to her surprise she found not a window but a mirror staring at her. Ravenhair smiled at the face in the reflection and began to twist at a strand of her hair, still wishing she had her ribbon with her. But the face that smiled back was not her own but Ashblossom's pale features.

Ravenhair gasped, but the face in the mirror made no response, just stared at her, steady and unblinking. Ravenhair took one step closer to see what she was seeing. Perhaps there was no mirror, but really a window after all and Ashblossom was on the other side. But no, Ravenhair could see the rest of the room clearly reflected: the bed, the walls, the tightly locked door. And as she stepped forward, so Ashblossom retreated, further and further, back into the reflection of the room. Ravenhair watched her go, but as she watched, Ashblossom changed. Her legs grew longer, her back arched forward. Her face extended until she was not a woman but a deer. Not a deer in a forest, running free, but a deer here in this room.

THE WOMAN IN BLUE

Ravenhair turned quickly but the room was empty. She turned to look in the mirror again and the deer began to tread the floor, and as she did so, she felt herself rise up taller and her mottled coat turned from brown to a vivid white. She raised her head and gave out a cry, the cry of a mare that needs to run free, as she tossed her mane and her eyes flashed wild, then turned darker than dark. And her coat was grey and shaggy and she howled an anguished howl to the moon which she could not see, and then crouched down again, her belly and her long red tail pressed vixen-tight to the floor.

Ravenhair was deer, she was mare, was wolf and vixen. Until none of these anymore as she felt herself rising, intense and powerful, to the top of the room. She watched in the mirror as her wings beat there, eagle-proud but trapped in the space beneath the white ceiling. And then she heard a knocking on the door. She landed softly on the bed and sat there, breathless and shaking, clinging on to her dress which hung around her like a cloak of sweat as she heard the sound of the key in the lock and the door swing slowly open. Ashblossom stood there in her long blue dress, a curious smile on her face.

Ravenhair didn't know what to say. She wasn't sure if Ashblossom was her, or whether she was Ashblossom, and where all the creatures had come from. And so she just nodded and said nothing at all as Ashblossom smiled and closed the door behind her and left. But this time she didn't lock it and Ravenhair rushed across the room and drew the black curtains over the window which was a mirror. She was too tired and confused now to want to go looking for her grandmother's ribbon and so she pulled back the silver covers of the narrow bed, and without even bothering to undress, fell fast asleep between the cool crisp sheets.

The next morning Ravenhair woke, her long black hair tousled all around her, across the soft white pillow. She sat up and stretched. She was still in this room. Light seemed to spill from beyond the curtains, but she did not want to open them. She was sure it must be morning, but suddenly realised she could hear no sound from outside: no birds singing, no rain, no rattle of wheels passing in the street. No voices anywhere, not from outside nor here in this house.

She tiptoed to the door and tried it. To her relief it opened easily and she stepped out into the corridor. The walls were white and pale and the floor felt cold beneath her feet. In the distance she could hear the harp playing again and hurried quickly down the stairs towards it. One door stood open at the end of the corridor and Ravenhair saw it was the dining room where she had eaten the night before. The table was set for breakfast, but this time only one place, which she assumed must be for her. There was no sign of Ashblossom anywhere.

Ravenhair lifted the silver cover to find a dish of porridge, just the way she liked it and gobbled it up before anyone could stop her. The harp music swelled louder and seemed to be leading her away from the dining room, with its sparkling lights and crystal chandelier, into the corridor of mirrors. But she did not see the creatures there. She did not see Ashblossom in her long blue dress. She did not even see herself, just the plain white walls of the corridor, stretching on and on.

Ravenhair hurried as quickly as she could until she

reached the other end. The music stopped. There was a door before her painted dark blue and covered in a pattern of stars. Ravenhair paused then opened it. For a moment she thought she saw Ashblossom sitting there, cradling the moon in her hands and staring intently at nothing at all. Ravenhair opened her mouth to speak, to offer her greetings, to thank her for sheltering her and giving her food, to ask her what she might do today. But before the words could form themselves, Ravenhair realised the room was empty. Just a scatter of cushions with bowls of brightly coloured sweets left temptingly around. Ravenhair tried one but its taste was bitter and she spat it out again.

Her head was spinning now as she ran away down the corridor. Each led to another one and as she ran she glimpsed room after room decorated sumptuously and filled with all manner of brightly painted toys, musical instruments, embroidered dresses and flowing robes - everything she might wish for. But Ravenhair felt trapped. She wished that she had not come here at all. She wished that she was running free, back in the fields at Brunt Boggart.

The harp played on, louder and louder. Ravenhair only wanted to escape, to find her way out to the streets again, to breath fresh air and find her way to her room in the lodging house at the other end of the city. She rattled at windows which were all painted white, but none of them would open. She tried door after door, but each one led to another room until she was at the end of the very last corridor. Before her stood one last door. She seized the handle carefully and slowly pulled it open.

She stepped out into a garden. Not a wide elegant

garden, such as she thought might surround a house like this, but a small overgrown back yard, filled with nettles and dock leaves and tall straggling daisies. From the other side of the wall she could hear the sounds of the city morning - the cries of the market vendors, the clatter of wheels, the chatter of birdsong. Ravenhair rushed to the rusty gate and quickly flung it open and raced, as fast as ever she could, out into the noise and hubbub of the street.

As she looked back, she felt puzzled. She thought she might see a splendid white mansion rising above the narrow buildings. But all she could see was a shabby door, leading to a narrow house, just like the door she had passed through the night before.

Ravenhair shrugged and rubbed her eyes. As she pushed through the crowded market stalls, vendors grabbed at her, trying to sell fish so fresh she could taste the brine, oranges brighter than the sun, yams as long as her own right arm. Ravenhair hurried on. She had no money for any of this. She just wanted to get back to the lodging house. But then she paused in front of a stall that sold bracelets and pendants and shiny rings. Hanging from the awning was a mirror. Ravenhair hardly dared to look in it, fearing what she might see. But she caught sight of a girl, just a girl, just herself, though her hair hung long and matted from when she'd washed it in the fountain the night before and slept with it uncombed on the bed in the mansion's room.

As she raised her hand to run her fingers through the tangled tresses she realised that her ribbon, the dark black ribbon that Grandmother Ghostmantle had given her, was still lying where she had left it on the wall beside the fountain, back in the grand surroundings of the house.

"Can I help you?" asked the stallholder, a small gap-toothed man who dangled a handful of bracelets before her. Ravenhair shook her head. She wasn't interested in trinkets, she only wanted the ribbon her grandmother gave her. She had to go back to the house again, no matter how much she had wanted to escape. She pushed her way suddenly away from the stall, so quickly that some of the women stared after her, wondering if she might have stolen a trinket from the counter.

But Ravenhair didn't stop to answer their cries. She ran through the jostle, fled from the market to the festering silence of the dull narrow streets. But which was the street where the grand house had been? And how would she know it? Ravenhair looked all around. The streets were just a maze now - there was no way of telling which way she had come. And then, from the entrance to an alleyway littered with rotting oranges, a creature came tottering on long spindly legs. It lowered its head and gazed at Ravenhair with huge dark dewy eyes. Ravenhair stopped in surprise. It was the deer she had seen in the mirror the night before. Ravenhair gently stroked the animal's neck and fondled its long soft nose. The deer gazed longingly at the girl, then reared up its head and jerked away. Ravenhair followed. She realised the deer was leading her, away down the narrow street towards the house where she had slept the night before.

The deer began to move faster, turning first one way then another until Ravenhair found herself running, scampering after the creature who did not look back, just kept moving faster, faster than Ashblossom had taken her the day before.

Ravenhair stopped. She was out of breath. The deer had turned another corner. Ravenhair took one gasp of air then rushed on to find just another narrow street, but the deer had gone. Ravenhair sat down on the nearest step, gasping and panting. Her head was spinning as she looked around. She must be closer to the mansion house now, but despite the deer's help, the way was no clearer. Ravenhair hung her head in despair, her long black hair sweeping down to the ground.

What could she do? Ravenhair parted her hair from her face and looked up - and to her surprise saw a tall mare standing there, nostrils flared. The mare shook her withers and tossed her mane as Ravenhair gripped her neck and swung up onto her back.

The horse pranced and bucked and then cantered away with Ravenhair hanging on tight to the mane. They seemed to be turning back along the way Ravenhair had come. Which one was right and which one was wrong? Had the deer led her astray or was the mare trying to trick her? They galloped on, faster and faster as the morning sun beat down on the windows of the houses until they gleamed like an avenue of mirrors, and in each mirror Ravenhair saw Ashblossom riding on a pure white horse. Each time she glimpsed her, she looked the same, but she looked different, first smiling that stern fixed smile, then laughing, then crying, then pleading and begging and beckoning Ravenhair to join her, but then throwing up her arms to send her away. And then the horse stopped. They had left the houses far behind and returned to the gaudily painted tents that stood at the quayside by the river where Ravenhair had first met Ashblossom. The crowds of beautiful women and children were surging out again, holding up their silken robes to stop them trailing in the mud.

Ravenhair dismounted and patted the horse. She was curious to see inside the tents and lifted one of the ragged flaps. A face stared out at her, a face dark and strong. Ravenhair recoiled as the wolf sprang out, forcing her over, its breath hot and fierce on her face. The wolf pinned her down but as Ravenhair struggled a spark came into her eyes as if she was back in Brunt Boggart again, by the hollow on the Green with the boys. And there they would wrestle and there they would play while the boys learned their strength and the girls tested their ways. So this was not wolf, she said to herself, was Crossdogs, was Bullbreath, was even Greychild - and Ravenhair had the measure of them all. And so it was here by the river - with one thrust of her foot, Ravenhair pushed the shaggy beast away. Howling, it slunk back into the tent. When Ravenhair turned around, she saw a fox stalking silently away, turning its head as if expecting her to follow. But before she could move, Ravenhair felt a rush of wings. The fox had gone. Ravenhair began to run, away from the river and the quayside and the tents.

As she ran, the eagle plunged and swooped around her. The flap of its wings cracked the air like a clap of thunder. Her arms beat in front of her face, trying to drive the bird away. But the bird dived again. Ravenhair stopped in despair. She was shaking, she was shivering. Then she felt a hard horny grip about her shoulders. Felt the eagle's talons graze her flesh, but gently, as if no hurt was intended. The great bird swept her slowly above the rooftops and the air rushed by as its wings beat hard and strong. Ravenhair smiled. The streets slipped by below her, but just as she began to enjoy the flight, the eagle let go.

Ravenhair looked back, startled. The bird was wheeling away into the clear blue sky above the maze of streets and she began to plummet down towards the chimney tops. But then she spread her arms and she felt a warm belly of air pillowing beneath her. Her legs spread behind her and she began to glide, flying slowly and strongly. The streets lay like a map beneath her as she floated. She looked down and there below her she saw white roofs and walls and guessed this must be the mansion house. Ravenhair descended gradually, landing with a spring before the steps to the door. She smoothed down her skirt and took a deep breath, then rattled the knocker firmly.

The door swung open. Ravenhair raced up the steps. Nobody was there. She rushed inside, eager now to see again the corridor of mirrors, the bed chamber, the fountain where she had washed her hair. She realised she was hungry. Perhaps there would be food again laid out on the long white table in the middle of the dining room. As she stepped through the door, it creaked shut behind her. Ravenhair blinked. It was dark inside. Dark and dingy and dusty. She found herself in a narrow passageway. The walls smelt damp. Cobwebs clung to the low ceiling. The paintwork was musty and peeling. Ravenhair shivered and sneezed.

Where was the corridor of mirrors? Where were the bed chamber and the dining room? There was no harp music now, only the dull hand of silence. Another door hung half-open. Ravenhair peered through. It was a kitchen, a tiny kitchen. The shelves were stacked with peeling packages and decaying food. A mouse skittered across the grimy floor. One stray fly buzzed up to the broken lamp which hung from the ceiling. In the corner sat a woman. It was Ashblossom, still smiling that same fixed smile.

"Come in," she said. "Don't be afraid."

Ravenhair stepped forward. Their eyes met.

"I knew you'd come back," said Ashblossom.

Ravenhair nodded.

"I knew that this was what you wanted," and Ashblossom turned around to reveal the ribbon dark as night tied tight into her own white hair which hung over her pale slender shoulders.

Ravenhair nodded again. "It belonged to my Grandmother Ghostmantle," she said. "She gave it to me when I was a child and I have worn it all my life."

As Ashblossom's nimble fingers picked at the ribbon and she let her hair fall, their eyes met again in the mirror on the wall. Her face was Ravenhair's face. Ravenhair gasped. Her fingers scrabbled through the tresses that tumbled over her shoulders.

"Who are you?" she begged Ashblossom, who was girl, who was woman, who sat there before her in the fading light.

Ashblossom held out her hands and replied.

"You are what I have been. I am what you may be. Like you I came to this city empty-handed." She handed Ravenhair the ribbon dark as night. "Now I have everything and nothing at all."

Ashblossom looked away. From the top of the shadowy house, a harp began to play.

THE GRIMMANCER

"Let me tell you..." said the Grimmancer as he sat in the empty house gazing up at a raddle of one-eyed crows who squawked and squatted along the open rafters, hobble-legged and broken-winged. "... let me tell you - there are places in the world where you have never been. I have never been there either, as long as I have lived. So far as I know, no-one has been there. So how do I know about them, you ask?

"Let me tell you... I have dreamt them. I have met people who have dreamt them. I have dreamt about people who have dreamt them. And so they are real, as real as our dreams - and our dreams are as real as our waking. Our waking is hazy and dread and dull. We drudge through the days to wait for our sleep. But our dreams come alive. Our dreams are filled with bright colours and laughter. And in dreams we visit the places in the world where we have never been."

The crows croaked harshly, their voices coarse with

the smoke of the street's cowering chimneys and the fog which rose from the river.

"What do we find there? Let me tell you... or perhaps it is you who should tell me, because for each of us it is different. I cannot dream your dreams and you cannot dream mine. But we can share them. Let me tell you..." said the Grimmancer as he slipped out into the darkness, thin as a dream himself.

Ravenhair flitted through the twisted streets, pulling her travel-worn shawl tight about her shoulders. In the glimmer of an alleyway she saw a child in a white dress, shivering, clutching a flower. Its petals were purple, darker than blood. The child's face was pale, as if she was dying, as if the flower which she held close was draining her life. Ravenhair stared into the child's eyes. Saw darkness there, and hunger.

She reached out to touch the child's hand. The girl flinched and turned away as Ravenhair stepped closer, wishing to embrace her, to share the frail warmth of her threadbare shawl, to shelter them both against the wind which rattled salt-fevered up from the river, from across the darkness of the depths of the oceans. But then as she touched the child's face, the girl was not there at all, but only the flower, fallen withered and still on the cold stone of the alleyway, the colour draining from its purple petals until it lay lifeless and limp. Ravenhair reached to pick it up, then sensed fetid breath on the back of her neck as a wiry hand gripped her shoulder. She wheeled around, gathering her shawl about her, and found herself staring into the Grimmancer's face.

"Come with me," he smiled, and led her to the house where the crows prodded and poked, pecking at the carrion of dead rats and rotted dogs.

The Grimmancer coughed like a crow himself, his tattered coat of matted fur clung about his frame, his ashen face distorted in a gap-toothed leer. He pinned Ravenhair in the corner.

"Tell me your dreams," he whispered.

"I dreamt a child," she cried. "A child that I birthed in the briars and the bushes all out in the wood by Brunt Boggart. I took him home and bathed him and showed him to my mother and she was pleased to see a new babe in the house and we clothed him and coddled him and then I gave him suck.

"He grew and he played with me, till one day he ran from the door and turned somersaults all out on the Green. Then when I looked away, he found the path from the Green to the woods - and there he sported with the boys, wrestling and racing and tug-o-war. And then I dreamed of him no more..."

The Grimmancer smiled and closed his eyes. Ravenhair slipped slowly to the floor, as drained as the flower that the girl in the alley had dropped. The Grimmancer watched, covering her over with his great matted coat. When she woke she tossed the garment to one side and wandered out through the door, not seeing the Grimmancer standing in the shadows, not hearing the racket of the crows high above.

The Grimmancer shuffled across to the place where she had slept and then lay there too, wrapped in his coat still warm from her body, and then he slept, and then he dreamed. He dreamed the dream of the child in Brunt Boggart. Dreamt that he watched the boy as it grew, followed it to the woods where it sported with all the other boys. The Grimmancer saw all this as real as the streets of Arleccra that he traced and trailed night by night.

Ravenhair ran from the shadows of the house into the arms of the waking dawn. She wandered dull streets and cobbled courtyards as if she was searching, as if she had lost something precious - but all the time she walked she could not remember what it was. She hurried on until she came to a wasteground, where dandelions and ragwort clustered between the broken stones. A group of children were playing beneath the empty buildings which loomed above them, their thin voices chanting:

> "A penny for your fortune,
>> A penny for your dreams -
> But you cannot drink the water
>> And you cannot swim the stream."

They ran across the rough rutted ground, their petticoats flying, caps tossed in the air as they snatched up the poppy heads and flung them into a basket.

> "Pick a poppy, slip a poppy,
>> Put it in the pot.
> Pick a poppy, slip a poppy,
>> Tie it in a knot."

One girl ran, clutching the blood-red flowers in her hand as she tried to touch an upright beam propped in the centre of the hollow.

> "Once around the kissing post.
>> Twice around the tree,

Touch the sun and back again -
You can't catch me!"

She raced and raced while the others chased her, till she clung to the post and raised her basket to the sky. Then a boy made a run, but this time they caught him and all the girlen kissed him and he fell down and lay on the ground. The game went on, and on and on till the sun set as red as the flowers and only one child was left standing beside the kissing post. Ravenhair stared into her eyes, as deep and as dark as the boy she had birthed in her dream. She felt the emptiness inside her. Now she knew the words she had wanted to say - but before she could speak, the girl laid the basket of flowers at her feet. Then the other children sprang to life again and they all ran away.

That night as Ravenhair lay in her bed, she felt the darkness press about her, but she was not asleep. Outside the window she heard voices calling as if she could hear children playing in the shadows. When she looked, there was no-one, but still she made her way down the dingy stairwell into the street, following the sound of their voices, though now all she heard was the dark wind stalking the spaces between the tall houses. Ravenhair followed. There was nobody there, the windows were shuttered but still she walked on. A lone dog loped in front of her, following the scent of a trail. She wandered through a web of alleyways where a woman stood in a doorway, dressed in a long flowing gown patterned with glowing red flowers. She fretted like a moth trapped in the shadows, running her hands across the surface of the wall, as if her fingers touched the weight of the mountains which had made the stones, the wind's breath and the tug of the rivers which honed them.

Ravenhair ran on through dank narrow gullies as warehouses rose gauntly on either side, so high that they blocked out the sky, the moon and the stars. Ravenhair felt trapped and yet not trapped at all, as it seemed that each time she reached a wall which stood in her way, then she rose and floated up and over, landing again in a maze of backyards. She clattered and crashed among stacks of timber, rubble and guttering, fearing that any moment someone would hear and chase her away. But nobody noticed her at all as she drifted on between crumbling outhouses and festering slop-pits, until there in Arleccra's darkness she heard the cries of the children again, trapped behind doorways, locked behind windows. Ravenhair cradled herself in her own arms for comfort. She was not cold. She was not warm. She was not awake. She was not asleep.

When dawn came she returned to her bed, then rose again as if she had just slept, although she had not slept at all. She spent the whole day in a waking dream. Night followed day, followed night and each night it was the same - soon as she took to her bed, she rose again and walked the streets till dawn. The moon waxed and waned until at last she wrapped her shawl about her, curled in her bed and slept. The night seemed long and terrible, not lit by any dreams, till she woke in the morning more exhausted than she had ever been before.

The Grimmancer lay in his basement, surrounded by girls in forests dark who were not girls at all but the daughters of sinuous serpents, writhing to the rhythm of the sea. He dreamt a child who stood beside him, with flaxen hair and a ragged shirt, eyes staring wide and round. The boy clutched a spinning top painted in hoops of yellow, crimson and green, but tug as he might at the string, he could not make it spin. The Grimmancer offered to try his hand, but as he fumbled with the toy it slipped to the floor and the young boy left without a sound.

The Grimmancer woke and shook his head. The boy was a dream, he knew it well, just as the girls who were serpents' daughters - and yet it was as if the child was still here. He could hear laughter echoing faintly in the air. The Grimmancer rose to open the door and saw a spinning top lying on the floor.

That day as the Grimmancer strode the narrow streets, he became aware of footsteps following him, scurrying, hurrying, but when he looked round there was nobody there. As he reached the top of a flight of stairs he heard laughter, just as he had when he had woken - and then as he turned to look, light footsteps hurrying away. Later in the day a voice whispered behind him, *"Touch the sun and back again - you can't catch me!"* But the Grimmancer wheeled round to see no-one at all, only the blinding glare of the sun reflected from an upstairs window.

At the end of a narrow alley, the Grimmancer spied a woman in a doorway, dressed in a long flowing gown patterned with glowing red flowers. Her frenzied eyes were alive with dreams, the Grimmancer could see them shining. But as he drew closer to touch her on the shoulder and whisper, *"Come with me,"* a shadow fell across his path, the silhouette of the boy-child he had seen in his dream.

"Leave me be," the Grimmancer moaned. "You know I have work to do." He turned to where the woman had been standing, but she was gone. Only the rustle of her skirt and an aching shimmer of the dreams that might have been.

"Will you let me alone, boy," he muttered under his breath, as the rattle of a spinning top clattered away. And then the laugh. And then nothing at all. The Grimmancer stood wondering where the boy might be - was he safe and did he need anything to eat? Then he turned to the alleys again, peering into unlit doorways, looking for dreams that were not deadened or tarnished - but none could he find. Instead he strayed into a shop to part with a silver shillen to purchase his meagre supper. Without thinking, he bought not one loaf but two and a double portion of cheese and set off walking quicker than before, ignoring the shadows which lurked about him.

When he reached his doorway he was startled, and yet not startled at all, to find the boy he had seen in his dream standing there waiting for him.

"What is your name?" he asked gruffly. "And what do you want?"

"I am Shufflefoot," said the boy, then said no more, but followed the Grimmancer inside.

The Grimmancer fussed around, spreading a cloth across the bare wooden table and setting out the bread and the cheese.

"Eat," he said, but Shufflefoot had started already, wolfing the food without a word, then staring about him, looking for more.

"Here," said the Grimmancer, pushing across his

own portion. "You may have this as well."

Shufflefoot smiled and ate slower now, staring at the Grimmancer between mouthfuls. The Grimmancer coughed and looked around.

"What shall we do?" he said.

Shufflefoot pulled a spinning top from his pocket. The Grimmancer remembered the dream, that the toy would not spin - but this time the boy seized hold of the string and ripped at it hard. The top spun around into a blur of colours, shimmering gold and a dancing trace of crimson and green that became the shapes of high waving trees - and through them stepped Ravenhair, out of the woods, calling:

"Shufflefoot, Shufflefoot, where are you? - Come home!"

"I am here," said the boy and ran to her, dancing and twining about and about. The Grimmancer watched as she ruffled up his flaxen hair and combed it again, then pulled the black ribbon out of her own hair and knotted it into his, before clapping her hands and untying it again, bunching back her long dark tresses.

"This is the ribbon my Grandmother Ghostmantle gave to me - and not for you to play with!"

Then Ravenhair looked at the Grimmancer, as if she had not seen him standing there in the shadows. The boy stood awkwardly between them.

"Whose child is this?" she asked.

"Whose dream did he come from?" the Grimmancer replied.

"You stole my dreams," said Ravenhair.

Shufflefoot scuttled suddenly and plucked at the door.

"This child is a dream no more but here true as true,"

the Grimmancer reasoned. "He followed me here today, and here he must stay. But you must stay with me too and help me to tend him and feed him."

And so Ravenhair stayed with Shufflefoot in that dream-raddled house. She dressed him and fed him and each day racked through her head for more games to play. The Grimmancer stayed awhile, but soon enough he began to slip away each day to return at night with a different stranger, whispering... *"Tell me your dreams..."*

Some dreams delighted young Shufflefoot, full of laughter and dancing and sweetmeats dripping with honey. But some dreams were darker, of a sharp-beaked crow and a lumpen stone and a man shackled to a wheel, until each night Shufflefoot would lie and cry until Ravenhair rocked him to sleep. One morning the Grimmancer woke, still riding a dream of a distant isle where creatures sported, their eyes glowing bright as burning coals, their backs as smooth as polished horn. His eyes were wild and troubled as he paced the room, roaring at Ravenhair and berating young Shufflefoot until the boy screamed and covered his ears and ran through the door before Ravenhair could stop him.

"He is gone," she said, "our child." But the Grimmancer scarely heard her as he continued his ranting, plagued by a land of ice and blood where pale birds circled the sullen sky, singing with voices pure as snow.

Ravenhair left him alone where he sat, pulled her shawl tight about her shoulders and set off through the streets.

"Shufflefoot! Shufflefoot!" she called his name.

But *"Shufflefoot... Shufflefoot..."* came echoing back.

No child could she find in the maze of dim-lit alleyways, until at last she caught a glimpse of him, standing alone at the end of a sun-filled street. She raced towards him, but as soon as he saw her he ran away. When she turned the corner she realised he was not alone but out on the wasteground between the towering buildings with the children all about him, their petticoats flying, caps tossed in the air as they sang:

> "A penny for your fortune,
>   A penny for your dreams -
> But you cannot drink the water
>   And you cannot swim the stream."

"Shufflefoot, Shufflefoot - come to me," Ravenhair cried, but it was as if he did not hear her. He was with the children now and they whisked him away, turned him away, all through the dandelions and ragwort, all across the uneven ground strewn with broken stones.

> "Pick a poppy, slip a poppy,
>   Put it in the pot..."

The chant went up and Ravenhair watched as the basket of bright red flowers was flung to Shufflefoot and he ran, jerking and twisting, to try and make his way to the upright beam which stood at the centre of the hollow.

"Once around the kissing post..." they shrieked. *"Twice around the tree..."* as Shufflefoot ducked and dived and twisted and span until he tripped down onto the cold hard ground. The children froze, motionless, as the clatter of the streets fell silent and across the empty

wasteground a girl in a white dress came. In her hand she held a flower, its petals purple, darker than blood. She walked in a rhythm slower than breath until she stood before Shufflefoot as the other children watched, and placed the purple flower between his clasped hands. As Ravenhair stared, unable to move, the colour drained from the flower and as it faded, then Shufflefoot was gone too and the children sprang back to laughing, chasing each other and singing:

> "Pick a poppy, slip a poppy,
>> Put it in the pot.
> Pick a poppy, slip a poppy,
>> Tie it in a knot."

Back at the Grimmancer's house, Ravenhair closed the door.

"I have no dreams now," she said.

"We are each other's dream," the Grimmancer replied, but Ravenhair pushed him away.

All about the room hung tattered rags and shriveled flowers, slivers of glass and tarnished bones.

"These are your dreams, not mine," she said.

Shufflefoot's spinning top lay between them on the floor. Ravenhair picked it up and tugged the string, but it would spin no more. From far away and away, she could hear a boy's voice calling:

> "Once around the kissing post.
>> Twice around the tree,
> Touch the sun and back again -
>> You can't catch me!"

ILANIA

Let me tell you... let me tell you - Greychild met Ilania on the ragged wasteground where buddleia hung in bruised bunches and brambles snagged between the broken walls. She sat cross-legged, her ashen face framed by flying hair as a host of cats crept all about, watching and waiting, their heads turning each time she moved.

A dark wind blew through the beds of dank nettles and the cats became restless, stalking and crawling, prowling and yowling as they chased the dead petals of lurid red poppies.

From the harbour came the creak and yawl of tall ships shifting on their moorings, while beyond the wasteland rats scuttled through the overflowing gutters and the smell of rotting sewage clung to the air.

"Let me tell you..." said Ilania, "in this city every step we tread has been trodden before. Each footfall touches someone else's memories till our limbs begin to ache with their sorrow and their voices rise in our throats. We turn endless corners until we stumble on ourselves coming the other way - but we never recognise who we are."

A gaggle of shadows shambled by dressed in old shabby tunics, hauling a trawl of tattered nets behind them. As they walked, they rolled and swayed as if the sea still swelled beneath their feet.

"Where are they going?" Greychild asked.

Ilania sighed.

"They pass this way every morning. They take their nets to the dockside and drag them back at dusk, like as if this was a fishing village still, though they catch no more than a handful and sell less than enough. They sit out the day in the blistering sun, their lips dry and cracked, their eyes closed over to slits so narrow they can scarcely see. Then at twilight they come back with their baskets and their nets, muttering songs that no-one else sings."

Greychild peered after the shuffling figures, but Ilania turned away as the hoists and the cranes swung and clanked on the quayside.

"The ships bring us everything we want, but nothing that we need. Here in Arleccra more people live than you could ever meet. Even friends do not know each other."

An open cart sped by carrying a clamour of drummers calling and chanting, beating cymbals and blaring a cacophony of raucous horns.

"Come with me," said Ilania and led Greychild away to an empty house nearby. At the top of the dusty stairs they entered a room with a high crumbling ceiling and broken floorboards. A harp stood in the corner between wells of dark shadow, its strings hanging slackly from the old warped frame.

A spinning top lay on the floor painted yellow, crimson and green. Pictures hung skewed from the smoke-stained walls - a mountain with a tongue of fire, a tree whose fruit burned bright as lanterns and flowers dancing in hidden caves, their petals twined tight with desire. A sift of rain fell gently through the open roof and a chill wind coaxed a mournful melody from the harp strings.

Ilania pulled her robe around her shoulders and opened a rusting casket. Inside lay a painted egg, a brightly coloured spindle and a putrefying orange. She sat with her head to one side as if she was listening, then moved distractedly, this way and that until her eyes lighted on a musical box. She frowned as she picked it up, carrying it carefully to the other side of the room before setting it down before the empty window.

Slowly she wound the handle until a tune uncoiled, disjointed notes stuttering into the gathering darkness, while the thrum of the wind in the harp played on. Then she began a languid dance, her arms entwined with her body, a pale smile slipping across her lips. She stopped beside a chequer board laid out on a low table and stared thoughtfully at the pieces until she reached out and shifted one to a different square.

"Are you thirsty?" she asked.

Greychild nodded and watched as Ilania poured tea into two tiny cups. It sparkled with a shimmer of blue and though it was refreshing it tasted sharp and bitter. He noticed Ilania's hands were stained the same colour as the tea as he slipped into a sudden sleep.

He woke, shivering. The door opened and a child

appeared, dressed just like Ilania - a long flowing robe and her hair tousled loose about her shoulders. She ran across the room, skittering and laughing, knocking the spinning top across the floorboards until she came to the music box which Ilania had placed under the window.

She picked up the instrument and carried it back to the corner where it had been. Then she turned the tiny handle until the music came and she danced and she danced, spinning faster and faster, all the time laughing until she fell down in a sprawl of dizziness, nearly scattering the pieces from the chequer board. She hauled herself up and stared at them, scratching her head and rubbing her chin. She reached out and moved one of the pieces just as the music stopped. Then she clapped her hand to her mouth and ran giggling out of the room.

Another night passed and another night more as Greychild woke and slept and woke again and first Ilania came and then the child and they danced to the music of the silver box and moved one more piece on the chequer board. But not once did they meet, not once at all.

Then one night when the moon was full came a scratching, came a pecking at the window frame. The girl looked up from the chequer board, then crossed the room. She pulled the sash slowly and there on the window sill sat a crow. She reached out and cradled it in her hands. Greychild watched as it jerked its head from side to side and then he realised the bird was blind.

He stepped forward.

The girl smiled at him.

"I am Ilania," she said.

"But...?" Greychild hesitated.

"She is my mother," the girl explained before he could ask his question.

The crow rolled its head back and forth as Ilania rocked it gently in her arms. Then with one hand she poured a cup of blue tea and let the crow drink. The crow stopped its fluttering and soon fell asleep. Ilania turned to Greychild.

"Are you thirsty?" she asked.

Greychild nodded and watched as Ilania poured tea into two tiny cups. Again he noticed that, just like her mother, Ilania's hands were stained blue. Without thinking he sipped the sweet bitter brew.

The crow rose up and flapped about the room. Greychild and Ilania followed it out into the darkness, skimming across rooftops, flying along the course of the river until they set down in a field filled with girlen and boys-who-would-be-men dressed in tatters, dressed in rags, smeared about with daubs of mud, their hair gaudied all with feathers. They danced in silence, their heavy limbs dragging to the beat of a drummer who sat hunched under a dark crooked tree.

Greychild watched as a gaggle of crows set upon the bird which had brought them there, strutting and pecking and driving it back to the safety of Ilania's arms. She stood shielding the crow as she peered at the dancers, till soon enough one of them came closer.

"Dawnflower, where are you going? What are you staring at?" the others called.

But Dawnflower took no notice, seeming to be gazing straight at Greychild, but when he stepped towards her it was as if she could not see him at all. He wanted to speak to her, wanted to embrace the girlen he left behind to go in search of his mother. Then she shook her head and suddenly danced away, to fall into the arms of Hamsparrow.

"I thought you liked the WolfBoy," he said as he kissed her.

"He was only a boy," Dawnflower replied. "He was only a boy and he's gone now. Now I got you."

Greychild ran towards Dawnflower just as the dancers set off to leave the Echo Field. The crows rose and swirled above them as under the lengthening shadow of the Fever Tree the drummer played on. Dark against the horizon stood the shuffling silhouettes of a fool, a fire-eater, a juggler, a knife thrower and a woman with a flock of circling birds, while behind them a bear and his keeper lumbered slow as slow.

Greychild turned away as the crow struggled in Ilania's arms. The other crows circled above them, their voices rising to a deafening crescendo until they swooped down, surrounding Ilania, Greychild and the bird. The darkness of their feathers blotted out the dying sun, but their wings were beating slow and warm. And then they were gone. Greychild and Ilania were back in the room. The blind crow flapped between them, but now its eyes were returned. It flew about the room cawing raucously, "On and on. On and on..."

The next night Ilania the mother appeared as usual. She threaded her way past the spinning top then picked up the music box and placed it before the open window. As she wound the handle to release its tune, the wind droned on through the strings of the harp. She moved the last piece on the chequer board.

The game was over.

The game was won.
She tipped the pieces into the rusted casket where they rattled and clattered as the music stopped. Outside a prowl of cats yowled in the alleyway while she sat and gazed through the open window and waited for her daughter to come home.

CELANDA

Let me tell you... let me tell you... Ravenhair dodged through unlit alleyways filled with three-card tricksters, burnt-sugar vendors and blind night watchmen until she came to the tree-lined avenues on the south side of the city. This was where the merchants once lived, but now the streets danced with drunken sailors who could find the way to their ships no more and the butcher boys with blood red aprons fresh from the slaughter yards and the killing floor. She chanced upon an empty house where once sweet music played, but now the dining halls stood empty - only high plaster ceilings fluted with ferns and the dangling remains of smashed chandeliers. All that she found was dust.

That night she lay down on the bare wooden boards, but no sooner had she closed her eyes than she was woken again by the sound of someone sweeping. Ravenhair looked all about, but she could see no-one in the darkness. The gentle brushing continued - and then came a voice singing softly, till Ravenhair was lulled back to sleep. When she woke in the morning and looked about, she saw all the dust was gone - even in the room where she had slept, leaving only a shadow in the shape of herself lying on the floor.

That evening Ravenhair returned from the windowless workroom where she spent all the day sewing button eyes onto pale faced dolls. The dust was as thick as before and all about were cobwebs, clinging to the ceilings and the corners of the walls. Again Ravenhair lay down to rest and again she was woken by the sound of sweeping - but this time the sound was accompanied not by singing but by weeping. Ravenhair lay still, wondering who this could be. She determined to stay awake, to see who would bring a broom to this room - but soon she fell asleep. In the morning when she woke, again all the boards were swept clean, but this time she saw a trail of tears stained across the floor.

Another night passed and another night more, until Ravenhair woke in the moonlight and this time she swore she saw a girl in a shawl of silver and grey, sweeping slowly towards the door. Ravenhair called out and then sprang up and rushed to the stairs to look for her - but the girl had gone.

In the morning Ravenhair rose and combed her long dark hair, before tying it up in the ribbon black that Grandmother Ghostmantle had given her. She became aware of someone standing in the hallway outside the room. She turned and looked, sure it was the girl in the shawl. Ravenhair turned to speak to her, but the girl moved quickly away, hurrying down the long tiled corridors until they reached the door to a stairwell. Ravenhair couldn't tell if the girl had seen her, but followed quickly as she lit a lantern and descended the stairs. Ravenhair stayed in the shadows and watched as the girl moved gracefully across the basement's cold stone floor until they came to a room hung with velvet curtains.

On a chair sat Bodran, a boy-who-would-be-man, scarce older than Ravenhair. He wore a robe of sleek purple satin and the dragonflies painted on his long blue nails shimmered and flashed in the room's dim light. He smiled when he saw the girl.

"Celanda," he cried. "What have you brought me?"

"Brought you what you asked for," she replied. "Brought sugared lilac dipped in honey."

Ravenhair watched, her mouth watering, as Celanda stepped forward and placed a bowl in front of Bodran. He stared at the sweetmeats, reached out languidly towards them, and then pushed the bowl away with a flick of his slender fingers.

"Do not want them now," he said. "Wanted them when I asked for them. Been waiting all this time. Do not want them now."

Ravenhair peered around the room. All about were scattered other bowls, each filled with different delicacies, some full, some half-eaten, some scraped clean as clean. A flurry of rats scampered between them, nibbling and preening then scuttling away as soon as Celanda came near them. In the corner sat a song bird, trapped in a jewelled cage. The light from Celanda's lantern seemed to waken the bird and it began to sing shrill and clear. Bodran covered his ears with his hands, his painted fingernails raking through his hair.

"Take it away!" he screeched, drowning out the bird.

"I cannot stand its endless din."

"But Bodran," Celanda reproached him, "you were so pleased when I brought you the bird. You said you needed a companion to sing you through the endless night."

Bodran kept his hands clenched tight to his head.

"Said I needed a companion, yes. But not this creature who torments me, singing when I try to sleep and stubborn and silent when I am awake. Take it away..."

Celanda seized up the cage. As soon as she did, the bird stopped its trilling.

"Wait," said Bodran. "This cage is so beautiful - and the bird is too. Look at her feathers, how they shimmer and shine. Leave her there. She is quiet now."

Celanda hovered about him, sighing and shrugging.

"Whatever you want, whatever you choose..."

Bodran clapped his hands.

"You may go now. What are you doing, standing round here, cluttering the place with your fuss?"

Celanda scurried away and Ravenhair stayed close behind her. As they reached the top of the stair they heard the bird begin to sing again and Bodran flinging lilac sweetmeats at its prison.

That night Ravenhair dreamt she was a bird, singing in a jewelled cage. Dreamt she watched Bodran, his sullen face, his sulking eyes. Dreamt that she might kiss him, although she could not, for the bars stood between them and she knew her beak would only peck at his beautiful puckered lips. And so she sang, but as she sang Bodran only hurled abuse at her and covered the cage with a discarded gown.

But it was *his* gown, and as she shook her feathers, beating her wings against the bars, she could smell his scent in the folds of satin. She tugged and jerked until she had pulled it aside and she could see Bodran again, lounging in the darkness, dragonflies flashing on his painted nails as his fingers flickered around bowls of marzipan and roasted almonds. Ravenhair watched as the door opened and through it stepped Celanda. She smiled at Bodran and sat with him. They fed each other pomegranates, all the while fingering each other's lips as the pips spilt out. In the cage, Ravenhair hopped up and down, stropping her beak and rattling her perch, warbling, chirruping and shrieking. But Bodran took no notice, he was so absorbed by Celanda. He gazed into her pale green eyes, he stroked her hair, he kissed her cheek.

And then she stood and she was gone and Ravenhair was alone again with Bodran. She sang her sweetest song to him, hoping that this would soothe him, for she could see that he was sad, now that Celanda had gone. But he turned to the cage in a rage, hurling a bowl of cashew nuts so that it dashed against the bars. And then he jerked his old gown away and instead threw a heavy blanket over the cage so that all Ravenhair saw was darkness.

Next day Ravenhair wandered through the house until she came to the room that must once have been the kitchen. There she saw Celanda, frowning. Ravenhair stopped. Celanda looked up and smiled a sour smile.

"I see you clear," she said. "Don't think I don't know you followed me, down to the cellar where Bodran lives."

Ravenhair nodded.

"Are you going there today?" she asked.

Celanda frowned again, twisting her fingers.

"Every day I go there to take his food and bring his milk. I do not want to go this morning, down to that cold dark basement - the sun shines so bright outside. All we ever do is sit and pick at pomegranates and listen to his stupid bird screeching from its cage."

"Nothing so wrong with pomegranates," Ravenhair replied.

Outside the blackbirds trilled as they flitted from tree to tree all along the avenue. Celanda kicked at the door with her foot.

"Today he says he wants oranges," she complained. "All I got is this."

She drew one fruit from her pocket. Ravenhair took it.

"Let me go instead," she said. "Lend me your shawl..."

Ravenhair stood nervous now, her dark hair covered by the grey and silver shawl. The orange fell from her hand and rolled along the length of the narrow corridor. As she grabbed it up she fell against a heavy wooden door and found herself tumbling down the spiral of steps till she landed on the basement's dusty floor.

"Celanda," Bodran called irritably. "What took you so long? I've been waiting."

Ravenhair approached. Today he wore a cloak of peacock blue. The dragonflies flashed on his fingernails as he beckoned her closer and stretched out his hand. Ravenhair offered the fruit. Bodran took the orange disdainfully and held it at arm's length, peering at it through long velvet eyelashes.

"It is bruised," he declared, scarcely giving her a glance. "Shrivelled and bruised. Give me another."

"I have no more," Ravenhair confessed.

"What do you mean?!" Bodran bellowed. "I asked for fresh oranges, not one putrid fruit."

Ravenhair turned her face to the floor. She was aware that Bodran was staring at her.

"Who are you?" he demanded. "Where is Celanda?"

Ravenhair looked away.

"She cannot come today. She sent me instead."

"But I do not know you," Bodran complained. "I have never seen you before."

"You have seen me now," Ravenhair declared. "And besides - there are many more girlen in the city outside. Have you never seen any of them?"

Bodran looked sullen and shook his head.

"No - I see only Celanda, when I feel to call her. I only eat the fruit she brings me. I only hear this one bird sing... and only then when it chooses."

The bird rattled its beak against the cage then sat in silence, ruffling its feathers. Ravenhair looked around.

"Don't you ever leave this room?" she asked.

"I was born here. I grew here," Bodran replied. "Never see anything else. All I know is what Celanda tells me when she comes to bring me food. I did leave once, but there was nothing there. Celanda had told me of streets and markets and ships at the quay all down on the docks and of other men parading in robes just as splendid as these..."

He twitched at the edge of his silken gown.

"... but there was nothing. Only whiteness, like as if the sun had burnt it all away."

"If there was nothing," Ravenhair reasoned, "then how could I come and bring you this orange, bruised and shrivelled as it may be?"

She took his hand.

"Come with me. Let me show you."

Bodran hesitated. He gazed about the basement.

"These shadows suit me well," he said. "There is nothing else."

But then the bird set up its ceaseless screeching. Bodran covered his ears.

"Come with me," Ravenhair enticed. "Let me take you away from that fowl and its stink and its endless din. Let me take you to the riverside, the market and the ships. Let me take you to all the places that Celanda has told you of."

Bodran's eyes turned to misted milk as he paced the cellar floor, across and back from wall to wall.

"I cannot come dressed like this," he complained, but the bird continued its screeching as Bodran cast off the robe that he was wearing, then tried on first one, then another and another. He stood before a rusted mirror and brushed his flowing hair. And then he paced the floor again and changed the robe that he had chosen to another glowing red. His gaze darted quickly towards the waiting door as he sat down slowly to lacquer his nails, highlighting the turquoise dragonflies with the tip of a fine-haired brush.

As he sat down brooding in his high-backed chair, the bird stopped its noise. Bodran gazed at Ravenhair who gestured him to follow, but he seemed settled now, in the silence of the cellar. Then the bird set up a furious flapping as it threw back its head and screeched. In one sudden movement, Bodran threw off his robe and strode towards the door. Ravenhair watched as he hesitated, as he waited as he turned around to gaze again at the dimly lit cellar.

"Bodran," she coaxed, as his eyes clouded over once more and he seemed about to return to his pacing of the floor. But as the bird's dreadful screaming rose to a crescendo, Bodran took one deep breath and then with shaking hands, pushed open the weight of the cellar door.

Ravenhair led him gently. She could feel his body quaking as she held him. They edged their way to the top of the stairs and along the dusty corridor. Then she paused before the front door.

"Are you ready?" she asked.

Bodran seemed eager now. They could hear the rattle of carts on the road and the cries of hawkers down on the quayside. Ravenhair reached out and turned the handle, then stepped out onto the street.

"What do you see?" she asked, expecting him to be amazed at the sight of the market stalls brimming with fruit and the sound of the blackbirds singing in the trees.

Bodran shook his head.

"I see nothing," he said. "Only white light, same as before."

"Come with me," Ravenhair reassured him. "I will take you to the riverside, just as you asked. There you will see the cargo ship which brought your orange to you."

Bodran smiled.

"Will I touch the wind?" he asked.

Ravenhair guided him into the street.

"You will stand on the riverbank and feel a breeze which has travelled to greet you across seven seas."

Bodran giggled and shrieked as he felt the wind upon his face, falling blossom brush his cheek and heard the cries of the flower sellers who thrust bouquets of sweet-smelling blooms beneath his nose. Ravenhair led them down a narrow side street, past a courtyard where old men sat playing chequers in the shadowy sunlight. They nodded their heads and scratched their chins, pondering over the pieces before making a move with a thoughtful clatter and click. Then out of an alley came the familiar babble of children's laughter and a thrumming of feet chasing towards them.

"Shufflefoot!" cried Ravenhair, seizing up one of the boys. "Shufflefoot, what are you doing here?"

Shufflefoot grinned and wriggled from her arms then weaved around her, leading the others in a winding dance. But Bodran stood rooted, staring blankly, first one way then another, as the children whirled around him, prodding and chanting.

"Stop!" cried Ravenhair, but they took no notice and began to pelt him with the husks of old hazelnuts and broken twigs.

Bodran held out his hands.

"Are these falling fruits?" he asked. "Do the children bring sweetmeats just as Celanda does?"

"Not sweetmeats," Ravenhair frowned, rounding on the children.

"Be off with you!" she cried. "Shufflefoot, I am ashamed."

But Shufflefoot was gone, hiding in the shadows, and Bodran was left standing alone.

"Why did you send them away?" he asked. "Bring them back. They were singing. They were my first friends."

Ravenhair led him on towards the river.

"Weren't friends," she muttered. "Just want to taunt you. Stay close to me now."

Bodran stood still. He began to sob. The tears fell like rain into his cupped hands. He held them out for Ravenhair to see.

"What is this?" he asked.

"Tears," she said.

"Where do they come from?"

"Come from inside you," she explained. "Taste of salt. Taste of the sea. They are all the journeys you never made."

The sun shone down on the tears that glistened in the hollow of Bodran's hand, until they formed a ball of glowing colours. The blue dragonflies on his painted nails glinted as he swung the globe above his head.

"I see the sky, I see the day!" he cried as colours and shadows swam through the whiteness which was all he had known before. "I see Arleccra, just as Celanda told me."

Ravenhair smiled as he led her on excitedly, tasting the vivid colours of the fruit upon the stalls, filling his nostrils with the aroma of spices which wafted out from kitchens and lofts. His ears were filled with dancing clamour as the city surged all around. But then he stopped. Ravenhair watched as Bodran's eyes darkened.

"The leaves on the trees are yellowing. They turn to brown..."

He held out one hand to catch them, though to Ravenhair the leaves on the trees were fresh and green as they had ever been before. Bodran began to shiver. He pulled his robe around him.

"The branches hang stark and naked," he said. "Is this the winter which Celanda told?"

Dancing and capering, the children surged out from the alley again. Bodran could see their faces livid with sores. Their eyes stared dull red and their skin was vivid white. He watched as their hair turned grey and fell away, their backs bent and hunched, their voices cracked and hoarse, as they sang:

"Pick a poppy, slip a poppy,

Put it in the pot..."

- as first one fell to the ground and then another, to lie there still and dance no more.

Bodran groped in his pocket for the orange Ravenhair had given him. As he drew it out he saw its rotted flesh seep through the cracked and mildewed skin. The dragonflies flickered on his painted nails as the fruit turned to dust and trickled through his fingers.

Bodran looked around to see Celanda step forward from the shadows.

"Come with me," she urged. "You have seen too much."

Ravenhair returned to the empty house on the tree-lined avenue where the merchants used to live. All about were cobwebs clinging to the fluted ceilings as she curled to sleep in the room upstairs where dust lay thick on the floor. That night she woke and heard the sound of sweeping, just as she had before.

"Celanda," she called, expecting to see her, but as she watched she saw Bodran, broom in hand, swathed all about in a shawl of silver and grey, brushing slowly across the floor. Ravenhair sat up and called to him, but Bodran did not hear. His eyes fixed straight ahead as he softly sang,

> *"Pick a poppy, slip a poppy,*
> *Tie it in a knot..."*

Then he looked down at Ravenhair, but she was fast asleep.

THE ROBE OF SMOKE

Let me tell you... let me tell you about Spidermind - how he woke one morning as he always woke in the overgrown undergrowth that edged around the scrub of empty ground where the children played at the dark streets' end. Beetles crawled through his matted hair, while tiny cobs wove webs around him, dragging him this way and that. His fingers fluttered like birds as he scurried hither and thither, blown by the wind, skittering out to run among the flowers that had long since gone to seed.

Spidermind crawled through the leaf-mulch. He could see the dreams of tiny woodlice as they crawled between the twigs. He could taste the colour of the fine rain at dawn before it even fell. His waking voice echoed the damp decaying sadness of the song of the east wind as it swirled through nets of gossamer:

"Throw me a shadow

that's lighter than air.
Throw me a shadow
that will run anywhere.
Chase me through sunshine
then hide in the shade.
Kiss me with silence,
slip slowly away."

Spidermind stopped. He pushed his wire spectacles back onto the bridge of his long straight nose, his eyes blinking and flickering in confusion. He sniffed the air, his long nostrils quivering. A smell of damp grass and rain on the wind. Spidermind thrust his hands in the pockets of a patched gaudy waistcoat, then tugged his overgrown overcoat close about his shoulders.

His spindly fingers fished deep into his pocket till he pulled out a snuffbox, tarnished and dented. He prized open the lid then tapped the corners carefully, gathering up one last pinch between his forefinger and thumb. Savouring the moment, he raised it to his nostrils, then held his breath and sneezed. Every bird on every bush and every tree rose suddenly upwards, taking flight and scattering in every direction. Spidermind closed the lid and smiled, slipping the snuffbox back into his pocket as he tugged the overcoat tight about him, set his face into the coming rain and trudged off towards the city streets.

Ravenhair hurried, hunched and huddled through the shadows of the overhanging buildings. She shivered as she ran to a low slatted door, pulled her shawl about her shoulders and slipped through into the darkened work room. The other girlen scarcely noticed her as she slipped to her place at the long wooden bench. Her fingers shook as she pinched each bright sparkling bead, threaded the needle and plunged its tip through the eye of a limp-limbed doll stuffed with rags. She sewed swiftly and deftly, tugging the thread tight before she tossed the doll aside and picked up the next one. And the next. And the next.

A thin sliver of light fell through one high window and crept slowly across the work bench. Ravenhair waited for the moment for it to vanish - and then she would know that darkness had come outside and she could creep home again through the sullen streets to her small box-shaped room in the boarding house.

As their fingers clicked, the girlen had little or nothing to say. When they did speak their voices were heavy and dull and soon as any of them started to chatter or sing, then Lollingtongue's son would appear to walk up and down between the long rows of benches until silence fell once again.

As Ravenhair picked up each doll, her fingers caressed its satin dress, purple and turquoise, with trimmings of taffeta. How she longed for a dress such as this, to swirl in, to twirl in, to sing and to sigh beneath the chandeliers in the houses that stood on the far side of the river. But all she had was a dust-coloured smock, same as had clung to her every threadbare step of her journey along the Pedlar Man's Track. How she yearned for fine clothes like these silent rag dolls - but all she earned here was a pittance of pennies.

As soon as she seized up a doll, she knew she could not hold it for long, just plunge her needle deep into its eye socket and sew in the bead which would gaze back at her, smirking, *"You will never wear a dress so fine as mine...*"

And Ravenhair could only snap the cotton between her teeth and pick up another, its dress more splendid than the one before - while Lollingtongue's son strode along the rows, running his hands across the girlen's shoulders and stroking their long tattered hair.

At the end of the day the girlen stumbled out through the doorway of the work room, into the darkness which had already fallen - their fingers numb, their voices near dumb though they had scarce said a word to each other all day long. Ravenhair clutched her shawl about her shoulders and as she did so another of the sewing-girlen set eyes on the withered root which hung about her neck.

"What is this?" enquired the girlen, running her fingers across its gnarled and twisted stem.

Ravenhair smiled.

"Tis a wolf's foot," she declared and the girlen fell back with a cry, but then all the others gathered around.

"Where did you find it?" they asked.

Ravenhair laughed.

"Twas given to me back in Brunt Boggart, the village where I came from. Twas given to me by Crossdogs. He was my one boy, true as true. And he was the Wolf Slayer in the village - for he could hit harder, throw further, leap higher than all the other boys-who-would-be-men. He gave me the wolf's foot all out in the moonlight one bright starry night, down in the meadow at Sandy Holme."

The girlen pressed closer, stroking the root.

"Let me touch it... can I wear it?..." they clamoured and wheedled.

"It would suit me so well..."

But Ravenhair pushed them back.

"Tis *my* wolf's foot," she said. "It is special to me."

"Must give you good fortune," said one of the girlen. "Must give you strong powers to cast over men folk."

"If twas mine," chimed another, "I know I would sell it. Take it down to Mother Pottam's shop down in Slopswill Alley. That's where all the women go who want to know their fortune. You can buy many a potion there that can change your luck with a man."

The other girlen nodded.

"Why, Mother Pottam she would give you near twenty shillen for a trinket such as this."

Ravenhair shook her head as she made her way down the maze of alleyways back to the boarding house.

"Twenty shillen," she said to herself. "Tain't worth nothing at all. Tain't even a wolf's foot, though they all believed me. Didn't even get it from Crossdogs - he ain't never give me nothing. Just found it down by the edge of the woods one dark rainy night when Silverwing and Moonpetal got tired of waiting to see if that was the night when the Wolf might come."

The tiny shop was grey with dust. Behind the counter an old woman coughed, shuffling and shifting the jars and phials ranged on the rickety shelves. Ravenhair stood for a moment, her eyes growing accustomed to the gloom. A stuffed owl stared down at her from high on a cabinet as she stepped forward hesitantly. Mother Pottam turned round slowly and peered at her.

"What d'you want?" she rasped. Her faded smock was patterned with peacocks but it reeked of garlic and snuff.

Ravenhair unpicked the knot in the string which held

the twisted root around her neck. The old woman turned it over and over between her fingers which were as gnarled and wizened as the root itself. She squinnied it closely.

"What is it?" she hissed.

Ravenhair paused.

"Girlen tell me tis a wolf's foot," she said.

Mother Pottam turned it over again. She sniffed it slowly and raised one eye.

"Tain't no wolf's foot," she said. "But I smell forest here. I smell bluebell and nettles, tall oaks and skies all mardied with thunder... maybe I even smell mandrake root."

She looked at Ravenhair again.

"And I do smell wolf too, somewhere deep in the woods... a powerful mix," she mused. "If twas only a wolf's foot like the girlen told you, then might be worth pennies - a shillen or two."

She cradled the root before her, closed her eyes and breathed in deep.

"But this, I could sell to those women who come here who dream of sweet journeys, who dream of mountains far beyond the sea."

Ravenhair smiled, then set her face straight.

"How much?" she asked, "how much will you give me? The root is full precious to me, given to me by my one boy, true as true, beyond the turning moon."

The old woman sniffed again, fondling the root as if she was loath to let it go.

"I give you twenty shillen," she whispered at last.

Ravenhair paused. She gazed along the shelves. She studied all the jars and read the prices inscribed on the labels in faded ink.

"Fifty," she said.

The old woman wheeled around.

"Fifty is too much," she moaned.

"Then give me the root." Ravenhair held out her hand.

Mother Pottam shook her head.

"Too much, too much..." Ravenhair heard her muttering, but then she felt something pressed into her palm. It was not the root. When she looked down she saw a worn leather bag lying in her hand. She tugged open the thong which held it closed and there inside nestled fifty silver shillen.

Ravenhair clutched the bag and ran out of the shop, hardly stopping to look at Mother Pottam behind the counter, who was unscrewing a tall dark jar to place the root inside. As Ravenhair ran down Slopswill Alley her shawl slipped from her shoulders, but she didn't care. In her hand she clutched a bag filled with fifty silver shillen and she headed straight on to the bazaars and arcades clustered all around the market square. Here gaggles of girlen pushed and shoved as they paraded up and down in dresses brighter and more dazzling than any sewed onto the blind-eyed dolls in the work-room's dusty shadows. But Ravenhair took no notice of their disdainful stares for now she knew she could buy a dress finer still than anything they could afford.

She looked first on one stall, then another and then another more, but nothing could she find that she thought might suit her complexion or her hair, the angle of her hips or the trimness of her waist. Until at last she stepped through a door to find high walls hung with mirrors - and everywhere she looked were dresses of every colour, cut from the finest silk. Ravenhair felt dizzy with choice, tugging and flouncing at each one in turn. The seamstress stepped out from between all the finery and stared disdainfully at Ravenhair's threadbare smock. Ravenhair met her eye.

"Here in this bag I have fifty silver shillen."

She rattled it under the seamstress's nose.

"I want a dress that is nothing like the other girlen wear. I want to parade out fine as fine!"

The seamstress smiled when she saw the bag of money.

"I have just the dress for you! Not for you the blue or green. Not for you the fiery red. I have a dress such as no-one has seen. They call it - the Robe of Smoke."

With that she brought a box tied with a fine white ribbon.

"Can I see? May I try?" cried Ravenhair.

But the seamstress shook her head.

"Trust me, the Robe of Smoke is special - it is not just any dress. You must take it home and open it when you are all alone. The Robe of Smoke will take on any shape you choose. No-one else must see you put it on."

Ravenhair was so eager to try this wondrous dress that she thrust the bag of shillen into the seamstress's hand, grabbed the box with its fine white ribbon and ran every step of the way back to her lodging house.

Ravenhair opened the door of her room and flung herself down on the bed. She could scarcely catch her breath, so excited was she to see the Robe of Smoke. She sat and looked at the box a while, and then a while more, then slowly, slowly her fingers tugged at the ribbon which bound it all about. The ribbon fell loose and she eased the lid open. What did she see? Was the dress yellow or purple or lilac? Let me tell you, the dress was no colour at all, but a robe of smoke, true as true. It rose in a cloud from the tissue which wrapped it. Ravenhair quickly pulled off her smock as the smoke wound itself smooth as cream all around her. She peered at herself in the makeshift mirror which hung upon her wall. The Robe of Smoke swirled about and clung to her body until it fitted perfectly, then was not a robe at all but a glimmering gown so smooth as she stroked it, then a coat of fur which flowed to the floor, then a cloak of darkness as black as the night.

"Why!" cried Ravenhair, clapping her hands in delight, "I can wear this robe any way I like, any time of day that I choose!"

She settled on a dress which flowed and swirled and as she looked down saw that even her shoes seemed changed by the robe, not worn and broken any more. With a smile on her face and her head held high she tripped her way lightly down to the alley, then set off out to the main thoroughfare, that all might admire her finery.

As Ravenhair walked, she saw old men gaze after her, and young men too - wifen and girlen and boys-who-would-be-men, their eyes all seemed to turn her way. Ravenhair smiled to see if they would smile, but they seemed so entranced that they only stood and stared. She stroked the length of the sheen of her dress and was pleased when others wanted to touch it too. They walked so close she felt they might embrace her, might even try to kiss her as she raised her mouth in a smile. But then they walked past and hurried away.

"Mayhap they are bashful and shy after all," she said to herself. "This dress is so fine they don't know what to say. Mayhap I should just wear a plain simple cloak that doesn't scare people away."

Before she could turn around, the smoke writhed and shifted to change to a cloak, trailing loose and long all down to the ground. Ravenhair stopped on the corner and smiled.

"Now the girlen and wifen will all envy me and the young men will step up and steal a kiss!"

The first young man who came along walked straight into her arms. Ravenhair smiled and held up her face, but it was as though he could not see her. His hands clutched her waist, not in an embrace, but rather to move her out of his way.

Ravenhair stood all alone as the crowds thronged around her. They did not look at her, nor at her fine cloak. They seemed to look straight through her.

"No-one can see me!" she cried.

Spidermind woke in the sultry heat, his head still filled with the east wind's song which had lulled him softly to sleep:

> "Wrap me in shadow
>> that's closer than night.
> Wrap me in shadow
>> that swallows the light.
> Follow the darkness
>> till dawn brings the day.
> Kiss me with dreaming -
>> chase sorrows away."

In the streets it smelt as if all the fruit, all the spices, all the carcasses that lay in the crates on the quayside were slowly rotting all together. Shadows crawled by, that was all he saw. Old'uns carrying baskets, young'uns chasing the sun, girlen in their dresses and bonnets. But he did not see them at all, only their shadows. He watched and he waited till one drifted close.

"No-one can see me!" Ravenhair repeated as she capered down the street, snatching flowers, snatching kisses, turning cartwheels and pulling faces at anyone she met. And then she spied Spidermind, picking his way along the gutter. At first she scarcely gave him a second glance, until she saw, plain as plain, the wolf's claw root dangling round his neck.

"That's *mine*," she tried to say, but Spidermind slipped away through the market, past the stalls of fly-blown meat, past the barrels of festering fruit, until he stretched himself out on a bench. Ravenhair sat right beside him and waited till he closed his eyes in the sun. Then she leant closer.

"Will he feel my breath on his face?" she wondered. "Will he feel the touch of my fingers on the back of his neck?"

Ravenhair picked at the cord which held the withered root - then froze still when Spidermind stirred, flapping his hand as if swatting away a fly before closing his eyes once more. Ravenhair returned to the knot which she had tied so many times before, but then Spidermind suddenly opened one eye and reached out to grip her hand.

"You can see me!" she exclaimed.

"Course I can see you," said Spidermind. "I can see dreams of woodlice and taste the colour of the rain.

Why wouldn't I see you?"

"That's why you can see me," Ravenhair replied. "No-one else sees me at all. I have become bird's breath and slip by as quietly as the shadow of the moon."

She reached out for the wolf's claw again.

"How did you come by this?" she demanded. "It's mine."

Spidermind turned away.

"Why would you want it, this twisted old root?" he enquired as he cradled the claw in his hands.

"Tain't no root," Ravenhair protested, "but a wolf's claw sure as sure."

"That's what the woman said who I got it off, all dressed from top to toe in vixen fur and her eyelids tattooed with turquoise butterflies. Told me she'd bought it from Ma Pottam's shop. Told me she paid a fortune for it. I told her it was worthless. I told her she was robbed. And then she wrenched it off her neck and flung it to the ground. '*You can keep it,*' she told me. '*I wouldn't want it anyway now you've touched it with your filthy hands!*'"

Ravenhair hung her head.

"Now she has nothing. And what do I have? I have this cloak trailing loose and long all down to the ground. But no-one can see it at all."

"I can see it," Spidermind assured her, and stroked her silken sleeve.

"But I have lost what I valued most," Ravenhair wailed. "I have lost my claw of the wolf."

"Tain't no wolf's claw," Spidermind reminded her.

Ravenhair reached out and touched the twisted stem.

"Twas given to me by Crossdogs, my one boy true as true."

Spidermind held the root to his nose.

"Ain't no boy ever touched this," he said.

"This root is all I have left to remind me of Brunt Boggart, the village where I was born," Ravenhair pleaded.

Spidermind stretched behind his neck and loosened the knot which held the root. He let it dangle for a moment, then dropped it into her hand.

Ravenhair clasped it to her neck. At that moment a plume of smoke swirled around her then rose and floated away, back towards Mother Pottam's shop. She looked down to see that she was dressed in her old smock again, same as she had worn all down the Pedlar Man's Track. She turned around to thank Spidermind, but Spidermind had gone. The street was filled with the sound of a fiddle band striking up a tune.

Ravenhair ran towards them, her feet dancing gladly in her old wooden clogs. As a crowd gathered round to watch her every step, they pressed flowers and shillen and bright sparkling pebbles into her outstretched hands. And from way and far away, she thought she heard Spidermind sing:

> "Cry me a shadow
>   that lies in the dust.
> Cry me a shadow
>   that creeps into dusk.
> Under the twilight
>   where hunger is laid,
> Kiss me with secrets
>   till the tears fade away."

THE CRYING IS DONE

Let me tell you... let me tell you... Ravenhair sat at the window of her room and gazed out across the roofs of the city. She could sense the season's moon, feel it throbbing in her head. Her limbs ached to dance, just the way she had in Brunt Boggart, around the fire on the Green. But she could not make out the stars, dimmed by the dazzle of a thousand moons - lanterns, torches, flares and beacons that lit the murky alleyways.

But the true moon was there, she knew it, hidden behind a mask of smoke and the sea mist fretting in from the river. She could feel its tug, feel its ache surging through the tides of her blood. Her feet began to tap, as if the Drummer was come from the Fever Tree - and she arched her back to the fiddler's dervish skirl. And then she danced all by herself, but as if Silverwing and all the girlen who ever went to the Echo Field were dancing with her too.

She danced down the rackety stairs of the lodging

house and out into the darkness of the alleyway. There she danced between the overhanging shadows, out across the cobbles of the square, her hobnails clattering, her fingers snapping, her hands clapping high above her head, until the clouds parted and just for a moment the full moon swam, urging her on. She danced faster, she cried out loud, but nobody stirred at the windows above. Nobody woke to watch her. Nobody came to join her. And then the moon was gone and Ravenhair sank down to sit upon the cold hard stone.

From a far away street, she could hear Crossdogs singing:

"Here the boys do not wrestle for sport –
    They only want to maim and hurt.
There is no scent of open fields,
    Only clouds of smoke and dirt.

The girlen do not laugh and kiss,
    Only cast you down to taste the dust.
There are no streams to leap across –
    Only gutters of grime and rust.

There are no skies where songbirds climb –
    Only grey walls which block the sun.
There is no dawn, there is no night,
    There is no dark, there is no light –
Only the din of loneliness droning on and on."

"Crossdogs!" she called, but he did not come, and when she looked it was Greychild she saw, standing shivering beside her. He placed a hand on her shoulder and slowly stroked her hair.

"Remember when you used to twine me with blossoms as we sat together on the Green?"

Ravenhair nodded.

"There are no flowers here," she said.

Greychild sighed and sat beside her.

"Why did you come here?" Ravenhair asked.

"I saw my mother in the Eye of Glass. I saw her there by the market stalls. I've been there every day. She's not here at all."

"You don't know," she said. "So many people here. So many houses, so many back entries. Could be anywhere, Greychild. Could be anywhere at all."

"When I find her," he said, "then I've fetched her this scarf."

It dangled from his hand - maroon and purple, moss green and black, all picked out in threads of silver and gold. Ravenhair smiled and ran the scarf through her fingers before draping it around his shoulders.

Greychild looked away. He could hear a howling somewhere close. Pale rain began to fall, that smelt of smoke, smelt of oceans. The howling came again, as if from high on the rooftops. Greychild sprang up.

"I must go," he said and left Ravenhair still sitting in the gathering rain, still watching and waiting for the stars and the moon.

Greychild followed the sound of the howling, sometimes near, sometimes distant. Sometimes one voice all alone, sometimes as if a whole pack ran ravaging through the streets. He darted down passageways, scaled over walls, scrambled along guttering, skirted backyards and out-houses.

The howling grew closer as Greychild listened. It

came from a dwelling whose door hung ajar. He ran soft across the silver cobbles then plunged inside. As he climbed the stairs the howling grew louder. At the top was an attic room, the skylight open, waiting for the moon - but still there was only blackness. On the bed sat a girlen whose arms and neck were scratched and bleeding as if she had been racked by thorns. When she saw Greychild she raised her head and he full expected that the howling would well from deep in her throat. But all he heard was a stifled sobbing as tears ran down her face. He cupped his hand beneath her chin and bent to kiss her, to soothe the tears away. But as he did, her lips curled back into a bare-toothed snarl and as Greychild darted towards the stairs her baying followed him as she wrenched and jerked at the chain which held her to the wall.

Greychild ran. He ran to the pulse of a drum that he could feel but could not hear. He ran through gullies dank with moss and across wide cobbled squares. He ran to stand in the empty market, beside the boarded stalls. There he let out a baying cry as he stood all alone and gazed upwards while pale clouds scudded across a silent moon.

As he sank to his haunches he felt a hand, soft upon his shoulder. Was this his mother, come at last? He turned around. There was not mother, but Dawnflower, true. She took him in her arms, ran her fingers through his hair - just as if she was holding him still back by the stream in Brunt Boggart.

"Oh my boy," she cried. "Why did you run? I have come all this way to find you."

She twined a dark poppy into his hair, just as she ever

had before. As she rocked him in her arms her breath was hot against his cheek.

"*Coddle me,*" she whispered. "*Coddle me, coddle me, my darling boy...*"

But Greychild pushed her away.

"You are not my mother," he said.

She held him firmly at arm's length.

"Greychild, listen - I tell you true. Your mother is gone. I am all the mother you have now."

And then they came, the girlen of his journey, each and every one. Saffron, touching an orange to his lips, singing, "*Coddle me, coddle me...*" to add to the refrain.

A wind blew soft across the square.

"*I'm leaving you here till the crying is done...*" Mystra continued.

"*I'll bring you sweet milk and I'll fetch you fresh bread...*" Ashblossom promised, her long white hair wrapped close around him.

"*The trees are your chamber, green moss is your bed...*" Jessimer lulled Greychild almost to sleep as she plied him with first an apple, then a damson, then a peach.

They ruffled him and tussled him and tousled his hair. They planted him with kisses, here and there, there and here, as they tossed the scarf he'd brought for his mother from one to each to another. They took him in their arms and they spun him all around as their feet drummed across the cobbles with scarcely a sound. Greychild sighed and Greychild cried and then he laughed and ran with them.

"*We are all your mothers now,*" the girlen sang as they swung him one to each across the market square.

Greychild clapped his hands - and as he did the moon

loomed out from behind a bank of scudding cloud. Its light reflected pale silver on the haze of mist and Greychild stared straight into its eye and clapped his hands again. The moon held his gaze, drinking him in, until its eye saw everything and yet saw nothing at all, only brightness, only darkness, only skeins of crystal light which drew him on.

For an instant all in the city were wolves - old'uns, wifen, girlen - their eyes ablaze, their yellow teeth snarling, dripping saliva as they ran, as they prowled, as they howled. And Greychild, the WolfBoy, was boy true and true, running from them wildly, running to find the arms of his mother. But only an instant and then all was as before and Greychild stood shaking, wondering which way to turn.

Could smell blood, could taste blood, everywhere he went, roaming in the alleys, howling at the flood of the moon. Could sense Wolf wild on the wind. Wolf that was not wolf, was the scent of trapped tracks, running in the gullies that led to nowhere. Then not Wolf but mother, her arms wide open, her breast soft and warm, the caress of her breath as she held him, singing, *"Coddle me, coddle me, my darling son..."*

Then not mother but Wolf, true as true, standing at the back of the alleyway, the light hard behind her. But as he stepped forward was not Wolf at all but only shadow, cold and grey, only smoke, only dust. Then not even shadow but nothing, only emptiness, only aching, only loss.

He made his way to the quayside where pale-eyed children shuffled towards him, holding out their hands while from the unlit doorways beggars called, clutching their empty bowls. In the shadows stood the knife-sharpener, the butcher boys and the flower-seller, the gamblers, the wastrels and the sailors who reeled neither drunk nor sober.

They poured onto the dockside and watched as the great ships lowered their gangplanks and down clambered a raddle of horn-backed creatures, their eyes smouldering wild as volcanic fires. They moved among the crowd, handing out painted eggs to the pale-eyed children who stared in wonder at the pictures of cities and deserts such as they never had seen, of mountains lit with tongues of fire, trees whose fruit burned bright as lanterns and flowers dancing in hidden caves. Then from the eggs black crows broke out, each clutching an eye in its beak. They swooped and harried, swirling around until they circled into a wheel of raucous squawking.

"On and on," they screamed. "On and on!"

Louder and louder - until out from the very midst of them stepped the stooped and wizened figure of Marsh Brunning, cradling his hurdy-gurdy in the crook of his arm. One knotted hand turned the droning wheel while with the other he fingered the rattling keys as a mournful dirge echoed from its belly. The notes spilled out in a sighing whisper and then grew louder, raw and harsh as it sang of the lowlands, fields and streams.

Gulls swirled around, shrieking at the crows, then the grey-necked geese drawn in from the mud-flats. The birds meshed together in a skirl of bone and feather, driving the children up the long gang-planks and onto the boats where the geese strutted the decks while the crows and the gulls perched up in the rigging, spitting tongues of fire which set light to the sails. The ships hauled away, all out of the harbour, wreathed in flames and yet not burning at all as the children stood on the deck and waved to the crowd clustered there on the quayside while the horn-backed creatures turned to girls who were not girls at all but the daughters of sinuous serpents, writhing to the rhythm of the sea.

Marsh Brunning played on, wilder and louder. Then first came Homminy, beating a sheep's bladder, making one and all roll laughing with the wisdom of his wit - then Whisper, who straightway lit not one torch, but two and three until a whole fistful whirled around as he tossed them in the air and caught them. He spun around and around once more then plunged one plume of flame full deep into his throat. He pulled it out, a blackened stick - then opened his mouth and the flames shot up, lighting the faces of the gathering crowd.

Slipriver stood tall and elegant all on her one leg as she threw first wooden discs, then cups and spoons then balls of ice high up and higher into the sky.

Marsh Brunning played on, delving out a melody that he used to play, back along the flat-lands, as Downfeathers stood beside him, singing clear and high:

> "Here is the shadow
> That follows the wind.
> We know where she's going,
> We see where she's been.
>
> Now that we've found her,
> She turns to the sun,
> Which will hold you so tightly
> When you are alone."

At that Marsh Brunning set aside his hurdy-gurdy to embrace Downfeathers, then Slipriver, Whisper and Homminy - and finally Hobknockle and Lumbucket the bear who came ambling through the crowd to greet them all. They placed down the five stars they carried: the star of twisted twigs, the star hewn out of stone, the star of hammered metal, the star of plaited rushes and the star of pure light.

As the points touched each to each, Marsh Brunning stepped into the very centre of them all, his knotted fingers quivering still as his breath hung white in the cold night air. Greychild stood and watched as this breath took shape and first it seemed like a tree in blossom and then it seemed like a sudden fall of snow. And then on the quayside it was like a sheep that had lost its way and was sheep no more but changed to a naked man, running and running and running until he fell to the ground as Marsh Brunning turned the wheel once more and his hurdy-gurdy let out a sighing sound.

As he turned, the sky above them spun around and around and they were not on the quayside no more but back at Brunt Boggart, all down on the Green. They were all there, the boys-who-would-be-men: Hamsparrow and Bullbreath, Larkspittle and Longskull, Shadowit, Scarum, Scatterlegs and Crossdogs too, as if he'd never been away. And the girlen singing in a ring: Silverwing, Moonpetal, Dawnflower and Duskeye, Scallowflax, Dewdream and Riversong - with Ravenhair linking onto Crossdogs' arm. Old Granny Willowmist and all of the old'uns, Nanny Nettleye and Old Nanny Ninefingers - while Snuffwidget ran amongst them, serving up Corbin Night-thorn's Morning Sunrise and Oakum Marlroot stood and glowered.

From the midst of them all, Thunderhead rose and brandished his staff while Skyweaver caught up the tune on his fiddle and the Drummer set in with a familiar rhythm. Marsh Brunning played on and on as each and every one of them all began to sing:

> "When five stars shine as one
> The journey has begun,
> All the way down the Pedlar Man's Track
> To take us here and bring us back -
> To help us find all that we lack.
>
> Moon of Sky and Moon of Earth,
> Moon of Blossom, Moon of Blood -
> Lead us onward as we run,
> Now the journey has begun,
> To help us find all that we lack
> To take us here and bring us back -
> All the way down the Pedlar Man's Track."

And then they stilled, as the moon above them rose. Marsh Brunning stepped forward.

"I know this place," he said. "I came this way an age ago. I know this Green, these cottage rows. I know the dark woods that lie beyond the fields, where I've tarried a while and a while."

Slowly he struck up a melody and Greychild joined in, for it was the tune to the song his mother sang when she brought him food out under the stars: *"Coddle me, coddle me, my darling son..."*

Greychild stepped forward to stand beside him.

"Did you find a girlen here?" he asked, trembling at

the thought. "And did you leave her to fend for herself, same as she left me?"

Marsh Brunning sighed as he placed a hand on the young lad's shoulder and looked him in the eye.

"On and on," he said at last. "On and on..."

*

Let me tell you...

when we are asleep, we are not asleep. The dreams are real. The waking is a dream.

Let me tell you